Being herself is more dangerous than ever.

Stanzie's job as Advisor to the Great Council is discovering other people's secrets. When those secrets are being kept by the ones she loves most, can she find the courage to expose them?

Under orders from a Councilor, Stanzie journeys to Dublin and the MacTire pack. Her mission: warn her estranged bond mate, Liam Murphy, to abandon his overzealous search for the man responsible for the death of his first bond mate. Not only is he endangering himself, but also disrupting the delicate balance between opposing factions in the conspiracy threatening to tear the Great Pack apart.

Liam needs Stanzie's help to protect their Alpha, who has entangled himself in the conspiracy's deadly web. But he also desperately needs her back. In a race against time, Stanzie and Liam discover enemies often wear the faces of friends.

Books by Amy Lee Burgess

The Wiolf Within Series
Beneath the Skin, Book One
Scratch the Surface, Book Two
Hidden In Plain Sight, Book Three
Inside Out, Book Four
About Face, Book Five
Across the Line, Book Six

Published by Kensington Publishing Corporation

About Face

The Wolf Within Series

Amy Lee Burgess

LYRICAL PRESS
Kensington Publishing Corp.
www.kensingtonbooks.com

Lyrical Press books are published by
Kensington Publishing Corp. 119 West 40th Street New York, NY 10018

All Kensington titles, imprints, and distributed lines are available at special
quantity discounts for bulk purchases for sales promotion, premiums, fund-
raising, and educational or institutional use.

Special book excerpts or customized printings can also be created to fit
specific needs. For details, write or phone the office of the Kensington
Special Sales Manager:
Kensington Publishing Corp.
119 West 40th Street
New York, NY 10018
Attn. Special Sales Department. Phone: 1-800-221-2647.

Kensington and the K logo Reg. U.S. Pat. & TM Off.
Lyrical Press and the L logo are trademarks of Kensington Publishing Corp.

First Electronic Edition: April 2013
eISBN-13: 978-1-61650-450-2
eISBN-10: 1-61650-450-1

First Print Edition: April 2013
ISBN-13: 978-1-61650-856-2
ISBN-10: 1-61650-856-6

Printed in the United States of America

This one is for Kim Murphy. She has been one of my most staunch supporters and loyal beta readers. Whenever I need technical help, especially when it has to do with all things Irish, she's the one I go to. If I need a shoulder to cry on, she's always there for me--whether it has to do with my current book or my life in general. And, remember, Kim--I named Murphy for YOOOOOU!

Acknowledgements

As always, thank you to Lyrical Press for all the hard work and believing in me and my Stanzie novels. Special thanks to Antonia Tiranth who stepped in to edit this one. Editors never get enough credit and theirs is a pretty thankless job. People like me really need them. Eternal gratitude to my beta readers Nerine Dorman, Kim Murphy, Portia Scott Palko and Chris Wilbanks. You guys rock!

Chapter 1

"You don't look happy." Lauren's first words after she and Jason dropped the bombshell, possibly added up to the understatement of the frigging century.

"You're damned right I'm not happy," I snapped—and cursed when Lauren cringed in her seat and her hyacinth-blue eyes filled with tears. If she let them fall, this would be the sixth—no, seventh—time today she'd cried.

I beat a fist against my thigh when the first tears dribbled down her cheeks.

"You're going to ruin your makeup," I said.

With a choked gasp, Lauren leaped from her chair and raced out of the dining room. I held my breath and waited for her to fall and break her ankle. She wasn't used to platform pumps with four-inch heels. My father had preferred more sensible, lower-heeled shoes.

Jason Allerton watched her, too, his fingers tight around his soup spoon. I knew if she fell, I'd be in deep shit with him. I stole at look at his handsome face. Deeper.

Half the diners in the private room of the small seafood restaurant also watched Lauren's floundering progress.

They were all Pack, shape-shifters, like me, so no doubt they'd overheard everything, but with true Pack discretion, they all paid scrupulous attention to their appetizers. To most of them, the news would not have been a bombshell, but, rather, good news. This was a Regional Gathering and people expected announcements like the one Lauren had just made.

The table next to ours, full of members from Nightclaw, the premier pack in Connecticut, made no pretense they hadn't overheard. Perhaps they considered themselves exalted and therefore exempt from the conventions of lesser packs. They eyed me askance as if I'd done something ridiculous by objecting to what they would have considered an honor.

Let them think what they wanted. Lauren wasn't *their* mother.

I sat at the table in my new silver-pleated chiffon cocktail dress and fancy new silver sandals, my hair curled into waves that brushed my shoulders. Up until forty-five seconds ago, I thought we were having yet another of our friendly dinners.

Lauren was radiant in a grape sequined V-neck dress. I'd picked out her shoes—Jimmy Choo sparkling anthracite platform pumps. If I hadn't, we'd still be in our motel room while she agonized over every pair of shoes we had between us, still unable to make up her mind.

The problem with Lauren was that she could not make a decision. At least she couldn't unless I gave her an hour and patiently listened to her fears and doubts and dealt with tears and pleas for me to do it for her.

This was not entirely her fault. Thirty years under my father's pack bond and his refusal to let her think for herself was to blame. But sometimes I suspected she'd always been weak. Other times I just thought she needed time.

What she didn't need was another man in her life to tell her what to do, especially a man like Councilor Jason Allerton.

"What exactly are your objections?" Jason set down his spoon and regarded me with his cool blue gaze.

I put down my own spoon and lamented the fact the clam chowder was ruined for me now. It had been damned good, too. Why wouldn't it be? We were in Providence, Rhode Island, within spitting distance of the Atlantic Ocean. In fact, if I glanced to my right I could see the waves—pewter gray in the twilight—as they curled to the rocky shore right outside the back windows of the seafood restaurant.

It was the first Friday in August and this was the kick-off dinner to this year's New England Regional Gathering for the packs that held territories here.

Jason and I were attending because of Lauren and my past association with two of the New England packs. He was from Silverlake, the premier pack in Montana, and, for the moment anyway, I belonged to Mac Tire of Dublin.

Since his bond mate died of a stroke, he'd had three months to find a new one, by Pack law, in order to retain his pack and Great Council status. He'd obviously arranged to extend it so he could take advantage of the New England Regional and my mother as well.

At the bonding ceremony tomorrow night he and Lauren were going to become bond mates, and she would leave Mayflower in favor of Silverlake.

That was the bombshell. Jason Allerton, my boss, member of the Great Council, was going to bond with my fragile, damaged mother. Just when she'd taken her first tentative steps to reclaim herself, he was going to bond with her and I knew she'd defer to him the same way she'd always deferred to my father.

She still had a month before she lost her Mayflower status, but it hardly mattered if she did. Unlike Jason Allerton, she had nothing to lose.

"One of them is that you're rushing her so you won't lose your seat on the Great Council or your pack status and land in Silverlake." I glowered at him across the table and he glared back. Jason Allerton rarely glared. A shiver ran down my spine, but I refused to back down.

"Another is that she's finally starting to find herself and now she's going to lose it all so she can cater to you. Everything she's accomplished in the past eight weeks is going to fall to pieces. Congratulations, Councilor, you've got yourself a doormat you can wipe your feet on and order around instead of an equal and someone with her own mind. Good job."

"Do you really think I'd undo all her progress simply because I became her bond mate?" His question was sincere, but his blue eyes were glacial. "You think I'm doing this for expedience's sake and not because I genuinely care about Lauren?"

"That's exactly what I think. You've known her two months. How can you possibly care about her? You're in a rush to get a bond mate. You didn't expect Kathy Manning to turn you down. Now you're scrambling and my mother is the convenient pawn in your game."

Jason became very still. The anger radiating from him was white-hot but I was past caring. This was my mother we were talking about, not some stranger. He'd blown it with his mistress, Kathy Manning, and now my mother would be sacrificed on the altar of his power. This was so not fucking right.

"She said yes when I asked her to bond with me." It was a warning to back down, but I ignored it.

"Of course she did. What else could she say?"

"Are you saying I coerced her?" His eyebrows drew together in a dark slash.

"You're like the godfather making her an offer she can't refuse. This is Lauren we're talking about. And you're a Councilor. How's she supposed to say no?"

"Do you dare suggest I used my position to force her into this?" His voice was frigid. "Constance, you are overstepping your boundaries with me and I suggest you back off now."

"You see? You're using your position with me right now. You do it by default, like you're on autopilot. Jason Allerton, Councilor. You're not Jason Allerton, potential bond mate to her. How could you be? She doesn't know you."

"We've been virtually inseparable for the past month."

"Oh, hell, twelve dinners and a handful of lunches are not the basis on which you make the decision to bond together for life."

A small voice whispered inside my head that I'd used even less of a basis to decide to bond with Liam Murphy. I hadn't known him even one week before I'd joined with him during a bonding ceremony at the Great Gathering in Paris last November.

And look how fucked up that idea turned out to be. Guilt and a surge of painful love seethed inside me and my stomach roiled.

Jason's angry, clipped voice brought me back on target. Focus on Lauren.

"Pack law gives us three months to bond again after the death of, or separation from, prior bond mates. How long do you suggest we wait before you are comfortable? Four months? Seven? Two years? Meanwhile, life goes on, and all our pack benefits are stripped so we can make a decision we could have made in the allotted time just to allow you some dubious peace of mind. Lauren and I are both well into our fifties, we're not inexperienced youngsters."

"For all intents and purposes, that's exactly what Lauren is. She bonded with Paul when she was twenty and he's all she's known for over thirty years. You generously gave her two whole months to get over that? How magnanimous. She's not in any rush to join a new pack. She's got me and the condo in Boston. You're the one who's in the rush, and you know it. Don't make her suffer for your agenda."

"What do you suggest I do? I have found the woman I wish to bond with, and we both wanted your blessing. But make no mistake…we don't need it, and we will go on with our plans, regardless of your objections. You've already said enough to me. Please spare your mother your vituperative comments and at least attempt to be gracious."

"You're not listening to me at all, are you?" Tears scalded my eyes. "What is the point of asking me for my objections if you don't intend to pay any attention to them at all? Why don't you just tell me to shut the fuck up and deal?"

"Shut the fuck up and deal," he said.

It was quite possibly the first time I'd ever heard him drop the f-bomb, and it brought me up short for a moment.

"You do this and I quit. I won't be your Advisor if you go through with this bullshit bonding," I declared, and Jason's face darkened.

"So be it. You are released as my Advisor," he said. And just like that our nine-month association was severed. Everything I'd accomplished for him and the Great Council all meant shit next to his pride and his determination to bond with my mother.

I threw my napkin on the table and jumped to my feet.

"Stanzie." Maybe there was a glimmer of regret in his eyes, but it was too late. He'd said it. Just as my bond mate Murphy said it to me almost four months earlier when he'd walked out on me and just as my Alpha, Paddy O'Reilly said it to me when he'd left with Murphy.

Three for three. No job. No bond mate. No pack. I was alone. Again.

* * * *

Two hours later I stopped my mindless trudge across the cold, wet, packed sand and calculated my bearings.

My sandals dangled from my fingers and the strap of my expensively flimsy evening bag wouldn't stay lodged on my shoulder.

Night had descended and the lights from the beachfront hotels, homes and businesses cast a yellow light over the sand, but where I was at the water's edge was shrouded in shadows.

The briny smell of the sea clogged my nostrils. I sidestepped a glistening, dark strip of seaweed only to step squarely on a goddamned pointy rock.

"Shit." I swiped at the tears that had streamed down my face for the last half mile or so. I was such a baby and an idiot. I'd just cut off my last lifeline to the Great Pack.

I was still Murphy's bond mate, but my birthday was in ten days, and it was my chance to break the bond. Pack law gave everyone the right to reassess relationships and break bonds on birthdays. I could wait and let him do it on his birthday but why should I humiliate myself even further by letting him break our bond when my birthday came first? Once I did, the clock would start to tick on my membership within Mac Tire because no unbonded adults over the age of twenty-six could remain in the pack.

I would have three months to find a new bond mate. By mid-November, if I wasn't in a new relationship, I lost my pack.

"Been there, done that," I muttered and wiped my eyes again.

He'd let me go. Jason Allerton had insinuated himself into my life since Paris. He'd given me sanctuary and a job as his Advisor and interested himself in my life. He'd been the one to maneuver me into bonding with Murphy.

Ostensibly, he put us together so we could investigate the weird, untimely deaths of young pack members worldwide, but also another agenda, a more personal one. He'd wanted us to bond together and be happy after we'd both suffered the deaths of our original bond mates.

Amidst everything I'd been through in the past nine months, Jason Allerton had been a comforting father figure.

And just like that, in the span of three seconds and one sentence, it was all undone.

I'd trusted him with my mother. When he'd taken a hotel room in Boston after my father had been exiled and I'd taken Lauren back to my condo, I'd thought he was looking after me.

He'd seen me struggle with Lauren as I'd tried to give her space to reclaim herself and yet keep my sanity at the same time.

Every decision was agony for her. What to wear. What time to get up and go to bed. Which flavor of jelly to spread on her toast.

He'd taken us out to dinner more nights than not. I'd cooked for him.

His calm, comforting, authoritative presence had become a given in my life over the past eight weeks.

To think I'd been grateful when he'd suggested he take Lauren out to dinner on his own so I could stay home and relax. Or go out.

Yeah, right. With who? My best friends, Vaughn and Jossie, lived in Vermont and my cousin Faith and her bond mate, Scott, were two hours away from the city.

I'd expected to see more of them the past couple of months, but people got busy. Faith was pregnant and had a pack to rebuild after my father nearly destroyed it.

Jossie was convinced I wanted to bond with her and Vaughn and make a triad—and invented excuses to keep us all apart.

So I spent those nights alone. I had time for a luxurious soak in the bathtub with a delicious murder mystery. I could watch a movie while curled up on the sofa as the lights of the city glowed through my living room window. I had opportunities for walks around the block in the summer darkness so I could ease the tension out of my shoulders and take deep breaths as I marshaled the inner strength to deal with Lauren another day.

Now after this Regional was over, she'd go to Montana with him and start her new life, and I'd have every night alone in Boston. Every morning and midday, too.

"You selfish bitch," I whispered to myself in amazement and for a clouded moment wasn't sure if I referred to me or Lauren.

The lights and music from a waterside bar attracted my attention. It was a small place, gray shingles, a wooden deck in the back so patrons could watch the ocean as they pounded down beer and shots and figured out who they would go home with that night. It was full of Others, not Pack, but screw it. No way I wanted another night alone. Those would start soon enough.

* * * *

My eyes felt gritty and full of sand when I fluttered them open the next morning. I had no idea where the hell I was or why the sunlight had a weird dappled effect across the sheet that covered my nude body.

My head thumped, and my mouth tasted sour. I held still, afraid I might be sick, until the queasiness passed.

Someone's bare foot brushed my ankle. I jerked away in shock, clutching the sheet to my neck like a virgin in a bodice-ripper.

Holy shit, it stank. The man in bed with me reeked and his scent was all over me. I was fucking disgusting.

The smell decided my rebellious stomach and I lurched out of the bed. I had no idea where the bathroom was. I estimated I had about thirty-five seconds to figure it out.

I looked around to orient myself and discovered I was in a small studio apartment. Outside, seagulls screamed over the relentless crash of waves. Sheer green curtains with an odd texture fluttered in front of a half-open sliding door that led to a weathered deck. The dappled effect was explained.

Dirty dishes were piled in a porcelain sink near the front door. A rickety table and two chairs squatted in front of the sink. More dishes were on the table as well as a thick accumulation of junk mail.

A battered sofa with the arms duct-taped to keep the stuffing from spewing out rested against one wall bookended by two tray tables. A drop ceiling and cheap fluorescent lights completed the shabby decor.

No bugs, just the cluttered detritus of a young bachelor.

A half-open door with chipped paint to the left of the front door was either a bathroom or a closet.

I didn't have time to care so I bolted.

It was a bathroom. Not filthy, but certainly grungy. I prayed to the porcelain goddess over and over but still couldn't get that foul stench out of my nose.

I'd slept with an Other.

I even thought I remembered his name. Don. Or maybe Ron. Ron. Almost definitely Ron.

To be fair, he didn't stink because he was unwashed. He just wasn't Pack. He wore Obsession cologne. I could smell it the bathroom cabinet and faint traces in the damp towels on the rack.

Some Pack could sleep with Others and get over their strange, sour scents. I'd never been one of them. I could work with them, ride the subway with them, buy food and clothes from them, but I could not be intimate with them.

Until the fourth or fifth Long Island Iced Tea, apparently.

Just the thought of the sweet drink loaded with six different kinds of alcohol made me gag again until I was reduced to dry heaves that twisted my stomach and choked my throat and nose.

Murphy had walked out on me four months ago and I'd painted my condo. Jason Allerton dropped me as his Advisor and I'd rushed out, gotten drunk, and fallen into bed with some young Other man.

What the fuck was wrong with me?

I needed to take a shower so I could rinse the stink off me, and wash away the hangover.

Breath held, I twitched the grungy shower curtain aside to reveal a mildewed plastic shower stall. It was not exactly the Ritz, but whatever.

The water pressure was for shit and the temperature fluctuated between icy cold with spurts of stinging hot. I endured it until I'd soaped my entire body and washed my hair with Ron-or-Don's combination shampoo and body wash. Only men could be so lazy as to combine two such different products. The gel smelled like a guy, too.

Once I was done, I realized I'd have to wrap one of his used, Obsession-scented towels around me to dry off. The entire point of the shower was undone.

Curses spilled out of my mouth in a steady stream as I dried off with as little of the damn towel as I could manage and not stay dripping wet.

When I walked out of the bathroom, Don or Ron was awake and hastily doing dishes as if I gave a shit what his hellhole apartment looked like.

Last night in the bar, he'd been almost a dead ringer for Liam Murphy, except he was shorter and younger. This morning he didn't even remotely resemble Murphy, except maybe a little around the eyes. He wasn't fat, but he was loose in places Murphy was tight. And his hair wasn't right. It was blond. It had looked darker under the black lights in the bar. Everything about him looked different under the lighting and the influence of those fucking evil Long Island Iced Teas.

His voice was wrong too. It was deeper, with a Rhode Island accent, not an Irish one.

"Hey, do you want breakfast? I can make eggs? I don't have bacon, but I think I have toast?" Everything he said was a question. I remembered bits and pieces from the night before. At one point I'd told him to stop asking me so many questions and he'd said, "Am I asking you lots of questions?" I'd cried, "There's *another* one right there!" Then I'd kissed him to shut him the fuck up.

We'd still been in the bar then, but I guessed after it closed he'd brought me up to his apartment. Empty beer bottles littered the countertop, and I devoutly hoped they weren't from last night. My stomach rolled again, so I looked away.

"I need to go." I was pretty close to panicky as I searched the room for my clothes. Aha. My dress was wadded up on the sofa. It seemed we'd had a very heavy make-out session there. My bra was under the coffee table, and I grimaced at the thought of wearing it after it had spent the night on the grubby, stained carpet.

One sandal was by the front door and the other was by the kitchen table. My purse was on the table. I had no earthly idea where my panties were, and I wasn't sure I wanted to stick around to find out.

"You don't have to?" Ron-or-Don made the statement into a question. I wanted to scream, but didn't. "I mean, I'd like it if you stayed, okay? Unless…you have a boyfriend, right? You kept telling me last night you didn't, but you do, don't you? Can you stay for ten minutes to eat something? Please?"

As he spoke, I shimmied into my bra and last night's cocktail dress. I spied my panties tucked half under one of the sofa cushions. Disgusting. With a grimace, I plucked them free and debated whether I wanted to put them on.

"Oh, I just wanted to tell you? I used a condom, okay?" He gave me a sheepish smile and then turned back to the eggs on the stove. They smelled gruesome, and I pressed my lips tightly together to keep from gagging.

The way he looked at me made me think he expected some sort of response. Congratulations, perhaps? Gratitude? A high five for quick thinking even while inebriated?

"Safe sex, you know?" he added. I didn't even remember getting laid, let alone whether there was a condom involved.

"I have to go," I repeated as I slid on one of my shoes and lurched for the other, one leg magically longer now, thanks to the four-inch heel.

"It was a mistake, wasn't it?" Ron-or-Don asked. "You wish you'd never met me, don't you?"

My head hurt. I massaged my temples with the fingers of one hand while I braced myself against the door with the other and slid my foot into the second shoe.

"I was drunk and so were you." I was aware I wasn't being kind and the poor bastard hadn't done anything wrong. He looked at me in the harsh morning sunlight and more than ever did not resemble Murphy. What the *fuck* had I been thinking?

"Look, I'm sorry, I can't stay. You're a nice guy."

That made him wince. I guess Others didn't like being called nice. I had no time to figure him out. I didn't want to figure him out. It did seem as if our roles were reversed. Generally, wasn't it the guy who rushed out the door in the morning and left the girl to feel guilty and used? Or maybe I was being sexist. I didn't have a clue.

"You know what? Can you tell me your name? Can you believe I forgot it?" he confessed as I unlocked the door. Perhaps this was his attempt at a cheap parting shot? I flashed him a rueful smile over my shoulder on the way out.

"That's okay, I can't remember yours either."

* * * *

Lauren's makeup was spread out in a vast confusion across the bathroom vanity when I walked into our motel room just after five PM that afternoon.

She wore a peach-colored slip, and her hair had obviously been styled at a salon. Her finger and toenails were colored a darker peach than the slip. Summer color.

As soon as I walked in, a radiant smile lit up her lovely, perfect face, and she was in my arms a second later. She smelled like Chloe and Calvin Klein's Escape because, of course, she hadn't been able to choose between them. I'd thought I'd been so clever. I'd gone through her suitcase before we'd left and taken out all but two perfumes—one for day, one for evening. I should have known she'd wear them both.

"I thought you'd left. When I came back to the room this morning, your bed wasn't slept in, and I thought you walked out." She burrowed her soft face into my shoulder and, as I hugged her, I thought how inverse our relationship was. She was more like the child and I, the mother. It had been that way since my teens, and that aspect hadn't changed in the past two months, even though I'd desperately wanted it.

Oh, for a mother I could confide in. What would it be like to have one who would listen to my woes and thoughts and hopes and offer advice, comfort, understanding? All Lauren ever did was look to me to fix things, to approve, to give sanctuary. I did those things ungrudgingly, but I wished sometimes our roles were reversed.

I was also a little weirded out she'd spent the night with Jason Allerton. Thoughts of their naked bodies entwined in passion made me strangely uncomfortable. Lauren having sex didn't bother me. No, Lauren having sex with Jason Allerton was the issue. What did he look like without his Armani suit and tie? Did he drop his authoritative, commanding personality in bed? Was he strictly a missionary position kind of guy, or did he like to experiment?

I squeezed my eyes shut and banished that shit straight out of my mind.

When I opened them, Lauren had tears in her eyes that turned them nearly purple. She looked so goddamn young and vulnerable in her lacy peach slip and bare feet, her hair twisted up into a breezily perfect updo that had taken at least an hour to arrange.

My heart contracted the way it always did when she looked at me like that.

"Silly, did you really think I'd miss your bonding ceremony?" When I hugged her, I dropped the three shopping bags in my hands. The first two contained a new dress for tonight and shoes to match. The third bag held my cocktail dress from last night. After I'd left Ron-or-Don's apartment, I'd gone to the Providence Place mall, straight to Gap for a pair of jeans and a t-shirt. Then I'd gone to Victoria's Secret.

A new pair of Skechers had replaced the silver evening shoes, which were in the bag with the shoes that paired with my new dress.

Shopping, especially for shoes, cleared my head of all the crap that haunted me since the moment I'd opened my eyes in Ron-or-Don's bed.

At least until I'd walked into the motel room and had to face everything again. That's the problem with shopping. The stores eventually closed, and I had to go home.

Now I needed a shower and time to pull myself together before the ceremony at seven, and Lauren would need me to reassure her and help with her makeup and...

Breathless, I contemplated the depth and complexity of my selfishness. What did it matter what I looked like tonight? She was going to bond with Jason. They were going to start a new life together. And I ran out on them the night before.

My cell phone was full of both voice and text messages, mostly from Lauren, although Scott and Faith both left a few. A notable exception was Jason Allerton. He was royally pissed at me, I guessed. Big deal. I was furious with him, so we were even.

"You don't want me to bond with him." Lauren's voice was subdued, and she walked away from me so she could look out the motel window at the shore beyond. I wanted to remind her she was in her slip, but I bit the inside of my cheek. I wasn't her mother, no matter how much she looked to me for support. She was fifty-eight years old, even if she didn't look much past thirty. She could decide for herself if she wanted to stand in front of an open window in her damn underwear.

"Lauren, are you sure this is what you want to do? You don't have to, you know."

"Oh, but, Stanzie, I *do*!" She turned away from the window with such exquisite happiness on her face I took an involuntary step back. I had never seen Lauren Newcastle look like this before. "Jason is the kindest, gentlest and most understanding man I've ever met. I *want* to be with him. Every minute I spend with him I just keep thinking how much I like him. How much I want to show him who I am. I feel like I'm eighteen years old and back in Aspenmoon with my family. Happy.

"Do you ever think about a time in your life when you were so happy you couldn't even imagine what anything else felt like? When unhappiness was missing your favorite television show because you'd stayed outside in the twilight too long chasing lightning bugs with your twin sister?" She giggled. In that moment, she was heartbreakingly beautiful.

"I know you don't have a twin sister, but you know what I mean, don't you?"

Murphy's face flashed before my eyes, damn him, and my eyes burned. I had to nod because I couldn't speak. Lauren didn't notice. She was too caught up in her own feelings.

"I can't wait to leave Massachusetts and go to Montana. I've never been farther than Louisiana, and that was just for a week. Jason says the forests there are deep and dark and the streams are so clear you can see your wolf's reflection if you stand still. And it tastes sweet and pure, and it's so cold it freezes your tongue, even in July. Can you imagine, Stanzie?"

I thought the forests in New England were wild and wonderful places, but I wouldn't say that to her. I tried to imagine this conversation she'd had with Jason about the forests in Montana. He'd never once even referred to his pack or his home in all the talks we'd had together.

I'd known he was from Silverlake because it was the premiere pack in America, even if it wasn't the oldest. He was one of the most influential and powerful Councilors in the United States and among the youngest ever appointed. He'd joined the Great Council when he'd been only forty-seven, which was nearly unheard of in the Pack.

He'd been an Advisor from the age of twenty-four and Alpha of Silverlake at twenty-six. He'd served on the First Midwestern Regional Council for ten years before joining the Great Council.

Someday he would head the Great Council, I was confident.

All the things I knew about Jason Allerton's life, I'd learned from Murphy or picked up through the Pack grapevine. He'd never shared much about himself with me, and I'd never questioned that. I'd been too busy looking up to him as a father figure to ask him anything about himself.

I bowed my head. Tonight I'd vowed to suck it up and stand behind Lauren as she joined with Jason. I'd planned to put aside my reservations and fury and be there for her, even if I couldn't believe she did the right thing.

Now I was ashamed of myself. For two months she'd been falling in love, and I'd only seen a woman who couldn't make a decision. A woman I wanted to morph into a responsible, nurturing mother who would make me feel as if I mattered as my life slowly fell to pieces around me.

So goddamn selfish. I, I, I. Never a thought for her except in terms of how she related to me.

Maybe Jason did care about her. Sure, he'd been on a search for a new bond mate, but perhaps Lauren had been a real candidate, not someone convenient.

He'd only known her for two months and already reached her far more deeply than I had after thirty-two years.

"Wren, I'm going to miss you so much, but I am so glad you're happy. Of course I want you to bond with Jason. You two are going to be great together." Tears spilled down my cheeks as I looked at my mother and knew I was once again going to lose her.

Her smile was incredulous, and she crossed the room to fling herself in my arms.

"Stanzie, you just wait. Everything will be different now that I'm with Jason. I feel like I've got a second chance, and this time I'm going to do it right."

Somehow the scent of Chloe combined with Escape worked with Lauren's chemistry. Either that or my throat was too clogged with tears to really smell.

"Come on, I'll help you with your make up, okay?" I took Lauren by the hand and led her to the vanity. I wanted her to look especially beautiful tonight.

Chapter 2

The room glowed with candlelight. Golden light shimmered against the soft cream paneling and danced in circles across the ceiling.

Six people stood in the front of the room before Kathy Manning, who was dressed in her ceremonial Councilor's robe of dark blue trimmed with white.

As the highest-ranked Regional Councilor in attendance, she would perform the bonding ceremony.

Her serene expression gave no clue to her actual feelings. It had to hurt to be the one to preside over her ex-lover's bonding ceremony to someone else he'd just met two months previously. Someone he couldn't keep his eyes off.

Jason Allerton was smitten, there was no escaping that fact. How I hadn't seen it before tonight, I wasn't sure. Perhaps he hadn't allowed himself to look at Lauren the way he did tonight.

They were the center duo, facing one another hand in hand, and simply drank each other in as the candlelight enveloped them in a soft, amber glow.

The other duos were younger—first-time bonding for both of them—but Lauren and Jason were the ones who drew our gazes.

The families and packs of the duos stood behind them as witnesses, and beyond us were several round tables with pristine white tablecloths and summer floral centerpieces. The sweet fragrance of tiger lilies perfumed the room.

I'd managed to hop in the shower, wash my hair, throw on my new red dress and black spike pumps. My hair had even cooperated with the curling iron, although I was pretty sure all the curl would fall out halfway through dinner. It didn't matter.

When I took a deep breath, I must have made a wistful sound because my cousin Faith, who stood beside me, moved closer so her shoulder brushed mine. She took my hand and gave it a gentle squeeze.

I hadn't seen her in two months, and during that time her pregnancy had started to show. She had a definite baby bump beneath the wine-colored Empire maternity gown draping her body. She placed my hand across her abdomen, and I felt a tiny, fluttering movement. Had that been a kick?

"My God," I whispered and turned to her in excited shock.

"I know." Her whole face glowed. She was beautiful. "Grandmother Carolyn says it's twins, Stanzie. Can you believe it?"

"Twins!" I pressed my forehead to hers and grinned. "You are so lucky, Faith."

"Scott wants two boys, but I think one of each would be nice." The babies, or at least one of them, fluttered beneath my hand again, and Faith went still so I could feel it better.

"Alpha female, surely the Pack prospers because of you." The words were traditional, but I'd never said them before. They felt strangely right to say to my cousin who was Alpha of my birth pack.

"Someday I'll say the same to you." She seemed convinced, but I wasn't. Hard to be Alpha without a bond mate.

I twined my fingers with hers as Kathy began the ceremony.

Halfway through I started to cry, thoughts of Murphy and Lauren and Jason tangled together in my head, impossible to sort out and laced with a bittersweet ache that tingled through my whole body.

Scott Charest—my cousin's bond mate, Kathy Manning's Advisor, and my friend—wrapped his arm around my waist and pulled me close. Faith kept hold of my hand. Alan Perrault, another friend from Mayflower, moved close behind me, his body warm against mine, his breath soft in my ear.

I remembered us in bed together, the first step of his wolf's initiation, and leaned back against him as Lauren fastened her new bond pendant around her throat and Jason Allerton did the same with his.

* * * *

After the ceremony we feasted on baked stuffed shrimp and Maine lobster. I sat at the table with Jason and Lauren, Faith, Scott, Shane, Samantha and Todd.

Todd was Faith's father and Shane and Samantha were his bond mates.

The rest of Mayflower ate at nearby tables. No one from Silverlake was present, and I wondered if that bothered Jason.

He and I sat on either side of Lauren, but we didn't talk. He and my mother were very wrapped up in each other, but he made the effort to chat with Faith, who sat on his other side.

Lauren had chosen the baked stuffed shrimp for an entrée, as had Jason, but I saw how she cast wistful looks at my lobster.

I put one of my lobster claws on her plate, took half a baked stuffed shrimp in return, and her face lit up.

"I couldn't decide what to order," she confided in my ear with a little laugh. "So I ordered what Jason did, but when the lobsters arrived, I realized I should have ordered that instead."

"Always order something different than what Jason does," I suggested. "Then you can share, and you won't be disappointed. That's what I always did when Murphy and I went out to dinner."

I bit my lip as I remembered the many restaurants we'd visited on our road trip from Texas to Massachusetts. We'd gotten to know each other as bond mates during that time.

We'd made a thirty-hour drive last nearly four weeks. If we liked a city or town, we'd stayed there for as long as we liked.

We'd remained nearly a week in New Orleans. It was there we'd figured out the rhythms of each other's bodies and the sex became intense. The third day there we hadn't even gotten out of bed until after sunset, and then only because we were starving.

It was there, too, we'd vowed to share our food and always order something different so we could try more than one thing. From appetizers to desserts, we never had the same thing, and we shared it all.

"I wish you'd work things out with him," Lauren whispered as she dipped a succulent piece of lobster claw into the melted butter on my plate. I moved it to her plate because I never put butter on my lobster. I loved the taste of it plain.

"Who?" I pretended ignorance and she sighed.

"I know you're thinking about him. You just said his name. Murphy, your bond mate. You always get that same starry-eyed, wistful look on your face when you think about him."

"Wren." I wished I'd ordered wine with my meal but I hadn't because I was still slightly hungover.

"I know you don't like to talk about him, but I think it's a shame. It must be really hard to see all the duos and triads together tonight and be alone."

I winced, the ache inside me so raw it hurt.

Amy Lee Burgess

"I'm fine," I gave her a bright smile that didn't fool her. "Anyway, tonight is about you. You and Jason and the other two duos who bonded tonight. You better drag him on the dance floor because I want to see if he can keep up with you."

Lauren giggled and the whole table looked indulgently at her. Sometimes I couldn't believe this perfectly stunning woman was my mother. She seemed so unearthly, and I was so very grounded and real. It was as if a fairy had given birth to a peasant girl.

My appetite gone, I gave Lauren the other lobster claw and excused myself to go to the bar for a drink. Hangover be damned.

* * * *

Once there, I pulled a Lauren and couldn't decide between a mixed drink or wine.

The back of my neck tingled as someone moved close behind me and then came to stand beside me. Scott. He gave me a grin and stood close so our shoulders and hips brushed together.

He studied the twinkling bottles of alcohol behind the bar and frowned. Then he saw the beer and wine list and brightened.

"Two Labatts." Scott decided for me, and the bartender bent beneath the bar to retrieve the bottles from the mini fridge.

When she'd opened them and moved down the bar to attend to another guest, Scott turned to me and said, "Hunt with me tomorrow night."

My stomach flip-flopped, and it wasn't all due to the fact Scott was gorgeous as hell. It mostly had to do with waking my wolf now that she was supposedly normal.

"What if she won't come out?" Scott was possibly the only person on Earth I felt comfortable with talking about my wolf. Comfortable was not even a very good word. He'd been there the last time I'd tried to shift and couldn't do it.

"It was the pack bond holding your wolf back, Stanzie." He nudged my beer closer to my hand with his bottle. Ice-cold condensation dripped down the brown glass. "It's gone now. She'll come out."

I cast him a doubting look.

"And if she doesn't, I'll be there with you. Look, we'll shift away from the rest of the hunt. That way if there's an issue, no one will know. But there won't be."

Shift away from everyone else. I took a sip from the bottle. The beer tasted bitter as my thoughts. I hadn't participated in many Regional hunts, but when I had, I'd always shifted away from everyone else and gone the opposite direction, with Grey, Vaughn and Elena, my former pack mates, chasing after me.

Now my wolf was theoretically normal, and Scott, unwittingly, proposed the same basic concept. Screw that.

"I don't know." I took another sip and watched as his gray eyes filled with both compassion and exasperation. "What about Faith?"

"Have you seen her?" he said and then laughed. "She's not shifting again until after the twins are born. She says it's too uncomfortable."

There was no medical reason to avoid shifting during pregnancy, but most women did prefer to avoid it after they got bigger.

"Why don't you go with someone who you know will be a good hunt partner," I suggested.

His seductive mouth twitched. "That would be you."

"We may be good Advisor partners, but I don't know about hunting, Scott."

"Well, I do." He put his hand on my arm, and the weight of it was so soothing I wanted to melt.

"You smell good, you know that?" I didn't mean to say it, but the words escaped me anyway. He did. He smelled like Pack.

"Faith got me this new cologne. Made me wear it tonight." Scott rolled his eyes.

"Pussy," I said and he grinned.

"Hey, if it gets you to agree to hunt with me, I'm fine with it." He gave my arm a squeeze. "At least give it some thought, Stanz, okay?"

I nodded, but I was pretty sure I wouldn't do it.

"You're going to have to do it sometime," was his parting shot before he walked away. "Why not do it with a friend who understands?"

"I thought you were such a dick when I first met you." I shook my head in amazement.

Laughter was his only response.

I turned back to the bar and squared my shoulders. Maybe Scott was right. Hell, he was. I had to face my wolf. If the worst happened and she wouldn't come out, Scott would be the only one to see it. And he understood. He was Alpha of Mayflower. He knew how my father's pack bond had dominated the pack for thirty years and made everyone who'd activated the bond into slaves. I'd run from my birth pack and never activated the pack bond. It had remained an invisible wall between my psyche and my wolf. The reason she'd been childish and stubborn and so different from everybody's wolves was because she couldn't get past the pack bond.

For years I'd let her do whatever she wanted. I'd never tried to reach her. I hadn't known about the pack bond. I'd just thought she'd been different and hadn't wanted to force her to be like other wolves because I didn't think she could.

Then I'd met Murphy and he convinced me she could be changed. From the start my wolf had adored his wolf. For him, she'd tried to change, but had been so frustrated because of the unactivated pack bond. The more we pushed, the more she suffered. She'd been so mad at me and her circumstances. She refused to come out the last time I'd tried to shift. But there was nothing holding her back now. Scott was right.

If we hunted together, she'd come out, she'd be normal. And what the hell would that be like? Even if she did look for Murphy's wolf and he wasn't there, she could handle it as a normal wolf. After all, I was handling it as a normal human.

I snorted and drank more of my damn beer.

* * * *

"Can I talk to you?" Jason Allerton approached the dessert table at the same time I did. Neither of us was aware of the other until we both reached for the same piece of cheesecake.

When I spoke, he let his hand drop away in an indication I should take the cake.

"Please?" I added when he didn't say anything.

Behind us the dance floor was full of couples moving sinuously under flashing strobe lights. Faith's laughter rang out above the music as she and Scott danced together and he whispered crazy, naughty things in her ear.

Alan hadn't left the floor since the music started. He'd had a different partner for nearly every song, including me once. He was full of confidence, brimming over with excitement.

"I've met more people tonight than I have my entire frigging life, Stanzie," he'd confided to me as we'd danced together.

"Found a hunt partner?" I'd teased, and he blushed.

"*She* asked *me*," he whispered, awestruck, as if the thought of it was too weird to be possible.

He'd changed so much from the frightened, sheltered boy he'd been when I'd visited Mayflower two months ago.

"Who's initiating your wolf?" I'd asked him and he'd grinned.

"Dorothy. Can you believe it? She asked me if she could. She remembered when I'd asked her and she'd turned me down because of the pack bond. But there is no pack bond now, so she asked me. It's going great, Stanzie."

I remembered I'd told Scott about Alan's preference for a teacher and wondered if he'd had a hand in Dorothy's recent offer. I suspected he had. He was a good Alpha.

The slice of cheesecake was the last one. Bright red strawberries decorated the creamy frosting, and I could smell their juice above all the other desserts. My mouth watered at the thought of sinking my teeth into one of the plump, ripe berries.

"Not tonight." Jason's voice was cold, as if he didn't even know me and I was some stranger who wanted an audience when he had better things to do. Right now better things to do translated into what dessert should he choose now that he couldn't have the cheesecake.

"Take it." I pushed the cheesecake in his direction. "I bet you're getting it for Wren. Cheesecake's her favorite. She never got it much. Paul preferred chocolate cream pie."

He pulled his hand back from the piece of chocolate cream pie he'd selected and I walked away.

* * * *

I needed air so I pushed open the reception hall door and walked out into the salty breeze.

A wooden deck overlooked the sandy beach. Moonlight streamed down upon the glassy black waves and made a path of shimmering silver.

A woman stood by the stairs that led down to the sand and gripped the rail, her head bowed. She had pixie-short brown hair highlighted with streaks of dark gold and wore a nude-colored sheath dress with a black colorblock hem and black Jimmy Choo pumps. Diamond drop earrings glittered from her earlobes.

She'd taken off her ceremonial robe and looked small and vulnerable as she huddled against the rail.

"Kathy," I whispered and she swung around guiltily as if she'd committed a crime instead of gazed at the ocean.

"I did the right thing." She made no pretense that I hadn't caught her almost in tears. "But it's still hard to watch the way he looks at her. He used to look at me that way."

Before I could stop myself, I went to her and put my arms around her. The strength of her return embrace hurt, but I held her as she buried her face in my neck and we rocked together.

Our eyes were wet when we drew apart, but some of the wild sadness had lifted from her face.

"It would never have worked." Her tone was conversational as she slipped her shoes from her feet and waited for me to do the same thing. We left them on the deck and descended the wooden stairs to the rough sand.

In common accord, we moved toward the black expanse of the restless ocean, which muttered secrets to itself that grew louder as we approached.

"He wanted me and Matt to leave Darkhunt and join Silverlake. I would have had to leave the New England Regional Council. He told me he believed I would be appointed to the First Western Regional Council, but he couldn't guarantee it. He knew damn well Matt wouldn't leave Darkhunt. He was counting on that, counting on us severing the bond. He had no real interest in a triad but was willing to compromise on that for me. His exact words. Can you just hear him saying it, Stanzie? The colossal gall of the man." Kathy linked her arm with mine as we turned parallel to the ocean and continued to walk. We left bare footprints in the wet sand behind us.

"The First Western Regional Council is bigger and more influential than the New England one." I spoke before I thought as usual. Kathy just laughed.

"Do you really think I would have been appointed? As Jason Allerton's bond mate I would have had two strikes against me as the Council leaned backward to avoid making it seem as if they took orders from Jason and the Great Council. And the third strike would have been that I knew absolutely nobody in the region. How exactly was a stranger supposed to swoop in and become a Council member?"

"You could have pitched it as a fresh perspective that wasn't jaded with knowledge of the packs in the area."

Kathy laughed again and skipped nimbly over a slimy string of seaweed.

"I probably could have done that," she admitted. "But I have a life here. Should I give it up for him? Where was his compromise?"

"Matt."

"Who would never have come. Ah, I do like talking with you, Stanzie. You make me feel much better and reinforce my conviction that I did the right thing."

"I'm not his Advisor anymore," I blurted and was forced to stop dead when she dragged me to a halt. "I quit because I was so pissed at him for bonding with my mother. And he let me."

She forced me to tell her the whole story, and her blue-gray eyes grew darker and darker with every word. By the end of it she wanted to charge back to the reception hall and confront him. I grabbed her by the arm. It was like trying to hold back a whirlwind.

"I thought you'd laugh at me and tell me what an idiot I was." I hung on grimly to her arm, even though she'd stopped her struggle to break free.

"You are an idiot," she said. "But so is he. Does everyone around you eventually lose their minds, Stanzie? First Liam and now Jason."

When I heard Murphy's name, I let go and turned around so I could continue pacing along the shore. Kathy heaved a frustrated sigh, caught between returning to blast Jason and lecturing me.

She chose the lecture. I knew she would.

"Now it's more vital than ever you get your butt to Dublin and fix things with him. Do you know that exasperating man has changed his phone number? I tried to call and give him a piece of my mind and got some strange man in Revere instead. I suppose it makes sense that he wouldn't have his American phone number anymore now that he's gone back to Dublin, but it's still very annoying not to be able to get in touch with him. What did you do anyway, Stanzie, to provoke Liam into bolting for Ireland?"

"You know, that's just like you to take his side of it and not mine," I snapped over my shoulder. "Why does it have to be something *I* did and not something *he* did?"

"He's the one who left."

"That's just stupid," I said, which only made her smile one of her Kathy Manning patented smiles that always sent me sailing over the edge of my temper. "For your information, I didn't do anything except possibly give him shit because he didn't stay with me during the tribunal. And everybody, including you, you hypocrite, told me over and over he was wrong and I was right about that. So what? I'm not allowed to get mad at the bastard? Ever? Or he's justified in walking out on me? That's not fucking fair, is it?"

I tried in vain to modulate my damn voice, but it was impossible. The goddamn ocean amplified it and sent it shrieking back at me until I wanted to block my ears.

Kathy's smile never faltered. "When he walked out, what did you do? Stand there and let him?"

"I don't want to talk about it." I knew I sounded sullen and moody, but fuck it.

"Of course not," she said with an annoying-as-hell little laugh. I flipped her the bird, then stomped off. This time she didn't follow.

* * * *

Brooding alone in my room sucked. Dissatisfaction seethed within me until I wanted to punch something. Instead I pulled on a pair of sweats and a t-shirt and scrubbed the makeup from my face. Then I paced the confines of the little motel room that had become mine by default. Lauren's things were gone, only mine were left, and in two days I would drive back to Boston alone.

I couldn't sustain my fury but self-pity only annoyed me. I didn't know what to do with myself. So when someone knocked on my door, I sprang to open it with a small cry of relief.

I braced myself in case it was Kathy, but when I opened the door, I saw Faith and Scott instead.

She looked tired but determined, and he had a grin I didn't altogether trust.

"Can we come in?" Faith asked, and I stepped away from the door.

Their bond pendants winked in the overhead lights. I was supposed to wear mine since it was a Regional. Ever since I'd broken the clasp of my silver chain, I'd kept it in the small pewter box Murphy had given me the night we'd bonded in Paris. A hundred million years ago it seemed, although it had barely been nine months in reality.

"Look, if you came to talk me into shifting with Scott tomorrow night, save your breath. I'll do it, okay?" Up until I said it, I hadn't known what would fly out of my mouth. But once said I could not take it back, nor did I intend to.

Shifting was another step I needed to take to reclaim my life, and I damn well was going to take it.

"Whoa." Scott's face filled with pleasant surprise, and his cocky grin became genuine.

Faith took my hand. "That's great, Stanzie, but it's not what we came to discuss."

She examined my face as if I were under a microscope. Her scrutiny exposed my rawness. I was not at all sure I wanted to hear what she had to say.

"You need to go to Dublin."

For a wild moment I almost laughed. Of all the things they could have said to me, *this* was what they'd come to say?

"I had this dream," began Faith, and a blasting shock of coldness permeated my bones.

"Murphy? Was it about Murphy?"

Faith dreamed the future sometimes. Not often, but there had been enough episodes during my childhood where Faith confidently predicted what would happen and it had that I'd learned to pay attention whenever she said, *I had this dream*—because inevitably what she dreamed came to pass.

Once she dreamed our pack mate Darren would get caught robbing someone's house, and three nights later the homeowner walked in unexpectedly, and Darren had barely escaped before the police arrived.

Another time she'd dreamed Samantha, her father's bond mate, would have a baby boy and name him Alan and he would have blond hair and blue eyes. Eight and a half months later, she had.

I always tried to be skeptical about Faith's predictions. For instance, the law of averages demanded that cat burglar Darren's luck run out at least a few times. That it had a few nights after Faith said it would didn't definitively prove she was precognitive.

And it was a fifty-fifty shot Samantha would have a boy, and since she and Shane, the third member of her father's triad, had blond hair and blue eyes, what else would he have? Perhaps Faith had heard them talking about names for potential children.

At the time of Faith's dream, Sam had been Alpha female, and the whole point of being Alpha is to procreate. How far-fetched was it for Faith to have predicted a baby boy?

However, no one knew Samantha was pregnant when Faith related her dream to me, and no one knew for sure whether Shane or Todd was the father until after Alan was born and looked like a carbon copy of Shane.

"Tell me about your dream," I demanded. Why would I need to go to Dublin? Faith's dreams were indiscriminate; she foretold both the pleasant and the not so pleasant future. I wondered which category this dream fit.

Scott's face held no clues except that he was skeptical. Enough uncertainty shone in his eyes to let me know his doubt was eroding. Faith's accuracy tended to do that. I wondered what she had dreamed for him that had come true.

Faith frowned, and I went cold again. It wasn't going to be good, I just knew it. She hadn't had some hearts-and-roses reunion dream. No, of course not.

"I was tired from the party, and I took a nap about an hour ago and dreamed. I woke up and knew I had to come tell you about it. My dream didn't make much sense, but I remember he had an Irish accent. I can't remember much of what your bond mate said except that once he said,

Now do you believe in me again? You were there, and you were crying, but I don't remember why. You said, *Yes, I believe in you. I belong to you.* And he smiled, but it was so wistful and haunting." Determination filled Faith's voice. "I think it was a dream about your bond mate and how you need to be together."

I frowned. *I belong to you?* That wasn't something I'd say to Murphy, but it did remind me of something that had been said to me once. The bastard.

Suspicion made my voice prickly. "What did he look like? My bond mate."

Faith frowned in concentration as she struggled to bring up the dream memory. Scott shifted his weight and sighed.

"Dark curly hair. Oh, and one blue eye, one brown eye. He looked like a really nice guy, Stanzie." Faith bit her lip and might have gone on, but I interrupted her.

"It wasn't a dream about Murphy. That's Paddy O'Reilly you're describing, my Alpha. And I'd never say that to him. I don't belong to him, the lying bastard."

"Whoa, are you saying the Alpha of Mac Tire has curly dark hair and different-colored eyes?" Scott was shaken. I nodded.

"Goddamn it," he said. "Faith, she must have told you about him."

"No," Faith denied. She put a hand on his shoulder, and he almost, but not quite, shrugged it away. "Now do you believe I dreamed I would meet you at the Regional? I did, you know. Down to the Red Sox baseball cap you wore to the meet and greet."

"Bullshit," he whispered, but more of his skepticism fell away. He took a deep breath.

"Maybe you'd better go, Stanzie," he said, and my heart performed a strange dance in my chest.

"Paddy O'Reilly is a lying bastard." I was furious with Faith's damn dream. I would never tell that man I belonged to him. Ever. Paddy had betrayed me when he left me behind. He told me I was family and then not even a week later walked away.

Scott recovered his equilibrium and grinned. "Jesus, why don't you tell us how you really feel about this guy?"

"Shut up, Charest," I snapped, and he winked at me.

"Maybe I should try that line out on some of the Mayflower ladies. You belong to me!" He made his voice sound like Bela Lugosi's in *Dracula*.

"Fuck off, Scott."

"Yeah, that's pretty much the response I'd probably get. I guess I'm no Irish heartthrob Alpha, huh?" He laughed. But he sobered at the look on my face.

"It's not funny." I was so pissed at Paddy if he'd been in the room with me I would have spat at him. Scott's lame sense of humor only made my humiliation worse.

"Okay, okay, I'm getting that now. God, Stanzie, it was just a joke. How could you take a line like that seriously? Oh, hell, you did. He said it, you took it seriously, and he fucked it all up. Now you're going to kick my ass, right?"

"Just stop talking about it," I rumbled, so close to tears I could taste them. *I belong to you, my ass, Paddy O'Reilly.*

Faith's expression was somber. Alarm bells zinged down my spine, and I tried to fight them. There was something about the dream she wasn't telling me, I just knew it. "Stanzie, I'm sorry. I really thought it was about your bond mate. I still think you need to go to Dublin. I woke up thinking that. Just because he's not your bond mate doesn't change that. He's your Alpha, lying bastard or not. Maybe you'd better skip the hunt and go tomorrow. I think he needs you."

"Needs me?" I scoffed, but a thread of disquiet wormed down my spine. Goddamn Faith and her stupid-ass dreams. I was *not* going to Dublin.

Faith gave me one last look before she took Scott by the hand and led him out the door.

I still think you need to go to Dublin. Faith's words reverberated in my head until I wanted to scream. *Need.* Why did she have to say *need*? Was he in trouble? Was something wrong?

"I do *not* belong to you, Paddy O'Reilly," I announced, but even to my ears my voice sounded weak and unconvinced.

Goddamn dreams.

Chapter 3

"May I sit down?" Startled, I glanced up from my solitary breakfast of eggs and bacon to see Jason Allerton with his hand on the chair opposite mine.

Next to the motel was a small diner where many of us ate breakfast before attending the day's activities at the Regional. However, it was barely past six o'clock, and until Jason's arrival I had been the only Pack person there.

I nodded, and my breakfast began to congeal into an uncomfortable lump in the pit of my stomach.

Outside a light rain misted the diner windows, but the sun was attempting to burn through the cloud cover.

Jason sat, but before he could say anything, the waitress hurried over to take his order. The Sunday morning rush was still two hours away, and she looked bored.

He asked for coffee and a ham-and-cheese omelet, and I decided my breakfast was over. To keep my hands busy, I pulled my coffee cup closer and pretended I needed cream.

"I owe you an apology, Stanzie." My hand jerked at the unexpected words, and most of the cream ended up on the Formica tabletop, where it began a race toward my lap. I hastily swabbed at it with my napkin and cursed my clumsiness.

Jason's scent was apologetic. At least I detected no anger. That surprised me, too, and I gave him my full attention.

"You're absolutely right. I do default to Councilor mode. I've been one for so long now, it's automatic. How dare anyone challenge me? You weren't speaking to me as Councilor Allerton, you were talking to me as Jason Allerton, the man who swept into your mother's life and went behind your back to court her.

"Something that had developed between us over a two month span was dumped into your lap as fait accompli in two seconds over what you thought was an innocent dinner. You see, I thought my personal life was none of your business."

"It isn't." My throat was dry, and I wanted a sip of water in the worst way but couldn't move.

"It is if my personal life intersects with yours through your mother."

"She's fifty-eight years old," I reminded him.

"We did it wrong. We should have told you earlier. Lauren followed my lead. I wanted everything private, the way I always do with my personal life. I thought perhaps she might have shared her feelings with you, but she didn't, did she?"

"No. Looking back, I guess I knew she was keeping something from me, but mainly we talked about how I envisioned her life was going to go. No wonder she got so nervous and upset when I'd talk about fall foliage tours we'd take in Vermont when she knew she'd be in Montana. Or at least suspected it. No wonder she couldn't make up her mind about anything."

I looked across the table at Jason's face. As always, I found his aristocratic good looks intimidating. I thought of how kind and gentle he'd been to me at my tribunals and most recently with everything that happened in my birth pack, Mayflower. I wanted to believe in him again.

"Maybe I was willfully blind. I wanted her to stay with me. I didn't want to be alone. So maybe I ignored the signs she was trying to show me."

Affection tinged with sadness made his eyes very blue. "I think most of the blame for this rests squarely upon my shoulders. I was so affronted you'd question my motives that I didn't share with you how I felt about Lauren. I did nothing to address your valid concerns. I anticipated you'd be pleased. I believed you trusted me and would know your mother was safe with me."

"Maybe I wanted more for her than just safe." I looked away from him as the waitress returned with his omelet and a fresh pot of coffee. She filled his mug, reheated mine and rushed to intercept a new customer. I wished I had her energy, but I felt thick and slow.

He pushed the cream and sugar in my direction and gave me a wistful smile. I didn't like Jason Allerton to be wistful. As a Councilor he ought to be above such emotions. But he was more than simply a Councilor.

"You're wrong," I blurted, and his eyes widened. "About me appealing to you as Jason Allerton the man, not the Councilor. I never do that. I don't like to think of you outside of your Councilor role because you make me feel safe when you're the Councilor. When you're not, when the mask slips, I get nervous."

His smile was warm. "I am in love with Lauren Newcastle. I am her bond mate, and that puts our relationship, yours and mine, Stanzie, in a different category than previously. I'm not going to be the Councilor for you all the time anymore."

Yeah, great. When would I ever see him now that I didn't work for him? Did he think I would visit Montana? Would there be an annual Christmas holiday now where'd we play the happy family? Maybe he'd intend it at first, but in my life, people had a way of slipping through the cracks. Montana might as well be the moon for all I'd see of him or my mother after this weekend.

"I saw that you did at the bonding ceremony. All I wanted to say to you last night was that I was sorry for doubting your motives. I didn't know you really cared about her or that she loved you."

Or that he could get over Kathy Manning in the space between one breath and the next.

I'd mourned for my dead bond mates Grey and Elena for two years. I still missed them sometimes so much it felt like a stab to the heart. And Murphy? Ha. I couldn't stop loving him no matter what I did. But Jason Allerton just decided to be over one woman and in love with the next in the blink of an eye. And in the middle of it all deal with the grief of a dead bond mate. Yeah, sure, she'd been insane for years, but he must have cared about her at some point in his life. Must be nice to be him.

I fumbled in my wallet for money to cover my check and dropped it on the table. I had to get out of there before I bawled like a goddamn baby.

"Where are you going?" He put a hand on my wrist, and I froze.

"I was going to go for a walk on the beach." Just anywhere away from him.

"Please, let me join you." He got his own wallet out.

"You didn't finish your breakfast." Finish—hell, he'd never even started.

"I need to talk to you about a job I want you to look into for me." He reverted straight back to Councilor mode without a pause. Or did he? I peered suspiciously at him through the hair that had fallen across my face in my rush to get the hell away. I brushed it back with impatient fingers.

"But I don't work for you anymore."

That made him smile, but there was also a plea in his blue eyes. "I hoped we could erase that part of our previous conversation. The Great Council knows nothing of it, and unless you've told—"

"Kathy," I finished for him.

He sighed, and a look that was half irritation, half amusement crossed his face. "That's no matter. I can smooth it out."

"Like you smoothed out her life's ambitions?" The words escaped me before I could help it, and I waited for his expression to turn cold and hard against me.

"Would you like me to confess to you I handled that situation poorly as well? I can do that. It's the truth after all."

I gaped at him. "It is?"

"It is. It was very unfair of me to expect her to uproot her entire life while I gave up nothing in return. I believed she loved me and would agree to my vision of our lives together. The truth was she did love me but didn't share my vision, nor should she have. Three months later I'm in love with another woman, and I'm an arrogant, manipulative bastard. Okay? Can we get past that and work together, or are you done?" His words were clipped and concise. Cold.

I got to my feet, this time sure he would let me leave, but he pushed back his chair to follow me until the conversation was concluded to his satisfaction.

"Jason, I want to go to Dublin," I heard myself say past the ringing in my ears. Up until that precise moment, I hadn't realized I'd made up my mind. This did not mean I wanted to belong to Paddy O'Reilly. There was a perfectly valid reason other than him to return to Dublin, and the dream just gave me the impetus to try. "I want Murphy back. I know it might be too late, but I've got to at least try.

Trepidation and elation warred within me, and black pinpricks of light danced before my eyes as my vision narrowed and my heart rate accelerated in a dizzy burst of adrenaline. I hadn't given myself permission to even think it was possible to reconcile. Was I setting myself up for a disastrous disappointment? What if he pushed me away?

"Can I work for you after? Will you give me a few days to try to sort things out with him?"

"Stanzie," he said. "Sit down."

I sat. Jason handed me a napkin, and that's when I realized I was crying. That figured. I always cried. He reached across the table to put his hand on my arm. His fingers were warm and comforting, his face full of concern and affection.

"The job is in Dublin. I want you to help Liam either find Mick Shaughnessy or give up the search gracefully. It's become an obsession with him and he'll put himself and his pack at risk if he's not careful.

Now do you believe in me? Paddy's face swam before my eyes. Could he need my help with Murphy? Is that what Faith's dream meant?

"He's not thinking clearly lately. You, my dear, I suspect are the cause of that."

Mick Shaughnessy. The name sent a shiver down my spine. Four years ago Murphy placed him in a janitorial job at the lab where Murphy's bond mate, Sorcha, worked nights. Grandfather Mick repaid the generosity by arranging her death in the name of the conspiracy. Once his cover had been blown and his role in the conspiracy revealed, Mick Shaughnessy disappeared. Murphy was chasing him down? That was so dangerous I wanted to scream.

"Murphy's not running around Dublin spouting off about the conspiracy, is he?" I was scared. I knew Murphy when he had his mind set on something. He was single-minded and relentless. He threw his personal safety to the wayside.

"Not quite yet, thankfully." Jason gave my arm a squeeze and sat back. He cast a hungry look at his omelet, and I pushed the salt and pepper shakers toward him.

"Eat. Do you want ketchup?" At his horrified look, I let go of the bottle and then decided my eggs needed more and dumped a red blob of it onto my scrambled eggs. They were cold but still delicious.

Jason tore into his omelet with the appetite of someone who had spent the previous evening occupied with strenuous exercise. I didn't really want to think about him and my mother thrashing around passionately between the sheets, so I forced my attention back to my plate.

We ate in silence for a moment, and the less I thought about Jason and Wren, the more Murphy crowded into my thoughts. What if the asshole did something stupid? Fatally stupid? The conspiracy already tried to take him out with an overdose of narcotics. Would they hesitate to act again if Murphy threatened them? I didn't think so.

"Someone told Grandfather Mick the Council knew he'd been involved in Sorcha's death," I said when my plate was empty. Jason's was, too, except for a few lone breakfast potatoes. "Someone in Mac Tire?"

"Presumably." Jason set down his fork and gave me his full attention. "The problem with Mac Tire is that it's a very large pack and is not confined to simply Ireland and Northern Ireland. England, Scotland and Wales have to be considered as well. Mick's obviously taken refuge somewhere, and he's nowhere to be found in Dublin. At least not yet. Liam doesn't believe he's there."

"So you two are in contact? You authorized his search efforts?" My coffee mug was lukewarm between the palms of my hands. Outside the diner, the rain had intensified, the sun blocked by a raft of ominous dark clouds. Heavy droplets spattered against the window and combined to smear the glass so I could barely make out the wavering shapes of the cars in the parking lot. Maybe the hunt would be a wet one tonight, but it seemed more and more likely with every passing moment I wouldn't be there to find out.

"We're in contact," Jason confirmed, but frowned. "But the colder the trail, the hotter his pursuit. Maybe you could distract him."

Murphy had been focused on finding Sorcha's killer for nearly four months. Would I be a distraction he would brush off easily? I'd never been able to compete with Sorcha, even four years into her grave, why in the world would I be able to start now?

But I had to do something.

Chapter 4

"Where the hell do you think you're going?" A bulky shadow detached from the brickwork near the green door of the pub and resolved itself into the shape of a very tall, extremely muscular man.

The glow of the streetlights illuminated his green eyes and bright red hair. His expression was not exactly welcoming.

The sign above the pub doors read *An Puca,* and I was pretty sure I was in the right place. Although, after a hellish twelve-hour delay in Philadelphia due to some damn mechanical malfunction in one of the plane's engines, I wasn't even sure what frigging day it was anymore.

Instead of arriving in Dublin at just before eight in the morning with time to find a hotel and get my bearings before setting out to find Mac Tire's pub, the plane landed just after eight PM, and I'd taken a cab straight from the airport to the pub.

My eyes were scratchy and dry, my throat ached and my stomach rumbled. I was sleep and food-deprived and pretty damn close to a meltdown. Whether it would be a temper tantrum or tears I wasn't exactly sure, but I'd had enough.

Now this goddamn red-haired giant couldn't even be civil?

"This is a pub, right? Don't pubs want people to drink in them?" I curled my lip sarcastically which only made the red- haired giant angry. Good one, Stanzie.

"Can you not read the wee sign in the window that says *Private party tonight*, maybe? Or do they not teach reading in American schools these days?"

"Your big, goddamn hulking shoulders blocked the wee sign in the window," I muttered rebelliously.

The red-haired giant cracked his knuckles.

"Excuse me?" I tilted my head to the side and regarded him with growing incredulity. He was not going to threaten to beat me up, was he? I wished I'd worn my six-inch spiked heels with the steel-tipped toes, but all I had were a comfortable pair of leather boots. "Look, I don't know your name but I do know you're Pack. And so am I. And if the private party tonight is for members of Mac Tire, well, then, here's a funny thing—I'm a member of Mac Tire. So can I go in now? I'm fucking tired and I want a drink."

Meltdown verged in the direction of temper tantrum. That was interesting. Most times it was tears.

"Well, I can smell too, can't I now?" The giant sneered. "But, if you knew the first thing about Mac Tire, which I'm almost positive you don't, you'd know we have pack jewelry, which, incidentally, I'm not seeing on you. And I'll betcha my left nut you don't have the jewelry because you're not Mac Tire. Because if you were, you'd never take it off. Brilliant, isn't it?"

Yeah. Brilliant. Of course I didn't wear the damn ring. It was a lie. Paddy had put it on my finger and told me I was family and it was a fucking lie.

"I'm going to lose my temper," I announced. The giant might be bigger than me, but I knew I could scream louder.

"I don't give a fuck." The giant crossed his beefy arms over his chest and smirked.

I cursed the fact I hadn't let Jason alert Paddy or Murphy I was coming to Dublin. In my irrational fear of everything, I'd thought maybe they wouldn't have let me come, but they could hardly object once I was already there.

I'd come armed with the name and address of the pack's pub. That was all I'd let Jason give me.

Damn the man, why hadn't he gone behind my back and called anyway? Of all the times to let me have my way, why now? Bastard.

"Look, I have the damn ring. It's in my luggage. I am Mac Tire, I swear." It galled to say that because I did not feel remotely as if I belonged to the pack, but I needed to get into the pub. I was tired, hungry, miserable and about to collapse.

"Doubtful." The giant made no move to move aside and let me in.

"Do you want me to tear apart my suitcase? Jesus, I don't believe this. I think you get off on hassling people." I began to unzip my suitcase.

He guffawed, but did not uncross his arms. "What's your name, woman? But I have to tell you, we don't have Americans in Mac Tire."

"Ha," I crowed. "That's just a goddamn lie. Because you do have one. Me. My name is Constance Newcastle."

I don't know what I expected. Maybe not that he'd break down into abject apologies, sweep open the door and personally escort me in, but at least some glimmer of recognition.

"Doesn't ring a bell. Why don't you fuck off? Right now I'm bored, but I'm edging toward irritated and there's a thing you don't want to see, I promise you."

"How about Liam Murphy? You know him?" I spat out his name and hated myself for sinking so goddamn low.

One bushy red eyebrow elevated. Paddy could do that trick too. Was everyone in Mac Tire a direct descendent of Mister Spock or something?

"Him I know." That figured. Murphy was an ex-Alpha after all.

"Then do you know he's bonded with an American?" I prompted, my lip still curled.

"I know he showed up here four months ago without her and never talks about it. Rumor has it you two are on the rocks only he won't face up to it." The giant gave a huge shrug and his green eyes gleamed with protective ire. "Tell you what. You give me the real story of it and I'll think about asking if you can go in. Fair's fair. Liam Murphy's a favorite in this pack and you're some flighty American twat nobody knows or gives a damn about."

Won't face up to it? What the fuck? *He* walked out on *me*. I don't know what showed on my face, but the red-haired giant's expression altered and for the first time he looked unsure.

"Look, let me call Paddy and..." he began, but I couldn't stand the sudden pity in his eyes. I guess he'd figured out I wasn't the one who walked out. Fuck.

"Oh, screw this." I wheeled around and stomped off. I ruined my exit though because I forgot my goddamn suitcase and had to scurry back to retrieve it and the backpack full of shoes.

The giant attempted to help me, and I slapped his meaty hands away, my cheeks on fire with mortification.

"Did you come to try to work it out with him then?" He didn't seem to feel the stinging slaps on his hands, and pulled the strap of the backpack over my shoulder even as I fought against his help.

Where was my goddamn anger now? Mortification rapidly turned into blinding tears. My eyes burned.

"None of your fucking business." I stomped away.

"Hang on," he called after me. "Just let me call Paddy and maybe I can…"

"Fuck you," I screamed over my shoulder and turned my head away before he could see the tears on my cheeks. But I think he saw them anyway. Goddamn streetlights.

* * * *

Two blocks later when I was about to shove my damn heavy suitcase into the middle of the street and watch it get demolished by the terrifying traffic that traveled on the wrong goddamn side of the road, my cell phone rang.

"This blows," I announced as the backpack of shoes fell off my shoulder and dragged me by the elbow half into the gutter. I gave my suitcase a kick and it tottered a moment before it fell over—straight into a puddle.

Pedestrians gave me a wide berth, and once again I wished I had my steel-toed, spiked heels.

Instead, I dug into my purse, fatalistically convinced I would miss the damn call, and pulled out my phone. I pressed Talk.

"What?" I barked, and there was a strange silence on the other end, as if the person debated whether or not to gently hang up and say to hell with it.

"Where the hell are you?" The person on the other end obviously had no fear of death, but I wondered how he felt about death by disembowelment. Slow disembowelment.

I looked around at the unfamiliar street. A pharmacy. A men's tailor. A shoe store. I knew I was not in a good mental space when not even the slightest desire to drift closer to the shoe store window passed through my head. In fact, I felt like throwing my backpack through the damn thing. Bad place. Stanzie was in a bad, bad place.

"I have no fucking clue," I replied because I didn't. Some street in Dublin. I smelled food—something thick and meaty like stew—and nearly wept, I was so damn hungry.

"Turn your ass around and come back to the pub."

"Is that a direct order, Alpha?" I snarled. Paddy, who was on the other end of the phone, damn him, made a strangled noise halfway between laughter and a roar of outrage.

"You know what? Just shut up and frigging stand there. I'll find you. You can't be far, Colm said you didn't have a car."

"You have got to be kidding. A car? Everyone drives on the wrong side of the road, Paddy. I almost had a fucking coronary in the cab from the airport and had to put my head between my knees and close my eyes for most of the ride. The cab driver thought I was freaking insane, and there's a distinct possibility he may be onto something. A fucking car. Please."

"Are you gonna go ballistic if I start laughing now?" Paddy definitely struggled against hysterics, I could hear it in his damn voice. Fury, dull and hot, pounded through my veins and made my head hurt.

I heard traffic noises from his end and suspected he was outside. "Where are you?"

"Grouchy," he commented. "I'm walking down the damn street, Stanzie, where the hell else would I be? I told you I was coming to find you. Do you suppose you could describe your surroundings? Give me a bit more than the cars are driving on the wrong side of the road?"

"Pharmacy, men's tailor, shoe store," I recited obediently, although I really wanted to reach through the phone and strangle him.

"Let me guess. You're standing outside the shoe store and drooling over the Jimmy Flus or whatever the bloody hell they call them."

"Choos," I snapped. "Jimmy Choos. You're fucking with me on purpose, aren't you?"

"Maybe a little," he agreed, and I growled.

"Did you just growl at me?"

I did it again and gave my suitcase another kick. It was still on its side in the puddle, and I bet all my damn clothes were now soaked in dirty Dublin rainwater. Fuck. Me.

"Just for my own edification, what might be the name of the pharmacy? Or the men's tailor? Or the bloody shoe store?" Paddy was the one who sounded grouchy, and a grim smile flickered across my face.

"Boots, John O'Toole's Menswear and Shamrock Shoes. That's the dumbest name I ever heard for a shoe store, by the way. What's next? Emerald Isle Organic Market? Blarney Stone Cosmetics? Jesus. H. Christ."

"Hey," groaned my Alpha. "Don't be making fun of my culture, woman. It's not nice." Then he snickered. "Blarney Stone Cosmetics. You horrible bitch."

I almost laughed myself. It was kind of a good one.

I saw him then as he rounded the corner. Black curls ran riot over his head, black jeans, black t-shirt, black jean jacket, black boots.

"Who are you? The Dark Lord of Dublin?" I eyed him up and down as he approached, and he rolled his eyes at me.

"And you? Who are you? The Bedraggled Bitch of Boston?" His gaze was equally derisive as he took in my jeans, t-shirt, gray hoodie and boots. My hair was a dreadful mess and my makeup long since worn off.

We glared at each other for thirty seconds before we both burst out laughing.

"You do look like shite," he said when he'd recovered, but he sounded concerned, not derogatory. I shrugged and remembered what a bastard he was. The warm moment between us evaporated, and he sighed before he righted my suitcase. It dripped, and he grimaced. He shook his head but didn't say anything, although I suspected it half killed him to keep his mouth shut.

"Did you not sleep at all on the plane?" He started back the way he'd come. My suitcase bumped along behind him, and I was forced to follow him if I wanted it back.

"I can't sleep on planes."

"Jaysus," he muttered. "What is with you and your dire distrust of all methods of modern transportation?"

"It's not just modern. I'm kinda afraid of horses, too," I admitted, and he snorted.

"Well, doesn't that figure."

"Walking and running are the two best ways to get anywhere, Paddy."

"If you never want to go more than a couple miles or get someplace in less than a month, I suppose."

"I also like bikes. The ones with pedals."

"Aren't you awful scared you might hit a pothole and fly over the handlebars and break your arm, maybe?"

"If I'm that damn stupid not to avoid the pothole, I deserve to break my arm. Haven't you figured out yet I distrust putting my life in the hands of someone else? Someone who may fall asleep at the wheel or screw with his cellphone just as the light changes?"

"Control—you just don't like to give it up. Have you always been this way, or is this a recent character flaw?" He threw me a suspicious look over his shoulder.

"Define recent? You try growing up with a father who takes every last decision out of your hands and makes you feel like you're too stupid to figure shit out for yourself, and top it off with killing your bond mates in a car crash—and *you* tell me why I don't like losing control. Control makes me safe, Paddy O'Reilly, and I don't think it's too much to ask to feel safe, do you?"

"No." His tone was subdued, and I became aware I'd screamed at him and, also, surprise, surprise, I was in tears.

More pedestrians scattered out of my way, some of them even went so far as to turn away so they didn't have to meet my gaze and perhaps become infected with my special brand of crazy.

"Look, I'm tired and starving to death and all I wanted to do was come into the pub. Only I wasn't wearing my damn pack ring, so that giant bastard wouldn't let me in. Why should I wear my ring? You don't give a shit about me. Apparently the whole frigging pack thinks I left Murphy and not the other way around." I swiped at my eyes with my sleeve and cursed myself.

"A little advance warning would have been nice, Stanz." Paddy slowed his pace so he fell in next to me and tried to put his free arm around my shoulders, but I shrugged him away.

"You want to watch me kick Colm's ass? I didn't have time to do it on my way out the pub door, but I'd definitely planned on it."

"Violence doesn't solve anything. I just think it's stupid you have to be Mac Tire and wear a goddamn ring to get into a fucking pub. Why isn't being Pack good enough?" I felt my blood pressure skyrocket, and Paddy groaned.

"Because the pub's private, woman, but..."

"What the hell kind of bullshit elitist crap is this? A pub just for your own pack members and to hell with the Pack at large? Padraic O'Reilly, you sonofabitch, what kind of pack is Mac Tire anyway? Fucking private pub? Unbelievable."

"Will you shut it, goddamn it?" Paddy cast a nervous glance around, but there were no pedestrians in the vicinity. Not anymore. Anyway, I hadn't screamed. I had used a very vicious whisper.

"Why? What in the name of hell for?" Incensed, I grabbed his arm and forced him to stop his forward motion.

"Mac Tire's a big enough pack as it is, Stanzie, and—" He broke off and pushed his hand through his unruly curls. His fingers stuck and with a grimace he yanked them free. "I'll not be standing on the street discussing pack politics with you, damn it. The pub's private and there's a reason for it and to hell with you if you don't like it. You don't have to like it, do you? You aren't—"

"Going to be a member much longer? Yeah, well, screw you, too. Bastard," I hissed and would have taken a swing at him, but he stepped prudently out of reach.

"If you'd let me finish my sent—" he began, until I hissed, "Bastard" again under my breath, and he shut his mouth.

We stared at each other for a good forty seconds.

"I was gonna say Alpha, you annoying twat. You aren't Alpha. Next time let me finish my frigging sentence!"

"Sure. I wouldn't want to stop you from swearing at me and calling me derogatory names in these unfinished sentences, Paddy."

"Oh, and *bastard* is a compliment then?" We glared at each other again until the silence was broken by my goddamn growling stomach.

"Tell me you ate something on the plane, Stanzie."

"So now you want me to start lying to you? I'm sorry I'm not as good at it as you are, but maybe with practice I could get better."

He squeezed his eyes shut and I swore I saw his lips move as he counted to ten. "Da always told me never to argue with a starving woman. So I'm not saying anything at all to you until you eat something."

"Fine with me! Who the hell wants to listen to your bullshit, anyway?" I shoved my backpack back on my shoulder so I could follow him the few paces left to the door of the pub.

The red-haired giant had obviously eavesdropped if his expression of complete astonishment was any indication.

"Were you the freak of nature who called Paddy and told him I was here?" I snarled into his chest on my way past. I didn't feel like tilting my head back enough to look him in the face.

"Ye—es?" He didn't sound very confident and I rolled my eyes.

"Thanks for nothing, asswipe."

"For fuck's sake, will somebody shove some food down this woman's gullet before we're all doomed?" Paddy yelled, and the entire pub went eerily silent.

"We have shepherd's pie or fish and chips tonight." A redheaded woman with eyes the color of green sea glass stood behind the bar. She looked between me and Paddy with a curious expression and the barest hint of a grin.

"Bring both up to my office," Paddy ordered. "And Guinness as well. And be goddamn quick. And don't even think about turning that sly smirk into laughter, Alannah, or I'll have Fee pull all that red hair out of your skull for you."

The woman turned away and covered her mouth, but we all heard her stifled snickers anyway.

"Goddamn it," swore Paddy and stomped up a flight of old wooden stairs just inside the door. A red velvet rope stretched across the bottom, but he had long legs and simply stepped over it.

I was not as tall and had to hang onto the banister to keep my balance, but I managed not to trip over my feet.

At the top of the staircase was a door marked *Private*. To the left was a small, very antiquated bathroom. Paddy shoved open the office door and stomped toward an old rolltop desk piled with papers and a desk calculator. He threw himself into a leather chair on wheels that squealed in protest and nearly bashed into the brick wall behind it.

A battered sofa, two armchairs with the stuffing coming out, an ancient coffee table and a set of built in bookshelves crammed haphazardly with books and magazines made up the rest of the furniture.

A grimy window covered with curtains in a faded red chintz pattern overlooked a dark alley.

"Very film noir." I brushed off the seat of one of the armchairs before dubiously taking a seat. "Are you a private eye or a publican? All you need is a fedora and a fifth of rye stashed in your desk drawer, and you could be straight out of a Mickey Spillane novel."

"Shut it," Paddy advised and put his head in his hands for a moment.

"Dramatic bastard." I looked around the room and grimaced at the grime on the window.

"I take it by your comment outside that you're here to sever the ties with Liam?" Paddy moved his squeaky chair so the desk didn't block me from his sight.

"Actually, the opposite. I came to work things out. Just when you thought it was safe to go back in the water, right?"

"Huh?" He gaped at me, and I rolled my eyes.

"That was a *Jaws* reference, you dumbass."

He continued to stare.

"American movie from the seventies? About a huge shark that ate half the damn town and then got blown up with an air tank and a lucky-as-hell rifle shot?"

"What the hell are you blathering on about now? You're delirious— you do know that, right? You need to eat something and maybe then we can have a genuine conversation. Jaysus." Paddy rolled the chair back behind his desk and began to sort through the phenomenal mess spread across it.

"This office is a joke. You can't seriously run a business out of here. How can you possibly keep track of anything with it thrown all over the desk like that?"

"I have a system." Paddy gave me a defensive glare and I shook my head.

"And I have nine lives like a cat. My ass, you have a system," I sneered and something pounded the desktop. Possibly his fist.

"This is not the Stanzie Newcastle I remember," he muttered. "Step one foot on Irish soil, and it's like a fucking banshee possessed you."

I settled back in the armchair.

"So where is he? Murphy?" My voice was casual, but I didn't fool either of us. I thought of Faith's dream again and wanted to beg the man to tell me Murphy wasn't in over his head, but I had to play it just a little cooler than that. If I could. Subtlety was not one of my better talents.

"No," he decided. "We are not having this conversation until after you eat and after I drink copious amounts of beer. Not gonna happen."

"I know he's giving everyone in the pack the impression I walked out on him. Or maybe that was you," I accused and Paddy's mouth fell open.

"Me?" he bellowed. "I'm not in the habit of blabbing pack members' private business all over the place."

"Fine. It was him, then." I tried to keep the hurt out of my voice but I knew I failed. "That red-haired giant hurt my feelings," I yelled. "I wasn't in half so bad a mood before he treated me like shit and talked about the pub being fucking private."

"I told you I'm gonna kick his ass. Why do you have to take it out on me?" Paddy shouted.

"I'm also mad as hell at you! Worse than I am at the giant!"

"His name is Colm, damn it," snapped Paddy. "And why the hell should you be mad at me?"

My blood pressure zoomed again at his treachery.

"You said I was family. After my father disowned me at the tribunal, you took me aside and told me I didn't need him because I had a family. You. Mac Tire. You fucking lied to my face, Paddy, and what's worse, I believed you. I believed *in* you. And then you just walked away. You couldn't even look me straight in the eye the day you and Murphy left. And in four months not a phone call or an email to see if I was okay. Nothing. Not one goddamn thing."

"Fuck." Guilt spread across Paddy's face, but I was unmoved. Then the guilt turned to anger, and he yelled, "And why the fuck has it taken you four months to get your ass over here anyway? I didn't think it would take you even four days, but no, you've got to be a bitch about it!"

"Me? A bitch? What?" I spluttered, unable to form a coherent sentence due to the rage strangling me.

"You heard me. You sat there and didn't say one word when he said he was leaving, and how the hell do you think that made him feel? Like complete shite, that's how it made him feel. And here I am, having to pick up the pieces for you, and now you have the gall to be mad at *me*, woman? I'm the one who should be mad, and I am. I am good and frigging mad, so don't you glare at me like that. You tell me what the hell took you so long to get here."

"*He* left *me*," I screamed. Rage burned up and down my spine and all through my blood until I thought I might spontaneously combust. "How many times do I have to keep telling people that? Why is everyone blaming me? *He* walked out on *me*, and I'm supposed to come crawling after him to beg him to take me back? Fuck you! Oh, you arrogant bastard, I cannot even believe you!"

"Where in the hell did you hear me say the word *crawl*? Stanzie Newcastle, will you calm your ass down and shut the fuck up for one minute? I can't even hear myself think." Paddy tore at his hair with his hands, and his cheeks were so red I thought he was close to combustion too.

Affronted, I turned away from him and stared at the damn brick wall. He wanted me to shut the fuck up, did he? Fine. I would not say a word.

The office door banged open, and the redhead from behind the bar walked in with a tray of food and Guinness. My stomach rumbled, and she flashed me a smile I didn't trust an inch. Too many teeth.

"I'm Alannah Doyle," she introduced herself as she set the tray down on Paddy's desk. "My bond mate's Declan Byrne."

"Constance Newcastle." I took a deep breath. "At the moment, anyway, my bond mate is Liam Murphy." I wanted to throw up or crawl beneath the sofa, but I managed to look her in the face, braced for pity or ridicule.

"What took you so long to get here?" she demanded, hands on hips.

"*Thank* you," Paddy yelled rudely.

"Does this shit happen all the time in Mac Tire? People walk out on other people, and other people chase after them, even though they were the ones that were walked out on?" My tone was snotty, but, honestly, what the fuck?

"For three years every eligible female in this pack and some not so eligible chased after Liam, and he spurned us all. So forgive me, woman, for being a bit pissed the female he finally does choose deserts his ass at the first sign of trouble. It's been a terrible thing to watch him these past few months. At least after Sorcha died we didn't have to see him because he ran away to Belfast, of all fucking stupid places, and we weren't constantly exposed to his sad, pitiful face day after day. Has the man smiled even once in four months, Paddy?" Alannah turned to him, and he looked up guiltily from his Guinness and swallowed the wrong way.

"Stop drinking that and participate in this discussion. It's important." Alannah stomped a small foot on the wooden floor, but by the way Paddy cringed I would have expected her to be an Amazon or at least brandishing a weapon.

More and more it seemed my interpretation of Faith's dream was dead-on. Paddy needed my help with Murphy. Only, was I the one who could give it? That man never took anybody's help—why the hell would he take mine?

"How many goddamn times do I have to say that *I* am the one who was deserted, not the other fucking way around?" I wanted to get up and kick her pretty face in but somehow controlled myself.

The look of scorn she directed at me could have stripped paint.

"What are you doing here, then?"

I didn't say anything, and she blew out her breath in impatience. "You silly cow. Why can't you admit you want him back? Bloody stupid, prideful Americans. You get on my nerves."

"Did you—you did not just call me a *cow*." My face heated. I turned in Paddy's direction. "Did that bitch just call me a cow?"

"Jaysus, I want to eat dinner in peace. Woman, get your ass back to the bar. You're the one who wanted the job, didn't you? Begged me for it, in fact. And now you've got the job, what do you do? Stand around in my office, badgering poor Stanzie. If she doesn't want to answer you, she doesn't have to. Why should she tell us her strategy anyway? You're gonna spoil all the fun we'll have watching her."

"I did not beg you for this job." Alannah tossed her red hair as she moved for the door. "Declan fucked Fee for it, you bastard."

I waited until the door was shut before I said anything. Spoil the fun, would she?

"You made her bond mate fuck yours so she could have a job behind the bar? Oh my God." He ducked when I threw my boot at his head.

"Stanzie. It was a joke! The stupid kind between brother and sister? Alannah's my half sister, for Christ's sake. Her ma was bonded to my ma and da."

"She introduces herself as Declan Byrne's bond mate but conveniently leaves out the part where she's your sister? Unbelievable. And rude. And you didn't say anything either, you bastard." He ducked again when I threw my second boot.

The lure of the food on the desk was too much to resist. On sock feet, I padded over.

He kept his hands prudently out of the way as I made my choice between the shepherd's pie and the fish and chips. I retreated back to the armchair with the shepherd's pie and a foamy glass of Guinness.

Before I dug in, I gave him a dark look, and he groaned.

"Okay, so we're frigging rude barbarians here in Mac Tire. From now on I'll make sure to give you everyone's family ties before I even tell you their names when I'm introducing you. I will never understand women. Particularly American women. I don't even know why the hell I try to reason with any of them. Ever." He muttered the last bit to himself and abruptly grabbed a fistful of chips from the plate and stuffed them in his mouth.

"All right then," I allowed after I savored a forkful of the delicious shepherd's pie. It was spicy and warm, and hit my empty stomach like a welcome friend.

"Glad to have the royal pardon, your Majesty," he mocked, and I flipped him off because my mouth was too full to yell at him.

I decided to concentrate on my food and not Paddy because he'd just ruin my appetite, the sonofabitch, and I was starving. I applied myself to my plate, and by the sounds he made, he practically made love to his fish and chips.

Replete, I leaned back in the armchair. My plate was incredibly empty, and so was my glass. Paddy remedied the latter by refilling it from the pitcher on his desk.

He studied me for a moment as he stood before me. "You've got some color back in your face. Non-choleric-rage-related color, that is." He reached down to brush some hair from my face, and I flinched. His mouth tightened.

"I know you think I'm some sort of complete, unfeeling bastard, Stanzie, but—"

"I don't think—I know," I interrupted.

He sighed and stomped back behind his desk. Faith's dream had to be bullshit. There was no way I would forgive this man for abandoning me after he told me I was family.

"So where is he?" At my question Paddy nearly dropped the pitcher of Guinness and set it down carefully. "Paddy?"

"Belfast," Paddy told me, although by the look on his face he'd rather have eaten glass than answer me. "He got an offer for his cottage, and he went to the closing. He'll be back soon. I think." His tone was doubtful.

I thought about the cottage in Belfast. I'd never seen it, but Murphy and I had had plans to go there together for weekend getaways after we made our home here in Dublin. We were going to keep my condo in Boston and his cottage in Belfast, and now he'd sold the cottage. It shouldn't have hurt because the man walked out on me four months ago, but it still did. Now I'd never see it. Of course, it could be cover for his investigation into the whereabouts of Mick Shaughnessy, but I could not blurt that question in case Paddy didn't know about the conspiracy.

Besides, Murphy wouldn't have to put the cottage up for sale to support his investigation of Grandfather Mick. If anything, he'd want to keep it as a base away from home as he traveled around the UK. My stomach soured, and I wished I hadn't wolfed my food so fast.

"Well, I guess he's not planning to leave the pack and grow vegetables this time around," I remarked, chin jutted.

After Sorcha died he'd left Mac Tire, bought the cottage, and escaped. After he left me, he'd sold the cottage and apparently planned to say in the pack. Which meant…

"Who is she? He's got someone new, hasn't he?" My heart beat painfully in my chest, and I wanted to rip it out and stomp on it to make it stop.

"Don't be daft," Paddy advised. "Sure and he'll have to bond with somebody if you don't figure out a way to get back with him, but you heard Alannah, didn't you? He's been scowling and moody the whole bloody time he's been here. Snapping at people or more likely ignoring the crap out of them. If he's got somebody new, she's a masochist for sure." Then a grin spread across his attractive face. "You're jealous."

"You're fucked in the head," I snapped, and he laughed, the bastard.

"You do want him back," he crowed.

I scowled at him. "Well, duh, that's why I'm here. But you don't have to get all smirky about it. So I admit it. I want him back. But since I wasn't the one who walked out, I don't see how what I want means shit."

"Then why are you here?"

Because of you, mostly, I thought to myself but didn't say since Paddy didn't know that part. *Ask him, Stanzie. Ask him if Murphy's in bad trouble.* But I wasn't sure it was the right time. I wasn't even sure that's what the dream meant. I wasn't sure of any goddamn thing.

"I'm tired. Do you know any good hotels? Since Murphy's not here, there's no sense in me sticking around here tonight." I yawned and stretched my arms over my head.

An affronted expression made Paddy look like a mule.

"A hotel now? You'll be traveling all this way, and you being Mac Tire and asking me if I know any good hotels? You rude little bitch."

"What?" I glared. "What did I do now?"

"Mac Tire don't stay in hotels in Dublin, woman," Paddy roared, and if they didn't hear him downstairs in the pub, it was only because everyone had gone deaf.

"Where would you suggest I stay?" I made my voice as sweet as I could, but he still grimaced as if I sounded like nails down a chalkboard.

"Not a hotel," he barked. He fished in his pocket and came up with a set of keys. He extracted one from the main keychain. It had its own keychain, one with a small Eiffel Tower dangling from it. My heart gave a lurch in my chest.

"Here," he tossed it to me, and I caught it automatically. My mind flashed back to a windy afternoon in Paris when Murphy and I had sat together on a bench on the first level of the Eiffel Tower and drank coffee while we read case files Jason had given us.

I'd bought the keychain in the gift shop, and somehow he'd ended up with it. I'd forgotten all about it until I saw it in Paddy's hand.

"I'll give you a lift to Liam's place. You'll stay there."

"What if he comes home?" I said, panicked.

"Oh, the horror," Paddy screamed in a girlish voice. "The man you want to get back with comes home and finds you sleeping in his bed. Whatever would you do?"

"Shut up," I snapped. "You're such a bastard, Paddy."

"If you continue to hurt my feelings, I'll make Alannah give you that lift," he threatened, and I gritted my teeth.

Paddy watched me drink my Guinness. His eyes fascinated me. I'd never seen anyone with different-colored eyes before him. I wondered if his wolf's eyes were two different colors and tried to remember if I'd noticed the afternoon I'd had to shift for the tribunal. My mind had been focused on other things—like how my wolf had refused at first to come out, so it was no wonder I didn't have a clue.

"I meant what I said, you know." He had that wistful, remorseful look on his face again—the one I didn't trust because he was a lying, manipulative bastard. "About you being family. About how you belong to me." The possessiveness in his voice was not overtly sexual, although there were undertones since he was an Alpha male and I was a fertile female. Instead he evoked feelings of protectiveness—feelings I fought because they weren't true.

Was this the prelude to the scene from Faith's dream? Would he open his mouth and say, *Now do you believe in me again?*

I hoped not because I sure as hell didn't feel like saying I belonged to him. Maybe I ought to put the dream aside and concentrate on dialog that actually took place versus the stuff of Faith's unconscious imagination.

But if Murphy was in trouble, Paddy would know it. And he'd tell me, I hoped. So maybe the dream had nothing to do with Murphy and everything to do with me and Paddy. Somehow I was supposed to learn to trust him again? Was that it?

"You want me back with Murphy, don't you?"

"Right," he agreed.

"Then I'm only family if I'm with Murphy, is that it?" I guessed bitterly. "I only count if I'm Liam Murphy's bond mate."

He shifted uneasily on his squeaky chair. "I told you before, you've got to prove yourself to this pack. You don't just waltz in and take your place near the top of the ranks without a struggle."

"Who says I want to be near the top?" I whispered.

He scowled at me. "For fuck's sake, Stanzie, you're an Advisor to a member of the Great Council. And, yes, you are Liam Murphy's bond mate, at least for a little while longer—hopefully more if you get your head out of your ass and kick his. Fee and I have been Alphas for three years. We've got another two to go, and then this pack will choose a new Alpha pair. And there's every chance in the world it will be you and Liam if you play your cards right.

"So people like Alannah Doyle and Declan Byrne, your main competition, are not going to quietly let you sneak ahead of them in the ranks. No matter what I want or what Fee wants, our votes only count so far. The pack has a say, too."

"The main contender for the next Alpha female is a barmaid?" I spoke without thinking and Paddy groaned and threw up his hands dramatically.

"A barmaid who's my sister, remember, you horrible bitch? What the hell do you want her to be? A nuclear physicist? Stanzie, for Christ's sake, since when do we judge who should be Alpha by their damn day jobs?"

"I figure this is a huge pack and it doesn't just revolve around the fertile duos and triads, so there has to be more criteria than that. Why not day jobs? Sorcha was a scientist, wasn't she?" I wanted to throw my Guinness at his face, but it was too good to waste.

"A lab technician with delusions of grandeur." Paddy's voice was flat.

I wanted to argue. She'd been murdered by the conspiracy, so obviously she'd been more than a simple lab tech. She had to have been.

"She was working late to impress her bosses. She was taking classes and wanted to move up, and maybe she would have, but all that would have been put on hold so she could have her baby. She shouldn't have even been working still, the stubborn bitch, but nobody could ever tell her what to do. Liam begged her to stop working and act like a real Alpha female, but she laughed in his face. He's the one who carried that duo when they were Alpha, and everyone in Mac Tire knows it. So they're going to be doubly hard on you. For all they know, you're the next Sorcha. Maybe you won't even stop being an Advisor when you're pregnant."

Paddy talked like it was a done deal.

"And when they find out about my wolf, game over, wouldn't you say?" I looked him in the eye, determined to brazen it out. Did he know my wolf was normal now? Or supposedly so. I inwardly winced when I remembered I'd just taken off for Dublin and hadn't told Scott I wasn't going to hunt with him after all. That was rude. I made a mental note to call to apologize, but meanwhile I stared Paddy down.

"Do you not think your Alpha has kept track of you?" Paddy's eyes burned with triumph, and I knew my bluff had failed. Damn that Jason Allerton.

"Well, since my Alpha never called me once in four months, how the hell was I supposed to know? Who told you? Allerton?"

"I have my sources." His smile was enigmatic, and I really wanted to slap him hard.

"So Murphy. He told you." I felt my face turn sullen, and Paddy rolled his eyes.

"He and Allerton do communicate, being that Liam's his Advisor and all."

"What's that got to do with me?" I bunched my hands into fists and looked around for something to pummel. Murphy knew about my wolf. Why did he get to know everything about me even when he'd walked out on me?

Until that moment I hadn't realized how much I'd wanted to be the one to tell him about my wolf. He'd helped me so much with her. If anyone in the world had ever initiated my wolf, it was him with the help of his wolf.

What had he thought when he'd found out? Had he been pleased? Indifferent? Maybe he'd changed the subject because it didn't matter to him anymore.

"So you know about the pack bond, too, then," I said, my voice hard.

"Only the bare bones of it. Just that that bastard father of yours was exiled, mostly because of you figuring it all out. But not the specifics of how you did it or what you felt like going through it." Paddy's voice was soft and encouraging. As if I'd tell him anything.

"Well, it's no wonder you seem to want me back with him. Now that I'm normal and a real contender for Alpha. You're such a treacherous bastard, Paddy, you know that?"

"Goddamn it," he swore helplessly. "I never thought your wolf would hold you back even before the bloody pack bond thing. Liam was working with you, and that was good enough for me. I saw what your wolf did for the bloody Council wolves. It wasn't an issue with me."

"Maybe not you," I said through gritted teeth. "She's normal now, and I'm still apologizing for her. Still making excuses for her."

"Yeah, and I don't understand that at all. Nobody in Mac Tire knew about your wolf anyway."

"Why not?" I thrust my chin out angrily. "You kept it a dirty secret, didn't you? Afraid it would ruin my precious chances at Alpha? What if I don't want to be Alpha? Normal wolf or not?"

"You don't want a baby?" Paddy asked. "Because I don't believe you. I saw the way you looked at your friend's baby daughter, and I heard what you said about the subject. I was there, remember?"

"I'm tired, and I want to go to bed." I knew I was being a coward, but fuck it. I couldn't even think straight, and maybe I was getting belligerent for no reason. But I was not going to fall for his Irish charm and his bullshit lies. I wasn't.

Chapter 5

Paddy had a red Mini Cooper with black cloth upholstery. I huddled in the passenger seat with my eyes closed for the entire drive and hoped I would keep my dinner down. The car had a manual transmission, and every time Paddy shifted gears, I tensed. By the time we pulled up in front of a four-story brick apartment house, I was sick to my stomach and so tightly strung every muscle in my body ached. Rain drizzled down and smacked against the windshield. Paddy told me to wait in the car until he got my suitcase and backpack out, but I didn't listen to him. I wanted out of that damn car in the worst way.

He made no move to give me my suitcase and instead led the way to the glass door entrance.

Inside it was dark, but motion sensor lights picked up our movements, and dim lights lit up to show us the way to the elevator. Since this was Dublin, I guess it was called a lift.

The back wall of the lift was mirrored, and Paddy leaned against it with nonchalant ease while I stood stiffly near the front.

"I could find it by myself." I knew I sounded churlish, but he only shrugged.

Murphy's apartment was on the top floor. Paddy led the way down a narrow, carpeted hallway past two light brown doors until he reached the third one at the end.

I had the key, so I unlocked the door and walked in first, but he was right behind me and switched on the lights so I could see.

The apartment was small, with light cream walls and darker tile flooring. The living room and dining room were one long room combined. Twin couches covered in burgundy tweed were propped opposite each other against the walls. Two large prints of the Irish seashore in dramatic golds and bronzes hung above them. One depicted sunset, the other sunrise.

A French door shielded with flat burgundy blinds led out onto a balcony. Small windows with diamond inset beveled glass were set on either side.

Beyond the couches was a dark hardwood dining table with four ladder-back chairs placed around it.

The galley kitchen had stainless steel appliances and granite countertops beneath sleek, modern cupboards the same color wood as the dining table.

A door to the right of the kitchen obviously led to the bedroom. It was closed, and I couldn't see what lay beyond.

A flat-screen television on a swiveled arm was bolted to the wall opposite the dining table, easily viewed from anywhere in the room.

A wooden coffee table was placed precisely between the sofas on a rectangular burgundy rug. White radiators were mounted to the walls on either side of the room, one by the sofas, one closer to the table. End tables sat on either side of the sofas and had modern brass lamps with soft white squared-off shades.

Nothing personal was displayed on the tables, but I saw a wine rack on one counter in the kitchen full of Murphy's favorite cabernets and merlots.

"It's a bit stark," muttered Paddy as he watched me take it all in. "He's still decorating. You could give it a woman's touch."

"You really think I'm going to stay?" I was pessimistic. What would Murphy say when he saw me? Maybe he'd tell me to leave. He sure wouldn't greet me with open arms, or why the hell would he have left in the first place?

"Get some sleep, Stanz." Paddy propped my battered suitcase against the wall by one of the end tables. Raindrops glistened in his curly black hair. He looked tired.

"You were the one who got me through the tribunal," I whispered, my throat clogged with tears. "And then you left me behind. I wanted so much to have an Alpha I could believe in."

He reached out and drew me into his arms. I buried my face against his shoulder and squeezed my eyes shut. If he'd said it then, *Now do you believe in me again*, I was so tired and sick at heart I would have told him I belonged to him. So I could belong somewhere again. But he didn't say it, and I didn't know how to make him.

* * * *

After he left, the apartment echoed with silence. I picked up my suitcase and crossed to the bedroom door. It was a strange, European door with a shiny finish and a thin silver handle that moved up and down instead of twisted.

The bedroom walls were the same modern cream, but the floor was carpeted in pale gold. The bed was huge with a sleek wooden headboard screwed into the wall matching the built-in wooden floor-to-ceiling cupboards.

The drapes were a shade lighter gold than the carpet. A white, down-filled duvet covered the bed, and a thin burgundy blanket was folded across the bottom.

Mounted to the wall across from the bed was a small television, and beneath it, a compact wooden desk with a laptop and a banker's lamp with a burgundy-colored shade.

Mail had been carelessly tossed across it. A wooden shelf hung to the side of the desk, and it held a few paperback and hardbacks novels.

One other thing rested on top of the desk—a small box covered with creamy brown shells. My heart slammed against my ribs as I picked it up, unable to keep from looking inside.

His bond pendant was there, the silver link chain carefully arranged so it wouldn't knot. The peridot I'd bought and had mounted next to the lustrous pearl he'd had since he'd been born gleamed under the electric lights.

Of course he wouldn't wear it anymore. Why would he? My own bond pendant's clasp was broken, and I'd never fixed it. It was in the small pewter box Murphy'd given me the night we'd bonded in the chateau just outside Paris.

I remembered a time when neither of us had taken off our bond pendants except when we'd shifted or showered.

I put the shell box down and crossed to the clothes cupboards. The second I opened them, I smelled Murphy. The sterile apartment filled with his unique scent, and before I knew it, I was on the floor with one of his shirts in my hands, my face buried in it so I could drink him in with my olfactory sense.

My heart bumped painfully in my chest, and I heard it even above the strangled sound of my sobs.

She found me that way, crying into his damn shirt so hard I didn't even hear the door open.

The sharp intake of her breath alerted me. I lifted my tearstained face and saw her.

The first thing I noticed was that she looked eerily like Murphy, only her features were softened and more feminine, and her hair was blond, not light brown. Her eyes were hazel with flecks of amber, different than his forest brown, but they were the same shape and size.

The second thing was she was pregnant. She wore a pair of maternity jeans and a loose purple top with a leather jacket that glistened with rain. Her hair was long and straight and slightly damp, even though I could see a half-furled umbrella in one hand.

She could only be one person on earth. Fiona Carmichael, Murphy's twin sister and Alpha female of Mac Tire. Still I asked, "Who're you?"

"Now that's a damn silly question," she scolded, and our gazes locked.

Sometimes it clicked between two people and an immediate friendship formed. No need to speak or even for introductions. A look created an instant bond and the two people just knew how it would be between them. That's how it was with Fiona Carmichael and me—we were friends before she finished that first sentence and we both knew it.

She had a bag of groceries in her free arm, and a small bouquet of wildflowers poked out of the top.

"I like to take care of my stupid brother because if I don't, nobody will. Isn't this apartment like a small corner of a very neat and clean version of hell? Maybe you'll put some personality into it. I keep trying, and he just erases it all. Help me arrange these flowers, will you?"

She walked into the living room and I followed, Murphy's shirt still in my hands.

"Here, let me." I dove in front of her as she tried to bend to rummage in the cupboard beneath the pristine stainless steel kitchen sink for a flower vase. I estimated she was at least seven, probably closer to eight months along, and although she carried well, it couldn't be easy to bend at this point.

She gave me a grin disturbingly reminiscent of Murphy's and began to unload the groceries. Small colorful oranges went into a glass bowl on the counter, coffee beans into the freezer, cans of soup into the cupboard, and a loaf of fresh rye bread into one of the drawers that held the heel of another one, which she threw away with a grimace because it was rather moldy. Milk and eggs went into the refrigerator.

I found a large modern burgundy glass vase, which I filled with water and a teaspoon of sugar while Fiona snipped the ends off the flowers with a pair of scissors.

We worked together seamlessly, and a few moments later the flowers were arranged in the vase and placed in the center of the dining table.

She helped herself to a glass of cold water. I decided I needed a cup of tea and plugged in the electric kettle.

We sat at the table while we waited for the water to boil. She sipped her water and stared at me. I knew I looked like shit—how could I not after a twelve-hour layover and a long flight with virtually no sleep and no change of clothes.

"I won't stay long, you look knackered," she said with another Murphy smile. "So you love him, don'tcha?" Forthright hazel eyes locked with mine. I slowly nodded.

The woman found me sobbing into one of Murphy's damn shirts. A person didn't do a thing like that unless they were in love. Or psychotic.

"I knew it," she crowed. "That stupid brother of mine is so damn dense you could use his head to knock down walls."

"How come I didn't know you were pregnant?" The electric kettle shut off with a sharp click, and I rose to make my tea. Murphy had two kinds—Irish breakfast and chamomile. I went with the latter since I didn't want to delay sleep any longer than a short soak in the tub after I drank it.

"I wanted to surprise you both when you finally dragged your asses to Dublin." She watched me pour boiling water over the tea bag as she sat at the table and drank her water. "You fucking ruined the moment, though."

"Not my idea." I held up a placatory hand, and she grinned at me and brushed some of her sandy-blond hair away from her face. The earrings she wore were handmade and beautiful. Twisted silver, they formed dangling spirals that twirled from her earlobes and glittered in the light. They were reminiscent of the abstract design of the Mac Tire pack ring she wore on her right middle finger.

I touched the empty space around my finger as I waited for the tea to steep.

"Boy or girl?" I wondered as I scooped two teaspoons of sugar into a white ceramic mug and stirred.

"Hell if I know," she replied. "I do know it's just the one though. Glenn and Siobhan were convinced it would be twins since they're both twins and Liam and I are twins, but the pack doctor's sure it's just the one. Can't say I'm upset about that. Twins are a terrible lot of work, don't you think?"

I shrugged because I'd had no experience with twins. Both the children born in Mayflower after me had been singles, and there had never been a baby in Riverglow at all, let alone twins.

"Paddy's a single. Can you fucking imagine more than one of him? Jaysus." Fiona went off into gales of infectious laughter. "If this baby's anything like him, the world's a lucky place it's just the one."

The way she spoke about him let me know how much she loved him. Her hazel eyes danced with the same warmth that lit Paddy's when he talked about her.

"The three of us grew up together. He's two-and-a-half years older than we are, so he thinks he's the boss, but he's not. That would be Liam. Didn't he get to be Alpha before us, and didn't we bond a year before he ever even heard of Sorcha, damn the bitch."

"Not a fan, huh?" I brought my steaming mug of tea to the table and took a sip before I sat. It was hot and sweetly comforting.

"I hope she's fucking burning in hell. Not that I believe in such a place. But the otherworld is too good for her. Bitch. The only time Liam ever stayed mad at me longer than an hour was the day I begged him not to bond with her. He didn't speak to me for three fucking months. Ignored me if I walked into the same room. And, of course, Sorcha laughed her skinny ass off, the little cunt. I couldn't stand her. Can you tell?" Fiona's voice dripped poison, and I tried not to grin.

"I hate her too, and I never even knew her," I admitted. Fiona threw back her head and laughed in genuine amusement. I liked her more and more with every minute.

"So what did you fight about? I'm not trying to be a nosy bitch, I know my stupid brother, and I'll help you figure out a strategy. It's been four months, and he's miserable, so maybe he's forgiven you, but just in case, I can help you if you let me."

I wrapped my hands around the hot mug of tea and willed myself not to wince when it burned. The pain focused me.

"We didn't fight. He just told me he wasn't happy and walked out," I admitted and waited for her to blame me just like everybody else had.

Fiona's eyes narrowed as she tossed this idea around. It seemed to be the last thing she'd expected to hear. It was clear Paddy had not said a word to her. Anger rushed through me again. Bastard men. Why did they keep each other's secrets from their own bond mates? We would have told them in a heartbeat.

"Bollocks," she said, and I smiled a little because it did sound like nonsense.

"I was mad at him because he didn't stay with me at the tribunal. He went to the archives in Virginia to search for a precedent, and I wanted him with me. I was pissy to him when he finally did show up. Cold and distant, but I told him I just needed some time to get over it, and I would have. When he walked out two days after the tribunal, I was almost all over it. Now I can't even remember why I was mad. He was still with me even if he wasn't in the same goddamn room. I guess I was a bitch, but I don't know why it was wrong to want him with me. Was it wrong?" I held my head very still so the tears in my eyes wouldn't spill down my cheeks.

"Only a complete bastard would have gone to the fucking archives instead of staying by your side. I would have screamed bloody murder if Paddy tried any such shite with me. He wouldn't because he knows better. Liam really wasn't there?"

"Paddy didn't tell you?"

"He and Paddy cover each other's asses. Always have, always will. When we were kids, if Paddy fucked up, Liam'd take the blame or cover for him, and it also went the other way, but Liam wasn't one for getting in trouble. Paddy was always the troublemaker of our trio.

"Well, then there was me, but they both covered my ass, so I hardly ever got blamed for anything I did. One or the other of them always got whipped instead." Fiona's grin was infectious, and I imagined Murphy as a young boy with his twin sister and curly-haired best friend and remembered my own childhood with Mark and Faith.

Despite myself, I let out a prodigious yawn. Fiona was on her feet as quickly as she could move her pregnant body.

"I'll pick you up tomorrow morning around ten," she said as she walked to the front door. "We'll go shopping, out to lunch. Girl stuff. Unless my stupid brother comes home, but let's not hold our breath on that one. Good night, Stanzie."

I waved goodbye and watched her leave, then I took my mug into the pristine bathroom. Gold tile covered the floor and walls. The pedestal sink gleamed white with chrome fixtures. A glass door shielded the soaker tub and shower, and I drew a bath as I sipped my tea.

Murphy did not have bubble bath, but he did have Epsom salts—most Pack did because the day after we shifted could be a sore one. I poured a healthy amount into the warm water, watched it dissolve and then let my clothes fall to the gold tiles.

The water, scented like eucalyptus, was warm and enveloping. I closed my eyes and lay submerged to my neck. When I next opened my eyes, the water was clammy cold, and my fingers and toes were pruned.

Murphy had not changed the sheets before he'd left for Belfast, and I hugged his Murphy-scented pillow tight to my chest as I curled beneath the duvet and let sleep sweep me under again.

Chapter 6

"This doesn't look like a shoe store." I surveyed the pretty, terraced row houses with suspicion. We weren't even in Dublin proper anymore. The four houses were semidetached with a wide swath of green grass and attractive flagstone walkways leading to the front doors. Fee—she insisted I call her by her nickname since the only time anyone called her Fiona was when she was in trouble—laughed and thrust open the car door.

"Get off your ass, you chickenshit, and come meet my parents." She waddled down the walk of the row house on the end, the one with the kelly green door.

"Fuck me," I muttered, but I followed her. Damn Alpha female bitch.

The door opened before I made it to the front steps, and a tall, blond woman stared past Fee's shoulder straight at me. Her eyes were hazel, like Fee's, but I would know this woman as Murphy's mother anywhere. She even had his arrogant stare, the one he never used on me anymore. Or, at least, he hadn't before he'd left me.

My stomach clenched, and for a moment vomit burned the back of my throat. Damn Fee. Damn her. I wasn't ready for this.

"Siobhan, this is Constance Newcastle. Stanzie, this is Siobhan Carmichael, my mother." Fee performed the introductions with a breezy smile, but there was an undertone of worry buried in her voice.

"Well, I'll have to meet you properly some other time. I'm off to do the marketing." For the first time I noticed Siobhan had her purse slung over her shoulder and keys in her hand.

"Siobhan," said Fee with a sigh of impatience. "What the hell? Your son's bond mate shows up on your doorstep and you're off to the market? Why don't you just spit in her face instead of this passive-aggressive shite?"

Siobhan Carmichael's expression remained frozen and polite. Now I had a facial expression to add to the tone I remembered from the phone calls.

Every Sunday before Murphy left me, he'd called to speak to his family. He'd told me that on Sundays the family gathered for dinner at Siobhan and Glenn's house. After Sorcha's death, when he'd lived in Belfast, he'd called to try to convince them he was fine living alone. After he bonded with me, he'd called to tell them how happy he was with me.

"Not happy enough to bring you home to the pack," Siobhan had observed once. Murphy spent five minutes telling her how happy he was before he'd handed me the phone. It had been the only thing she'd said to me before she'd passed the phone to her chattier daughter.

Siobhan Carmichael blamed me for keeping her son away from his pack, and now she probably blamed me for Murphy's return without me. Her next words proved it.

"I'm not rearranging my schedule for a woman who decided after four months it might be nice to come visit Liam. Her birthday's this month. Liam told me. So you know she's here to break the bond. I don't care to disrupt my day to meet my son's soon-to-be former bond mate. Now if you please, move aside so I can pass. Using your belly as a barrier is a terrible atrocity, Fiona Carmichael. I taught you better than that, I hope."

"I'm not using it as a barrier, damn it, I'm just huge," snapped Fee. She moved aside, and as her mother swept by, she rolled her eyes at me to make me laugh. I didn't find it remotely funny.

I wanted to tell Siobhan I wasn't here to break the bond with Murphy, but when she sailed past me, the spit dried up in my mouth, and my vocal cords shriveled. Speech was impossible, tears a distinct possibility.

"Is Da inside?" Fee yelled after her mother.

"Why don't you go in and find out instead of bellowing like a cow in the street in front of my neighbors," Siobhan screeched back.

Fee gave her the finger.

"Is that any sort of a gesture to give your own mother, you little viper?" Siobhan didn't turn back and kept up her brisk pace.

"How the hell can she see behind her? Does she have eyes in the back of her frigging skull?" Fee muttered.

"I don't need to see you to know what you're doing. Don't be such a dimwit." Siobhan increased her speed and disappeared around the corner.

Sputtering, Fee stalked through the open doorway into her parents' house.

"Well, come on, goddamn you," she screamed back at me. My feet were rooted to the sidewalk. This was pure hell.

"You don't have to shout," I yelled. Somehow, I managed to move forward.

Inside, it smelled of apples and spice.

"Pie!" Fee made a beeline for what I presumed was the kitchen.

I followed, reluctant to be left behind in the narrow hallway crammed full of occasional tables topped with knickknacks—mostly glass and china. The walls were crowded with photographs of Murphy and Fee. They got younger as I advanced. By the time I reached the kitchen doorway, they were babies in blue and red sailor suits complete with dorky hats. Baby Fee slept peacefully, while baby Murphy scowled. It was probably gas, but I preferred to believe even as an infant Murphy would have hated that hat.

His pictures jolted me. I wanted to see him so badly it was like a missing piece in the puzzle that was me. What would his first words to me be? "Go away?" "I'm glad you came?" Maybe he wouldn't even speak—he'd just turn and walk away. He might even refuse to see me at all.

My bottom lip quivered, and I bit it, the traitorous thing. I was not going to be reduced to tears by the sight of Murphy in a sailor suit. No way.

A tall, ruggedly good-looking man sat at the kitchen table, a plate with pie crumbs in front of him next to a mug of steaming tea. He was reading a book about golf, but when I walked into the room, he set it aside so he could look at me.

Fee was at the kitchen counter greedily dishing herself a slice of apple pie. Pregnant Pack women were bottomless pits. We'd just had lunch and she'd eaten half of mine.

"Pie, Stanz?" She called over her shoulder. I wanted to slap her for being so goddamn nonchalant, but she was pregnant and my Alpha. If I ever got to be pregnant and an Alpha, *I* would never use either one against a defenseless pack mate. *I* would be above that shit.

Ha. The chances of me ever being bonded again, let alone pregnant and Alpha, were about as remote as Glenn Murphy's brown eyes. I gulped.

"Hello." He rose to his feet. Although taller than his son and huskier, his voice was so like Murphy's I wanted to cry. "We finally meet in person, Constance."

He held out his hand for me to shake. If Murphy had been the one to introduce us in person would he have hugged me? Probably.

"Hello, Glenn." He had a firm, practiced handshake. I remembered then he was a Regional Councilor. Had I blundered? Should I have referred to him as Councilor? It was tricky since I was bonded to his son.

Fee deposited two plates of pie on the table and sat down in the chair next to her father's. She'd pushed my piece across the table so I'd have to sit on his other side. Bitch. Why couldn't I sit at the perfectly good chair at the foot of the table?

"Sit down." Glenn gestured at the chair, and I sat, but I didn't eat. It was all I could do not to puke. "What precisely are your intentions? Why are you here?"

Fee choked on a bite of her pie. "Da, let the woman eat her pie before you interrogate the shite out of her. You bloody Councilors are all the same. She's not facing a tribunal. This is a family visit, for fuck's sake."

"It's all right, Fee." I found my voice somehow and stared straight into Councilor Glenn Murphy's brown eyes. "I'm here to try to fix things between me and your son."

He met my gaze and held it for an excruciating moment. If I looked away first, I was a liar, but goddamn, he had an Alpha's stare, and it was so hard not to bow down.

A slow, attractive grin spread across his face.

"Well, that's fine," he said. "I think I'll have more pie before I go back to my office."

"His office is upstairs in the spare room," said Fee as she happily chomped her pie. "Being a Councilor has its perks. He could work in his pajamas if Siobhan would let him."

"I've tried," he agreed with a laugh as he pushed back his chair. "No dice. Apparently even over the phone people would be able to deduce I was in my robe and slippers."

Fee snorted and something twisted tight inside me loosened just a little bit. Enough so that the pie on my plate looked appetizing.

After we finished our pie, Glenn Murphy took me into his den while Fee insisted on washing the dishes. I went with him, and without Fee as a buffer, all my confidence drained away. This was Murphy's father. I wanted his family to like me. Hell, I wanted them to love me. I wanted a family.

The den was small and very masculine. Lots of plaid and brass. A huge desk took up most of the room, and for a moment I thought he might sit behind it. If he did, I knew I'd shrivel into a ball of desperate humiliation. He was already intimidating enough.

Instead, he led me to a plaid sofa and sat down beside me. Up close I could see the fine lines radiating from the corners of his eyes. He looked like a man approaching his forties, which made him in his sixties from a Pack perspective.

He didn't look like Murphy, except they had the same forest-brown eye color, but when he spoke, it was as if Murphy were in the room with me. I could listen to him talk all day. As long as he didn't ask me hard questions.

"What in the world is wrong between you and Liam?" A hard question. Goddamn it.

I studied the brown carpet with increasing desperation, aware of my thundering heartbeat and the stench of guilt rising from my skin.

"I don't know," I confessed, but it was the wrong answer. Glenn Murphy frowned. He smelled like cherry tobacco, and I looked around the room. Yes, there on the edge of the desk in a large green glass ashtray was a pipe.

"You came here to make it up to him, didn't you?" He used his Councilor's voice, and a flare of resentment stabbed through me. I was family, not some fucking witness at a tribunal.

"*He* left *me*, Councilor," I said and the man frowned again.

"Will you not call me Glenn? What's this Councilor shite?" He got up and began to pace restlessly.

"This feels like an interrogation," I said.

"It's a bloody conversation." He shot me a dark look, and I wanted to leave the room in the worst way. Damn Fiona. Damn her Alpha female meddling ass. Why couldn't introductions to her parents have waited until after I'd worked things out with Murphy? If I did. He wouldn't have left me alone with his father to be badgered because if we were together again, it would be water under the bridge.

"He left me," I repeated. I stared at his shoes, not him. He had on brown loafers that needed to be thrown out. What was it with the Murphy men that they had to wear shoes until they begged to be put out of their misery? "I have no idea why."

"Bollocks." He sounded so much like Murphy my heart skipped. "A man just doesn't walk away from his bond mate without both of them knowing the reason why."

"I'm here to get back with him. Isn't that enough?" My hands clenched into fists, and the apple pie rolled around in my gut until I suspected I might puke on Councilor Glenn Murphy's brown carpet. And I was damned if I'd be the one to clean it up either.

"Liam had a rough time of it with Sorcha and after her death. He needs someone stable in his life, not some flighty American girl who can't even look me in the eye. I'm a Councilor. My experience has taught me that people who can't look me in the eye have something to hide. What are you hiding? If you're here to make a mess of his life again, I suggest you go back where you came from."

"Do you know how hard it was to come here?" The words cut like ground glass in my throat. I forced my gaze to meet his. "Do you have any idea?"

"No," he answered. "I don't. Because I don't know you. You seem nice enough on the surface, but I want to know what's beneath it. Liam needs a good woman. He deserves one. I don't know the particulars of how you two came to be together, but Jason Allerton had a hand in it, and that disturbs me."

"Jason Allerton is a good man. He tried to help us." Now I was pissed.

Glenn Murphy, incredibly, smiled at me. "So you do know how to be loyal. That's the first positive thing I've seen today. You just might be good enough for my son, woman, but you'll need to prove yourself."

"How?" Goddamn Mac Tire males and the way they believed everyone had to go around proving themselves all the damn time. Why couldn't we just be who we were instead of constantly trying to prove our worth to other people?

"By making the poor bastard smile again for starters," he said. "He's been back for four months, and I can count the conversations he's had with me on one hand. None of them deep, all of them short. He talked to me more when he was gallivanting through America with you. Get him to talk to his da, and I'll be happy. Stick with him, and I'll be happier still."

"I'm not the one who left," I whispered. I looked into Glenn Murphy's handsome face and wished I knew him better. Would he become a good friend in time? Or would he set obstacle after obstacle in my path? Make me jump through hoops just like my father had? I was so tired of jumping through hoops.

"Well, see that you're the one who stays," he suggested.

Chapter 7

The red-haired giant, Colm, was on duty outside An Puca again. He saw me with Fee and opened the green pub door.

"Still no ring," I muttered, waving my ringless fingers in front of his face on my way past him

"Anyone with the Alphas gets in," he informed me, and then he winked. His green eyes were frankly appreciative, and I knew I looked a hundred percent better than I had the night before. In fact, I looked damned good.

A new pair of black ruched leggings with a black sleeveless scoop neck tunic fitted me to perfection. They were new purchases from my Fee-inspired shopping spree. After we'd left her parents' home, I'd splurged on myself in the vain attempt to push Glenn Murphy out of my head. My favorite purchases of the day were my new black platform ankle boots with dull gold buckles and a dark purple leather hobo bag. I'd braided my hair to the side and wore my bond pendant on the thick silver evening chain. It and a pair of silver studs were my only jewelry.

It was a cool night so I wore a purple leather jacket, also a new purchase.

Inside the pub it was warm, and I left my jacket and purse at the table near the bar where Fee held court. Before she could sit all the way down, a plate of sausage and mashed potatoes was on the table and a pitcher of water.

Alannah Doyle looked at me. "Bangers and mash, the same as Fee?"

I nodded. I'd never heard sausage referred to as bangers before, but this was Ireland. A sudden stab of homesickness assailed me. What the fuck was I doing here?

"I'll bring you a Guinness too." Alannah winked at me and bustled away to get my dinner.

The pub was boisterously crowded with people. My pack mates, but the only ones I knew were Fee, Alannah and Paddy.

Paddy appeared on the stairs about forty-five seconds after we walked in and joined us at the table.

He gave me an appraising look and grinned. "You look beautiful tonight, Stanzie."

I rolled my eyes.

"And so do you, my adorable pregnant bond mate." He turned his attention to Fee, who wrinkled her nose at him before she dug into her plate of bangers and mash.

"You're so full of shite," she muttered around a mouthful. She was beautiful. Her green dress brought out the amber highlights in her eyes, and she'd pulled her hair back into a silver Celtic knot design barrette so the angles of her face were sharply defined.

"Any sign of my stupid brother?" Fee gulped at her water, and when she set her glass down, Paddy poured more from the pitcher.

"No, and the bastard's not answering his frigging phone either."

"Gobshite." Fee's exhaled breath sounded more like a growl than anything else.

My meal arrived then, and I hid behind my Guinness so neither of them could see my expression.

A flat-screen television bolted to the wall showed a soccer match, although the sound was muted. Soft pop music floated above the animated chatter of the pack. On the television, one team scored a goal, and a yell of outrage went up from the crowd.

"You like football, Stanzie?" Fee asked as she followed my gaze to the television.

For a minute I was confused because I forgot in Ireland they called it football.

"I'm not much for sports, especially played by Others," I admitted.

"Do you watch television? Go to movies?" Paddy raised one of his eyebrows in the way he had, and I had this mad desire to run to the ladies' room and practice in the mirror. How the hell did he get only one brow to rise at a time?

"Sometimes."

"Shopping with her is a trip," Fee told him. "Surrounded by a sea of Others, Stanzie acts like she's the only one at the shops. She barely deigns to meet the sales clerk's eyes when she presents her credit card, and I don't think she's ever heard of small talk."

"I couldn't understand half the people today. Goddamn Irish accents," I protested. A bloom of warmth stole across my face. "I'm not mean, am I?"

"No. More like oblivious." Fee reached out to pat my hand reassuringly. "You're a queen among paupers, love."

"That doesn't make me sound oblivious, that makes me sound patronizing and elitist."

"Nah, just sheltered. I don't think you did much shopping until lately."

"I usually order online from catalogs. It's easier," I admitted. "Except for shoes. I have to try them on. That's half the fun."

"But shoe shopping is normally something you can do without some Other fluttering along in your wake, asking if she can help you."

"Until I started buying designer. They keep all the shoes in the back except for the ones on display. It's fucking maddening." I bit my lip to shut my damn mouth. I *was* patronizing and elitist. Others didn't matter much to me. Even when I'd worked in an office, I'd kept to my own cubicle as much as possible and done my solitary work without bothering with my coworkers unless I had to.

"Oi, who's this, then?" A man with jet-black hair and vivid blue eyes slid into the empty chair at our table and stared at me with curiosity bordering on rudeness.

"Declan Byrne, this is Stanzie Newcastle." Fee's voice was prim. "My stupid brother's bond mate, so keep your pecker in your pants, okay?"

Paddy snickered, propped his elbows on the table and leaned forward as if to watch a sports match.

The black-haired man winked at me. "I'm not in the habit of whipping out the family jewels before I'm properly introduced, so no worries, Fiona, calm down."

Fiona stuck out her tongue and gave me a long-suffering look. "Declan thinks he's God's gift to women, Stanzie."

"Paddy, did you put Fee up to this blatant cock-blocking act, or should I feel flattered she still wants me for herself?" Declan grinned in Paddy's direction, and Paddy laughed.

"Stanzie's her stupid brother's bond mate, Byrne, you figure it out."

"Ah, he's not here. And he's made it plain he thinks she wants out of their agreement. Tell me you're here to find a new bond mate, love. Ever think about a triad?" He leaned across the table to smile at me, and I resisted the urge to spit a mouthful of Guinness at his arrogant face.

"Not since both my bond mates died in the twisted metal of what was left of my car after I crashed it," I said, and both Paddy and Fee winced.

Declan Byrne's flirtatious smile faded. "You kill 'em on purpose?"

When I picked up my glass, Paddy grabbed it. I guess he thought I was going to throw it in Declan's face. Really, all I wanted was a sip of beer.

Although the thought of tossing the contents in Declan's smarmy face had crossed my mind, I'd planned on resistance., No matter what Paddy thought.

"Fuck off, Declan," said Paddy. "Jaysus, try not to be such a bloody moron. I know it's a stretch, but surely you can just about manage it."

"I'm not the one who started it. She did," Declan protested.

"Because you're an asshole not letting her finish her damn dinner before you're crawling halfway across the table so you can look down her shirt close up. Have some pride, man." Paddy gave him a shove and Declan grabbed the edge of the table to keep from falling out of his chair.

"Well, how in the hell many people has she killed? I only knew about the psychopath whose throat she ripped out, but she killed her bond mates too? Bloody hell, Padraic, are you letting just anyone into the pack on Liam Murphy's say-so? You know damn well his taste in women is frigging awful."

"Piss off." All of Paddy's goodwill evaporated, and his eyes narrowed. "You're so full of shite, Declan. Stanzie and Liam are your biggest competition, so we all know you're only here to divide and conquer. You think with a triad you'll be in even better position as Mac Tire's next Alphas?"

"Not if I bond with a bitch who kills people right and left like this one. Bollocks to that." Declan's handsome face twisted into ugliness as he shoved back his chair and stomped away. Good thing Paddy had grabbed my glass after all.

"Sorry about that, Stanzie." Paddy's eyes gleamed with ire. "Why the hell'd you have to say that about your bond mates, anyway? Why are you giving him ammunition? Didn't you listen to anything I told you last night?"

"I'm just trying to eat my dinner, Paddy," I said, but the truth was I couldn't eat another bite. What I wanted to do was get up and walk the hell out, but I couldn't do that either.

Pack politics were such a bitch, and I'd never played them right. Tonight was no exception.

"What the hell'd you ever see in that bastard?" Paddy rounded on Fiona, who calmly forked up the last of her mashed potatoes and ate them before she answered.

"It's a girl thing," she said and Paddy groaned.

"You say that every single bloody time you fuck up. Why can't you admit you fucked up for once?"

"Because I'm not convinced I did." Fiona set down her fork and looked contemplative. "The sex wasn't that great. I kept waiting for it to get better, but it never really did. So, Stanzie, don't waste your time, love. You want good in bed, take Paddy. The man knows what do with his tongue when he finally shuts the fuck up and puts it to other uses besides bitching."

I flashed back to my tribunal when we'd all shifted so my wolf could meet the Council's wolves. Images of Paddy with his head buried between the thighs of one of the Advisors filled my mind, and I wriggled a little in my chair.

Paddy saw me do it and grinned, the bastard.

"Sadly, she has scorned all my advances, Fee," he lamented, and Fee looked highly entertained.

"Good things come to those who wait, love." She patted his arm consolingly, and he sighed.

"Fiona taught me everything I know as far as tongues go," Paddy said, and he and Fee watched my face and burst into laughter.

"We're always looking for someone to practice on together," he added, and Fee gave me a wink.

"Hell," I said. "My Guinness is gone. This night has gone from awful to tragic. I might cry."

"Fee and I could make it better," Paddy teased, but he got to his feet and took my glass to the bar for a refill as I'd intended.

"We're terrible flirts, Stanzie. Tell us to fuck off, and we'll stop, I promise." Fee heaved herself to her feet. "I can't even drink half a bloody glass of water without feeling like I'm drowning in my own piss. Being pregnant is bollocks, I swear." As she muttered to herself, she waddled for the ladies room.

"Sexy," I mused. She cursed the group of men crowded beneath the flat-screen television, blocking the way to the restrooms. They scattered once they realized who swore at them. One of them tried to help her, and she almost took his head off.

Paddy put my beer on the table and, laughing, took a seat.

"Mother of God, that baby can't come quick enough. I swear she's waddling like a frigging duck lately. That only started this week. Normally, she's graceful as a swan."

"So says the pig who knocked her up in the first place. Your compassion is overwhelming, Alpha." I took a healthy swig from my beer, and Paddy grimaced at me.

"Killjoy."

The speaker system shut off, and the pop music died. I looked around and saw Declan Byrne at a control panel behind the bar. He moved toward a small stage on the side of the pub and pulled the cover off a gorgeous twenty-two string Celtic harp. It could have been the twin of the one I'd once owned.

Declan Byrne was the musician of the pack, apparently. He sat behind the harp and fiddled with the strings and levers a bit to tune it and then launched into a cheerful Irish song that showcased his technical prowess. He was definitely no stranger around the strings. A few members of the pack gathered around and began to sing. I turned my chair around so I could watch. He played with an easy grace that must have taken him years to develop.

After three tunes he switched to a guitar for some rowdy Irish bar songs, and more people began to sing along, including Paddy and Fee. I knew some of them, but I kept silent, my gaze fixed lustily on the harp.

After an hour of continuous playing, Declan took a break and went to the bar. Alannah drew him a beer and he gulped at it. I slid off my chair and walked over to him, aware Paddy and Fee both watched me.

"You prefer the guitar or the harp?" I leaned my elbows on the bar as he finished off his beer in three long swallows and set the glass down. Alannah whisked it away for a refill.

Declan ruminated for a moment. "Not sure I have a preference."

"I play the harp." I knew by the way his eyes lit up I sounded too eager, and I wanted to slow down. But it had been three years, and for some reason tonight, the music had torn a hole inside me that I needed to fill. "Could I play?"

He stretched his mouth into a sardonic grin and took his refill from Alannah before he gulped at it. He looked around the pub for a moment, his blue eyes alert.

"Yes. I reckon everyone's drunk enough they won't hear your mistakes. But I will. And I'm gonna point out each one afterward. That's the price of admission. Too steep, woman?"

Three years was a long time away from the strings. I was bound to make some mistakes, but I didn't give a shit if the bastard pointed them out to me. What the hell did I care? I'd hear them, too.

"No problem," I said, and his grin widened into derision. I'm sure he planned to rub my nose in every wrong note.

When he shrugged toward the harp, I needed no further invitation.

My heart trip-hammered as I stepped up onto the small platform stage. A hush spread over the pub when everyone saw me. I had expected an audience, but I hadn't anticipated the complete quiet. Declan must have gestured for their attention when my back was turned, and not a person in the pub moved or spoke.

I sat still for a moment and let the music steal into my fingers. I didn't plan on what I would play; I let my fingers choose.

Three years they had been forced into submission. They'd stood idle, and their calluses had disappeared from disuse, my skin smooth and soft where it had once been hard and tough.

Declan had played fast and lively tunes, but I was sad and wistful, so I wasn't surprised when I heard the first strains of *Carolan's Farewell to Music* drift into the silence.

I suppose it was risky—maybe even cheeky—to play a tune by the man venerated as the last of the great Irish bards. Declan might believe I did it to impress, but I didn't do it for that. I did it for my fingers and my soul, denied the music for so long.

The strings were sharp against my soft skin, and I knew I wouldn't have the stamina to play an hour straight as Declan had, but I could last the four and half minutes it took me to play the one song.

Over the years as I'd become adept with the harp, I'd learned to feel the music beyond the technical composition. This song was one of my favorites, and the way I played it was different than most harpists. I slowed the tempo and added hesitations most did not. The music breathed through my fingers.

The song was committed to muscle memory, so I had no need of sheet music. I didn't even have to think, just play. My connection to the harp came back in a gratifying rush, and I felt my soul's music open up. The place where it resided had been squeezed tight ever since Grey and Elena died and my harp had been destroyed.

The emotion that swirled through the pub was not all my own. I'd affected the pack on a metalevel, and when I looked up after the song, they were one and all within my grasp. They existed inside and beside me in the unique way that came with music's gateway. I'd played at Regionals before, and this was the intoxicating feeling I remembered. Everyone was linked together like we were during group sex before the Great Hunt.

An incredulous smile of joy lit Paddy's face as he stared at me from the table with Fee. She was very still, her face transported with a bittersweet wistfulness. She understood the music the way I did—I felt that. She knew how it affected me.

Declan Byrne, from his vantage point in front of the stage, shook his head as if to clear it from my influence.

"How many mistakes did you count?" My question broke the spell that bound us all. Our connection shimmered in the air and was gone in an instant.

"Fuck you. Mistakes. I never heard it played quite that way, but there were no mistakes. Where the hell'd you learn to play like that? And me thinking you just took a few lessons in your spare time like a spoiled American brat. You bitch—*Carolan*? You played *Carolan* for *this* crowd? You're insane, you are, but you got away with it, damn you." Declan was torn between fury and reluctant admiration. I saw him seesaw on the edge of his temper, but his love of music won out, and he grinned at me.

For a second I sensed the attraction he must have held for Fee. And for his bond mate, Alannah Doyle.

"My mother taught me," I answered and thought of the years of lessons with Wren. At first I'd tried to play like her, and then she tried to play like me. Eventually she had declared I was so beyond her own skill that she would take lessons from me and not the other way around anymore. "I played professionally for years. It's how I made money for my pack before I became an Advisor."

"Her not telling me a word of this, and me thinking she would embarrass the fuck out of herself. I've been played, I have. Alannah, get this woman a drink," Declan bellowed, and the crowd erupted with laughter. A few of them called out for me to play something else. Some asked for specific songs by name, and when I heard one I knew, I played it. My fingers were sore, but I had a few more minutes left before I started to bleed.

* * * *

Protests rang out loudly when I stood up, but my fingers were numb, and I really wanted a drink.

Several people grabbed my arms and helped me down, and I don't think my feet touched the ground more than twice before I arrived at the bar and slid onto one of the stools.

Paddy materialized beside me and slung an arm around my shoulders.

"Are you sure you're not Irish, woman?" he demanded and gave me a kiss. His lips were light and teasing against mine, but he wanted more, and I nearly gave in and opened my mouth for his seeking tongue, but cold beer spilled over my hand and startled me, so I pulled away.

"Sorry," said Alannah with a wink as she mopped up the spill with a bar rag. Paddy gave her a suspicious look, but she just laughed.

"This is what I meant by proving yourself to this pack, woman. You had us all eating out of the palm of your hand. You'll be a fucking brilliant Alpha," Paddy whispered into my ear. He swirled his tongue around the lobe and sent a shiver down my spine. "Where'd you learn all those Irish songs, and you not being Irish?"

"Only someone Irish can play an Irish song?" I countered and gave his chest a push so he would stop doing wicked things with his tongue and my ear. "Besides my grandfather's last name was Callahan, so you tell me if I'm Irish or not."

"Callahan," Paddy shouted and those around us all came to attention. "This woman's a Callahan!"

A roar went up from the crowd, and I rolled my eyes, both embarrassed and shocked.

"A quarter," I yelled above them all. "At best a quarter. And Grandfather Neil and his family have been in America for decades. I'm not Irish."

"You're a Callahan," insisted Paddy and tried to kiss me again but Declan Byrne shouldered into him and threw him off balance.

"Tell us, Stanzie, what does it feel like to rip out a man's throat with your wolf's teeth?" Declan's voice rang out above the noise of the pub, and there was instant silence.

Paddy muttered something in Irish under his breath, his face suffused with wrath.

He turned to snarl at Declan, but I put a hand on his arm. No one needed to fight my battles for me, fuck that.

I looked straight into Declan Byrne's vivid blue eyes. "I answered that question for the Councils at my tribunal, Declan, and the only thing you need to know is that I was cleared of all charges. If that's good enough for the Great Council, surely it's good enough for you, right?"

"She wasn't just cleared, you bastard—she was commended." Paddy couldn't keep his damn mouth shut, and I resisted the urge to smack the back of his head.

"Was there a tribunal after you killed your former bond mates in that car crash you were telling me about earlier?" Declan asked.

Paddy cursed beneath his breath again, his hands curled into fists.

"I was cleared at that one, too," I said and Declan snorted.

"How the hell many tribunals have you faced, woman?"

"Just the two so far," I replied.

"How'd you avoid one after that poor German bastard croaked on you at the Great Hunt in Paris?" Alannah's face was spiteful as she formed a tag team with her bond mate. He grinned at her.

"They never figured out how he died. It's hard to hold a tribunal when you haven't got anything to charge a person with." I tried not to think about Rudi's empty eyes but it was impossible.

"So maybe you didn't kill him, but I'd say you were bad luck, wouldn't you? Your bond mates died, that German guy died, that American Alpha sure as fuck died, and maybe Liam Murphy doesn't want to be the next one whose time runs out while he's standing next to you. Maybe he dumped you instead of the other way around. Can't say as I blame him. Who wants to try his luck with the Black Widow here?" Declan turned around to speak to the whole crowd, who kept silent.

Guilt kept me silent although I knew I hadn't killed anybody. If I hadn't wanted to go out on my birthday, Grey and Elena might still be alive. Nate had deserved his fate, but I still didn't like to think about my wolf tearing his throat out. Rudi's murder had nothing to do with me. I'd witnessed it, not caused it, but I still couldn't shake the way he'd said my name before he died as if he thought I could help him. If only I could have.

Declan did have a point. People died around me. I couldn't refute it.

"Piss off, Declan Byrne, you bastard. Leave off the woman. You're just jealous she plays the way you know you never will because you lack the fucking soul to pull it off. Black hair, black heart, that's you." The red-haired giant stood just inside the pub door, his meaty fists clenched. The crowd parted a little so he could get through quickly if he wanted. They seemed eager to see a fight.

"You offering to bond with her? You check that with Deirdre? It's not every woman who'd want to make a triad with a murderess." Declan Byrne's expression turned arrogant, and he clenched his fists, too. If there was a fight, my money would be on the giant, no contest.

"It wasn't murder, you arrogant prick. You don't get commendations from the Great Council for acts of murder. I'm sure as hell not listening to any more of your shite, Byrne. Now shut it, or come out back with me. Which will it be?"

"Looks like you've got at least one fucking idiot willing to risk his luck and bond with you, Stanzie, good for you. But Colm is hardly worth your while if you ask me."

"Lucky for me I didn't ask you," I snarled. "The day I need a bond mate broker, Declan Byrne, I'll be sure to knock on your door, but until then why don't you go screw yourself."

"Ooh, I struck a nerve." Declan's grin was irritating as all hell. The grin turned bloody when Paddy popped him one in the mouth with his fist.

With a furious roar, Declan Byrne threw a punch back, and the fight was on. They crashed into the table behind them, and Fee barely got out of the way in time.

I dove toward her and dragged her to the side before she got hurt.

"Why don't you all just fucking stand there and watch your Alpha get trampled, damn you," I shouted at all the idiots around us who just stood there with their heads up their asses. One and all, they were riveted on the fight, but at least a few could have helped Fee.

Of course, as soon as I yelled, several of them helped me pull Fee in back of the bar, although I didn't like all the glass around. I wanted to go into the kitchen, but Fee fought that too hard.

"If either one of them comes across this bar, you hit the floor, understand?" I yelled in Fee's ear above the roar of the crowd. I couldn't see over their fat heads, but Paddy or Declan must have landed a good one by their response.

"Move your asses so I can see!" Fiona bellowed and tried to heave herself on top of the damn bar for a better vantage point.

"Shit," I shouted as I struggled with her. "Stay off the bar, Fiona Carmichael, you fucking idiot. You're pregnant, remember?"

"Yeah, like I can ever forget. You fucking get up there then and tell me what the hell's going on. They're fighting over you in the first place," Fiona shouted back. Somewhere in the melee her silver barrette had fallen out and her hair was all over her face. She pushed it back irritably and shoved me at the bar.

"Don't you dare stand on my bar, you bloody cow." Alannah Doyle threatened me with a bottle of Jameson's. It was only half full, but it still would have hurt. I didn't want to get on the damn bar in the first place, but the hell some redheaded bitch would tell me what to do. Especially when she called me a cow.

I boosted myself up onto the bar and ignored her scream of rage. She took a mean swing at me with the bottle and Fiona snatched it away.

"Back the fuck off now," Fiona yelled, and Alannah snarled at us both before she flounced to the other end of the bar.

Declan Byrne was a dirty fighter. He'd picked up a shard of broken glass and slashed Paddy's arm with it. The first thing I saw when I stood up on the bar was the blood all over the floor and Paddy. The edge of the glass was bright red, too.

Declan Byrne's lips were drawn back in a snarl of fury, but Paddy was laughing, even though I'm sure his arm hurt like a bitch.

"You never could fight without a weapon to hide behind," he sneered and ducked when Declan lunged at him. The glass sliced a thin line across his cheek, and more blood spattered onto the floor.

They circled each other warily, and I clenched my fists in rage. I willed Paddy to pick up a piece of glass and make the fight even, but he didn't. He danced back out of range and continued to laugh.

Declan Byrne lunged again, and more blood flew, this time from Paddy's throat. It was just a nick, but it enraged me. Declan had his back to me, and before I could think it through, I leaped off the bar and landed on him.

He wasn't expecting it, and we went down hard. I had time to hope he landed straight on the glass, and then things went a little fuzzy because my head hit the edge of a table on the way to the floor.

The next thing I knew, Paddy loomed over me and blocked out the light while someone else threw water—no, beer—in my face. Alannah. Being helpful.

Declan Byrne was out cold on the floor next to me. Woozy as I was, Paddy's face wavered in and out of focus. I blinked and his worried eyes became clearer.

"Paddy, you're dripping blood all over me," I remarked. It was true. A steady patter of red droplets dripped on my face and, worse, my new shirt.

"What? Oh, shit. Sorry about that." Paddy drew back and clapped a hand to his bleeding face.

"That's going to scar." I tried to sit up, but the fucking world tilted in the most sickening fashion, and I decided it was not such a hot idea after all.

"Won't be my first." Paddy leaned close again and smiled at me, although his eyes were still worried. "If you want, I'll show you me others later tonight. What do you say, Stanz?"

"Sounds like a plan," I agreed, and things went dark for a little while.

* * * *

"I never saw anything like it." Fee giggled in the car on the way to Murphy's apartment. She was behind the wheel, and Paddy slumped in the passenger seat with a blood-soaked bar rag pressed to his still-oozing cheek. The earthy smell of blood filled the interior of the car, and it added to my general nausea.

I lay in the backseat with a bar rag full of dripping ice pressed to the lump on the side of my head. I was relatively sure I wasn't concussed, but my ears hadn't stopped ringing since I'd hit the damn table.

"Stanzie was like some sort of huge flying squirrel in platform boots sailing through the air to land on Declan Byrne's back. And didn't he go down like a ton of bricks, the bastard, and him not expecting it? You should have seen your face, Paddy, you didn't know whether to laugh or scream at her."

"Normally I can fight my own battles," Paddy remarked from the front seat. "Some Alphas might have found Stanzie's theatrics a little insulting. Luckily, I'm not one of them. I thought it highly entertaining, although I do wish she hadn't smacked her head so hard on the way to the ground. Couldn't you see that table coming, love?" He craned his neck so he could look over the back of the seat.

I extended my middle finger, and he laughed as he reached back to pat my leg.

"I'm flattered you cared enough to fling yourself into the fight, woman. But it's what I would expect from a Callahan. Never met one who could keep out of it once a fight broke out."

"Oh, for Christ's sake." I blew out my breath in exasperation and gritted my teeth when Fee shifted gears and the car lurched around a corner. "I will never get used to being on the wrong side of the damn road. This is hell."

"No, tomorrow morning will be hell when you wake up with a head bigger than a house," Paddy predicted. "Maybe I should stay the night with you. Help you through your agony."

"Oh, God, that's just what I need." I groaned. "Fee, help me!"

"Paddy, you're coming along home with me. I might need some help through my own agony. You'll never know how I felt watching that bastard slice you open like a ripe orange, and me eight months pregnant with your child."

"Knowing you, you were cheering the bastard on. You love a good fight, Fiona Carmichael, don't you dare lie to my face." Paddy was unmoved, especially when she burst into merry laughter.

"So does he get away with fighting dirty like that?" I asked. "Or is what he did normal behavior for Mac Tire?"

"Normal behavior for Declan Byrne, which is why nobody will fight him but my idiot bond mate." Fiona shifted gears again, and I grimaced.

"I had to or Colm would have, and I'll not be having him cut to ribbons just because he's trying to impress our Stanzie," Paddy defended himself. "He's too pretty for scars, the big bastard."

"Colm does have a thing for you." Fiona glanced into the rearview mirror and grinned at me. I gritted my teeth and hoped like hell she'd remember to look at the road before we crashed into something.

"I think it started when Stanzie called him a freak of nature last night."
Paddy's tone was jovial as he searched for a clean part of rag that wasn't
saturated with blood already.

"You never told me she started it between them," Fee accused and I
groaned.

"Since when is calling someone a freak of nature flirting?"

"He is cute as hell," Fee mused. "I wonder if his cock's as big as the
rest of him?"

"I can't believe you of all people haven't found out firsthand." Paddy
laughed.

"Not for lack of trying on my part. But between him being your half
brother and lately me being the size of a small whale, he's just not making
it easy."

"Wait. What? He's your brother?" I sat up and smacked Paddy in the
back of the head. "Haven't we talked about this? It's hard enough to
navigate through the twists and turns of a pack's blood ties, but when you
deliberately withhold information like Colm is your brother, you're just
fucking with me, Paddy."

"Maybe just a little." Paddy rubbed the back of his neck and gave me a
reproachful look. "It never came up. He and Alannah are twins. Couldn't
you see the resemblance?"

"He's so goddamn tall I can't crane my neck back enough to look at
him up close," I muttered and Paddy snorted.

"Well, if you do get him into bed, you'll have to let me know if he's as
big as I think he is," Fee ordered.

"Woman, from the way you're running your mouth, I'm thinking
you're in the mood. But you're killing mine, discussing my own brother's
bait and tackle with me sitting right beside you. Wasn't last night's romp
enough for you? You need more?" Paddy's grin was seductive, and he
reached out a hand and put it on Fee's thigh.

That made me nervous because she was supposed to be driving, not
flirting.

"Ah, that was charity, you fucking idiot, to keep you from crawling
beneath Ellen Maguire's skirt. She's on her period and begged me to
distract you." Fee swerved around something in the road. I gulped and
squeezed my eyes shut.

"Damn nicest charity I've ever gotten," Paddy said happily. "You think
I could have another donation tonight?"

"Fuck off, you pervy bastard."

"Well, then, you're forcing me to stay with Stanzie. And what's Liam going to think, him walking in on me fucking his bond mate seven ways to Sunday and her begging and screaming for more? You're going to get me into trouble, Fiona Carmichael, unless you take off your knickers for me, I swear."

"I'll take them off and strangle you with them. They're big enough," she threatened, and they both laughed.

"Is Murphy coming back tonight?" I asked, and their laughter faded.

"I don't know, love," Paddy answered.

"Maybe you better stay with her. She hit her head pretty damn hard. I heard it even above your bloody sister's screeching. Maybe we ought to find Andrew and have him take a look."

"Who's Andrew?" I was immediately suspicious.

"Andrew Brody. He's our pack doctor. One of them, anyway. He's going to deliver this fucking idiot's baby when the time comes."

"You aren't going to let the women be with you? Don't you have a midwife?" While it wasn't uncommon for Pack women to have male Pack doctors examine them during the pregnancy, it was almost unheard of for a male to be in the room when a baby was born. That was the province of the women of the pack. Babies were almost never born at a hospital.

"I'll not be letting that cow near my vagina," snarled Fee and Paddy groaned.

"Don't get her started, please, Stanzie. It's my bad luck Fee's been in a lifelong feud with Sheenaugh Donovan, and her being the pack midwife just like her mother and her mother's mother. If she has a daughter, she'll be a midwife, too."

"Ha. The bitch has to get to be Alpha before she can spawn, and I'll not support that." Fee's voice was laced with such poison, I decided I'd never want to be on her bad side. Fuck that.

"You know anything about midwifery?" Paddy asked with a hopeful look in my direction.

"Are you fucked in the head? Where the hell would I have learned anything about babies? I was eleven the last time one was born around me, and I kept as far away from that scene as I could when Samantha went into labor."

"But you'll be there with me just the same," said Fee with perfect confidence. "And with Andrew and Siobhan and Paddy's mother."

I thought about Faith's mother, Lily. My aunt. How she'd died in childbirth and I'd watched, hidden behind a chair.

"I'm bad luck, remember? I'll wait outside," I said. "Who says I'm even going to be here by then? Despite what Declan said tonight, I'm not on the lookout for another Mac Tire bond mate. If Murphy keeps avoiding me, I'll be back in Boston before two weeks are up."

"My stupid brother better show up before then, Padraic," Fee warned, her tone shrill. "You hear me?"

"What the hell are you screaming at me for?" Paddy gave her a dismayed look. "Do I look like I'm the one holding the other end of his damn leash, Fee?"

"I wouldn't put it past you. You two always cover for each other."

"I want him back here," Paddy whined. "Jaysus, I want him back with Stanzie, too."

"Then get his ass back here. I'll not be buying that crap about him not answering his frigging phone much longer."

"He's ignoring your calls, too, woman," Paddy rumbled and yelped when Fee smacked him.

"Shite. That's my sore arm, the one Declan Byrne half amputated. Watch what you're doing."

"I'll be the one amputating more than your arm, Padraic, if you don't stop being a preposterous bastard," Fee vowed.

"Why don't you call him, Stanzie?" Paddy pouted over the back of his seat, and my head really started to throb.

"Before I can call him, it might be helpful to have his frigging phone number," I muttered.

"Oh, yeah, he changed it. That's right." Paddy's voice was less than convincing, and he yelped again when Fee smacked him.

"Who's the ridiculous bastard who didn't give the woman her own bond mate's phone number?"

"You didn't give it to her either."

"Because I didn't know you didn't give her the new one."

"Why is everything my goddamn fault?"

Their bickering was done affectionately, but it still made my head spin. Paddy turned around and winked as Fee said, "You're too stupid to live, I swear."

She slammed on the brakes for a red light that I'd wondered when she'd see.

* * * *

Fee decided I didn't need Andrew Brody unless my head was really bad the next day. She also decreed Paddy would stay the night with me, mostly so she wouldn't have to deal with his whining and blubbering about his wounds.

"And you give Stanzie my stupid brother's phone number," she yelled as her parting shot before she pulled the Mini Cooper back into the street and disappeared in a flash of red taillights.

Once inside Murphy's apartment I made Paddy strip off his shirt so I could put peroxide on his cuts.

"And keep your roaming hands to yourself, damn it, or you'll have more injuries than just what Declan Byrne gave you," I warned him as I slapped his fingers away from my chest for the fourth time.

He chuckled and then shouted in pain when I splashed peroxide on the cut on his forearm. "Bloody fuck, that hurts!"

"Well, we're even. My headache just got ten times worse, thanks to you screaming in my ear," I snapped as I wiped away the blood and peroxide.

"Well, it hurts, damn you." He hissed in pain when I put more peroxide on the cut on his cheek. "Is it really going to scar? Jagged or straight?" He seemed fascinated, not repulsed by the idea, and I rolled my eyes.

"Straight," I told him as I cleaned it with a wet washcloth. "It will make you look like a fucking street thug and not romantic at all, so stop smirking like that."

"Why in the hell did you fling yourself on the bastard's back?" Paddy continued to grin, and I sighed when he gave my braid a gentle tug. "Could it be you give a shit about me, after all, Stanzie Newcastle? Maybe just a wee little bit?"

"For God's sake." I upended the peroxide bottle on the wound on his throat, and he squeezed his eyes shut in pain. "You're my Alpha, all right? I can't believe I'm the only person in that whole damn pub who took offense at Declan Byrne using a weapon when you had none."

"You got Fee out of the way, too," Paddy mused, and his fingertips caressed my earlobe until I shivered. Ears have always been one of my erogenous zones, damn him. "Don't you like to watch a good fight?"

"Not particularly." I rummaged through Murphy's medicine cabinet until I found some antibacterial salve, which I slathered onto all three of his cuts. I was vitally aware he was half naked and very male. Sure, I'd had sex with Alan Perrault in Willoughby, but that had been over two months ago and hardly satisfying for me, as it had been his first time.

Then I remembered Ron-or-Don, the Other, and shuddered. All thoughts of Paddy's masculine appeal vanished in a rush of self-loathing.

"What did I do?" Paddy sensed my revulsion and let his hand fall away from my ear. A shamed expression washed over his face. "You'll never forgive me, will you? For walking away?"

"Did Murphy leave because I'm bad luck? Is that why? Was he really freaked out by what my wolf did to Nate?" My voice shook, and I wouldn't look him in the face. "People do die around me a lot, Paddy. Declan's right. I am bad luck."

"Oh, for fuck's sake." Paddy took my face between his strong hands and made me look at him. "Don't you give that black-haired bastard the satisfaction of taking his spiteful words to heart, you hear me?"

"You didn't want me in Mac Tire at first," I reminded him. "The first time I ever met you, Murphy was pissed at you because you wouldn't let me into the pack because of my past. Because of Grey and Elena. And Rudi."

"Bollocks." Paddy gave me a gentle shake, mindful I'd given my head a hard knock earlier. "Jason Allerton asked me to hold off on letting you both back in. I thought you'd twigged to that, you idiot."

"Did Murphy know that?" Had that whole scene been an act? Jason Allerton was a master manipulator, and I wouldn't put it past him to assign everyone roles, some knowing, some oblivious, like me.

"Nah." Paddy shook his head and pulled me closer so our foreheads touched. His breath smelled, not unpleasantly, of Guinness. "He had some fucking master plan. Part of getting you to be his Advisors. At least that's what he told me. I don't know what good not being in Mac Tire at first did for him, but he asked me to hold off letting you back in the pack. I didn't want to do it, but how can you say no to a Councilor?" Such bitterness crossed his face that I sucked in my breath.

Did he know about the conspiracy? Now was the perfect opportunity for him to say something, but he acted completely clueless.

"I made him swear not to let you two join any other pack until you knew damn well you were welcome back here. And later he called to tell me I was free to ask you back, and I called Liam straight off."

"Do you know why Murphy left me?" I wanted to crawl onto his lap and let him hold me, but I wasn't so damn weak. Instead I pulled away and walked into the bedroom.

My shirt and leggings were filthy—both with blood and the detritus of the pub floor. I tore them off and threw them in a corner. Murphy's sterile apartment was rapidly becoming infected with my untidy personality.

I kicked Paddy out of the bathroom so I could take a shower. Afterward, wrapped in a towel, I rummaged in my suitcase for a pair of yoga pants and a t-shirt and put them on. When I turned around, Paddy was on the bed in just his boxer briefs. By the look on his face, he'd been avidly watching my ass as I'd dressed. The bastard.

"I take it by your smarmy silence you have no intention of telling me why Murphy kicked me to the curb." I winced as I pulled my fingers through my wet hair and tried to avoid the knot on my head. When I retreated beneath the covers on the other side of the king-sized bed, I made sure to keep maximum distance between me and the bastard in boxer briefs.

"I love your American sayings." Paddy's eyes danced with amusement. "Kicked to the curb. He didn't kick you to the curb. That sounds mean and vindictive, and that's never been Liam Murphy."

When I opened my mouth to demand he tell me the reason why, he lifted a finger, and I reluctantly kept quiet. "You'll need to discuss this with him. I'll not be telling you his reasons. I wish I could, Stanzie, but it has to be between the two of you."

I could tell by his face he knew exactly why Murphy had left, and he wanted to tell me, but I couldn't get him to break the friendship code, damn it.

"It's what my wolf did, I know it." Tears burned my eyes. "That's the first thing anyone ever asks me now. How did it feel to rip out a man's throat, Stanzie? Did your wolf really kill someone? Why would anyone want to be bonded to a psycho like me?"

"You were commended by the Great Council," Paddy reminded me.

"Yeah, that and two bucks gets you a ride on the T in Boston." I hunched beneath the covers and felt very sorry for myself for at least thirty seconds until I got sick of my defeatist attitude. "I'd fucking do it again, too. Screw everybody who doesn't understand. Including and especially Liam fucking Murphy."

Paddy had been very quiet, but now he burst into laughter. "That's my Stanzie."

"I'm not your anything, Paddy O'Reilly."

"Yes, you are. You're my pack mate. I meant it when I said you belonged to me. I meant it when I said you were family. And you can rail and scream at me all you like about being abandoned and me not bothering at all about you the past four months, but I know the truth of it.

"I never fucking expected you to take four bloody months to get your ass over here. I was halfway convinced you wouldn't even let Liam leave in the first place. That's why I agreed to his asshole plan to leave you behind. I told the man you'd be coming after him and, worse, he believed me. He waited for you, Stanzie. The first week we were here he carried his phone around in his hand, and more than once I caught him checking flight times from Boston. He even bought ketchup. Does that sound like a man who kicked you to the curb?"

"Ketchup." Murphy remembered how much I loved ketchup. He never touched the stuff himself. I would not cry over fucking ketchup. No way. But a few tears leaked from the corners of my eyes anyway, damn them.

"But you didn't come. You didn't call. And then one day he changed his phone number and started leaving the phone here in the apartment more often than carry it with him. And the light died out of his eyes. That sounds poetic as hell, but I don't know how else to describe it. And I wanted to call you and reach through the phone and wring your neck, but I didn't. I couldn't."

"Why?" I croaked. "I was the one left behind, goddamn it. Why couldn't you reach out? That's all I would have needed. How was I supposed to know what to do? Nobody's ever left me before. I mean not on purpose. Fuck you, Paddy. You make this so hard."

"*I* do?" Paddy was incredulous.

"And I still don't understand why he left in the first place. If he wanted me to come after him, why did he even leave? Sure, I was mad at him for not being at my tribunal, but I was getting over it. I knew I asked too much from him."

"Here's the part you talk to him about." Paddy leaned over to switch off the lights. The room plunged into darkness. When he reached for me beneath the covers, I didn't resist when he drew me onto his chest so I could rest my head on his shoulder.

We twined our legs together and I spread my palm flat on his chest so I could feel the steady thud of his heartbeat. He was a bastard, but he was my Alpha.

Chapter 8

"Damn it, man, your timing is horrible. Can't this wait?" Paddy's irritated whisper nudged me from a light sleep. His side of the bed was still warm, but he wasn't there. The bedroom door was half open, and I saw his shadow from the living room. I couldn't hear who he talked to, so after a moment I presumed he was on the phone.

My heartbeat, which had sped up because I'd thought Murphy might have come home, slowed. Massive disappointment left me limp.

"Fine, fine. I can be there in ten minutes, but this has got to be quick. I want to be back here before she wakes up, damn you."

Maybe because I still didn't trust him entirely, I feigned sleep when I saw the bedroom door swing open. Paddy hesitated in the doorway for a moment, and then I heard him stealthily get dressed.

The moment the front door closed behind him, I was up. I grabbed a pair of sneakers and slipped them on as I made my way to the door. My purse was on the dining table, and I snatched the apartment key and my gray hoodie off the back of a chair before I went out the front door and sprinted for the stairs.

The lift was old, and I was able to cover the five flights of stairs in just about the time the lift took to reach ground level.

When I pushed open the street door, Paddy was nearly across the road. I waited until he was all the way across before I went outside. I shrugged on my hoodie and pulled up the hood to conceal my hair and face.

With purposeful strides, Paddy walked a block until he reached the River Liffey. He made for a bridge, and I clung to the shadows of a building until he was halfway across.

If he'd been in wolf form, he might have scented me, but he wasn't. Plus I was downwind.

It was early, and traffic, both car and pedestrian, was light.

I bent to tie my sneaker, and when I straightened, I judged he was far enough across the bridge and sprinted across the street.

His hands were stuffed in the pockets of his leather jacket, and his hair was a riot of curls on his head. He walked at a steady, deliberate pace, but I could tell by the set of his shoulders he was irritated. He strove to ease the tension with a series of shrugs and shifts, but there was only so much he could do to work out his frustration.

Once across the street, he ducked down a narrow, cobblestone alley and I cursed. I crept to the edge and carefully peered around the corner, most of my body pressed to the damp brickwork of the building to the right of the alleyway.

He wasn't there, but another alley branched out about forty yards down, and unless he'd climbed over a rusty chain-link fence or swarmed up a fire escape, that was the way he'd gone.

I heard their voices just before I got to the second alley. A convenient rubbish bin lurked just around the bend, and I retreated behind it. The smell was putrid, and I covered my mouth and nose with my hand, but when I saw the man Paddy had come to meet, all thoughts of stenches, revolting or not, flew out of my head.

The old man who faced Paddy looked to be in his late sixties, but looks were deceiving with Pack. He could have been anywhere from one hundred to one hundred forty, but he'd long since left his actual sixties behind.

He had iron-gray hair and uneven bristly stubble across his sunken cheeks. His hand was out, and Paddy had his wallet open.

I watched as Paddy gave the old man a fistful of colorful bills, which the old man counted with shaky fingers.

"You old bastard, it's two hundred pounds. All I've got at the moment. And I just gave you a hundred last week. What are you doing with it?" Paddy's voice was quick and impatient, and the old man stuffed the bills into the pocket of his windbreaker.

"Never you mind, Padraic O'Reilly. I've got me work cut out for me avoiding that mad bastard you call a best mate, don't I?"

"If you'd get the hell out of Ireland like I told you to, you wouldn't have that problem, would you?" Paddy snarled.

"I'll not be leaving my home," said the old man, affronted. "He won't give up, Paddy. You've got to do something."

Paddy's face darkened. "You'd better not be suggesting what I think you are, or..."

"What?" interrupted the old man. "Or you'll what? You're not going to let a friendship compromise everything we're building, are you?"

"Of course not," Paddy sneered. "But I'll not be lifting a hand against Liam Murphy, Mick Shaughnessy, and that's that. He'll give it up. Soon. He won't be thinking of you for much longer, not once he knows his bond mate's here and wants him back."

The old man sniffed with contempt. He spat a wad of phlegm onto the cobblestones and shuffled off toward the other end of the alley where it opened up onto a main thoroughfare.

I sagged against the filthy side of the rubbish bin and would have sunk to the ground if there'd been room between it and the brick wall. Acidic vomit burned my throat and blocked a primal scream of denial and betrayal.

For centuries, the Pack existed on the fringes after the Others nearly exterminated us. We'd faded into the werewolf legends and no Other seriously believed wolf shifters existed. After the Paris Great Gathering, I'd become aware of the conspiracy to murder those of us who threatened our so-called safety by taking high-powered jobs with Others and moving more and more in their world. At first I'd thought it was the grandmothers and grandfathers who murdered younger members, but now I knew anyone in the Pack could be a part of the conspiracy. That had become crystal clear to me after Callie's suicide, but lying bastard or not, I would have never, ever suspected Padraic O'Reilly of being a part of it until I saw the proof with my own eyes.

If Mac Tire's own Alpha was a member of the conspiracy, how far did it reach down into the membership of the pack? Was it the reason for the privacy at the pub? Could it be that widespread, that insidious?

I couldn't breathe or move, and I struggled to do both. When I looked down the alley, both Paddy and the old man were gone. I knew I needed to get the hell out of there.

My cellphone was in Murphy's apartment, and I had no money with me, but maybe I could convince a pedestrian to let me use their phone. I needed to call Allerton, and he would tell me what to do. My feet itched to run the fuck away, but the rest of my body was heavy as lead and I couldn't quite move.

I closed my eyes and concentrated on making my muscles move. Just then, someone grabbed a fistful of my hair and yanked me off my feet.

* * * *

"Goddamn you, Stanzie. Why did you have to do this?" Paddy's face was inches from mine, and his fingers in my hair hurt like hell. "I can't believe this. Now what the fuck am I supposed to do?"

"Let go," I whispered. He had my hair so tight against my skull the lump I'd gotten from the table at the pub shrieked in agonized protest.

He did. Then shoved me against the brick wall so all the breath was knocked out of my body and black spots danced before my eyes. He took me by the shoulders and shook me until I thought my neck would snap. The smell of fear and fury blended in the narrow alleyway until it choked us both.

"What do I care if you give money to some old man?" I croaked, and he slammed me against the wall again.

"Nice try, but I know damn well you know what that old bastard did to Sorcha. You know about the movement, and you work against it every chance you get, just like Liam. So don't play innocent with me, damn you. It's too late for that!"

The world spun and staggered as I tried to focus, but I couldn't even draw a breath.

Paddy reached into his jacket pocket. Oh, God, I hoped it would be a gun, not a knife. Death by stabbing hurt more, and I wanted it to be quick because I was a fucking coward. Wren and Murphy's faces flashed before my eyes. I would have given anything for just a little more time, but I knew mine had just run out.

Instead of a gun or a knife, he took out a cellphone. His wary gaze fixed on me, he punched in a number and then held the phone to his ear.

"It's me," he barked even before the person on the other end could say hello. "You need to get your ass to the pub right the fuck now. There's a huge complication, and I don't have time to explain it. Twenty minutes." He cut the connection and shoved the phone back into his pocket.

Okay, so I would die in the pub instead of a public street. My time had still run out.

"Get going." Paddy gave me a shove. I sprawled onto the cobblestones and gashed both my palms open. The hot, iron scent of blood seeped into the air, and Paddy swore and dragged me up by the hair.

"You're hurting me." I tried to scream, but it came out a hoarse croak.

"Let me see your hands. You're bleeding."

I hid them behind my back. What the fuck did he care?

"Will you make it quick, Paddy?" Tears burned my eyes, but I refused to let them fall.

"Make what quick? You're the one standing around when we should be halfway to the pub by now, goddamn it." He curled his fingers around my forearm and dragged me for the end of the alley.

"You and whoever's waiting at the pub are going to kill me. I know. I just want it to be quick. Don't...torture me." For a moment I was back in Grandmother Emma's root cellar chained to a steel gurney, and black panic stole nearly all my reason away. I had not lived through that only to end up tortured in a Dublin pub, had I? Fate could not be so damn cruel.

He stopped short, and I would have fallen if not for his fingers dug into my arm.

"I don't want it to hurt," I begged. "I want it to be over quickly. Please. As my Alpha, please don't make it hurt."

"Get going," he said again.

He never let go of my arm, even when we got on the bus filled with early-morning commuters on their way to work. We sat in the back, me by the window, and as the bus chugged through its route, I looked out at the River Liffey and the baskets of blooming flowers hung from lamp posts and beneath building windows. I was so far from home, and everything was different and unfamiliar.

The stench of Others on the bus polluted my nostrils. Everything I looked at was all wrong and unfamiliar. Their Irish accents blended into a cacophony of scary noise. I didn't belong here. I didn't want to die so far from home. My ashes would not be scattered in a New England forest but somewhere here in Ireland. Would my restless spirit walk because I wasn't where I belonged?

I thought about screaming but didn't. What would Others do for me? Since I'd been a child, I'd been trained not to appeal to them, not to make eye contact unless I had to. They surely couldn't save me from my own pack unless I wanted to risk exposure. My life was not more important than the Pack's safety.

So I sat beside Paddy on the bus and wiped my bloody palms on my yoga pants so they left smears of red while Paddy held on to my arm as if we were boyfriend and girlfriend out to see the sights.

Paddy was my Alpha, and it was ingrained in me to follow his lead. I had never been the blindly obedient pack member some people were, but I always tried to follow my Alpha's lead—even Jonathan's, and I had never respected him. I did respect Paddy, or least I had until I'd seen him give that old man money. Even now I struggled to try to understand why he'd throw his lot in with the conspiracy. How could he be such a ruthless killer and such a gentle, understanding man at the same time?

Why weren't things black-and-white? Why did they always end up such an alarming shade of gray?

It was an overcast day, and sporadic raindrops splattered against the bus window. I tried to make peace with myself, but I couldn't help but tremble and wish I'd never woken up in time to hear Paddy's phone call.

Colm, the red-haired giant, was not in front of the pub's green door. A *Closed* sign hung in the window, but Paddy led me to the alleyway and the fire escape.

He pulled down the ladder so it touched the cobblestones and gestured for me to climb it and then take the stairs to the door that led to his office. I could see a light from the office window. Whoever waited there must have had a key. Would it be Mick Shaughnessy? Fiona? Declan Byrne? Someone I didn't know yet from Mac Tire?

"It'll be open," Paddy called from just behind me. Maybe I could bring myself to push him over the edge of the railing and make a break for it, but before I could, Paddy reached around me and opened the door himself.

He shoved me forward, and I stumbled inside, my gaze fixed to my feet so I wouldn't trip and fall.

Paddy stepped in behind me and shut the door.

When I looked up, my heart stopped.

Chapter 9

"Murphy," I whispered.

He'd grown a goatee in the months since I'd last seen him. A charcoal-gray crewneck t-shirt with long sleeves and a pair of off-black jeans fitted him like a second skin. He'd let his hair grow out, and he looked edgy, dangerous and sexy as all hell.

At first his face lit up when he saw me, but then he took in the blood on my pants and Paddy's no doubt dire expression and froze.

He was propped against the wall behind Paddy's rolltop desk, and now he moved around it with his quick, smooth grace, and the way the muscles bunched beneath his shirt flashed me back to so many memories of walking, driving, and making love together.

It both hurt and thrilled me, and yet above everything was the horrible realization Liam Murphy was a traitor and everything I thought I'd known about him was a black and filthy lie. This was a hundred times worse than Paddy. The enormity of it threatened to collapse my legs from beneath me. How could I have been so wrong about him?

"She saw me giving money to Mick in a back alley," Paddy confessed, and Murphy's whole face tightened, his eyes darker than I'd ever seen them even in the throes of passion.

"She thinks I brought her here so we could kill her." Paddy stepped past me, and I saw the grief and fury on his face before he stalked to the rolltop desk and kicked one of the legs right out from under it.

The crack of the breaking leg made me jump and the desk crashed to the ground. Papers flew everywhere. Paddy kicked them, too and stomped them to pieces. His breath came in sobbing gasps. Rooted to the spot, I couldn't tear my gaze away and watched him destroy the desk until it was nothing but broken pieces.

Murphy stared too. He stepped protectively close to me as if to shield me from flying pieces of wood.

When Paddy's rampage ended, the desk completely obliterated, he doubled over out of breath, and sweat and tears poured down his face.

Bent over, he rasped, "Now, for the love of God, Liam, will you tell her the truth of it like I asked you to four months ago? I can't do this anymore...I can't."

"You can," Murphy said, and his voice sent a shiver of recognition through my body. God, I'd missed him so much, it wasn't fair. "You've come this far with it, Paddy. You can finish it."

Paddy shook his head and sucked in a deep breath before he straightened. He pointed a finger at Murphy's chest.

"Tell her." The desk chair had somehow escaped his wrath, and he staggered over and collapsed in it.

Murphy turned to me. He was so close I could see his eyelashes and the silk-screen print of his shirt. He smelled of his signature cologne and something uniquely him that reminded me of autumn leaves on a crisp October day. His scent triggered a wave of longing within me that I tried in vain to smother. He was a liar and traitor. Everything we'd shared had been a lie.

His gaze traveled over the length of my body and back to my face, and I was sucked forward against my will, drawn by the power I'd given him over me. My heartbeat went crazy. I'd missed him so much.

"First off, we're not gonna kill you."

I spat at his feet and, shocked, he looked up from the floor to my eyes. I'd surprised even myself with my reaction. Fury, unreasonable and hot, flooded my system. After four months all he could say to me, in a condescending tone was *First off, we're not gonna kill you?* Epic fail, Liam Murphy.

"If you're not going to kill me, excuse me while I go call Allerton. Fuck you both." I wheeled for the door, but his next words stopped me in my tracks.

"Don't you even want to hear our side of it? What are you going to tell Allerton?"

"What am I going to tell him?" I turned back, incredulous, and tried to smother all the love I'd ever felt for him, but some of it refused to be killed. "For starters, that you're a double-crossing, traitorous sonofabitch and the Alpha of Mac Tire is a part of the conspiracy. Then I'm gonna sit at *your* tribunal, Liam Murphy, and watch you crash and burn. You couldn't be bothered to attend mine, but you won't be able to pay me to keep away from yours."

His eyes flickered, and I swore I saw hurt flash across his face.

I wrapped my arms across my chest. So cold. I was so damn cold.

"It's a long story, you might want to sit down." He gestured toward one of the armchairs and I curled my lip at him. More hurt flashed across his features.

"He gave that old man money. The one who killed Sorcha. And you know all about it and support it."

"There's a reason why we're doing the things we do. Please sit down, Stanzie. Hear us out, and then call Allerton if you have to. We won't stop you, but we need you to listen to us first. Give us a chance." His dark eyes were compelling as he stared at me. I'd seen his beloved face in my dreams and daytime fantasies for months. I'd missed him. Could I have fallen in love with a traitor? I knew he was stubborn and dedicated and protective. Secretive sometimes.

"You don't want me to call Allerton," I accused as a sickening sensation of free fall made me want to puke. "Not now and not after you explain. Do you? Because he has no goddamn idea what you're doing, does he?"

"Not exactly," Murphy confessed, and tears clogged my throat.

"He sent me here to try to convince you to tone it down because you're too conspicuous, but that's exactly what you're trying to be, right? You *want* them to come after you."

"It's complicated, Stanzie."

"Fuck complicated, Murphy. Just tell me the goddamn truth. For once? You and Paddy are playing a lone hand because for some reason you don't want Allerton involved which can only mean that you're doing something stupid and dangerous. And if you think I want any part of it, think the fuck again. No. No way."

"It's not stupid," Murphy said, his eyes narrow with anger. "It's Paddy's life, don't you get it? I'm not going to let anything happen to him, and I tried to keep you out of it, but now you're in it and, damn you, he's your Alpha, too. Stop arguing with me and *listen* to what I'm trying to tell you!"

We glared at each other until I stalked to a chair and threw myself into it.

Fear for him made me mean. "You have one minute to convince me you both aren't being complete assholes."

His jaw tightened. "No. I'm not going let you put me on some frigging arbitrary time clock. You either listen or you don't, but I'm not going to be rushed. There's the door. Walk out now, call Allerton, and reap the consequences—or sit there, shut up and listen to me."

We glared at each other again until I rolled my eyes.

"In case you hadn't noticed, I shut the fuck up about a minute ago, and now I'm just sitting here waiting." I gave him another baleful glare. "And I still reserve the right to call Allerton no matter what the fuck you say."

"Fine," he snarled and raked his fingers through his hair. The bastard had never looked sexier to me, and I cursed myself. Why did he have to grow a goatee? They were so damn hot. It was as if he did things like that to torture me.

"Look, let me tell her." Paddy sat straight in his chair, and tears glittered in his eyes. "You're all the time trying to clean up after all my mistakes, Liam, but let me tell this story."

Murphy looked at him for a moment and then abruptly glanced away. Tacit permission for Paddy to do what he wanted.

Fee had told me that Murphy was their little group's leader and how as kids, he and Paddy would cover for each other when they got into trouble. Mostly it had been Paddy who got into trouble and Murphy who took the blame for it. The dynamic had apparently not changed with the passage of time. Of course Murphy would protect and cover for his best friend. Paddy had been in his life since Murphy had been born. His loyalties to his Alpha and best friend would run deeper than his loyalties to a new bond mate he didn't even love.

Whatever Paddy was about to tell me, I was pretty sure I didn't want to hear, but this was why Allerton had sent me here. I was his Advisor and it was my job to listen to tales like the one Paddy was about to tell.

Paddy leaned forward and stared at me until I gave in and met his gaze. When I did, he shook his head, and his mouth twisted in self-derision.

"Five years ago my father came to me with a proposition. He was a man I'd respected and honored and tried to emulate all my life. He asked me to join him and a group of others within the Pack who had organized a movement geared toward preserving the old ways. They called themselves the Guardians. They'd formed in direct opposition of another group who called themselves Pack First.

"You see, Pack First wanted to move the Pack out of the shadows and into the modern world with Others. They'd started by encouraging younger members to get college educations and go out and get decent, high-tech jobs. They wanted them placed in positions of power and prestige so when they revealed that the Pack existed, we'd be so influential that the revelation would be smooth. We'd be accepted into society and not be forced to live behind the Others. We could live beside them at first and then, gradually, step ahead.

"We live longer, retain youth longer, heal faster, and we're stronger, more resistant to certain diseases and immune to others still.

"If we had the technology and the power base, we could take over. In theory. But my Da, he didn't believe it would work. He thought it was a path to disaster. We'd stayed in the shadows all these millennia for a reason, and that's because Others are violent by nature and distrustful and, above all, dominant."

I was frozen in my chair as I listened. Pack First? Guardians? The conspiracy was so much deeper than I'd ever suspected. Did Allerton know all this background? He must. Why hadn't he told me? Who the hell was I supposed to be able to trust?

Paddy stared at me for a moment as if he sensed my inner turmoil before he went on. "Why do you think the wolves were exterminated in Ireland all those centuries ago? Why do you think there's such an atavistic hatred toward wolves from the Others even today? It's because they knew about us once, knew what we were, and the only way they could tell us apart from them was by wolf form. So they killed wolves. They still kill them today, even though they don't understand why. To protect their livestock they say now. Because they're mean, nasty and vicious. That's the tale they tell, even though wolves don't attack humans and the weather kills more livestock than wolves do.

"They kill wolves because they are still trying, instinctively, to kill us. The Others would never allow the Pack to knowingly coexist with them, much less gain control, and since there are way fewer of us than there are of them, we don't stand a chance. We'll be wiped out as a species before we even begin to fight back."

I shivered and he gave me a sympathetic look.

He took a deep breath and said, "Kevin scared the shit out of me, Stanzie, because I could see it all unfolding just as he described it. There would be no halcyon period of Others and Pack coexisting. The Others would fight from the start, and our lives would be spent running and hiding. At least now we have places we can call home. We've perfected a system of blending in but never standing out. It's taken us centuries to get what little we have, and these misguided idiots would throw it all away for us unless something is done.

"The truth is, I still believe that. I still think coming out to the Others is the wrong thing to do, and I never joined the Guardians thinking we'd resort to killing our own kind. But people have been dying. Liam's Sorcha, your bond mates, Grey and Elena—may they be safe in the otherworld."

"Jesus." I rubbed my temples. My fucking head was going to explode. I hadn't known the first thing about the conspiracy. Where could I even start to untangle all the layers and layers of deception so I could find the truth of it all? "You joined the Guardians five years ago. What the hell took you so long to tumble to the truth of what monsters they really were? And why didn't you tell Murphy what you were doing?"

"I wanted to tell him, but my Da swore me to secrecy. We'd recruit him later, he told me. Then Sorcha died, and before I knew it I was Alpha."

"Yeah, Alpha because your father put you there by having Sorcha killed." My head was going to blow apart. I knew it. I put my hands to either side of my skull as if I could keep it from happening.

"I won't believe that. I won't believe Kevin O'Reilly had a hand in cold-blooded murder. All I know for sure is Mick Shaughnessy arranged it, and I didn't even know that until nine months ago when he came to me and demanded help to get him the hell out because his cover was blown. And after what he told me next, that's when I realized that the Guardians weren't all who I thought they were. All this time I'd thought I'd been doing something good for the Pack." Paddy squeezed his eyes shut and then opened them wide.

"Then Mick told me what he'd done to Sorcha. Told me it was on Guardian orders and that he'd done it to make me Alpha. Do you know what the hell that felt like, Stanzie? That I'd been responsible for her death? I half killed the bastard in a fury, and I was going out of my mind not knowing what to do."

"Orders from who?" I asked. "Your father?"

"My father's dead." Paddy's mouth trembled, and my heart gave a lurch in my chest. What the fuck?

"Dead?" I didn't want to face the implications of that, but I had nowhere to turn. "How?"

"The official story is a heart attack. But the man was only sixty-five. I suppose it could be true, but I have doubts." Paddy's answer made me gasp in outrage.

"What are you saying? He was assassinated? By who? Mick Shaughnessy? The Guardians? Because he found out the real agenda and couldn't go along with it?"

"I don't know." Paddy's voice was full of anguish. "That's the whole problem, isn't it, Stanzie? I don't know who I can talk to. I know other Guardians, but how do I know they're not in on it all? I can't believe everyone in the Guardians is a lying, murdering bastard. I know I'm not! Mick got his orders from someone. He didn't just decide to murder Sorcha to get me into the Alpha position. What am I supposed to do? I've been trying my damnedest to get that old bastard to tell me who he takes his orders from, but he won't talk. He tells me what happened to Sorcha could happen to me if I don't frigging cooperate. At this point I wouldn't put it past them to go after Fee. I can't risk it."

"Then you need to go to Pack First. Go to the Great Council," I said.

Why had I never questioned why people of the Pack would support what I'd called "the conspiracy"? I'd accepted a sort of half-assed belief that they rejected change. The idea of coming out to Others and then being exterminated for it had never crossed my mind. I didn't want that, obviously. However, I drew the line at killing my own kind to attain the means to an end. That was never the answer. There were so few of us, we could ill afford to lose anyone before his or her time.

Suspicion flared within me. I looked at Murphy. His expression was dark and angry. Of course he was furious. Why the hell hadn't Paddy let Murphy help? Why hadn't Murphy gone to Allerton?

My body temperature went so cold I couldn't move.

"Allerton's Pack First, isn't he?" I guessed. "We've been helping him unmask and destroy Guardians all along, haven't we?"

I would have run if I'd had anywhere to go.

"I don't think it's that simple," Murphy admitted and hung his head. "I'm pretty sure he's one of the Guardians."

I stared at him. Something wasn't adding up.

"If you think he's a Guardian, why would he be going after other Guardians? Have them put to death? Why did he send us out to find the truth? What the hell are we doing in his name?"

Murphy's face was pale, but his voice was steady. "What if we weren't the ones who brought it all out into the open, Stanzie? What if we were just Allerton's and the Guardians dupes? Cleanup squad. Who are we unmasking? Grandmothers and grandfathers and unstable, insane Alphas. People who are expendable. So he proves to Pack First that, no, all Guardians aren't like that, Councilors, and here's what I'm doing about it."

He closed his eyes for a moment and then opened them so he could look at me. "If that's how he's playing it, if we go to him with this, Paddy's dead, and we're most likely dead as well unless we want to wholeheartedly join. And I don't. Do you? I do not want to murder people, not even the

Amy Lee Burgess

ones who murdered others. I just want the whole fucking thing to stop and bring justice—Pack justice—to those who deserve it. I'm not a vigilante."

"Who are the other Guardians you know?" I looked at Paddy. He shook his head.

"That doesn't matter, does it? The less you know, the safer you are."

"You don't understand," I whispered. "There has to be a different explanation. We have to be able to trust Jason."

Murphy's face softened, and he took a step toward me. I stared at him as, one by one, the implications slammed home, and my whole life crumbled into dust.

Fear and fury made my voice shrill. "When did Paddy tell you all this shit? After my tribunal, right? And you *left* me there with him? You left me there when you thought there was a possibility Jason Allerton might be a murderer using his Council position to kill people? Using *me* to do it?"

I threw myself at him and pummeled him with my fists. "I *trusted* you. I *loved* you!"

Cheated tears streamed down my face so I could barely see. Murphy grabbed my wrists to keep me from tearing his face open with my nails, but at my words he dropped them and stood there, staring. Before I could rip his cheeks to shreds, Paddy leaped out of his chair and pulled me away.

I screamed and lashed out with my legs, but Paddy had a strong grip around my waist and pinned my arms to my sides so I was helpless.

Murphy's voice shook. "I was gonna get the proof and bring him down if that part was true. I didn't want you involved. You'd been through so bloody much, I didn't want you to go through any more. I never would have let the man hurt you. That's not what he wants to do with you, Stanzie. You were safe in Boston. Safer than you would have been here with me. And I'm not convinced Allerton's a bad guy."

"But you're not sure he's a good guy either!" I struggled against Paddy, but he was too strong. I managed to land a backward kick to his ankle, and he buckled but didn't fall.

"No," Murphy admitted. "I'm not sure of anything when it comes to him."

"He bonded with my *mother*, you bastard fuck," I shrieked, and I would have enjoyed the horrified shock that spread across his face if it hadn't been Wren in the crossfire.

"But what about Kathy Manning?"

"Kathy," I spat, a bad taste in my mouth. "If Allerton's dirty, so is she because she was there when Grandfather Tobias died. She mixed the poison herself. And she never wanted to bond with him, Murphy, she wanted a spot on the Great Council, but Allerton fucked her out of it, and it went to Rosemary Young instead."

Murphy tried to absorb this information and make sense of it, but by his expression he had a hard time of it.

"He bonded with your mother?"

I stopped struggling and Paddy said, "If I let go of you, are you gonna do something stupid, Stanzie?" For an answer I stomped on his foot, and he let out a yelp of agony, but he still let me go.

I stalked back to the armchair and fell into it so I could lace my fingers behind my aching head and press my forehead to my knees.

"Why does this shit keep happening to me?" I whispered. "All I want is to belong to a pack and have a bond mate and be happy like I used to be. What the fuck did I do wrong that *this* is what I get? I'm tired of it. This is so fucking unfair." For maybe the one billionth time I wished I could rewind my life and go back to the night of my thirtieth birthday. I wouldn't get in the car. I would tell Grey and Elena we should stay home instead. Screw dancing, we'd go to bed together. And then none of the bad shit would have happened, and I would still be bonded to them today and maybe even Alpha of Riverglow.

And I never would have laid eyes on Liam Murphy or Padraic O'Reilly. Never met Jason Allerton. Never ever.

"I'm sorry, honey. I don't know what to tell you." Murphy knelt by the armchair and put his hand on my leg, but I wrenched away from him.

"Don't touch me," I snapped. "Get the hell away from me. I wish I'd never fucking met you. I *hate* you!"

His brown eyes got very dark, and he got to his feet and moved away.

"No, you don't," Paddy said heavily. "You just need some time to think, Stanz."

"Don't you tell me what I feel or what I should do," I flared. His cellphone picked that extraordinarily inopportune moment to ring, and I curled my lip and sank back into the armchair.

Murphy stood with his back to us, head down. I hated him. I wanted to get up and pummel the shit out of him, but I also wanted to put my arms around him and make him stop being so despondent. I could be such a fucking idiot sometimes.

"Morning, my saucy pregnant wench." Paddy made his voice cheerful and innocent, and that only proved he was a lying sonofabitch and a fantastic actor. How could we believe anything the man said? "Stanzie and I went out to breakfast. Yeah, I know you just bought eggs and bread for your stupid brother, but we wanted to get out and stretch our legs a bit." He listened for a moment and then looked at me. "Fee's asking if you still want to go sightseeing today?"

I glared at him. The last thing I wanted to do was drive around Dublin to ooh and ahh at the sights. He had to be kidding. I mouthed the word *no* and flipped him the bird. He extended his middle finger back.

"Yeah, she's all for it. Excited as hell. You're gonna bring her to the Guinness storehouse and the Gravity Bar, I hope?" What an asshole. He really sounded as if nothing on earth was the matter. "Sure. You'll collect her at the apartment around ten. I'll see you at home later, love. I'm looking forward to you making me dinner like you said you would. Me, too. Bye." He stared at his phone for a moment and then tucked it into his back pocket.

I wanted to spit at him, but he was out of range. "That's just what I want to do. Sit around in a bar and drink Guinness. Does she know anything about any of this?"

Paddy shook his head, and I wanted to break his fucking neck.

"You sonofabitch. What if I get drunk and tell her everything?" I drummed my fingers on the arm of my chair and wished Murphy would turn around or move. Do something.

"Then you do. I wish you wouldn't, but what am I supposed to do about it?" Paddy moved for the fire escape door. He stopped by Murphy and gave him a nudge. "You coming, Liam? We need you to drive us back to your place. We'll drop her off, and you and I can go take care of some business, okay?"

I wanted to ask what the hell kind of business, but a look from him shut me up. How could I stop them anyway?

Murphy didn't say anything, but he moved to the door.

The metal fire escape rattled beneath our feet as we descended to the alley. Paddy brought up the rear so I was trapped between him and Murphy. As if I would have run away. Where the hell would I have gone? This was such a mess. Why was my life always in such a fucking turmoil?

Murphy's car, a gleaming black BMW without one splash of mud or mote of dust, was parked on the street half a block from the pub. I got into the back and buckled my seatbelt as he slid behind the wheel.

Paddy tucked himself into the passenger seat.

At the first stoplight I cautiously opened my eyes and tried to calm my galloping heart. I didn't think I would ever get used to driving on the wrong side of the road, not even if Murphy was the driver.

"You look like a frigging pirate with that slash across your face. What the hell happened, Paddy?" Murphy broke the silence to ask. I was sure he did it to break the tension, especially mine, because I was nervous in the car. He always knew.

"Had a bit of an altercation with Declan Byrne," Paddy admitted, and Murphy snickered, sounding genuinely amused. How could he laugh at a time like this? Were all members of Mac Tire idiots when it came to brawling?

"Let me guess. Knife."

"Nah, piece of broken glass. I started the fight, you see, so he didn't have time to plan for a real weapon."

Paddy and Murphy laughed as if the joke was a favorite one, and I shook my head. Unfuckingreal.

"You'll never guess what happened right in the middle of the damned thing. Stanzie here figured it wasn't a fair fight and decided to referee. So she climbs up on the damn bar in these frigging platform shoes—and how she did that without breaking her neck I'll never know—and proceeds to fling herself on Declan's back, screeching like a banshee, and—"

"I did *not* screech," I interrupted Paddy's hyperbolic description of the fight. "Jesus Christ, Paddy, if you are going to tell the goddamn story, tell it straight. Screeching like a banshee, my ass."

Paddy snorted, and Murphy bit his lip to keep from grinning, the bastard. I could see both their faces in the rearview mirror. How they could laugh at a time like this I'd never know.

"So Stanzie here flings herself on his back like a silent assassin," Paddy amended, and Murphy did grin when I loudly sighed. "Declan goes down hard as hell and is out cold for five fucking minutes on account of the way his bastard head connects with the floor. The crowd's cheering like mad—it's better than football. Of course, Stanzie, the silly bitch, also knocks herself out because she's too clumsy to avoid clipping the side of her head on the table on the way down."

"Well, I'm sorry. It was my first attempt at silent assassin. Next time I'll do better." I snapped.

"There's gonna be a next time?" Paddy bounced in his seat like a two-year-old who'd just spied Santa Claus.

"Well, it's a sure bet nobody else in Mac Tire will come to your rescue. They'll all want to see the blood if the way they stood around cheering instead of helping last night was any indication."

"Of course they'll want to see the blood. How can you not want to see the blood? And yourself being a Callahan and all? Your ancestors are spinning in their graves, woman."

"I am, at most, one quarter Irish, and I don't think that counts." Why did Paddy have to be such an idiot sometimes?

"It counts." Paddy turned to Murphy. "Doesn't it, Liam?"

"Callahan?" Murphy repeated with a grin. "One drop of Clan Callahan makes you Irish, let alone being a whole quarter."

"But you'll need to work on your accent, love, because it sucks," Paddy declared, and I gave him the finger.

"I'm really touched you hauled ass onto the bar to save me from Declan Byrne," he said, and Murphy snorted, before the two of them went off into gales of laughter.

"That wasn't my intention." Goddamn idiots, the both of them. That fight was not funny; it had been potentially lethal. "I hauled ass onto the bar, you bastard, to keep your massively pregnant bond mate from doing it herself so she could see over the heads of all the other idiots in the pack. Crazed by the bloodlust, she apparently forgot she's not a goddamn mountain goat. So in yet another attempt to keep the Alphas of Mac Tire from killing themselves, I got on the bar. I was only going to tell her what I saw, but when that asshole moved close enough and cut your neck, I got pissed."

"Aww, you'll have me in tears of gratitude in a minute, woman."

I reached over to smack Paddy in the back of the head, and the end of his sentence turned into a yelp.

"What was Fee doing in back? Why wasn't she up front?" Murphy asked, and Paddy burst into laughter again, so I was forced to smack him a second time.

"I dragged her in back of the bar to get her out of the way. Crowds watching bar brawls can be rough, and she is pregnant, remember? I was trying to get her into the kitchen, but the bitch wouldn't go. The back of the bar was as far as I could get her," I huffed.

Murphy looked at Paddy. Paddy looked at Murphy. Hysterics ensued to the point I was convinced Murphy would drive off the goddamn road.

"Her being massively pregnant and not at the top of her form is probably the only reason you got her as far as you did." Paddy wiped tears from his eyes and Murphy's shoulders shook as he obviously tried to regain control. "Otherwise if you'd pulled that stunt, there'd have been another bar brawl last night and you'd have gotten your ass kicked, Stanzie."

"How do you know I'd be the one getting my ass kicked?" I demanded angrily, and Murphy's shoulders started to really shake.

"Hating the sight of blood and all, you can hardly be a practiced brawler. Unlike Fee who could probably kick my ass if she put her mind to it," Paddy replied.

"From the way you were fighting last night, Mickey Mouse could kick your ass." I wanted to stay angry at both of them, but it was hard not resist them when they laughed. Murphy especially. When he lost it again at my words, a strange, suffocating wave of love swept over me.

Paddy laughed, too, but he pretended to be offended. The gleam of amusement in his eyes gave him away.

"I was just letting the bastard warm up. I was having fun, Stanz."

"Which is why you spent half an hour last night screaming and swearing while I poured peroxide all over your bleeding body, I guess."

"It was my arm, my neck, and my face, you horrible bitch. It's not like I was covered in gore and slashed to ribbons. Jaysus, now who's exaggerating?"

"It was a lot of blood. Murphy's going to find the bloody washcloths on the bottom of his tub to prove it," I maintained.

"Great," Murphy's tone was wry. "Anything else I ought to be on the lookout for in my apartment?"

"A shit ton of shoes," muttered Paddy, and I smacked the back of his head again.

* * * *

The appetizing smell of roasting chicken greeted me at the door of Murphy's apartment. The television was on, and the sound of an Irish-accented newscaster underscored, again, how far away I was from home.

Murphy stirred gravy in a pan on the stove in the galley kitchen. The table was set for two, and a bottle of white wine rested in a silver ice bucket. One wineglass sat on the table, but the other, half full, rested on the counter at Murphy's elbow.

"Thought you might need some food to balance out the Guinness." His cheerful grin didn't quite reach his eyes.

I put down the bag of Guinness souvenirs I'd bought and looked around for the things I'd left in the living room. Mostly, I'd left shoes. There was no trace of me at all, and the room looked freshly dusted and sterile as the night I'd walked through the door.

"Fee couldn't drink, so I only had the complimentary pint at the Gravity Bar."

He'd obliterated my presence and it itched at me. Just like the dust, I'd been swept away.

"Nice of you. I would have drunk hers, too," Murphy said. "There's wine. You want some?"

What I wanted was to run out the door and straight back to Boston, but instead I forced a smile.

"I'll just go put my souvenirs in my suitcase." I went into the bedroom.

My suitcase was gone, too. So was the mail on the desk. The shell box was still there, and I resisted the stupid urge to look inside. Of course his bond pendant was still inside. We were not together anymore. The fact he'd cleared away everything that was mine proved that. He'd staked his claim to this apartment and I had no place in it.

The bloody clothes I'd left in the corner were gone as well as all my other shoes. The bed was made, the curtains drawn, and I smelled the lemony scent of cleanser from the open bathroom door.

Maybe he'd moved my stuff to a hotel and he planned to give me a ride after I choked down the meal he'd made. A dinner guest, that's what I was.

I took the bag with my Guinness t-shirt and chocolate truffles back into the living room and set it by the front door so I wouldn't forget it on my way out. I didn't even know why I'd bought them. Why would I want souvenirs to commemorate one of the worst times in my life?

"Thought you wanted to put that away?" Murphy carried his wineglass into the living room and stared in confusion at my stupid Guinness gift shop bag.

"Couldn't find my suitcase. I thought maybe..." I trailed off as I realized how idiotic and pathetic I sounded.

"I threw it out?" He finished for me, even more confused. "I unpacked for you, seeing as you're going to stay for a while, right?"

When had I decided that? My throat squeezed shut and I didn't know what to do. Unpacked for me? He hadn't cleared me away, but instead had integrated my things with his? Without asking me first?

"When you didn't call Allerton or tell Fee, I figured you'd decided to stay and help." He took a sip of wine and watched me cautiously.

"How do you know what I did or didn't do?" I asked, unnerved.

"Easy. Allerton didn't call me to discuss things, and Fee didn't rush home to slit Paddy's throat for him and then come gunning for me."

I blew out my breath. He had me there. He was right. I hadn't called Allerton, nor had I said anything to Fee. Instead, I'd pretended to enjoy the fucking Guinness tour and gulped down my free pint in the bar.

"How exactly are we going to do this, Murphy, without getting killed or hauled up in front of a tribunal?" The smell of roasting chicken made my stomach growl. The thought of sharing a meal with Murphy, of something so intimate after months apart, threatened my fragile sense of self. This was too fucking confusing.

I went to the French doors and unlatched them so I could step out onto the small balcony overlooking a side street. It was functional and large enough for two chairs. Anything to get away from the scent of food. I sat in the chair on the right. It provided a sweeping view of the Dublin street below. Did Murphy sit here at night and look out into the dark? Did he ever think of me?

After a moment he joined me. He handed me a glass of wine and took his to the railing so he could look down.

"We can do this if we're very careful," he said.

I contemplated my wine for a moment and took a sip. It was clear, crisp, and cold. No doubt expensive. Where did Murphy get his money and his expensive tastes anyway? Resentment of his wealth churned my gut. Until I'd become an Advisor, I'd had to scrimp and save, especially after I bought my Boston condo with Elena's legacy. I'd paid cash for it so I wouldn't have a mortgage, but it had wiped me out financially and there had been many months I'd spent eating peanut butter and crackers two times a day in order to have the money for the utility bills.

This damn apartment probably cost twice as much as my condo, even if it was smaller. Yet, he still had money left to buy designer jeans and fancy wine and modern furniture that didn't come in a box ready to be assembled like most of mine had.

As an Advisor, I now had money, but it was blood money, most likely. I was living the high life off the murders of Guardians of the Pack. Yes, they were murderers themselves, but everything seemed black and wrong.

What had I gotten myself into?

"Your father was Paddy's mentor, wasn't he? And he's neck-deep in this mess, too, isn't he?"

At the railing, Murphy froze, every muscle in his body going taut.

All day long I'd been keyed up by thin, anxious energy and thoughts of him. Now he was here three steps away from me, and I didn't know whether to laugh, cry or fling my damn wine in his face. I had to concentrate on the conspiracy, not on how damn great he smelled or how much I wanted to bury my face in his throat as he held me. That was bullshit. We were in danger and we were broken up. So what if he'd unpacked for me? It made no difference. He'd walked out on me and I'd built my life back up without him. What the fuck had I come here for?

"No," he denied, but there was no force to his tone. His shoulders slumped.

"You don't want to expose him, even though you have to if you want to save Paddy," I accused, and he turned toward me, mouth tight.

"I'll do what I have to do. But I am not convinced my father is in this."

"Oh, bullshit, he's a Regional Councilor. He's in this somehow, and you have to face it."

"Stanzie, I don't want to talk about this." His words came out in a growl of exasperation and fear.

I wanted to kill him almost as much as I wanted to fold him into my arms and croon in his ear that everything would be okay. What the fuck was wrong with me?

"Just wanting to keep things status quo is not a crime. If the Guardians only wanted that and were accomplishing it by fair means, all Paddy's got to prove is that he had nothing to do with Mick Shaughnessy and the killing faction. If your father's not part of that, maybe he could help us."

"It's not that frigging easy." Murphy stared at the street. "How does Paddy know who to trust within the group? And what if it's all a setup, Stanzie? You reel in people one at a time by telling them one thing, and before they know it, it's an entirely different animal—and by then they're in too deep to get out. Who would believe him when he says he had no knowledge of what goes on beneath the surface? He's paid Mick money for months now and…"

"Blackmail. It's blackmail," I protested.

"Says Paddy. Mick Shaughnessy would never agree that's what it was. If we could even find him to ask." Murphy blew out an impatient breath and went inside to rescue something from the stove.

I helped him put the food on the table and tried not to brush up against him in the close confines of the kitchen.

When we were seated at the table, the scent of Fee's wildflowers competed with the chicken, peas, and potatoes.

I tried to eat, but fear formed a lump in my throat.

"Everything seems so hopeless." I set my fork down on my plate and took deep breaths to calm myself. It didn't help.

Murphy watched me, his eyes dark. "Stanzie, we're going to fix this, okay?"

When I pushed back my chair and fled from the table, he came after me. I reached out for the handle of the French doors, and he took hold of my arm and forced me to turn around.

His mouth was hot and demanding as we slammed against the doors hard enough to make the glass rattle. I opened my mouth and met his tongue with mine, and he tightened his fingers on my shoulders with a possessive strength.

He was kissing me. His lips were familiar, but the kiss sizzled. Electric. He tasted so good. Wine and warm spice. How could I have gone without this for so long?

To prove this was real and not a mirage, I pushed my hands beneath his shirt and spread my palms flat against his hot skin. His chest was smooth and hard, the contours familiar yet somehow brand new. With a groan, he yanked me closer even as he helped me strip off his shirt.

God, he felt good. I'd missed him so damn much.

His cock was rock hard against my lower belly and I slid my hands down to his ass and pressed against him as hard as I could.

Murmuring my name, he swept me up in his arms as if I weighed nothing, kicked the bedroom door open, and tossed me on the bed. His dark gaze locked to mine, he peeled off his pants and threw them on the floor.

On fire, I watched him. I wanted to scream in frustration because we weren't touching. All I wanted was his cock buried deep inside me. The four seconds he was away from me seemed like aeons.

With a growl, he leaped on top of me and slid his hand beneath my t-shirt so he could rake his nails across the sensitive skin on my belly. I wriggled my hips to help him strip off my jeans and panties, then he buried his face between my legs, and I dug my fingers into his hair.

His goatee was soft yet bristly against me. This was a new sensation between us. Sensing I liked it, he rubbed his rough cheek against the tender flesh of my thigh and I bucked beneath him.Wickedly expert, he licked me until I screamed. He watched me as I came, even as he continued to suck and swirl his tongue. He had two of his fingers buried inside me, and I wanted more. I needed more.

I loved him so much it ached.

He moved so his body covered mine and looked down at me. I kissed his chin, scraped my tongue across his goatee, and he shuddered.

"I love you," I whispered. Tears trembled on the edges of my lashes. "I missed you so much."

"God, I want to be in you so bad. I want to fill you up, feel you come." He kissed me, and I tasted the dark honey of myself on his lips. We thrashed together on the bed, until I thought I would go crazy.

When he slid into me, we both gasped into each other's mouths and everything went blurry.

I came again, hard, and he held me as I cried out. Waves and waves of love crashed through me and left me limp. His feverish caresses revived me, and we shifted to our favorite position, with me on my knees, braced against the headboard, him behind me, my hair pulled tight in his fist, my head turned to the side so he could kiss me until I was breathless.

With each thrust, he talked to me in Irish, and I never wanted it to end.

"Come for me, Stanzie," he coaxed and bit my earlobe, which always sent me over the edge, and he knew it.

I screamed his name, and when I came, he did, too. His whole body shuddered against mine as we collapsed to the mattress, soaked with sweat and out of breath.

Bliss. This was bliss. Perfection.

His weight against me was comforting and wonderful, and I tried not to move so he wouldn't either.

He whispered something in Irish and stroked my hair. I closed my eyes to savor the sweet afterglow, and when I opened them again, I saw he'd fallen asleep.

My own eyes slid shut, and the last thing I did before sleep claimed me was entwine my fingers with his.

* * * *

Our fingers were still linked when I opened my eyes hours later. The bedroom smelled of sex—of us—and while he wasn't snoring, Murphy's breath was slow and heavy, the way I remembered from the nights we'd spent together in America.

For a moment I was filled with such aching happiness I almost expected to levitate off the bed. But then I remembered everything, and black despair bit into me so hard I wondered I didn't bleed.

He'd rolled off me at some point, but we were still on top of the covers. I let go of his hand and slid off the bed. I found his t-shirt and my panties, put them on and fled to the living room.

The remains of our dinner had congealed on our plates on the table. The lights were still on, and I got as far as the sofas before my legs went out from beneath me and I couldn't breathe through the tears that poured down my face.

Murphy appeared like a ghost in the bedroom doorway. His eyes were very dark.

"Can we talk about it, Stanzie?"

"What's to talk about?" I drew one of the throw pillows defensively close to my stomach. I loved him but he didn't love me. I'd tried so hard not to let that overwhelm me and make peace with it. Of all the people in his life he protected, I was the last on the list and that's not where I wanted to be. "You chose Paddy and Mac Tire over me, and I guess I get that, but it hurts."

"I had no idea you loved me." His tone was raw and desperate. "I thought I was doing the right thing. You didn't need to be put at risk in this, and I thought I could—"

"Fucking what? Don't lie to me, Liam. You didn't want me involved because you're going to do something stupid to save Paddy and your father. Why should you martyr yourself for them?"

"Paddy came to me for help," Murphy shouted and the muscles in his face strained as he struggled to regain control. "He had nowhere else to turn, don't you see? It's not like I could tell him to go screw himself. He's my best mate."

"But it's okay to tell me to go screw myself, I guess. I'm your bond mate. You wouldn't come to my tribunal. You threw me out like so much garbage when Paddy told you his problems. And you couldn't even tell me why. You're so hell-bent on saving everybody, but it's always on your terms and you have to be the one to give help—you never want it in return. I would have helped you. I would have done anything for Paddy— he's my Alpha—but you decided what was best for me in your typical high-handed Liam Murphy fashion, and to hell with what I thought, what I wanted.

"And then tonight you take advantage of the fact I love you so you can, what? Have sex? Haven't you fucked anyone in four months, or have you just fucked people over?"

His face blanched of all color, and he stared at me, his dark eyes bottomless.

"That wasn't just sex. Did that feel like just sex to you?"

"No, not to me. I love you. But that's what it was to you. Will you please leave me alone? I'm tired and I want to go to sleep."

"Stanzie, I know you're tired, but we've got to talk about this."

"In the morning. Maybe." I turned away from him because I couldn't stand to look at the entreaty in his eyes. In a heartbeat I'd be across the floor to him, and fuck that.

He abruptly gave in. "Look, you take the bed, I'll sleep out here."

"No, I'll stay out here." I was ten seconds from tears, and I wanted him gone so he wouldn't see.

"Stanzie, take the bed."

"No," I shouted, and the damn tears poured down my cheeks. "It smells like *us* in there, don't you get it? And *us* is a lie. Just let me do what I want, goddamn it."

He opened his mouth to argue, but then, defeated, retreated and did as I asked.

Chapter 10

She hit me hard the next morning as I scraped the remains of our dinner into the garbage. The plate slipped from my hands and crashed to the tile. I would have fallen, too, except I managed to grab the edge of the counter.

A shocked, agonized cry escaped my lips, and purple fire clawed me from the inside out until I couldn't breathe.

Murphy skidded around the corner as he frantically pulled up his jeans. His hair was tousled, his eyes wild with fear.

"Stanzie, what's wrong?" He stepped distractedly around the broken shards of glass and put a hand on my arm. A thin, whistling scream burst out of my lungs at the contact. She clawed at me again, and it took everything I had to push her back down. I was scared shitless.

"Muh-my wolf," I said between clenched teeth. "She wants out, and I can't…I don't think I can hold…her. Mur—phy, God, it hurts. It fucking hurts!"

The fear left his eyes, and he became incredibly calm. This time when he touched me, it didn't hurt, his fear didn't infect me. Instead, his touch soothed, and I squeezed my eyes shut in relief. But she clawed at me again, and I tasted blood when my teeth shredded my bottom lip.

"They suh—say she's nuh-normal now, but I haven't shifted suh—since I took the elixir. I cuh—can't shift here, it's too small. What if I can't control her? Fuck, this hurts."

"You're fighting her," he told me.

I screamed, "Well, Jesus Christ, of course I am! She can't come out here. Murphy, where can I go? I can't stay here."

"Stanzie." He took me in his arms and hugged me, and I clung to him so I wouldn't disintegrate into a ball of cold, tingly, purple flame. The onset of shifting always felt like a cool crackling in my veins. I pictured it as a sweeping purple ball of flame that built higher and higher until I couldn't contain it any longer.

I moaned aloud and Murphy said, "Just hold on, honey. Can you hold on for forty minutes or so? I can drive you somewhere, but you need to hang on. We can't have you shifting in the car, can we?"

"I've never felt like this before. I don't know." I lifted my face beseechingly to his. Of course he didn't want me to shift in the car, but I had no idea if I could control my wolf and prevent that.

"We're gonna get dressed, and we'll leave." He walked me back to the bedroom and helped me put on my jeans and sandals and he found another shirt. The whole time he talked to me in a calm voice and told me what we were going to do next and how we were going to do it. His voice was melodic and mesmerizing and I focused desperately on it so I could drive out my rising panic. If he hadn't been there, I don't know what I would have done.

Donadea Forest Park was approximately thirty miles from Dublin, and Murphy did his best to get me there as fast as he could. We weren't going there, precisely, from what I understood of Murphy's explanation. We were going to private Mac Tire land abutting the forest. Murphy told me generations of Pack wolves had hunted there far enough away from the public forest that no Other ever heard a wolf howl. After all, there were no real wolves left in Ireland, just us.

I reclined in the passenger seat, my arms and legs stiff and full of agony, face squeezed tight against the pain of fighting against my wolf.

Once we had to wait for a train to cross the road. I whimpered when I realized we couldn't get around, and Murphy put the car in park. He smoothed his fingers along the side of my face and through my hair as he whispered it would be okay.

"So when's the last time you shifted?" he asked in an attempt to distract me.

"The tribunal," I said. "I tried once after that, but she wouldn't come out. This was before I drank the elixir."

"With who?" There was something weird in Murphy's tone, and I opened my eyes to read his expression, but there was nothing there but concern for me.

I tried to focus, thankful for the distraction and even more grateful for the touch of his hands on my face and in my hair. "Alan. He's twenty-one, member of Mayflower. When I was there, he asked me to initiate his wolf. It was all fucked up in Mayflower because of Paul. Alan asked me, and I said no because of my wolf. But Scott and Faith, the Alphas—Faith's my cousin—they convinced me finally to do it. Scott said he'd stay with me and my wolf and Faith could look after Alan. Only Faith couldn't sleep with Alan because their fathers were in a triad with Alan's mother and so even though they weren't the same blood, they were still like brother and sister, you know?"

"I understand." Murphy's thumb brushed something wet from my face. Tears. "But she wouldn't come out?"

"No." My voice was forlorn. "And your wolf wasn't there for her, to help her come out."

He pressed his forehead to mine. "I'm so, so, sorry, Stanzie. But my wolf's here today for you. And any time you ever want him, okay?"

"I wish I could believe you." I said. But I couldn't.

* * * *

Rain drummed on the roof of the car as Murphy drove through huge iron gates that opened when he punched a code onto a keypad. Once past, we stopped briefly at a gatehouse with another checkpoint. This time there was a guard, obviously a member of the pack, who waved us through into a small car park.

Oak trees stretched up to the sky, and beyond the car park I could see the gray gleam of a lake. A long gravel drive led to a fountain and a small castle. Any other time I would have been fascinated by the thought of a real-life castle, but my mind was too crowded by my wolf.

Before Murphy switched off the ignition, I all but ripped off my seatbelt and fell in a heap when I tried to get out of the car. My legs wouldn't support me because they wanted to shift.

Murphy picked me up into his arms and ran through the pelting rain into the forest. When I screamed at him to put me the fuck down, he did. We both tore at my clothes. My fingers were more like claws, and then…

* * * *

The rain is wet on my fur. I shake it off, but it feels good on me. I am free. I am whole. It is no longer hard to think. That is an oak tree. That is an oak leaf on the ground. Before it fell, it belonged to the tree. On a branch of the oak tree, there is a bird huddled against the raindrops. That bird is a crow. It looks at me and makes a sound. Caw is the sound. I growl, but I only play. I cannot reach the crow in the oak tree and we both know it. He caws at me again, but I do not want to play with him. Crows are not as fun as other wolves. Like me.

I smell him. I smell my Friend, and he is so beautiful. He has silver-gray fur and a white chest. One front paw is white. The others are gray. He has a thick tail he waves very fast because he is with me again. He was gone before, but now he is here. I thought he went away the same as Him and Her, and I was sad, but he did not. He is here.

Once, a long time ago, I ran with Him and Her. Their real names were Grey and Elena. They are dead, but I do not know how they died. One day they were with me when we ran through the forest, and the next time there was only Friend. But he is enough.

My heart beats fast when I look at Friend. He grins at me and waves his tail. His whine is excited. He runs and I run after him. I can run faster and I will beat him. My legs blur beneath me as I stretch into the run. I run so fast he is left behind. I hear him howl behind me and I lift my nose and howl back, but still I run. He chases me. Friend chases. Should I let him catch me? I do not know this forest, it is not mine. I think it must be his, but I can smell there are no roads ahead. No Others. The rain feels so good on my fur. The air is full of good smells. I want to roll in the wet leaves, but if I do, Friend will catch me. Maybe I want him to.

I roll. I roll and make snuffle noises. Friend pounces on me. We roll together. He snaps his teeth at me, he bites my ear, but it does not hurt. I snarl at him, but I am playing. We roll. We roll together. Friend gives me his throat.

I remember. I remember the throat of the bad man. The taste of his blood in my mouth. I do not like this memory. I make it go away. I take Friend's nose in my mouth. No, not nose. There is another, better word. I think hard, and I will find that word. I squeeze Friend's nose- not nose, still I think of better word—with my teeth, but I do not hurt.

I let go. Friend takes my muzzle—yes, that is the better word- in his mouth. He bites but it does not hurt. We roll. We roll together. I want to run, but I want Friend to play with me. I feel the rain on us and I have never had the glad feeling like this. It is so much I cannot keep it inside me. I must let it out, and I hope Friend feels it, too. I love Friend.

* * * *

Cold rain against my face. Human again. My wolf was gone. Naked, I surged to my feet and saw Murphy beneath the sheltering limbs of an oak tree. He had on his jeans, but that was it.

I found my shirt and put it and my panties on. My clothes were wet with rain and clammy against my skin, but I was still filled with the wonder of my wolf.

Murphy watched me dress. As was his habit with important things, he allowed me to speak first. Waiting for me to say something was probably agony for him, but he stood there in the rain and was silent.

I zipped my jeans and turned to him with a huge smile. Joy spiked through my veins. Huge, life-altering elation the likes of which I'd never experienced before. "Oh, Liam, She could think in full and complete sentences. And she knew all the words. Some didn't come as fast as others, but she didn't get mad, she knew they'd find her eventually. Oh, the best part—the really, really, really best part—was she could see in color. Does your wolf see in color?"

A tremendous smile lit up his face. "You never saw in color before?"

"No. Did you know your wolf's eyes are the most beautiful orange amber? They're almost like Faith's, but deeper gold somehow. What color are my wolf's eyes?"

"Very, very bright blue. With flecks of silver. They're gorgeous. And your wolf's fur is almost white."

"Like Kathy Manning's?" I whispered, entranced.

"Prettier. Darker. There's a lavender glow to it, and the tips are silver-gray. Never seen a color exactly like it." He edged closer to me.

"My wolf can't be more beautiful than Kathy's. Her wolf's the most beautiful I've ever seen." I smiled to think of her.

"Ah, Stanzie, why will you never take a compliment from me?" A bittersweet smile tugged the corner of his mouth.

"Don't I?" I was momentarily thrown as I tried to remember.

"Never," he said. "Not once. I guess I don't give compliments properly."

"Bullshit. You give them right and left. The waitresses in almost every restaurant we ever ate at, the girls behind the counter at Target—you know damn well how to give compliments," I countered.

"Ah, but then why don't you take them from me?"

"I would if you meant them, but you just say them because that's how you are with all women. Pack, Others, it doesn't matter."

"You think I'm lying?"

"No," I said. "Just force of habit."

"Any compliment I've given all these multitude of women, have I exaggerated? Told a homely woman she was the most gorgeous girl on earth? What?"

I thought back. His compliments to other women had been generous, but definitely fair.

"No," I admitted.

"So why, if I tell you your wolf is the most beautiful one I've ever seen, do you automatically dismiss it? Why, when I tell you that you stole my breath away the first time I saw you in that sexy red dress, do you think I'm full of shite?"

Uncomfortable in my own skin, I shrugged. I wished he'd change the subject. "I don't know."

"It's not just my compliments either. I've seen you brush off sincere compliments from any number of people— Kathy Manning, Allerton, Paddy. It doesn't seem to matter. You don't believe them. Tell me, when Grey told you that you were beautiful, did you believe him?"

Please change the damn subject. "Well, I always thought Elena was the beautiful one, but I didn't tell him that."

"I've seen pictures of Elena, and she was beautiful, but so are you." His smile turned wistful. "You don't trust people anymore, do you?"

"Sure, I do," I argued. Most of my wolf's magic dissipated and I shivered in the cold rain. "I trust everybody until they lie to me."

"*Until?*" He stressed. "Why not *unless*?"

"Because." I came to a slow, horrible conclusion. All my wolf's joy evaporated and left me despondent. "It's always *until* now. *Unless* died in the car crash with Gray and Elena. Everybody lies to me eventually. Even you. Especially you."

"When have I lied to you?" He stepped closer so he could search my face with his dark gaze.

"When you left. When you said it was for the best. How was that the truth when I was left behind? When you took everything away?"

"I didn't know you loved me." He moved close and took my face between his hands. "I thought I'd give you the chance to have what you said you wanted. A pack. A bond mate. To be happy like you used to be."

"But *you* were my bond mate." Tears slid down my cheeks and mixed with the rain.

"I thought you'd go to Vaughn and bond with him and Jossie. He used to be in your pack, and you loved him. I thought he could give you more than I could. He could keep you safer for sure."

"Vaughn and Jossie?" My mouth trembled. "After my father's tribunal, I took Wren to Maplefair, to Vaughn and Jossie. I wanted to confront my fears. I went down into Grandmother Emma's root cellar all by myself, and I walked around and knelt in the dirt where I'd killed Nate, and I took away his power to scare me. And when I came back up, Jossie was there, and she very politely hinted that I ought to take Wren and leave because Vaughn was going to ask me to bond with them, and she didn't want that. She wanted him to herself. Anyway, all I'd ever have been with them is spare to the pair. I wanted what I used to have, and I was not the spare to the pair.

"I thought I would come here and work things out with you and everything would be like it was before my wolf tore Nate's throat out. But it can't be, can it?" More tears leaked out of my eyes, and I tasted their warm salt on my lips.

"I guess they can't be the way they were. Too many things have changed, you're right. Your wolf, for one." He pulled me against his chest, and I buried my face in his neck. I inhaled his unique scent, and it fucking killed me.

"Thank you for all you did for her," I whispered. "For initiating her."

"Is that what I did?" he mused. "Whatever I did, it was a two-way street. Your wolf was so happy today. I haven't seen her this happy since the first time we shifted together in France. Remember that?"

"I remember your wolf growled at me," I sulked, and his fingers dug into my side until I couldn't feel low anymore and shrieked with laughter. The bastard knew just where I was most ticklish.

* * * *

"I don't like it because it makes me feel like one of them," I said. Murphy paused as we made our soggy way back to the car park. Mud squished between my bare toes. I'd only been able to find one of my sandals. I hoped the other one was by the car, but if not, I could always go shoe shopping. Besides, sandals were not the right shoe for this weather or terrain.

Murphy had on a pair of Doc Marten boots I'd never seen before. I wasn't sure I liked them—they added to his new edgy and dangerous look and danced him just out of reach of the Murphy I remembered from Boston.

His hair stuck up in strangely compelling spikes. He looked as if some salon professional had labored hours over his hair for a scene out of some supernatural drama set in the woods, whereas, my hair was plastered to my skull in unbecoming chunks, and yesterday's makeup clung to the corners of my eyes and lashes.

"When you compliment me," I clarified because, while our previous conversation had gone on in my mind, he'd apparently stopped thinking about it. "You make me feel like just another pretty girl in a long line of them. Nothing special. Sorcha wasn't beautiful. She wasn't even pretty. But she was mysterious." I knew my voice turned bitter on that last word. It had galled me for months. "No matter how hard I try, I can never be mysterious. You always know who I am and what I'm thinking."

"Why do you want to be like Sorcha?" He pitched his tone low and calm, but I could see the turbulent flow of emotion in his dark eyes.

"That obvious, isn't it? So you'd love me back. Doesn't it fucking kill you to think you're in the exact opposite position you were with her? Cause it kills me if I let myself think about it too much."

A strangled noise escaped him. Was the man laughing at me?

"Stanzie, I have been madly in love with you since New Orleans."

There was no sound for a long moment but the ragged patter of rain against the oak leaves.

"New Orleans." Was he kidding me? He'd loved me since New Orleans? Rage warred with exultation inside me. "But that was before *Christmas*. This is August. Why didn't you ever tell me?"

"Why didn't you?" he countered.

Oh, wrong answer, Liam Murphy.

"Because you said you didn't want anything from me!" The volume of my voice made him grimace.

"When did I say that?"

"At the safe house in Hartford after you bashed my head against the wall when I tried to show you how I felt." Remembered shame and grief slammed into me and left me shaky.

He winced at my bluntness. "I meant pity. I didn't want your damn pity. Because that's what I thought it was. How the hell was I supposed to know any different? That's all I ever got from Sorcha—why wouldn't you be the same? I spent ten years trying to get that woman to love me, and after that I figured I was just unlovable, that there was some sort of fatal flaw inside me that prevented people from loving me back.

"And anyway, I tell you all the time how I feel. It's not my fault you don't speak Irish."

I gaped at him. "You—you tell me you love me in *bed*, Murphy? In a language I don't even speak?" Unbelievable. Did I even know this guy at all? "All this time I've been thinking you're talking to her mostly, but it's been me?"

"Why the fuck do you persist in thinking every time I'm inside you I'm screwing Sorcha, too?" Murphy's yell roused a nearby crow. It rose squawking from the branches and flapped away. "That woman only crosses my mind when you shove her there."

"What a lie that is," I shouted back, fists clenched. "You're after Mick Shaughnessy and the conspiracy because of her. She has to cross your mind a hundred times a day!"

"She doesn't! She doesn't, Stanzie. I'm worried to death about Paddy, Fee and my father, not frigging Sorcha. How many times do I have to tell you she's dead before you'll let her lie in her grave where she belongs?"

I could see the car park between the tree branches ahead on the path.

I rubbed my face and tried to focus, but my thoughts scattered in fifty thousand different directions.

"So you loved me and left me anyway?" One by one my thoughts disintegrated until there was only one left. One monstrous thought that was full of betrayal.

His face fell. "I left you *because* I loved you."

I began to walk again, and he was forced to move, too, if he wanted to keep up with me. Dark emotions churned in my stomach like battery acid. How the hell was I supposed to deal with that statement? He left me *because* he loved me? Were we in some sort of fucking Oxygen Channel movie? What kind of a stupid idiot did that man think I was?

"That is the sort of declaration that sounds noble as hell but means shit when you really break it down and think about it." I waited for him to unlock the doors to the BMW. "You wouldn't have left Sorcha behind, and you know it. The truth is you didn't want to love me. You just wanted to play knight in shining armor. So you sacrificed your love for me to save me and thought yourself quite the great man.

"Well, in my eyes, Liam Murphy, you're a fucking pathetic piece of shit. And you've ruined everything. Good job." I threw myself into the passenger seat.

He stood there a moment in the pouring rain, driver's side door open, frozen and oblivious of the torrential downpour before he got in.

"Not how I wanted this conversation to go," he remarked.

He sat there for a moment and then pounded the steering wheel with his fist once, twice, three times, until I thought the damn thing would break and we'd be stuck in this miserable rain forever.

* * * *

Paddy sprawled across the sofa in Murphy's apartment, his gaze fixed to the comedy on the television.

I stalked, dripping wet, for the bathroom and a hot shower while Murphy stood just inside the door and stared at Paddy.

"I used Fee's key," Paddy explained. "Gave mine to Stanzie, didn't I?"

"Did I say anything?" Murphy asked.

Paddy straightened up on the sofa. "Where the hell have you two been? You're drenched."

"Brilliant deduction, Sherlock," I muttered.

"Oi," shouted Paddy, "I'll not have that tone directed to me as Alpha!"

"Is this better?" I extended my middle finger.

"Marginally," Paddy decided and winged a throw pillow at me. I dodged it and slammed the bathroom door behind me.

Breakfast smells greeted me when I emerged in dry clothes. I had a slightly better handle on my temper, but I was still pissed off.

The idea that Murphy loved me should have had me walking on the moon with delirious happiness, but instead I wanted to break something. Preferably his head. It wasn't fair. The four months I'd spent alone, agonizing over what I'd done wrong, had been hell. He loved me and didn't think I loved him back. He'd left because he didn't want me involved in the shit mess of the conspiracy. Did he truly believe I'd think him noble for it? I wasn't some weak, doe-eyed girl. I didn't run screaming into the night when confronted with nasty shit. How many times would I have to prove I was a strong, capable woman before any Mac Tire man would fucking get it?

Paddy stood at the stove over a pan of frying bacon while Murphy whisked eggs in a white ceramic bowl on the granite countertop.

"Take over." He handed me the whisk so he could have his turn in the shower. Quarters were tight in the galley kitchen, but I didn't think he had to brush quite so much of his damn body against mine as he squeezed past.

I stared after him for a second and then turned to the eggs. The mouthwatering scent of bacon nearly drove me to my knees, but I gamely began to whisk.

"Liam said you shifted and your wolf was fantastic." Paddy flipped several slices of bacon over in the pan and gave me a grin.

"So what," I snarled and his grin faded.

"Jaysus, woman, isn't this what you wanted? Your wolf to be normal and you and Liam back together?"

I grimly beat the damn eggs into a froth.

"You did tell me you came here to make it up with him. I'd say shifting proved you made up with him considering you can't shift without having it off with each other. People who aren't together don't screw, do they?"

"You're so fucking eloquent, Paddy." I brandished the dripping whisk, and he ducked, obviously recalling the many objects I'd thrown at his head since we'd met each other.

"Why are you here?" I looked around for a frying pan so I could scramble the eggs, and Paddy prudently backed away, his gaze fixed on my hands, presumably so he'd know when to dodge.

"Can't a man have breakfast with his best mate?" He ripped off a few sheets of paper towels and arranged them on a plate to soak up the grease from the bacon.

"Are either of you going to tell me anything about how we're supposed to save your sorry ass, or I am just here to scramble eggs and be emotionally manipulated?" I dumped the eggs into the heated frying pan, and they hissed against the bubbling butter.

"Is that how you feel? Manipulated?" Paddy's expression was sympathetic, and half of me wanted to fling myself into his arms and sob into his chest while he murmured horrible things about Murphy into my ear and told me it would be all right. The other half of me snorted in derision and continued to stir the eggs.

"You know what that bastard said to me?" I shook the spatula I used to stir the eggs at Paddy, and he flinched but held his ground. "He told me he had no idea I loved him and that if he had, he'd never have left me behind. Can you believe the fucking gall? As if it wasn't apparent I trailed after him like a lovelorn idiot? *You* saw it, didn't you?"

"Yes," he agreed warily. "I wouldn't call you a lovelorn idiot, Stanz, but the way you felt about him was clear. Every time someone would bring him up at the tribunal, your face got all funny and wistful and hurt and we all knew. He's the idiot. Never seeing what's right before his eyes.

"I know it's my fault what happened between you and I'm sorry. I'm not sure what to do to make it better, or even if I can, but if you want me to take his sorry ass out back and thrash him, I'm your man, okay?"

"Why is it that your first answer to any problem is a fight?" I rolled my eyes, but there was a secret part of me that felt absurdly cheered at the idea Paddy would kick Murphy's ass for me.

"Because it's a damn good fix to most things that are broken." Paddy crunched a piece of bacon between his white teeth. "And because I love a good fight, of course. The smell of blood is better than coffee, to my mind."

"Barbarian." I turned back to the eggs and rescued them before they could burn.

I set the pan on a cold burner and moved to the refrigerator so I could get milk for the coffee. The carton was on the door beside a glass bottle of unopened ketchup. I froze, and a huge lump rose in my throat.

"You don't know me at all if you thought I'd come after him." I turned around with ketchup in one hand, milk in the other. Paddy saw my expression and stopped laughing.

"Why'd you tell him I'd come after him? You shouldn't have done that."

"You're here, aren't you?" He reached to shut the refrigerator door behind me.

"Because Allerton sent me."

"Bollocks." Paddy followed me to the table with the plate of bacon. "You wanted him back. You still do. And he wants you. So why not go for it? Stop fighting. Stop playing the blame game, and just move on."

"Easy for you to say. You weren't the one left behind. You don't have to live in the shadow of—"

"If you say 'a dead woman' or 'Sorcha,' I'm out of here." Murphy stood in the bedroom doorway. His dark eyes sparked with anger. "The only one who gives a shit about that woman anymore is you, and I swear you use her as a shield half the time, a bludgeon the other. I'm through trying to convince you she doesn't matter to me anymore. *You* do. You don't want to hear it, maybe because you're guilty about loving somebody after Grey and Elena, or maybe because you think you're not good enough because of all the things that have happened to you.

"I could fucking kill Jonathan Archer and all of Riverglow for casting you out of your pack. You let them take every last shred of self-worth you had and flush it down the toilet. You know why you can't take a frigging compliment? Because you don't think you're worthy. And everything you do, you're screaming for people to listen to you, to look at you, and when they do, you push them away.

"You have to figure yourself out…before we really do give up on you. Nobody likes to beat their brains out against a brick wall forever."

A dreadful silence descended over the room. I stood there with the bottle of ketchup in my hand, Paddy with the plate of bacon. Murphy took a deep breath before he grabbed his leather jacket and slammed out the front door.

Chapter 11

"Classical music's for practicing your technique, woman, not for a night in an Irish pub." Declan Byrne managed to roar his criticism so loud everyone in the pub broke off what they were doing—and many of them had been listening to me play Mozart on the harp—to stare.

From his perch on a bar stool, Paddy made a rude gesture behind Declan's back, but I didn't grin as he'd no doubt intended. The Mozart had been an attempt to cheer myself after a brooding day in Murphy's apartment watching movies with Paddy and Fee.

We'd fled to An Puca in search of food, and the lure of the harp had proved too much for me again. Maybe I could play out my melancholy and confusion, but no, Declan Byrne had showed up and decided to be an asshole. Or perhaps, as I was beginning to suspect, that was his default setting.

"I exhausted my repertoire of sprightly Irish pub tunes the first night I played. Not much call for them at WASP-y New England weddings and upscale business receptions. Go figure. You're so bored, Declan, you take over." I smothered my regret with irritation and stepped off the platform onto the sticky pub floor. If I ran this place, somebody'd be out with a mop more than once a week or whatever Paddy's cleaning system might have been. The way he kept his desk organized, I wondered if the pub even owned a mop.

"Boo, Declan, you bastard. Some of us were enjoying the Mozart," yelled a pretty brunette with warm, sherry-colored eyes. "Hey, Stanzie, you ever hear the one where Mozart was Pack?"

I grinned, cheered despite my irritation with Declan and my humiliation at Murphy's hands.

"If all the ones I've heard about famous people being Pack were true, there'd be no Others left."

"Just the stupid ones. No, wait, that's all of them," deadpanned the brunette's companion, a gorgeous young man in a dark shirt that molded to his muscular arms and chest. God, why did Irish men have to be so sexy?

A raucous roar of laughter went up around the pub, and I tried not to let it bother me as I picked my sticky way to the empty stool beside Paddy at the end of the bar.

"You're frowning." He slid his Guinness in my direction. I tried to catch Alannah's eye to get my own, but she developed an urgent need to wipe the other end of the bar clean with her dirty bar rag.

"This whole pack makes fun of Others?" I gave in with a sigh and took a sip of Paddy's Guinness. Of course, the minute I did, Alannah flew down to our end and drew Paddy a new one. Me, she ignored. Probably a good thing because who knew what she might have accidentally deposited in my glass. Flinging myself on her bond mate's back like a silent assassin had probably not been the best method of kick-starting a friendship with her.

Paddy chuckled as he took a healthy swig.

"In our whole lives she's never treated me this good." He gestured toward Alannah who sent me a glowering look through lowered red eyebrows before she turned to take someone's drink order. "She's two years older than me, right? And that's made her act all superior until, of course, I sweep Alpha out from underneath her. Suddenly, nothing in the world's too good for her little half brother."

"Well, maybe if she and Declan were making deals with the devil in back alleys like you, they'd be Alpha now."

Paddy winced, all the good cheer erased from his expression. I wished I'd bitten my tongue. I thought again of Faith's dream and the man with different-colored eyes who needed my help. Some help I was.

"You really believe we should be kept to minimum-wage jobs and only the Alphas of our packs ever having their hands on real money?" I was honestly curious.

Paddy took a deep breath as he considered his reply. "Anyone in Mac Tire who needs money has it. We all contribute from our minimum-wage jobs. Not all of them are minimum-wage either."

"I'll bet that Andrew Brody went to med school but doesn't practice medicine except within the pack. He might even have a low-paying job somewhere to make ends meet, since I'm sure no one in the pack pays him for services rendered."

"You'll not be advocating Pack pay for medical benefits like the frigging Others?" Paddy's eyes snapped with outrage.

"Of course not. He spends his life paying back his med school expenses by donating services to the pack," I replied. "Doctors are just one example. Mac Tire must have at least one lawyer to deal with your real estate operations. I mean, that *is* how you invest most of your money, right? In land?"

"Liam took you to our compound," Paddy said. "You'll know that's not cheap to upkeep. The castle's a safe house, so all the packs in the UK and Ireland contribute, and the Councils, but most of the land is ours. With a dearth of forests in Ireland, we need all the land to run in we can find. A place for our wolves to howl and not scare the damn natives. There hasn't been a wolf in Ireland for centuries, and that's because Others wiped them out trying to eradicate us.

"What'll you have us do, Stanzie? Go right back to that? Just when we've built ourselves up to a decent world population, you want us to step forward and announce our existence to the very people who nearly exterminated us?" Mouth twisted with bitterness, Paddy took a swig of beer.

"We're not in Dark Ages anymore," I said. "Others are not the superstitious, witch and werewolf-hunting peasants they used to be."

"Don't you believe it," lectured Paddy. "Others haven't changed in anything but fashion, architecture and technology. Beneath the skin, they're still the same terrified, torch-waving mob waiting to rip apart anything that's different."

And we're different, that's true, Paddy.

"You really want us to take over the world? You think Pack First is a grand idea, do you?" Paddy stared at me as if he didn't know me.

"No," I denied. "I just want us to be able to get decent jobs without being murdered for them. All Elena was trying to do was design fun games for people's computers. She wasn't trying to take over the fucking world. And neither was Grey or any of the other men and women who have been killed the last few years."

"You buy into one part, you buy into it all." Paddy's gaze bored into my face—penetrating and uncompromising. "Which is why there's no excuse for what I've gotten myself into. I know that. I'm trying to fix that. But just because I'm fighting, doesn't mean I've shifted allegiance to the other side. Have you?" He pointed a long, accusing finger at me.

"What do you want with a high-paying job you need a college education to get? You play the most beautiful music I've heard in a long time. You don't need college for that. You don't need a high-powered executive position to play. You don't even need to play for Others for money. You give back to the pack, Stanzie. Tonight I'm appointing you Mac Tire's bard. Declan Byrne be damned. *He* can play when *you* give him leave. You own that harp and that stage. And you can do a damned sight more for this pack by playing your tunes than you can being a fucking Advisor."

"Not true," I argued. "I've done a lot of good as an Advisor."

"Have you now?" He shook his head, mouth tight. "And what have you got for it? Hauled up in front of a frigging tribunal for protecting that poor girl in the only way you had left to you. Nightmares from seeing your former Alpha's brains splatter all over the ceiling when she shot herself in the head because of you and your Advisor job. Putting an old man to death as the Hand of the Council. An old man who loved you. Not saying he didn't deserve his death, Stanzie, but you didn't need to be the one to serve it to him in a cup of hot chocolate.

"Jason Allerton is no hero in my book. If you truly belonged to me the way I want you to, you'd be bard for Mac Tire and first in line for Alpha come the elections and you'd leave your Advisor days behind you for good."

"You can't make me give up being an Advisor." I gripped the edge of the bar so tightly my fingers went bone white. I'd fought too hard to get where I was to give it up, even for my Alpha.

"No, I can't," he agreed. "And I wouldn't even if I could. Everyone gets to choose what they want to do in my pack. But I can tell you what I'd wish for you, can't I?"

"Sure." I forced my fingers to relax their death grip and flexed them to restore circulation. He was being reasonable thankfully.

"Ah, this fucking conversation's too deep for a light night out at the pub. Forget it, Stanzie. Just think about what I've said, okay? I'm not asking you to give up a damn thing, just think a little about my perspective. Fair enough?"

His face under the dim pub lights was shadowed and mysterious. I had no idea whether he had a point or was full of shit, and the last thing I wanted to do was think about it.

But his words ate at my conscience like corrosive acid. Damn him anyway.

Chapter 12

Blankets and a pillow were piled on the end of one of the sofas when I walked into Murphy's apartment. He sat at the other end, a cup of coffee cradled between his palms.

"I'll sleep out here tonight," he informed me as he stared into his coffee. He lifted his gaze to find mine. "I changed the sheets."

A flush burned my cheeks. I locked the door and shrugged off my leather jacket. I tossed it and my purse onto the other sofa and took a deep breath.

"Why do you fight the conspiracy?" I worried my lower lip between my teeth, and he watched me but didn't say anything. "You know why I do?"

He shrugged, but I could tell by the tautness of his shoulders that he listened.

"I fight it so that bond mates won't run out of time like we did with ours. So that nobody has to feel the way we felt when they died."

"Yeah," he said as he clutched his coffee cup.

"Ever since Jason recruited us I've felt righteous about it. Terrified and reluctant sometimes, too, but above it all I've thought I've been doing the right thing."

"You have been, Stanzie."

"No. No, I don't think so. I don't want any part of revealing the Pack to the Others. I don't want to take over the world. I just want to live in my part of it without having somebody kill the people who mean the most to me. Paddy said if you support one part of something, you support it all, and he's right. We can't just pick and choose which part of the movement we're for.

"I'm so naive, I never even suspected there was something like Pack First. I never thought the conspiracy—the Guardians—came second, as a response to something else. Because that's how it happened, isn't it? People didn't just wake up one morning and think, Oh, hell, we've got way too many young Pack members with college educations and decent jobs these days, better start murdering some of them.

"Pack have been encouraged to go to college and get good jobs. They didn't just decide to do that on their own either. This has been going on for years, and we only know the tip of the iceberg.

"And we're going to let it tear us apart, aren't we? Because I can't come to grips with the enormity of the whole thing, I'm going to concentrate on my fucking bruised ego and let it kill what we have, aren't I?"

"You just need time to think, Stanzie. To sort yourself." Murphy's voice was low.

"What if we don't have time? What if we run out before I figure things out?" Tears trembled on the edges of my lashes, and I blinked them away. "I'm scared, Murphy. Scared of being alone, scared of being with you because you might leave me again. I don't know what to do."

He was off the sofa in a heartbeat, and in the next I was in his arms. I ran my fingers across his face and traced the bristly outlines of his goatee.

"Everything's so different. *You're* different."

He closed his fingers around mine. "You don't like the goatee?"

"It makes you look dangerous. Like a stranger."

"I'm not a stranger." He kissed my palm and then my lips. He had such a wicked mouth. When I opened mine to allow his tongue access, he groaned deep in his throat.

The kiss was slow, and his lips burned against mine as he murmured my name. I brushed my fingers over the planes and angles of his face. I rarely touched his face, afraid he'd flinch away from the intimacy, but tonight I didn't care. There was too much at stake to let anything come between us anymore.

We pressed tightly together, his erection hard against my lower belly, and I slid one hand down between his legs and made him groan again. His eyes were dark with desire, and when I walked toward the bedroom, he followed.

I peeled my clothes off as I went, and so did he. By the time we fell onto the bed together, we were gloriously naked.

His skin was hot, and I raked my nails down the broad expanse of his back as his muscles contracted in reaction to my touch.

He nipped my earlobe and then darted his tongue in and out of my ear with a teasing rapidity. He knew just what drove me wild.

I closed my fingers around his cock and positioned him so that the tip nudged against my warm wetness.

"I want to go slow," he protested as he tried to move my hand, but I wrapped my legs around his waist and guided him into me so I could feel his hotness inside me.

He groaned again, but didn't resist when I thrust myself up against him and forced him to join my rhythm. When he whispered something in Irish, I grabbed a fistful of his hair and pulled to get his attention.

"Say it to me in English!" Another yank of his hair. His body tensed with pain and passion, and he grinned against my ear before he bit it. Hard.

"I love you. I love being inside you. I love feeling your legs around my waist and the way you say my name deep in your throat. I love you so much, Stanzie. I'm yours. I—oh, God, I love you!" He rolled me over so I was on top and cupped my face with his hands.

My hair brushed his shoulders, and he shivered, his expression full of delight and wonder. There comes a time during every sexual encounter between a Pack woman and a Pack man when our eyes change and our wolves awaken.

As I stared into Murphy's dark eyes I saw them change. First, they began to glow and then they lightened from dark brown to golden amber. He became all at once mysterious and yet so very familiar.

"Ah, your eyes are so beautiful," he whispered and I knew mine had changed to blue silver. I didn't know if it was magic, science or some sort of strange combination, I only knew it felt right.

He skimmed his fingers down my spine and back up again as I leaned down to kiss him.

I rocked back and forth on top of him until his chest gleamed with sweat, and I licked it off. He tasted spicy, like Pack. I growled softly as he bucked beneath me and rolled so that I was pinned beneath him again, and he buried his face in the space between my shoulder and throat.

"Stanzie." I'd never heard him say my name with such perfect longing before, and then he went still against me. He lifted his head so he could see my face. "This is all right, isn't it?" Doubt and uncertainty filled his dark eyes.

I knew he was afraid I would get mad at him for this and accuse him of taking advantage of me as I had before.

"Liam Murphy, if you stop now, I'll kill you." I was so close to coming, and it was torture to be so still. I tried to move beneath him, but his weight held me down.

"Well, sure, you like it in the moment, woman." He gazed down at me, and I saw how much I'd hurt him, and my heart clutched in my chest.

"I love you," I whispered, and a wistful smile curled the edges of his mouth as if he didn't quite believe me. "I love you." I said it again and pulled him down so I could prove it with a kiss. After that, things got exquisitely hazy.

Spent and exhausted, we curled together beneath the sheets, his arm across my waist, my butt snuggled against his groin. His breath on the back of my neck was warm, and it was the last thing I remembered until morning light flooded the bedroom.

* * * *

I think it was the smell of frying sausage that pried me from sleep, but once awake I stretched into the sunshine bathing the bedroom through the open curtains.

Murphy's side of the bed was empty, but I could still smell him and see the indent of his head against the pillow. I hugged the pillow tightly to my chest and inhaled his scent.

When I went into the bathroom, I saw by the damp towels on the rack he'd been there before me. I marveled at how deeply I must have slept, because I hadn't heard a thing.

"Last night was probably the best sleep I've gotten in months," I announced when I walked into the galley kitchen in my bare feet, my hair still wet from the shower.

He had his back to me as he poured himself a cup of coffee, but when he turned, he revealed his smooth and shaved face. No more goatee.

My heart jolted. Here was my familiar Murphy. He even wore a t-shirt I remembered. His bond pendant gleamed around his throat, and I thought I would either die or burst into tears for a moment. Everything got very bright and hectic as if I'd been seeing the world in black-and-white and miraculously could now see color.

"Is it your wolf?" He was at my side in an instant, alarm making his voice deep.

"It's you," I managed. "You shaved your goatee."

He tweaked the tip of my nose with his finger, which startled me. He never did playful things like that.

"Let me get you a cup of coffee." As he squeezed by me to get to the cupboard, he snaked his arms around my waist from behind and gave me a gentle hug.

Murphy was never openly affectionate like that. He touched me either to calm me down or when we were in bed together.

I guessed things would change now he knew I loved him. Maybe he'd been as starved for casual touch as I had been, only afraid I'd reject him. Maybe it wasn't that he preferred to touch first, but that he didn't want to impose himself?

I turned around and hugged him hard, and he was stiff for a moment but then relaxed into me. He *was* hungry for touch—I could feel it. What idiots we'd been.

I opened my mouth to tell him this, and my damn cellphone chirped.

"Stanzie." Jason Allerton sounded more than a little ticked off when I answered. I'd called him when I'd arrived at the airport, and he'd asked me to keep in touch every day, and obviously I had not. Shit.

"Jason," I blurted in total shock. Behind me, Murphy nearly choked on a mouthful of coffee and hastily set his mug on the counter. Eyes narrowed, I knew he would listen in to the conversation. Pack hearing made eavesdropping on phone conversations a snap.

"You sound surprised to hear my voice." I could see Jason's sardonic expression in my mind's eye, and winced.

I floundered for an excuse and came up with a lame one, but I only had seconds. "It's just that it must be the middle of the night where you are."

"Wrong," he corrected. "It's a little after nine in the morning. I'm in London having breakfast before I head for Heathrow. One of the UK Councilors was returning home, and I decided to hitch a ride. I'm due to board a flight for Dublin in three and a half hours, and I would like you and Liam to pick me up at the airport this afternoon at two thirty." He gave me the particulars—which terminal and where—but I barely listened because of my struggle to draw a deep breath. Panic squeezed my throat nearly shut, and black spots danced before my eyes.

He could not come here now. Nothing was settled, everything was a riotous mess, and he'd make me tell him the truth—I just knew it. I could not deliberately lie to a Councilor.

"I'm sorry I haven't called you like you asked, but I don't know why you have to come here. I haven't done much. The reason I haven't called is because I've been working things out with Mur—"

"Constance." He used my full name. That couldn't be good. "I'm coming. There are things we need to discuss, and I prefer to do them in person. I'll see you this afternoon." The phone went dead, and I shook it as if I could make him reconnect, but it was useless.

I met Murphy's gaze with my own.

"Shit," I said. He opened his mouth to say something hopefully more helpful, but the street door buzzer sounded, and I almost shrieked aloud.

Murphy moved for the security panel by the front door and pressed the intercom button. "Yes?"

"Liam, it's Etain Feehery. Buzz me up."

"Shit." It was Murphy's turn to swear, but he pressed the button to unlock the street door and undid the locks on the apartment door so he could have it open by the time Etain Feehery, whoever the hell she was, arrived.

When she breezed into the apartment, I recognized her immediately as the woman from An Puca who had asked me if I'd heard the one about Mozart being Pack.

Her red-brown hair fell in attractive waves to her shoulders, and she wore tight jeans and a hand-knitted sweater. I recognized the pattern. Paddy had worn a similar one in Connecticut during my tribunal. I suspected she was a fabulous knitter and making and selling sweaters was her contribution to the pack and their funds.

Or maybe not.

Power surrounded her and made a path in front of her. Murphy stepped out of her way automatically, and I moved, too, when she looked at me, but instead of away, I moved forward.

"Ah, Stanzie, hello to you. Liam, your bond mate's one hell of a harpist. You should have heard her put Declan Byrne to shame with her clever rendition of *Carolan's Farewell*. Brought a tear to my eye, it did."

"Etain," Murphy began, but she held up a hand, and Murphy fell silent. Her pack ring glittered under the muted track lights.

"This is a serious conversation we're having, and I'm thinking we'd best use titles, Advisor."

"Councilor Feehery," Murphy corrected himself, and I paled. She was a fucking Councilor? Holy shit. "Would you like some coffee?"

"I wouldn't mind. Add a wee shot of Jameson's, too, please." Councilor Feehery strode to one of the sofas and sat. She patted the cushion beside her, and reluctantly I moved to sit beside her.

"I served on the UK Regional Council for nearly ten years before I was tapped for the Great Council," she told me, and my heart sank. She served on the Great Council. We were so screwed. "Have you got your eye on the Regional Council, Advisor?"

"I can barely handle being an Advisor," I muttered, and Murphy dropped a spoon in the kitchen. I couldn't help it. It was the truth. Advisors worked for Councilors. They did the legwork and gathered facts. Councilors decided what to do with the evidence. I was not ready for that responsibility. At all.

"Ah, you're new at it. But you're good from what I've been hearing." The Irish lilt in her voice was pronounced, and I had to struggle to keep up. I wondered if my New England American accent sounded flat and dull to her ears, and decided I didn't care. I had more important things to think about than frigging accents. Concentrate.

She leaned closer and put a hand on my arm. The thrum of power she emanated was like an electric tingle. She reminded me of Jason Allerton. "Ripping out the throat of that Alpha took real balls." When she said *throat* it sounded like *troat*, and I shuddered at the sudden spiky taste of Nate's phantom blood in my mouth.

"Did you come to talk about that?" My hands shook as I accepted a mug of coffee from Murphy. I hoped mine had a wee shot of Jameson's, too. I gulped some down. It did.

"No," Councilor Feehery said. "I came to talk about Pack First and the Guardians, of course."

I carefully placed my mug on the coffee table and tried not to shake apart.

"Don't carry on so," advised Councilor Feehery, and she patted my back. "I've been after knowing about it all along. Not surprising, is it, me being a charter member of the Guardians and all. I recruited Paddy O'Reilly and his father before him."

My heart performed such erratic and painful antics in my chest, I had to be experiencing the onset of a major heart attack. Hearts were definitely not supposed to do things like mine was. If Etain Feehery had recruited Paddy and his father, where did that leave Glenn Murphy? Was he fucking Pack First? A Guardian? A Guardian who condoned murder? Which part of the Guardians did Etain Feehery support? What a fucking tangled mess this was.

Murphy sat on the sofa opposite us, his eyes dark.

"This is no surprise to you, Liam, of course, but I see you've not been sharing with your bond mate. You're trying to protect her. Isn't that sweet of you." Councilor Feehery turned her gaze to his, and he met her eyes without fear, but his whole body was tense.

That revelation stung a little. Of course Paddy had told Murphy who his recruiter had been. I was the only one in the dark. As usual.

"Sometimes knowledge can be unsafe." Murphy's voice was a dangerous rasp, but Etain Feehery did not seem fazed.

"I agree, which is why I'm here to ask you point-blank what you plan on telling Jason Allerton when you collect him at the airport this afternoon." Councilor Feehery took a sip of coffee and made a low sound of pleasure deep in her throat.

Sensual woman, that one. My mind did one of its intuitive leaps, and before I could censor myself I blurted, "You initiated Paddy's wolf, didn't you? And you used that connection when you recruited him."

"He was well past initiation when I recruited him." Her tone was blandly innocent, but I knew the truth of it now.

"But you still used that past connection."

She regarded me over the rim of her coffee mug.

"Yes," she agreed before she set it down next to mine on the coffee table. "A lot of the young men of this pack want me to initiate their wolves, but I only choose the best and brightest. Every single one of mine has ended up Alpha. And only one boy turned me down." She gave Murphy a sultry smile. "And I'm still not over that, Liam."

My face felt hot as the implications slammed into me. Had she set up Sorcha's death to get Paddy in place as Alpha? Had she also been motivated by wounded pride because Murphy had declined her invitation to be initiated?

How was Murphy sitting so calmly across from her? How had he not throttled her ever since he'd discovered she was part of the Guardians?

"It's a decision I've regretted, Etain." Since she dropped his title, he dropped hers. "I wanted to be in love with the woman who initiated me, and while you've inspired a lot of emotions in me, love's never been one of them."

She threw back her head and laughed, and the scent of her shampoo— something clean and uncomplicated—drifted to me.

"Tell Allerton not to come." Her laughter dried up as if it had never been.

"You're well acquainted with Jason Allerton, Councilor. You tell me how I could get him to change his mind once it's made up?" Murphy looked sincerely interested and slightly amused.

But there was nothing funny about any of this. Was Murphy enjoying this? Did he like this sort of bullshit game?

I'd been his bond mate for close to nine months, and I hardly knew him at all, it seemed. And what did he mean by "well acquainted"?

"Don't tell me you were one of his mistresses, too." Appalled, I clapped a hand to my mouth, but it was too damn late.

Etain Feehery laughed again and patted my knee. What a condescending bitch.

"Do I detect a whiff of jealousy? You another ex yourself, love? I wouldn't have thought you were his type."

"What the hell's that supposed to mean?" I gaped at her. When it came down to it, I was prettier than she was. "Too young?"

"Too adoring. Adorable," she said and gave me another fucking pat on the knee. Next time she touched me I would—yeah, right, do nothing. She was a powerful Councilor, and I couldn't keep my damn mouth shut. "He can't afford to have mistresses who are too wrapped up in him. He has nothing to offer, has he?"

"Councilor Allerton is bonded to Stanzie's mother," said Murphy.

Etain Feehery's sherry-colored eyes widened.

"Oh, dear. You know, I knew about Erin. He did manage – just – to tell me after she died. I'd no idea he'd found a replacement yet."

"She's not a fucking replacement, she's a person," I muttered, and the damned woman patted my knee again. "What am I, your dog?" My temper snapped. "Next you'll be feeding me bones and wanting to play fetch. I'm more likely to piss in your shoes."

Murphy let out a strangled bark of laughter, and Etain Feehery regarded me for a moment.

"I'm sorry, Advisor," she said and, for once, did not pat my knee. "I can be a bitch sometimes. I meant well. Jason Allerton doesn't deserve someone like you. And if your mother's anything like you, he just got very, very lucky."

"I take it your affair ended badly?" I was slightly mollified but not enough to stop my curiosity.

She grinned and for a moment looked young and carefree, not like a powerful Councilor at all.

"Ah, it was a long while ago and I knew better than to fall in love, but I did anyway. It wasn't his fault he didn't reciprocate. He told me straight up how it would be with us, and I thought I could make it go my way, not his. More fool me."

"Why don't you want him here? Because of the past?" That probably wasn't true, but wouldn't it be nice? No more ugly complications with the conspiracy.

"Because he's sticking his nose where it doesn't belong." Councilor Feehery became all business again, and the warmth in her eyes cooled. "This isn't his territory, it's mine." The planes and angles of her face became predatory and harsh, and I shivered despite myself. This was not a woman to cross.

"I'm not happy he's got two of my pack mates for Advisors either. Paddy O'Reilly was a fool to ask you into Mac Tire. You don't belong here. After joining ranks with Allerton, you ought to have known better than to come back." Her gaze shifted to Murphy.

A muscle twitched in Murphy's clenched jaw. "We're not going anywhere, Councilor."

"Don't be too sure of that, Advisor." She rose to her feet and Murphy stood, too. They faced each other across the coffee table, and I tensed miserably. When Murphy's expression got all dark and dangerous like that, he scared me.

He followed her to the front door, and when she hesitated, he reached around and opened it for her.

"I'm telling you this for your own good, Liam. I didn't have to come here." Her voice was so low I had to strain to hear it.

"I don't respond well to threats." Murphy's tone was flat. "What happened between Allerton and this pack was a long time ago. I suggest you get over it. Everyone else has."

"Tell that bloody man to get back on the plane and go to America where he belongs." Etain Feehery gave Murphy one long, last look and stalked out the door.

"What happened with Jason and this pack?" I barely let Murphy lock the door before I pounced.

He faced the door for a moment as if gathering his thoughts and then turned. "His first bond mate's name was Erin Feehery."

"Councilor Feehery's—"

"Twin sister," he finished for me grimly.

"So Councilor Feehery wasn't one of his mistresses, was she?" It was a wonder the woman hadn't spat in my face.

"No," Murphy answered. "He met Etain first, but once he met Erin, all bets were off. He tore those two sisters apart. There was a lot of bad blood between Jason Allerton and this pack, Stanzie."

"Still is apparently," I said and Murphy's expression turned grim.

"God, no wonder Paddy didn't want to confide in her," I said.

"Now can you see how hard everything's been for the poor bastard?" Murphy asked and he looked so forlorn, I crossed the room to get to him so I could wrap my arms around his waist. He buried his face in my hair and we held each other for a long time, neither of us speaking.

Chapter 13

"Shit." Paddy's expletive was muffled. He had his face buried in his knees, his arms wrapped around his head as he sat on the dusty sofa in his office upstairs at An Puca.

I sat, tense and frustrated, in one of the battered armchairs while Murphy paced the length of the small room, his jaw and fists tightly clenched.

Paddy straightened. "I've got to tell Allerton everything." His face was chalky white, and he looked ready to be sick. I sympathized. I was close to puking myself.

"For fuck's sake, Paddy." Murphy's boots thundered on the plain wooden floorboards, and from the way they creaked in protest, if he didn't stop stomping, he'd end up a floor down, sprawled on the pub's bar. The goddamn pub had to be a hundred years old, and this was no doubt the original flooring. Did Paddy do no upkeep whatsoever?

"What?" The cords in Paddy's neck stuck out, and I winced at the volume of his shout. The goddamn walls would probably crumble next. If we all perished in an avalanche of rotted wood and plaster, that was one way out of our current dilemma. But not the solution I'd prefer. "You got any better suggestions, Liam?"

"Here's a suggestion. Calm the fuck down." Murphy and Paddy glared at each other, Alpha males to the extreme. I wanted to kick both their asses.

"So our plan is no plan at all?" My damn hair was in my eyes, and I dragged it back into a ponytail but had no way to keep it back so let it all fall back around my face again. "Allerton's plane lands in just over an hour, and I'm pretty sure it takes more than a couple minutes to get to the airport, so unless you know how to teleport, we'd better decide something soon. If we're not at the airport to pick him up, he'll—"

"Have to fucking wait," Murphy snapped, and I gave him the finger. "Oh, that's helpful, Constance. Why don't we all go to the airport and greet Allerton with extended middle fingers. That ought to solve everything."

"Shut the fuck up," Paddy said. "She's right. We don't have time for this shite. I'm coming with you to the airport, and I'm telling him everything. And I don't want to hear anything to the contrary, you bastard."

"You are not coming to the airport with us. Fuck that. Fuck that hard," shouted Murphy, and if I'd had something to throw, I would have aimed for his frigging skull. "I'm sorry I even fucking told you."

"You had to tell me. A, I'm your Alpha, and B, you wanted to tell me before Etain did. I know you, Liam, I know how you think, what you'll do, and how much you care about me, but I'm telling you it's gone past the point where you can do this on your own. We need the man's help."

"If I thought he would help, I'd be first in line to tell him." Exasperated, Murphy drove a hand through his hair. His sweater rode up and exposed some of his flat stomach. I could see the light brown line of hair that arrowed down from his bellybutton to beneath the waistband of his jeans, and I stopped wanting to throw something at him. Unless that something was me.

Now was definitely not the time to get all lustful. What the hell?

"Danger is such an aphrodisiac," I murmured and realized a split second later I'd spoken aloud. Murphy and Paddy stared at me, for once struck dumb.

"So what's your plan? Have a threesome on the office sofa?" Paddy drawled, and Murphy, surprisingly, laughed.

"I don't think it's big enough," he said.

"Are you fucking calling me fat?" I demanded and Paddy guffawed. Murphy flashed me one of his killer grins.

"I need a drink." Murphy walked out of the office, and I heard his boots clatter down the narrow staircase as he headed for the bar.

I got to my feet so I could look out the grimy window. I don't know what I expected to see, but the only thing outside the filthy glass was an even grimier alley.

I had to pass by Paddy on my way back to the chair, and he snagged my wrist and drew me down onto his lap.

He wrapped his arms around me and buried his face in my neck. His heartbeat trip-hammered against mine, and when I hugged him back, he shuddered and squeezed me tighter.

"It'll be all right, Paddy," I whispered and smoothed my fingers through his curly hair. His curls were soft and springy, and I could have played with his hair all day long.

"I'm so scared," he confessed. "I don't want nothing to happen to you or Liam or Fee. Or anybody. I've made such a mess of things. You must want to kill me. I know why you don't believe in me anymore. How could you?"

He lifted his face to mine, and I was horrified to see tears on his cheeks. I wiped them away with my thumbs, and when he kissed me, I let him because he wanted comfort and I wanted to give it to him.

His kiss was tentative at first, but he grew bolder when I didn't resist, and the flick of his tongue was warm and wet against my lips.

I smiled against his mouth. "Don't push your luck, you perverted bastard."

He laughed as I'd intended and broke the kiss so he could press his forehead to mine. He slid his hands up my arms and then cupped my face.

"You belong to me," he whispered.

"Jesus, I turn my back for two seconds," said Murphy from the doorway, but there was laughter in his voice. How long had he been standing there?

"Piss off. I'm just being an Alpha male." Paddy refused to let me leave his lap.

"You ever try that 'you belong to me' shit on me, and I'll mop the floor with your face," warned Murphy, and I giggled. I couldn't help it.

"Ah, you've been mine since before you could walk without landing on your bum," declared Paddy. "I don't need to tell you. You already believe it."

"Balls." Murphy thrust shot glasses of whiskey at us. He winked at me, and I giggled again.

"Here's to luck." He lifted his shot glass, and Paddy and I followed suit. I thought we needed a damned sight more than luck, but I drank the whiskey anyway. It burned like molten lava all the way down to my stomach. For a bad moment I didn't know whether my shocked gut would reject it.

"You all right then, Stanzie?" Paddy sounded wary. If I upchucked, he was in the direct line of fire.

I held up one finger until I was sure I wouldn't puke. "Okay. Yeah. I'm all right."

"Next time get her some girlie shot. Don't waste my best whiskey, damn you," Paddy ordered, and Murphy rolled his eyes.

"Stanzie, come on. We need to head to the airport."

Determination entered Paddy's eyes. "I'm coming, too."

"Not in my car, you're not." Murphy banged his shot glass down on the coffee table.

They stared at each other again, tension building. Paddy had one arm slung around my shoulders, and his muscles were so tight, my own ached in sympathy.

"Damn it. Then bring him here," he demanded.

"We're bringing him to the safe house, and I'll think about bringing him here later tonight. But I've got to think things through, and you're going to have to deal until I do," Murphy said.

"Who the fuck is the Alpha in this scenario?" Paddy bounced me on his knee and sounded aggrieved. My stomach did not like the jolting one bit.

"You are. And I'm doing my level best to protect you. Will you let go of my bond mate so I can get on with it, goddamn you?"

Paddy's arms tightened around me. "Maybe she should stay here with me. As a sort of hostage. Then you'll frigging bring Allerton here, won't you?"

A smile quirked the corners of Murphy's mouth. "Stanzie can come with me or stay with you, as she likes. Allerton said to pick him up. He didn't specifically state both of us had to be in the car."

"Stay with me. I'll make it fun for you. Sort of a Stockholm syndrome hostage scenario. I'll treat you real nice." Paddy teased my ear with his tongue, and I shivered. Damn him.

"You're such an asshole, Paddy." I cuffed him lightly on the shoulder and slid from beneath his arms so I could meet Murphy at the door.

When I looked back, he was grinning, but beneath the smile lurked fear.

* * * *

Jason waited by the doors outside of the baggage claim area. His blue pin-striped Armani suit was crisp and wrinkle-free, and he smelled of fresh soap and cologne when he slid into the passenger side of Murphy's BMW. Murphy took his luggage to the trunk, and for a moment Jason and I were alone in the confines of the car.

"How's my mother?" I asked, and he turned his head so he met my gaze with his.

"Sad that I didn't bring her. I'm not happy I had to leave her so soon after the bonding ceremony."

"You could have brought her," I said and he frowned. "Etain Feehery wants you to get on the next plane and go back to America. Is that why you didn't bring Wren?"

Murphy and I had talked on the way to the airport. My idea was that the best defense was offense. He'd snorted and declared I'd have to get out of bed a lot earlier in the morning to put Jason Allerton on the defensive. The man had a valid point, but I thought I'd give it a shot anyway. My idea was to throw Lauren in the mix because I knew Jason felt guilty about that situation.

"Etain Feehery doesn't want me near my own Advisors. For that reason alone I would have come, but coupled with your disturbing silence, I could hardly stay away." Jason glanced out the window as Murphy slammed the trunk and moved toward the driver's side door. "Are you all right, Stanzie? Is Liam in some sort of trouble? What has he told you about me that makes you afraid to trust me?"

Fuck. Fuck, fuck, fuck. My offense shredded in less than thirty seconds. Way to go, Stanzie.

Before I could answer, Murphy slid behind the wheel. He took in our expressions and the ringing silence and scowled. He'd probably heard every word. Cars are not exactly soundproof to Pack ears.

"Congratulations on your bonding, Councilor," he said, and a disconcerted look flashed across Jason's cool blue eyes. If I'd been in the front seat, I would have kissed Murphy.

"Thank you," said Jason. "I hope to return to my new bond mate's side as quickly as possible. In large part, I suspect that's up to you, Liam."

"Me?" Murphy gave a short bark of laughter as he twisted the ignition key. The BMW purred into life. I closed my eyes as we merged into traffic. Maybe in twenty years I'd be used to everyone driving like maniacs on the wrong side of the damn road, but I doubted it. "How do you figure that, Councilor?"

"What is the situation with Mick Shaughnessy? And I don't want any tap dancing around the truth, Advisor." Jason's voice was as cold as arctic wind, and I shivered. Shit.

"I haven't seen him," answered Murphy truthfully.

Rage gathered in Jason's expression. He had his face half turned so I could see his profile, and I gulped. I wanted to wind down the window to chase some of the angry stench from the car, but I couldn't move.

"I sent Stanzie here to talk reason with you. To give you another chance because I want you to succeed, Liam, in all the things you want in this life. But understand this much—I can't continue to turn a blind eye to the things you do behind my back. I give you a lot of freedom, a lot of rope, but you're going to hang yourself if you aren't careful. You're going to tie my hands so I can't help you. And you may very well bring Stanzie down with you. Is that what you want?"

Murphy's face suffused with color. I watched him in the rearview mirror. It was a low blow to use me as leverage. Jason Allerton was a nasty fighter.

"You're the one who dragged *us* into this," Murphy accused, and the whiskey shot came back to life in my stomach and sloshed around uneasily. Murphy would kill me if I puked in his pristine car. "You're the one with the secret agenda, not me."

Would Murphy's offensive tactics be more effective than mine? I held my breath and waited for Jason's response.

"That is a serious accusation. I'd like to hear your evidence to back it up."

Damn it.

Murphy didn't answer, and Jason turned his head so I could no longer see his profile.

Just when the silence had reached the level of excruciating, Murphy spoke. "You sent Stanzie deliberately into this situation. You're the one who'll bring her down if we're not careful, not me. And I can't forgive you for that."

"At least now you admit there is a situation," remarked Jason. "Did it work, Liam? Are you ready to talk now? Or you, Stanzie? I'm sure at this point you know more than I do. I'd appreciate it if you'd share your thoughts with me."

I bit my lip. When had Jason Allerton become the enemy? He'd looked after me, guided me, been my mentor and my father figure. And now it was all shifted and skewed, and I looked at him with doubt and, yes, fear.

I wanted to tell him everything. But how could I look Murphy in the eye if I did that?

Which side was he on? If I knew which side he was on, I would know if I could talk. But I couldn't ask him that question without giving everything away, without possibly endangering everyone I loved.

I turned to the window and barely registered the blurry scenery.

* * * *

The security gate swung open after Murphy activated it, and I saw the small castle near the gray lake just beyond the guardhouse and the parking lot.

The Mac Tire pack member in the guardhouse snapped to attention as the car approached. Obviously Allerton was expected.

Two figures waited on the stone steps outside the castle, and they became clearer as the three of us crunched along the tree-lined gravel path that led to the castle entrance.

One of them was Etain Feehery. The wind whipped her chestnut hair around her face and obscured her expression. The other was Paddy. The bastard had not stayed at An Puca as we'd agreed.

Murphy swore in frustration beneath his breath, and when Paddy began to descend the steps, he swore again.

He stopped dead in his tracks, and I avoided bashing into him by a narrow margin.

"Let him do this on his goddamn own," Murphy snarled at me as Jason continued to move forward. Etain Feehery remained on the castle steps, her eyes shaded against the bright Irish sunshine with one hand.

Murphy set down Jason's Gucci overnight case, and the wind blew a lock of his hair into his eye. Before he could, I reached out to brush it away, and a half smile tugged at his mouth. I could tell he was pissed and that he didn't know what to do. Neither did I. Short of rushing Paddy and tackling him, how the hell could we stop what he was about to do? He was my Alpha. I was supposed to trust and support him. But, oh, how I wish he'd waited at the pub as we'd arranged.

"I'm trying to maintain a high state of piss off here," Murphy said, but his expression was affectionate, and he brought my hand to his mouth without taking his gaze away from Paddy. The kiss he pressed to my palm felt like a delicious secret. Love, complicated and immense, twisted through my guts. Everything was in such turmoil, but I had Murphy's love and he had mine. God, would it be enough to get us through if things took an abrupt shift for the worse?

Paddy reached the gravel path, and Jason waited for him by a burbling stone fountain. The path curved around the fountain in a circle and narrowed again into one lane that led to the steps.

"I can't look. Kiss me so I don't have to look," I said and leaned forward. Murphy shook his head, but met my mouth with his. His lips were featherlight and warm and, suffused with love, I opened my mouth to invite him to twine his tongue with mine.

He pulled me closer into his possessive embrace, and supreme joy engulfed me, even as I knew I ought to be scared of what would happen after Paddy confessed to Jason what he'd been doing with Mick Shaughnessy. What of Etain Feehery? Was she complicit in Sorcha's death, and would Paddy's words condemn her? Did she still resent the fact

Jason had chosen her twin and not her? Whatever the case, she seemed content to wait on the stairs.

My damn cellphone buzzed to alert me that a text message had arrived.

"Ignore it," Murphy whispered into my open mouth, but I was curious. Who would text me?

The text was from my cousin, Faith. It read simply *Everything okay?!*

Jason had his back angled away from the trees lining the pathway. Paddy stood facing them. He seemed to do all the talking while Jason listened.

"I don't get it," said Murphy, frowning at the text, and a blur of movement erupted from the trees. At first I had no clue who it was, only that someone was running straight for Jason and Paddy. I was too far away to make out features clearly.

Paddy was close enough to see. Etain Feehery shouted something from the stairs. But did she shout before or after Paddy erupted into action? It was a question that would haunt me for a long, long time.

Paddy intercepted the blurred figure, which resolved itself into an old man.

They struggled for maybe three seconds before Paddy went down, clutching at his stomach. The old man turned in my direction, and I saw the knife clearly. The tip was coated with red. Paddy's blood.

Murphy reacted before me. He flew at the old man, boots scattering gravel in every direction. Bits and pieces of it stung my ankles and shocked me into action. I ran for Paddy. Jason already knelt by his side, and Etain Feehery was halfway down the stone stairs, her hair wild around her face.

The fifteen seconds it took me to get to Paddy seemed a fucking lifetime. I skidded on my knees the last two feet and shredded my jeans in the process. I felt nothing but a warm gush, which I didn't even realize was blood.

The bottom of Paddy's cream sweater was horribly scarlet. A fucking huge amount of blood pooled on the gravel beside and beneath him. Jason frantically tried to stem the bleeding with his hands, the cuffs of his Armani suit jacket drenched and dripping.

"Call the paramedics. Now, Etain!" he shouted at Councilor Feehery, who chanced one look at Paddy, paled and took off at a run back to the castle.

Paddy's eyes were half closed, but when I touched his cold face, they flew open. They were glazed over with pain and shock, far away and glassy, but the fingers he wrapped around my wrist were amazingly strong.

"Nuh—now do yuh, you believe in me again?" Paddy whispered, his gaze locked to mine. Blood coated his teeth, and a blast of horrified pity nearly flattened me. Flashback to Grey on the ground after the accident. His mouth had been full of blood, too. Faith's text message made sudden, awful sense. Had she known Paddy had been hurt in her dream? Had she been afraid to tell me?

"Yes, I believe in you. I belong to you." I had to choke out the words past the awful constriction in my throat. Incredibly, he smiled. I braced myself for him to die and for the light to pass out of his eyes, but his fingers remained strong around my wrist. "Goddamnit, Paddy, why didn't you stay at An Puca like we agreed?"

"Not—terribly good at—taking orders," he said. "Stanzie, please, don't leave me. I'm scared. I wanted—-so much to see—-my baby."

Tears strangled me, but I wouldn't cry. "I'm right here, Paddy. I'm scared, too, but I won't leave you."

"Pruh—promise me something?" Blood leaked from the corner of his mouth. The bitter hot smell of it burned into my sinuses.

"Anything," I vowed and moved his hand to my face. I kissed his bloody fingers and tried so hard not to cry.

"If it's a buh—boy—your wolf—I want your wolf to ini—initiate his? Promise?"

Pain and grief punched a hole in my gut. I wanted to scream, to howl in outrage.

"Paddy, it would be an honor," I whispered, and Jason pressed his forehead to my shoulder even as he worked furiously to staunch Paddy's out-of-control bleeding. With every beat of his heart more blood gushed and bubbled from the horrendous wound in his stomach. I couldn't look too closely at it because if I did I could see the pink rope of Paddy's coiled intestines. Or at least my shocked gaze told me I could. "You hang on, okay? Help's coming and we're going to get you the fuck out of here, you understand?"

"Tuh—tell Fee I'm sorry. I love her."

"Shh, Paddy, don't talk. Just breathe for me." I squeezed his hand. It was cold and clammy, and awful shudders spasmed through his body.

"He's going into shock." Jason had taken off his blood-drenched jacket and used it to press against Paddy's wound. The cuffs of his designer shirt dripped with gore, and I'd never seen his eyes so full of icy rage—yet they still radiated compassion. "Keep talking to him, Stanzie. He's responding to you. Keep him with us. Where the hell is Etain with that ambulance?"

"Paddy, I'm right here." I leaned down to whisper into his ear. I smelled his shampoo and cologne and something uniquely him. I remember waking in his arms, my ear pressed to his heart so I could hear the reassuring thump of it. He'd been there for me when no one else had, and I was damned if I'd let him go anywhere alone.

Gravel crunched behind us, and then Murphy knelt beside Paddy's head. There was blood on his hands and his t-shirt. He held a dripping knife, and his eyes were so grim and black with hatred my breath was stolen.

"I killed him," he said in a perfectly dreadful voice that sent shivers down my spine. At first I thought he meant Paddy, but Paddy was still alive.

Then Jason said, "No. He came at me with the knife again after Paddy went down. You wrestled with him for it and in the process he was stabbed. I'm swearing to that. There will be no tribunal, Liam. Not for you. Do you understand?"

Jason would cover for him. Gratitude washed over me.

"There was no struggle. I plucked it from his bastard fingers and plunged it into his black heart." Murphy's chest heaved as if he couldn't drag enough air into his lungs.

"You're mistaken. I saw what happened. I saw the whole thing," said Jason calmly. "Put the knife down, Liam, and go get Fiona. Meet us at the hospital. Do it now."

Murphy's face seemed to collapse in on itself, and tears glittered on the ends of his lashes.

"Fee?" Paddy's lips formed the word, but he had barely the breath to enunciate it.

Murphy's expression morphed into determination.

"I'm getting her, Paddy." He leaned down and whispered something in Irish that made Paddy smile and then he took off down the path.

Just beyond the fountain lay a crumpled, bloody figure that did not move.

Chapter 14

The paramedics didn't want me in the ambulance at first, but Jason barked something at them that made them go pale, and after that I was allowed on.

The ride was hellish. We lurched around corners and went at speeds so fast my stomach flipped, but I wasn't scared of an accident. I was scared Paddy would die before we got to the hospital.

Jason rode in the ambulance, too, ejecting one of the paramedics. He pulled rank because he was a doctor. Before he'd become a Councilor, he'd been his pack's doctor and he still kept up his medical knowledge, which was a damn good thing. He hooked up an IV and did medical things to Paddy I couldn't follow. I knelt by my Alpha's side and held his hand. I whispered things into his ear and at first I knew he listened because sometimes he smiled and sometimes he would squeeze my fingers back, but his grip grew more lax, and his smiles faltered and then stopped.

He was unconscious by the time we arrived at the hospital, and while they allowed Jason, as a doctor, to go into surgery with him, they wouldn't let me.

"I promised. I promised him I wouldn't leave him." I ran down the stark green-tiled hallway and kept pace with the stretcher even though a nurse and two orderlies tried their best to dissuade me.

"He doesn't even know you're there anymore," one of the orderlies told me. Brutal bastard. "You can't help him, you've got to let the doctors do it."

"But I promised!"

Eventually, one of the orderlies grabbed my arm, and when I started to scream and struggle, he wrapped his arms around my waist and manhandled me into the waiting room.

"Stop screaming, damn you, or we'll throw you out of here. Do you want me to call security, you silly cow?" he snarled in my ear.

"You fucking smell," I howled at him. He did. He reeked of Other stench. I thought about shifting and ripping his fucking throat out. That's when I went limp in his arms. I couldn't be like that. I had to get control.

"You're not exactly Miss Daisy Fresh yourself," the orderly hissed as he deposited my sagging form into a garish orange chair.

I uttered a short, shocked bark of laughter. No, I probably wasn't. The smell of Paddy's blood and my fear was so rank it clogged my sinuses, it was no wonder even an Other could be disgusted, too.

"Frank," remonstrated the other orderly. "Jesus, have some compassion, you gobshite. Look, miss, I'm sorry about him. You want coffee? Water?" He knelt by my side and tried to touch my arm, but when I yanked it away, he didn't get angry or flustered. He simply dropped it slowly to his side.

I shook my head.

"Okay, then. Look, I'm gonna sit over here for a minute. It's my break, and I have a few minutes. My name's Chris. You change your mind about the coffee or water, I'll be right over there." He pointed to a chair far enough away from mine that he wouldn't crowd me, but close enough to get to me if I needed him.

I hung my head and didn't acknowledge him, but he still went to the chair he'd indicated and sat. He pretended to be interested in an outdated magazine, but his gaze was sympathetic when he glanced up every few seconds.

I wanted Murphy in the worst way. Caged and confined, the awful hospital smells made me want to puke. Industrial cleanser, sick people, faint putrid whiffs of anesthesia, the overwhelming smell of Others, burned coffee and rubber-soled shoes combined in a nauseating whirl. The emotions were horrible, too. Fear, despair, fury, the soul-sucking glut of sheer hopelessness. How the hell did anyone work here? How could a person face this miasma of shit every single day? Especially someone Pack? How could Pack doctors deal with this?

Chris pressed a cold bottle of water into my hands, and I realized I'd been rocking back and forth keening to myself. Poor guy. He probably wanted to be so fucking far away from me.

"I'm okay." Such a fucking lie. I struggled with the cap, and he took it from me and twisted it off. He watched me swallow some water, which I only did to make him feel better.

"Is there someone I can call for you?" He knelt in front of me again, and I felt absurdly like burying my face in his shoulder so I could cry. But I didn't. He was an Other. I wanted Murphy. I wanted my pack.

"They're on their way," I whispered, my voice raw. I took another sip of water. "Thank you."

His face creased into an appealing, empathetic smile, and he rose to his feet.

"If you need anything, ask the nurse down the hall to get me. You cool?"

"Yeah. Thank you, Chris."

"It's no problem. Sorry again for my colleague. He can be an arsehole at times as I'm sure you noticed."

He gave me another subdued smile and walked out.

* * * *

I fucking detested hospital waiting rooms.

My bottle of water was half empty when Fee and Murphy staggered in. Glenn and Siobhan trailed after them, faces pale and grief-stricken.

Fee was in shock, and she clung to Murphy in a grip so strong I knew it must hurt, but he didn't even wince. He took her to a chair near mine and made her sit down, but she wouldn't let go of him, so he ended up with her on his lap. Glenn and Siobhan took the chairs on either side, and the family bent close together. Siobhan was in tears, and her hiccoughing sobs were the only sound.

Two accusingly empty seats separated me from them so I got up and moved next to Siobhan.

I put a hand on her shoulder and because the orderly, Chris, had been so wonderful to me, I wanted to be nice to her. I wanted to help.

"Can I get you some water or coffee maybe?" She moved away from me as if my touch burned.

"Please leave us alone. This is private," she told me. I knew she didn't like me, but I was a pack mate, and we were all in this nightmare together, weren't we?

She angled her body as far away from mine as she could, and I moved back to my original seat. It stung.

I waited for Murphy, at least, to say something, but he was so wrapped up in Fee he didn't notice.

Other members of Mac Tire began to trickle in. One of them, a woman with riotous black curls, took the chair beside Siobhan, and when she touched her, Siobhan burst into a wailing sob and clutched her in a tight embrace.

"Oh, Maureen, oh Jaysus, what are we gonna do?"

"It'll be all right, Siobhan," said Maureen. Her face was streaked with tears. I wasn't sure, but I suspected she was Paddy's mother.

Muffled sobs filled the air, and my face twisted with grief and incomprehension. I couldn't just sit in my corner alone. I got up and moved around the room. I asked several people if I could get them water or coffee, and a few took me up on it, but nobody reached out to me. They all petted and touched each other but made damn sure not to brush fingers with me when I handed them their cups.

It was irrational of me to take it personally, I told myself over and over, but it hurt just the same.

Once I tried to approach Fee and Murphy, but Siobhan shot me such a venomous look that I backed away.

Declan Byrne and Alannah Doyle blew into the waiting room bickering with each other. Alannah's face was tearstained and tense, and while Declan wasn't crying, he looked ready to fly apart at the seams.

I had just handed a grandmother a cup of horrid hospital coffee when they tried to get around me and I didn't move fast enough.

"Who are you trying to impress now? Giving grandmothers coffee! Jesus." Declan sneered at me. "The least you could fucking do is wipe the frigging blood off your face, woman!"

Of course. I had Paddy's blood on my face. I gulped and put instinctive fingers to my cheek.

"You're upsetting people. Don't you know enough to wash off his blood?"

"Where were you when my brother was getting stabbed trying to save that Councilor from assassination?" Alannah turned her frustration on me. "You should have been putting yourself between him and the knife, not Paddy! He's Alpha, he's not expendable like you."

Angry murmurs filled the stagnant air of the waiting room. People began to glare at me.

I liked to think I would have put myself between Jason and a blade, but I didn't know if I would have, even if I had been close enough. I'd frozen and watched until Murphy leaped into action, and even then I'd been behind him by a good margin.

Trapped, my gaze traveled around the accusing room. Murphy and Fee were still huddled together, her face buried in his shoulder, his in her hair. They were oblivious. It seemed as though Declan and Alannah had shouted, but maybe they'd only whispered. Not everyone in the room glared at me, only those in closest proximity.

"Get off with you, woman. Go wash your frigging face." Declan pointed toward the door, and with one last, longing glance in Murphy's direction, I fled.

Chapter 15

Jason found me in the hospital cafeteria. I sat with my hands wrapped around a swiftly cooling cup of coffee at a table tucked away into a back corner. Paddy's blood was on my hands, on my shirt and probably my jeans, although most of that blood was mine from my shredded knees. Confronted by the sight of his bloody finger marks on my cheek when I'd stopped in a restroom and found a mirror, I'd fled rather than wash them off. However tenuous, they were a connection to him—one I wasn't ready to part with.

My knees throbbed, a constant, dirty pain I tried to ignore.

"Here you are." Jason slid into the chair beside mine. His face was drawn and tired, and his blue eyes were haunted. He'd rolled up the sleeves of his designer shirt, but the bloodstains still showed. His hands were scrubbed clean. They rested on a manila folder he'd placed on the sticky tabletop. "You ought to be with your pack at a time like this, Stanzie."

I winced. I only wished.

"I wanted some coffee," I lied. He moved one of his clean hands so it covered one of my bloody ones.

"I'm sorry. Paddy died fifteen minutes ago."

What little shreds of hope I'd held disintegrated into ash. I was too tired to cry, so I just sat there and stared at nothing.

"Tell me what you're thinking," he urged with such compassion I wanted to throw my coffee in his face only I was too weary.

The mind-numbing lethargy began to drain away as a flush of resentful anger flowed through me. "Right now I'm thinking he wouldn't be dead if you'd just gotten on the plane and gone home. Or better yet, never come here in the first place. You were the target, not him. He just"— my voice broke a little but I controlled it— "got in the way."

"I wish you'd come to me. I could have helped. Paddy got far enough in his explanation of what's been going on that I can fill in the blanks of what you and Liam have tried to keep from me."

"I don't want to hear this!" I did pull my hand away and this time he let me.

"If you'd just trusted me."

"Trusted you? I don't even *know* you, Councilor Allerton. I don't know what side you're on anymore. Up until a few days ago I didn't even know how many sides there were, and maybe I still don't. All I know is I thought I was doing good things for the Great Pack, and now I don't know what to think. If you could have helped him, what does that mean? That you were on his side? That you were a fucking dupe the same as he was? I can't believe that Councilor Jason Allerton could ever be anybody's dupe, so nice try. You bastard. You lying, manipulative bastard!"

I refused to be affected by his awful, remorseful expression. Too little, too late, Allerton.

"You have done good things. You'll continue to do them. You knew from the start things were going to get ugly, and you said you were prepared to deal with them."

"Ugly?" I curled my lips back from my teeth in a snarl. "I never thought they'd get *this* ugly. They weren't supposed to get this bad. I always thought you, at least, were telling me the truth."

"I never lied to you," he said.

"Lying by omission is still lying. Do you think for one second I would have done anything for you if I'd known you were part of the Guardians, the group responsible for Grey's and Elena's deaths? Even if you opposed it? Do you think I would have agreed to be the Hand of the Council if you'd told me you were Pack First and hell-bent on eradicating the Guardians? Because if you do believe that, you're delusional!"

"All I have ever done is tried to stop the senseless deaths. On both sides. That's all I've asked you to do, and if you'd just believed in me and not let Liam and Paddy scare you, I might have been in a position to help. I understand your bitterness, Stanzie, truly, but now is not the time to give up. Now is the time the fight really begins, and don't you think you owe it to Grey and Elena, and now Paddy, to be there for it? Or have I completely underestimated you?"

"Don't try to manipulate me anymore. I'm not some naive fucking idiot. You can't just wave a patriotic Pack flag in my face and expect me to leap into battle. The past nine months have taught me to be cynical and secretive and not to trust anyone. Not anyone. You still haven't confirmed whether you're a Guardian or Pack First and, more importantly, no matter which side, what the hell's going on. You're still trying to confuse me. Screw you, Jason Allerton. I don't care if you're the most powerful Councilor in North America. I don't care if you're my mother's bond mate, although I wish to hell you weren't. All I care about is getting as far away from you as I can. I wish I never had to see your lying face again!"

He regarded me silently for a moment, then said, "I understand you're upset, and I'll leave you be now. Your pack is at An Puca, and you shouldn't be alone. Before you go, though, please look at what's inside this folder. Know that whatever you decide to do with it, I will support you one hundred percent. I cannot emphasize this enough. Also know you will come out of this without any repercussions. I will swear that you kept me apprised of everything you knew as you knew it and kept nothing out. Liam as well. Believe it or not, Stanzie, I've got your back. I always have, and I always will."

"Go to hell," I said and turned my head. When I looked back, he was gone.

I picked up the manila folder and my coffee cup and took them both to the trash, but in the end I couldn't throw the folder away without just one look inside.

* * * *

The news of Paddy's death had spread, and An Puca was crowded with mourning pack members. A steady background of muffled sobs accompanied me as I made my way to Fee's table in the front. The Alpha table.

Her face was pulled tight with grief, hazel eyes clouded with incomprehension as she clutched a glass of amber whiskey but didn't drink it. Murphy sat protectively close beside her, one arm around her shoulders. His whiskey glass was half empty, and his eyes were so dark an involuntary shiver sizzled down my spine.

His parents, Paddy's mother and her bond mate, Alannah Doyle, Declan Byrne, a petite woman with long black hair who must have been Deirdre and her bond mate, Colm O'Reilly, were squeezed tightly together around the rest of the table. The red-haired giant took up most of the room.

When my shadow fell across the whiskey glasses spread across the tabletop, everyone but Fee looked up. She was somewhere else, deep down inside herself. My gut twisted in sympathy. I knew that particular territory with bitter familiarity.

Declan Byrne's lip lifted into a sneer, but before he could spit whatever venomous words he had in mind, I raised my voice loud enough so everyone in the pub could hear me.

"Declan Byrne, by the power entrusted in me as an Advisor to Jason Allerton, who, in turn, represents the Great Council, I hereby charge you with the following crimes—conspiracy to commit murder, conspiracy to depose the Alpha male of Mac Tire and treason against the Great Pack. I hereby command you to appear before a tribunal and answer to these charges."

Someone whispered, "Fuuck" and then dead silence.

"Piss off." Declan reached out for his whiskey. Murphy adroitly snatched it off the table.

Declan gaped at him. "You can't seriously think that twat knows what she's saying, can you? She's delirious, Liam. This is just another ploy for relevance, can't you see that?"

"Maybe these will convince you I'm not talking out of my ass." I tossed two of the photographs I'd found in the manila folder onto the table. Despite himself, Declan glanced down, and his whole body convulsed into stillness.

Murphy snagged one of them and turned it so he could see. Every bit of color drained from his face, and the scent of his fury enveloped us all in an invisible cloud. Even Fee reacted. She turned her head to him, some of the mindless grief evaporating from her eyes.

I passed out two more to people at nearby tables, and there was silence as the photographs were circulated. Silence and the scent of escalating fury.

In all the photographs, Declan Byrne stood in a cobblestoned alley with an old man. His right hand was extended, and the object he held was plain to see—a knife. The old man reached for it, and his profile was clear and distinct. Mick Shaughnessy.

"Grandfather Mick stabbed Paddy," cried out a young man by the bar. Two nights ago, he'd sat next to Etain Feehery and made fun of Others. "Declan gave him the knife?"

Growls and mutters filled with air, and Declan paled.

"This proves nothing," he sputtered. "This could have been taken anytime. Years ago. It's not a crime to give somebody a knife. And who can prove it was the knife he used on Paddy?"

"You're wearing the same clothes in the photograph as you are right now," pointed out a red-haired man at a nearby table. His face was thunderous with suspicion.

"Grandfather Mick was wearing the same clothes today as he was in the picture, too," added Murphy, his jaw so tight, the tendons were clearly defined.

"Why? Why'd you do it?" Paddy's mother stuffed a hand to her mouth in horror.

"I didn't! I swear I had no idea what the old bastard was going to do with the knife. How the hell would I know?" Declan's blue eyes were frantic with fear. He could smell the violence and rage gathering in the pub. One word from me or Murphy could incite a mob who would rip him to shreds with their bare hands.

Nobody fucks with the Alpha.

I heard Jason's words clearly in my head. *Know that whatever you decide to do with it, I will support you one hundred percent. I cannot emphasize this enough.*

It was tempting as hell.

"What were you doing giving that man a knife, Byrne?" Colm demanded. "You know there's something funny going on with him. Nobody knew where he was, and we've been looking for him for months now. How'd you manage to find him, and why give him a knife instead of bring him here so people could know he was all right? We were worried about him, but what's really been going on is that you and he have been plotting all along to kill Paddy. You know you want to be the next Alpha. Weren't you just sitting here offering to bond with Fee, for the sake of her wee unborn child? Didn't you start a campaign to bed her a few months ago as well? So she'd turn to you in her hour of grief? This wasn't about Councilor Allerton at all. Paddy was the target all along. You plotted this whole thing, didn't you? Had to have a dupe to kill him for you so you could step into his shoes and be Alpha?

"Well, fuck that!" Colm knocked over his chair as he lumbered to his feet. Six foot six was very tall, and everyone's necks tilted back so they could maintain eye contact.

"You were offering the same damn thing, Colm," yelled Declan, but he was intimidated. Rank sweat beaded his forehead and his hand shook as he wiped it away. "You want to be Alpha of this pack too, don'tcha? It was between you and me. This was make or break time for you, wasn't it?"

"I'm not the one who gave that old bastard the knife, Declan," shouted Colm, his meaty hands clenched into fists.

"But your Deirdre's pregnant, and this would solve everything." Declan's twisted smile was full of triumph.

"Declan." Alannah's voice was soft and betrayed. She'd told him. Her twin had confided in him and she'd told her bond mate.

The petite, black-haired woman paled and I thought she might faint, but she gripped the edge of the table with both hands and managed to stay upright.

Colm looked at his twin sister in shock.

"If you take me away, you'd better take him, too. I'll swear he was in on it with me!" Declan pointed a finger at me. If I'd been closer, I would have snapped it at the knuckle.

"You can tell the tribunal any fucking thing you want," I told him. "They're Councilors. They can tell bullshit from the truth easily enough."

His face darkened and made him ugly.

I looked around the room. "I'm going to need two men to help me escort Mr. Byrne to the safe house. Any volunteers? We'll need a car."

Pandemonium as every man in the pub rushed to get to me.

Murphy's father jumped to his feet. "As a representative of the Regional Council, it's my duty to escort the man into custody."

At his words, Declan Byrne sagged in relief. My stomach clenched. Why relief? Because there was less chance of him being murdered on his way to the safe house if there were a Councilor along, or something more sinister—Glenn Murphy was a part of the Guardians and on Declan's side?

I wished I knew what Murphy's thoughts were, but his face was a frozen mask.

Surely a father wouldn't help engineer the death of his own son's bond mate and force him from the Alpha position?

Then I thought of my father, and all bets were off. Sometimes family meant shit next to personal glory or a so-called greater cause. Was Murphy's father one of those men? He'd seemed so nice and normal when we'd eaten pie together in his kitchen, but people lied. They schemed and concealed, cheated and plotted, murdered and covered up.

Glenn Murphy's gaze traveled around the room and settled on the young man by the bar.

"Ryan Kelly, you come with us." I was no longer in charge. The Councilor had taken over.

The young man came forward, fists clenched. He was extremely attractive with thick brown hair and eyes so dark they were nearly black. His cheeks and chin were covered with dark brown stubble. Wildness lurked beneath his taut body, and I wondered if Declan Byrne would arrive at the safe house with bruises and broken bones.

Murphy took a step toward me, but his father noticed the movement. "You stay with Fee, Liam," he ordered.

Fee took hold of his wrist and buried her face in his arm. Murphy sank back into his chair and pulled Fee closer so her head rested on his shoulder. I was on my own.

Ryan Kelly took hold of Declan Byrne's upper arm and marched him across the pub floor. People made reluctant way. Someone spat at him, and it struck his cheek.

"You fucking idiot," muttered Byrne, and if I hadn't stepped between him and the man who'd spat, there would have been a brawl.

Ryan Kelly managed to knock Declan's head against the wall on the way out the door. It was very nicely done, and Declan's roar of protest was drowned beneath a groundswell of muttered approval from the pack.

Some violence was necessary to bleed off the pack's collective rage.

Alannah Doyle sat stiffly in her chair. She'd made no protest when her bond mate had been dragged away, and as I left the pub, I looked back at her. Still frozen in place, her cheeks were bright with either humiliation or anger—I wasn't close enough to smell which.

She caught my gaze, and her expression sharpened into vivid hatred. I'd made an enemy today.

* * * *

Three hours later I sat across from Jason Allerton at a small table set beneath an arched window in his suite of rooms at the safe house. Before us on the polished mahogany surface were plates heaped with pork chops and mashed potatoes. A bottle of wine, half full, sat directly between us and made it difficult to look at each other's faces.

He ate while I moved food around my plate and waited.

Once in Glenn Murphy's car, I'd called Allerton and told him we had Declan Byrne in custody. He'd directed us to the safe house but advised us to stop for clothes along the way. We would all be required to stay at the safe house for the duration of the tribunal.

Ryan Kelly turned out to be Glenn Murphy's Advisor. He'd seemed furious enough at Declan Byrne on the long ride to the castle safe house, and I wondered if both he and the Councilor he served were Pack First. Perhaps that was why Murphy had not wanted to discuss his father or his possible knowledge of the conspiracy. If Glenn and Paddy had been on opposite sides of it, of course he would be the last person Murphy and Paddy could turn to for help.

I'd tried to call Murphy to let him know I wouldn't be home for a few days, but my call went directly to his voice mail. I ached for him to call me back. I had my phone on the table. It bothered Jason, I could tell by the glances he directed at it, but I didn't move it.

The first thing I'd done, after throwing my suitcases on the massive carved oak bed when we'd arrived, had been to run a bath with lavender Epsom salts.

The water had turned Paddy's dried blood on my arms and face liquid again. I'd watched the swirls of his red blood slowly dissipate into the bathwater and turn it a murky reddish brown.

Each crimson spiral had fascinated me. My last physical connection to my Alpha. My friend.

Now I'd never know if his wolf's eyes were two different colors when he shifted. I'd wished I let him tongue-kiss me at An Puca when I'd had the chance. I'd wished I'd stayed with him. If I had, I wouldn't have been sitting in a bath of his blood.

I'd tried to cry, but the tears wouldn't come. They were blocked somewhere deep inside me. My wolf scratched and snarled to be free. She wanted to howl her grief and run so fast it would be left behind. But instead I'd pulled the plug, watched the last of Paddy's blood gurgle down the drain and dressed for dinner.

Now, outside the arched window, sunset washed over the gray lake and the trees crouched around its perimeter. Beyond the lake was a vast field of heather. The slanting sun turned the field into a burnished glow of dark purple that hurt my eyes if I stared at it too long. I looked at it a lot.

"If you won't eat, at least drink some wine." Allerton nudged my wineglass closer, but I ignored it and him.

My wolf clamored for release. She wanted to roll in the heather, bite it, taste it, feel it beneath the pads of her paws.

"Excuse me," I said abruptly and shoved back my heavy wooden chair.

Halfway down the stone corridor, I started to run and kept running until I was out the castle door, down the front stairs where Etain Feehery had watched Mick Shaughnessy stab Paddy, and past the gravel drive into the manicured gardens.

I stripped off my clothes as I ran. First my blouse, then my skirt. My bra and panties went next, and I was down to my shoes, which I kicked off contemptuously.

I remembered my bond pendant just before I fell to the ground and managed to put it near a clump of clover.

The shift boiled over me like an assault, and I gasped with the pain of it. My fingers stiffened, then curled, hair sprouted in my palms. My legs twitched and arms flailed. My spine gave a terrific crack as I arched up like a Halloween black cat and then, just as the agony was too much to bear and I thought I would rip apart, I blinked out to complete the change in the soundless, black dimension that only appeared to me midshift.

Tonight instead of blackness, the light was silver, and it glowed. It seemed I hesitated there a fraction longer than usual, enough to make my heart seize, and then I was back.

Four legged and furry now, I lifted my nose to the setting sun and let out a mournful howl. From somewhere in the distance behind me, perhaps the guardhouse, someone howled back in perfect, grief-stricken understanding.

Then I ran.

* * * *

This is grief. This is pain. This is feeling bad, so, so, bad it hurts me. I want the pain gone. My Alpha! Mine! And I was his! Now, gone, all gone. Run? Run for him. Run for all the dead ones that cannot come back.

Hate. This is hate. This is fury. This is wanting to tear apart the things that hurt me. That hurt him. I want the hate gone. Run? Run? Yes! Run faster than everything and it will all be gone.

* * * *

When I emerged, naked and in human form, from between the small copse of trees near the gray lake, I saw Allerton. He sat on the small patch of clover, patient, not the least bit concerned with grass stains on his Armani pants.

He'd gathered all my clothes, including my bond pendant, which he silently handed me when I approached. He stood back while I dressed. He did not stare, nor did he avert his eyes. I pulled on my clothes but didn't rush. Let him get an eyeful. The moonlight illuminated the clearing almost as brightly as if it were day. What did he care? He'd seen me naked before, and we were both Pack.

He helped me fasten my bond pendant and plucked bits of grass and leaves from my tangled hair. Neither of us spoke.

When I was fully dressed, we set out for the castle. It loomed, ghostlike and huge, in the darkness. Some of the arched windows were lit, others dark and desolate.

"Which side are you on? I have to know." He'd matched his stride to mine and didn't falter at the bitter suspicion in my tone.

"The same side I've always been on," he replied, and I wanted to tear his handsome face to shreds with my fingernails. "I am against the Great Pack revealing itself to the Others. Against it with all my will."

I squeezed my eyes shut, and the bright moonlight disappeared. I used my other senses to guide my feet. Wind rustled in the trees to my right, whistled above the flat expanse of the gray lake behind me. The good, clean smells of grass, flowers, and night sky filled my lungs. The earth was firm beneath my bare feet. Everything seemed normal, but wasn't, the cold dampness of the grass, the small puckers and indentations of the uneven ground, the steady beat of my pulse.

Jason put a considerate hand to my elbow. I wanted to shake him away, but I knew he wouldn't leave my side, so I ignored him.

The same side as Paddy and his father before him. He was a Guardian. He was a part of it, and by extension, so was I.

"Which side is Etain Feehery on? Glenn Murphy?" I opened my eyes so I could see his handsome profile in the moonlight. He was calm, composed, but even so the thunder of his heart was loud as it pounded beneath the expensive linen of his Italian dress shirt.

"You don't know, do you?" I guessed. My resentment and fear were huge inside me. My own heartbeat drowned his out. "Someone had to have given you those photographs. That person must be on Declan Byrne and Mick Shaughnessy's side."

"Must they?" Jason's tone was neutral, but his fingers on my arm tightened.

"Oh, Jesus," I said. My head hurt. My heart hurt. *Everything* hurt.

"I found the folder underneath my jacket in the scrub room. Anyone could have put it there."

"So you really don't know? Murphy's *father* could have helped plan Sorcha's murder? Are you sure?"

"I'm sure of nothing," he ground out. "Except where I stand. Against revealing the Great Pack, but I do not and never will condone murder."

Even though I was relieved to hear him say that, I still didn't believe he was telling me everything he knew. Why did he always leave something out? Didn't he trust me? "You must have an idea!"

"The Guardians in favor of killing to get their way are not in the habit of advertising their fanaticism. Do you really suppose any of them have ever approached me to confess they've helped murder members of the Pack?" He turned his head so he could look me in the eye. His face was the perfect diplomat's face. It made me want to trust him. Vote him into office. Help him save the fucking world.

"All I know is both Etain Feehery and Glenn Murphy believe the same things I do. They're Guardians. We're supposedly on the same side."

There went my theory that Glenn Murphy was Pack First. In a way, things were now worse.

"At least one of them helped Declan and Grandfather Mick murder Paddy. Helped murder Sorcha."

"It seems likely but not necessarily true. Byrne and Shaughnessy could have acted together on both schemes without the help of a Councilor."

"Then who took the pictures, and how did they know to take them?" I demanded.

"You want everything given to you in a neat package, Stanzie, and I can't give you that."

"There's the Advisor, too. Ryan. Ryan Kelly. He could be in on it. Couldn't he?"

"Absolutely," agreed Allerton. "We could be dealing with a Guardian who believes in murder to weaken the Pack First agenda or one who doesn't and made a deliberate sacrifice of two who did."

I stopped in my tracks, and he halted, too.

"Just toss Declan and Grandfather Mick away like garbage? Killing an Alpha? A Councilor who was a Guardian? How is that not murder, too?"

Jason shook his head somberly. "Maybe no one was supposed to die and things went horribly wrong. Maybe they thought Paddy would kill Shaughnessy instead of the other way around. I don't know."

"Was Paddy the real target, or were you?" I felt tears prick my eyes but wouldn't let them fall.

"I don't know."

"Don't tell me you don't know. You don't seem to know anything! How can you know so much and yet not know anything about this? How am I supposed to take your word for it after all the shit you've led me to believe? I want answers, Jason. Real ones. True ones. Not this amorphous bullshit you're trying to hand me tonight. My Alpha is dead. Dead. And somebody has to pay for that!"

"Somebody will. Mick Shaughnessy already has and, thanks to you, Declan Byrne is not far behind."

"But the real power behind it will get away. We've got to bring down Etain Feehery or Glenn Murphy."

"In time, if either or both of them merit it, we will," Jason assured me.

"Time," I spat. The word tasted foul in my mouth. "Why not now? Why not at Declan's tribunal?"

"The tribunal is convened against Declan Byrne. And both those Councilors will serve upon it. I will as well."

"How can you possibly serve? You were the one Shaughnessy attacked. You wouldn't serve on my tribunal. Kathy Manning couldn't serve on mine because I acted in her name, so how is it fair that you could serve on the tribunal which accuses a man of conspiring to assassinate you?"

"Because the other serving members do not object. Because I have not recused myself from the panel. Because this is Guardian business and needs to be handled delicately." Jason faced me in the moonlight. A cloud obscured the moon, and for a moment his face became indistinct and shadowed, and then the cloud passed, and he was revealed again.

"This isn't a real tribunal, is it? It's some sort of fucking kangaroo court because you're all scared to death to let this get out." My mind reeled. I wanted the bastard condemned, but this seemed underhanded.

"Stanzie, we judge by the evidence and facts presented. Those photographs have nailed his coffin shut."

"You can't prove he's part of the underground movement in the Guardians unless he admits it. Not unless the one behind him comes forward."

"Which isn't likely to happen. But we're not trying him on conspiracy charges. The assassination attempt on me and the murder of an Alpha are enough to sentence him to death."

"But the whole reason for the attempt is the conspiracy," I whispered.

"Not exactly true." Ah, here it came. Another admission. One more lie of omission. How could I trust this man if he never told the basic facts?

Jason's blue eyes were wide in the moonlight as he faced me. "My former bond mate was Mick Shaughnessy's granddaughter. He's never forgiven me for taking her from Mac Tire and her family. For her going insane after our baby was stillborn. Declan Byrne was his great-nephew."

He waited for me to respond as I explored all the possibilities. The twisted family ties in this damn pack. Declan Byrne and Etain Feehery were cousins. Wouldn't it make perfect sense for them to use Jason in their plot to murder Paddy because he wouldn't stay join in with them or stay silent forever about his suspicions? That would work if Etain Feehery did believe in murder to further the Guardians's agenda.

I couldn't forget that Etain was Jason's first bond mate's twin sister. That made her Mick's great granddaughter. He was blood family. Had she been in league with him and once his complicity in Sorcha's death had surfaced? What if she wasn't part of the murderous movement within the Guardians? What if she'd merely tried to help her great grandfather by getting him money through Paddy? Maybe she wasn't a part of his treachery but because he was family she'd tried to secretly support him?

Was Etain rich? She'd dressed as if she had money and Grandfather Mick had gone through the money Paddy gave him almost as fast as he got it. Because he was used to having unlimited funds and had never lived on a budget?

"You inherited all your money from your former bond mate, didn't you?" My voice shook, and I struggled to control it.

A flash of his teeth in the moonlight. "What does that have to do with anything?"

A beat of silence.

"Is that why you thought I stayed bonded with her? For money?" He looked wounded, or maybe it was a trick of the moonlight. "Stanzie, I loved her."

"It didn't stop you from having a parade of mistresses. I also know you have history with Etain Feehery. I know she was your bond mate's twin," I said, but I was thrown. Why did the idea of his loving his dead bond mate surprise me so much? Why did I always believe whatever I was told?

"I'm not going to discuss my reasons for the women I've known over the years. It is truly none of your business and not germane to the situation at hand."

"Of course not," I said. "Anytime we ever get close to your personal life, your true feelings, you erect a wall a hundred feet high and hide behind it. But I'm supposed to trust you with my life and I'm supposed to do what you ask me to do simply because you ask me to do it. That's not good enough anymore. I thought you were a great and powerful man. And you are. You've helped me more than once, but does that make me your slave? Do I have to pay off the debt of your gracious charity?

"You're asking me to be your dog, Jason. Am I supposed to be okay with it because you don't ask me to lick your boots?"

"I was lonely," he said and the vulnerability in his expression hit me hard until I couldn't seem to draw a deep breath. "All I ever had after Erin went insane was my position on the Regional and then the Great Council. I dedicated my life to the Great Pack and to upholding justice and honor, but it's hard to sleep at night with justice and honor as bedmates. And it was never simply for carnal pleasure. Every woman I ever associated with was intelligent and sensitive and just for a little while my best friend.

"People in my position have many allies, but damn few friends. Every mistress was my friend first, and quite a few of them, most of them, are still. And there weren't as many as you obviously think. I can count all of them on both hands with fingers to spare. What have I left out? Do you want all their names? Testimonials from them? Will that make you happy? Tell me what you want of me, Stanzie, and I'll get it for you. Maybe then you'll stop looking at me as if I were a traitor. I'm not the enemy. I understand you're angry and you want answers, but I've given you all that I can.

"What will it take for you to believe that I don't know whether Etain Feehery or Glenn Murphy had a hand in this or not? Do you think this is easy for me? I was once very fond of Etain Feehery, she was my bond mate's twin, and the thought of her being a possible accessory to murder sickens me. Do you know how much it will take out of me to bring her down? I will if she deserves it, but you think I'm a bottomless well of resources, and I'm not. I'm just as weak as everybody else. Maybe more so because I have to be a Councilor every minute or people get upset.

"I can't be anything but a Councilor to you because that's what you want of me, what you expect of me. That's one of the things I treasure most about your mother. She doesn't look at me and see Councilor Jason Allerton. She sees the man, not the image. I've tried to show you the man, but you won't see. So if I seem distant and reluctant to share my personal life with you, maybe now you can understand why." He stared at me for a moment and then hung his head, as if in shame.

"I'm sorry. I don't mean to burden you with my problems. You're in pain, and I'm only adding to it. Forgive me." He turned away from me and gazed out over the gray lake.

I stood rooted to the ground. So many different emotions slammed into me until I wanted to sink to the grass and cower until they left me alone.

Chief among them was doubt of my own motives, my own grasp of the situation. I was such a fucked up mess, how could I interpret anything correctly?

I wished I'd stay in wolf form longer. Had any of us ever stayed that way permanently? Or made that shape the primary and this the one they used only sometimes? That would be a hell of a lot easier. Wolves didn't murder each other. There were no conspiracies in the grass or the trees or the wind in our fur.

I took a step closer to Jason so our shoulders brushed. I waited for him to move away, but he didn't. He continued to stare at the lake, which shone silver in the capricious moonlight.

"Don't you get it, Jason?" I fixed my gaze on the rocky shore and watched small waves lap over the stones then retreat. Waves were the heartbeat of a lake, I thought. Calm for the most part, but bring a storm overhead, and they would lash up into a froth of fury. Beat the stones and sand on the shore into dust.

"You're everything I ever most admired in my father without the pettiness, the autocratic posturing. But the thing is, I always wanted to please that man, and I never could. I try so hard to please you, but there's this part of me that won't trust you because you remind me so much of Paul. I try to brush aside those suspicions, but things keep happening, and I take your silence, your omissions, as a direct betrayal. I don't know how to stop doing that, especially when it seems as if everyone in my life betrays me over and over again.

"Bonding with Lauren, that really threw me. Of course she'd see the same things in you that I did. She loved Paul. Why wouldn't she be attracted to someone with the same basic qualities? And now I'm just waiting for you to turn completely into him and ruin everything the way he did." I clenched my fists until my nails dug into my flesh. "I can't trust anyone. Every time I try, every time I forgive and tell myself I'm the problem, something else happens, and I have to start all over again. I'm sure you've figured all this out by now. I wear my heart on my sleeve, I always have."

"Your instincts about Paul were correct," he told me after I'd all but given up the idea he would respond. "But I'm not Paul Benedict. I'm trying to help the Great Pack, not gather power to myself in the guise of pack protection."

"I want to believe that so much." The moon went behind a cloud again, and the world was shrouded in darkness, but my night vision allowed me to watch the waves upon the sand.

"I can't make you believe in me. I can only continue to act in accordance with my conscience and will. You have to make the decision whether your conscience and will are in alignment with mine. Perhaps you'd prefer to simply be a pack member, Alpha someday so you can have a child, content to live the exact sort of life I'm trying so hard to preserve. Or perhaps instead of living that life, you want to dedicate yourself to the idea of it, so others can keep it, and others still to come can have it in their time.

"That's your choice. But know that if people like me fail, the life you idealize will cease to exist. There will be war, there will be death, and I am certain our Great Pack will be annihilated at worst, driven into hidden corners at best. Small, scattered packs, people existing always in fear and always on the run. Pack First is a deluded ideal doomed to failure.

"Perhaps it won't occur in your lifetime. Perhaps you have just enough time to seize the opportunity to be one of the last of this generation who can have this life. Or, maybe, you're out of time and it will be ripped from under you anyway, no matter which route you choose. I can't give you that answer either."

He began to walk toward the gravel path that wound its way back to the castle steps. I stood for a moment more and gazed out at the gray lake. It had no answers for me either.

Murphy never called back that night.

Chapter 16

"Thought you might like a drink," Ryan Kelly pressed a glass of whiskey into my hand and gave me a tentative smile. We were in a small, rectangular chamber off the massive entrance hall of the castle. I sat on the cushions of a window seat overlooking the sweep of the manicured gardens. In the distance to my right I could see the cool gleam of the lake beneath the summer sky.

It was just after five in the afternoon, and we'd spent a grueling day. I'd delivered my story to Councilor Feehery while Jason arranged travel for one of the European Great Councilors who would join the tribunal.

We were in the fact-gathering stage. Glenn Murphy and Ryan had just come back from Dublin, where they'd taken Murphy's statement. They'd gone to him so Murphy could stay by Fee's side. As an Advisor to the highest-ranking Great Councilor on the tribunal, that should have been my job, but I was also a witness and the accuser, so my role would be somewhat limited.

I wanted to be allowed to leave once the tribunal got underway, but my hopes were not high.

Glenn Murphy stood by one of the windows, seemingly lost in his own thoughts, and Ryan's gaze never strayed far from his still figure.

Ryan sat beside me with his own tumbler of whiskey. We were waiting for the arrival of the Great Councilor. Whoever he was, he was high enough in ranking that both Councilor Feehery and Jason had accompanied the driver to the airport to greet him.

I suspected the Councilor was from England and the one Jason had flown overseas with, but I wasn't sure. Whoever he was, he was no doubt one of the Guardians as well. I only hoped that one day no one would accuse us of railroading Declan Byrne.

Would anyone do that? The death of an Alpha—no, the murder of an Alpha—was a serious thing. It cut to the heart of everything our society stood for. Even though Declan had not wielded the knife, it could be traced back to him. That was enough to create a debt demanding satisfaction. It would likely be enough to blot out any urge in the minds of Councilors on the tribunal to question the validity of how the proceedings were carried out. Still, it made me uneasy.

I took a sip of the blisteringly stiff whiskey and suppressed a gag. Whiskey almost always tasted like paint thinner to me. Murphy said it was an acquired taste, but damn, how long would it take? Would Ryan be offended if I tossed it back like a shot? Before I could make up my mind, he said, "I really admire you, Stanzie."

Saved by the conversational bell.

"My mother says Paddy thought the world of you." When he spoke Paddy's name we both winced. The dark scent of grief gushed from his pores and clogged my senses. I didn't want to be premature, but I had begun to believe Ryan Kelly, at least, was not part of the underground movement within the Guardians. However, it didn't preclude him from being a part of flushing out Declan and Mick.

"Your mother?" Did I know her? I cast my mind back over everyone I'd met in Mac Tire so far and couldn't even make an educated guess.

"Etain," he supplied when he noted the confusion on my face. "Councilor Feehery. She's my mother."

Shit. Shit, shit, shit. I scrambled for a diplomatic answer. Could I trust him after all? Just because Mac Tire was a large pack, it didn't make it unlike most packs – full of family connections. Could Etain have set up her own great grandfather and used Jason as bait so they could silence Paddy and move Declan in as Alpha? Maybe Glenn Murphy had orchestrated everything. But why? His pregnant daughter was Alpha, but if Paddy was poised to ruin everything, I guess he would have to strike fast and hard. Everything was so convoluted. Nothing made sense. Now Ryan turned out to be Etain's son as well as Glenn's Advisor? What role had he played in this drama? Did he have one or was he as confused as me?

My head hurt. Maybe Jason's theory that neither Councilor was involved and it was all a bid for Declan to become Alpha was the correct one. But, again, how did Declan know to tell Mick to find Paddy at the safe house? Or had he? Perhaps Mick had simply followed Paddy there?

How Mick had gotten past the guard had been explained. He was a member of Mac Tire, and the guard let him in. He hadn't notified anyone because he'd had no idea Mick was Sorcha's suspected murderer. Nobody did who wasn't aware of Pack First and the Guardians.

"I want to be more than just Alpha someday. First I want to be a Regional Councilor just like Glenn, and then I want to be a Great Councilor like Etain." Real hero worship colored Ryan's tone, and a stab of jealousy flooded through me. What was it like to have a parent worthy of such regard? And had she fucked that up by setting up Paddy's murder?

"You believe in everything she does?" I asked. Jason would probably have strangled me for being so blunt, but he wasn't there.

"About the Guardians, you mean?" Ryan was just as forthright, and I studied him for a moment to try to pinpoint his weaknesses.

He was very attractive. Thick chestnut hair, sexy five o'clock shadow, soulful brown eyes full of grief and a smoldering anger. He would make a good weapon for someone else's rhetoric. Just like me. It was a disconcerting thought.

"What else?" I took another tentative sip of whiskey. Yep, still tasted like paint thinner.

"I don't believe we should come out in the open to the Others. I know you don't." Ryan's face was full of passion, and he waved his whiskey glass around for emphasis.

"How do you know that?" I regarded him steadily, and for a moment confusion washed over his expression.

"Oh, come off it. You're bloody Jason Allerton's top Advisor. He's the frigging leader of the Guardians. He started them, didn't he? He wouldn't have someone from Pack First working for him."

Jason had founded the Guardians? He was the leader? Icy prickles of shock jolted down my spine. How could I have been so fucking naive? No wonder he was after the murdering Guardians. They'd betrayed him.

Glenn Murphy didn't turn from the window, but I was pretty sure he was listening to the conversation.

"I'm not Pack First, Ryan." When I said it, I knew it was true. I did not want our Pack to come out into the open. I wanted what Jason talked about last night. To continue our existence peacefully the way we had been for generations.

The question was did I want to fight? Did I want to be a Guardian? For one thing, I supported people in the Pack seeking out whatever job they wanted. A college education was not a bad thing and should be offered to more than just a handful of us. Did a high-paying job automatically mean that person was Pack First? Did it preclude membership in the Guardians?

I had so many questions I couldn't make up my mind what I wanted to do. All I knew is that I wanted the murders to stop.

Ryan's body sagged in relief and his shoulder brushed mine. I knew we both stole small comfort from each other. Pack were very tactile people. Touch made us feel better. I wanted Murphy desperately. The thought of touching him hurt. Did Ryan have a bond mate he missed, too?

"The Councilor on her way is Pack First." Ryan's expression turned dark and brooding.

I gasped. How would this tribunal work if the Guardians wanted to keep this all a secret and yet invited someone who was Pack First to serve on it?

"Not only is she Pack First, she's spearheading the effort to convince the Great Council that Pack First has the right of it."

How the hell did he know all this shit? Oh, yeah. His mother was on the Great Council. Nice discretion there, lady.

My estimation of Etain Feehery sank even lower. I'd spent the day telling her my story, and she'd been sympathetic, friendly and completely disarming, but I did not trust her. Not even if she had been the one who had given Jason the photographs and was playing both sides in the Guardians in order to flush out the traitors.

Maybe it was like Jason said, Declan and Grandfather Mick were sacrificed pawns. She hadn't wanted Jason on her territory. Why? So he couldn't get any of the credit when she unmasked Mick and Declan? Or because she was afraid Jason would discover she was part of a plot to make her cousin Alpha?

I got to my feet and looked around for a place to ditch my whiskey.

I paused when I heard footsteps on the slate floor of the entrance hall. Three sets. One man wearing leather-soled loafers, two women, both wearing heels.

Ryan sprang to his feet before they arrived, his expression stony.

"Well, Constance, in on yet another death, I see." Councilor Celine Ducharme strode into the room as if she owned it.

It had been nine months since I'd last seen her, but the sight of her brought the events surrounding our association into resentful focus. Once again the sting of her merciless interrogation pierced me. We might as well be back in the chateau with me accused of murder again.

Fury ignited within me and licked through my body. Without a thought or a shred of self-preservation, I let go of my whiskey glass so I could throw myself at her supercilious, stick-like body and batter her smug face to ruins with my teeth and nails.

However, just as I sprang, a large, hard form collided with me, and my nose connected with Ryan Kelly's jaw. I saw silver-bright stars and tasted hot blood. My fucking nose was broken, I just knew it.

"Oh, Jaysus, I'm sorry. Sorry,. I saw you drop your glass, and I thought I could grab it before it smashed. Bloody hell, are you hurt bad?" Ryan had me by the shoulders, his fingers dug into my flesh so hard I knew I'd bruise. "What the fuck are you doing, Stanzie?" he hissed into my ear so only I could hear.

All four Councilors were frozen in place like statuary. My watery gaze made out Etain's, Glenn's and Jason's expressions—they were horrified, but Celine Ducharme, the bitch, was smirking.

"My Alpha's dead and she's making fucking smart-ass jokes." My mouth twisted, bitter tears mixed with blood burned my throat. "I fucking hate her so bad. Let me go, Ryan."

"Will you shut it and calm down?" He squeezed my shoulders so hard I gasped. "Don't give her any ammunition. Are you crazy, woman?" He whispered in my ear again. He was furious—every line in his body radiated anger. Not directed at me.

"Is her nose broken?" Etain Feehery moved quickly across the length of the room to stand beside me. Was she lending me her support, or was I another pawn in her fucking game?

Jason was a doctor, but he simply stood there and didn't come over to me. Was I to infer from his inaction that he was angry at me? Well, fuck him. Who wanted his help anyway?

Celine Ducharme fluffed her straw-yellow hair and sauntered toward a chair. A pair of Louboutins graced her feet. Nude pumps with glittering crystals embedded in the low heel. They perfectly complemented her beige wraparound dress. So goddamn Parisian I wanted to bite her.

"Let one of the servants tend to her, Etain. We need to talk." Her tone was dismissive, and a slow flush crept over Ryan's cheeks. Etain Feehery kept her cool, though.

"I'm afraid we haven't got servants, Celine."

"Am I expected to make my own bed and do my own laundry?" Celine's smile was pure malice.

"Of course not. Someone from Mac Tire sees to the rooms and catering, laundry as well."

"Servants," said Celine with a Gallic shrug. She settled herself on the chair, glanced around the room with its heavy furniture and Celtic tapestries and wrinkled her nose as if she smelled something bad on the bottom of her Louboutin pump.

"Can you get one of them to bring me a glass of white wine? Slightly chilled, you understand, not almost frozen. And the sight of blood nauseates me. Please, take Constance somewhere and deal with her. You'll find, if you haven't already, she's quite a lot of trouble. Everywhere she goes, misery follows. Mostly in the shape of death." She pushed a lock of hair behind her ear and reclined gracefully against the back of the chair. "Isn't that right, Constance?"

I curled my lip, but Etain Feehery spoke before I could. "Constance has been instrumental in bringing our Alpha's murderers to justice. I've found her most helpful. Not troublesome in the least. You'll have to set aside your prejudice, Celine, in order to serve fairly on this tribunal. She's a key witness and is integral to the process. If you find the idea too much for you, I'll be glad to bring you back to the airport and book you on a flight for Paris." Etain directed a very diplomatic smile in Celine Ducharme's direction. How cool Councilor Feehery was when she talked about Paddy's murderers. If I didn't know better, I'd never have guessed they were her blood relatives. Is that what being a Councilor meant? Being so in control family ties were ruthlessly cut if it served the greater purpose?

Councilor Ducharme let out a trill of mocking laughter. "Oh, you won't be rid of me so easily as that, Etain. Someone with sense and clear vision needs to be on this tribunal."

"So you'll be going back to Paris then?" I snapped and Etain Feehery gave a snort of laughter. Even Jason's lips quirked. Ryan Kelly squeezed my shoulders again, and I pinched him hard as I could in the side. There wasn't much excess skin to work with—the man was built like a fortress— but I saw his eyes glaze over with pain.

"You ought to watch what you say, Constance." Councilor Ducharme's eyes narrowed aggressively. "Key witness or not, I will not tolerate insubordination from a mere Advisor. Tread carefully around me. Jason Allerton cannot protect you from me, so if you think you've got a shield, think again."

"I don't—" I began, incensed, but Ryan shook me and startled me. My fucking nose protested violently against the movement, and I saw stars again.

The next thing I knew, I was being dragged across the slate flooring.

"My wine, please," requested Ducharme, and I didn't hear Etain Feehery's hopefully snarky response because Ryan kicked the door shut behind us.

"What the fuck are you doing taking on the most powerful person on the Great Council, you feckin' idiot?" Ryan all but shoved me into a small bathroom and kicked that door shut as well.

"I don't give a shit who she is. She's a fucking bitch, Ryan!" I pushed his hands aside as he attempted to examine my bloody nose.

"You know her?" Ryan ducked down and retrieved a towel from a cupboard beneath the sink. He ran it under cold water and tried to staunch the flow of blood from my nose.

"She's the whole reason I'm bonded with Murphy." I snatched the towel from him, because he had all the finesse of a construction worker, and applied it gently to my nose. Biting pain swelled up and I growled low in my throat.

"Well, isn't that—wouldn't that be a good thing?" Ryan stared at me with his soulful brown eyes, and I cursed beneath my breath. "You were forced to bond? Is that why he came back without you? But the way he acted and avoided everyone, we all thought he was brooding because he loved you. Maybe you didn't want to bond with him? But how in the hell can someone, even a Councilor, force you to bond with somebody else?"

By making the alternative worse.

"I love Liam Murphy." I'd wanted it to come out forcefully, but the damn wet towel muffled my voice and made me sound pathetic.

"Then I don't understand," Ryan said with an exasperated sigh.

"Who asked you to try?" I gave him a belligerent glare, and he backed away, hands in the air, the universal signal of surrender.

"Can I look at your nose?"

"What a goddamn strange question," I snapped. "You broke it, now you want to admire your handiwork?"

"I don't think it's broken. I'd know for sure if you let me look at the damn thing, Stanzie. Jaysus God, are you always this frigging annoying?"

Grudgingly, I lowered the towel. Of course the damn thing was broken. It hurt like a bitch.

"You're not even going to have a black eye out of this. Just a bloody nose." was Ryan's prognosis.

He was such a liar. "Are you kidding me? It hurts. How can something not broken hurt so much?"

"Women are pussies with pain, that's why," said Ryan. I threw the towel at his face and he slapped it away, but there was a roguish gleam in his eye.

I swung to the mirror to examine my nose and make my own damn decision.

The bastard was right. The traitorous thing wasn't even swollen, just bloody. Ryan got me another towel, and I gingerly began to wipe the blood away. It wasn't even bleeding much anymore, just a small trickle.

"Listen, you're going to have to tone it down around Councilor Ducharme." Ryan's voice turned serious, and I grimaced at his reflection in the mirror. I looked like a gargoyle.

"I will if she will."

"No. You just will. She's a Councilor, she can be as bitchy as she wants. You have to sit there and take it."

"Who are you, my life coach?"

He sighed, and the room filled with the scent of his frustration.

"I don't know what sort of feud you've got going with her, Stanzie, but can't you concentrate on the tribunal? On getting Declan Byrne, the bastard, settled? That should be your top priority, not some contest of wills with a Councilor. I know you didn't know Paddy that long, but he was a good Alpha, a good man, and he deserves—"

"You don't have to sing Paddy's praises to me." In the mirror, I watched my face drain of most of its color. Furious grief made me tremble. "You don't know the first thing about how it was with me and him, so shut the fuck up."

Ryan sucked in his breath, and for a moment such stark misery shone in his eyes I had to look away before I burst into tears. Not fair. So not fair.

"I'm sorry. I thought you just met him," he whispered.

"Well, I didn't. He was there for me when nobody else was, including Liam Murphy, and he was my Alpha and nobody better question my loyalty or my grief. I'll fucking kill you, Ryan Kelly, I swear."

I swung around and tried to hit him, but he took me in his arms and instead of fighting him, I collapsed into him. We both burst into scalding tears and held each other up because if we hadn't, we would have fallen to the floor.

* * * *

By dinnertime I'd managed to get myself together. My nose was tender but, without all the blood, looked perfectly normal.

I put on a long black skirt and white t-shirt with a black vest, settled my bond pendant prominently against my chest, and pulled up my hair into what I hoped was an artfully messy knot.

Flat silver sandals and a pair of hoop earrings finished my ensemble, and I hurried down the carpeted hallway to the stairs.

The dining room was on the main floor and was, predictably since this was a castle, huge. Stone walls, mullioned windows, and a large rectangular table with an impossible amount of chairs around it made up the décor. An ancient Oriental rug took some of the chill from the slate flooring.

Beeswax tapers in elaborate iron candelabras sent out a soft aroma that did not clash with the food.

Celine Ducharme presided over the head of the table, and the rest of us spread out on either side. We didn't have nearly enough people to make someone sit at the foot—at least not and still be in conversational range.

Jason was impeccably attired in one of his Armani summer suits. It was cool enough inside the stone castle for him to keep his jacket on, and once again I marveled at how handsome and influential he looked.

The seat beside him was empty, and when I approached, he gallantly got to his feet to pull out the chair.

Celine watched with amusement as she toyed with a glass of white wine. Ryan, Etain Feehery and Glenn Murphy sat across from us as if we had squared off into rivaling teams.

My stomach knotted. Somehow I doubted this would be a hospitable affair.

Celine Ducharme picked at her salad as if it offended her. It was a basic salad. I'd eaten several just like it in France so I knew she was being willfully difficult.

When the main course, lamb shank cooked in red wine, was served, she sighed.

"At least it is not, how do you say it, bangers and mash," she muttered, and Etain Feehery grinned.

"This is a traditional Irish dish, Celine."

Celine looked doubtfully at a forkful of lamb before she ate it.

"I think it's delicious," I declared, and Ryan shot me a warning look, but Etain Feehery beamed.

"Thank you, Stanzie."

So far, Jason hadn't said a word, but now he lifted his wineglass and looked across the table at Etain. I tensed, wondering how they would interact with each other given their history.

"How are the pack members reacting to the idea that this will be a closed tribunal?" He took a sip of wine and set his glass down.

Etain Feehery shrugged. She didn't seem rattled at all to be in the same room with him or angry either. Then I remembered they had served together on the Great Council for at least ten years and decided this wasn't their first face-to-face interaction. "Frankly, they're so overwhelmed with their grief that if we do this quickly enough, they won't think to protest."

"Why does it have to be a secret?" I asked, and Councilor Ducharme gave me an indulgent look as if I were a child. A not very bright child.

"Would you have the whole of Mac Tire discovering the fact that there is a matter of great importance being debated among the Councils?"

Debated? What an interesting way to put it.

"People are dying. It's hardly a debate. People don't get murdered during debates."

Beneath the table, Jason put a hand on my arm, but I was sick of being ordered around blindly by Councilors.

"You think everyone in the Pack should know and take a side in this issue? How naive, Constance, but then I wouldn't expect anything else from you." Celine Ducharme set down her fork and pushed her plate away. She'd eaten three bites, the bitch. It was no goddamn wonder she was so stick-thin.

"The ones who have no idea what's going on are doing most of the dying," I pointed out.

"And knowing would make their deaths easier?"

My fingernails itched to claw the condescending smile off her face. "All knowledge would do is create discord and more violence. The common Pack member hasn't the necessary tools to understand the concepts or appreciate the greater picture."

"If you think revealing us all to the Others is a good idea, I doubt you have them either," I snapped.

"Constance," remonstrated Jason.

"You chose poorly in this Advisor, Jason." Ducharme's smile was brittle, just like her bones and overtreated hair. "Usually you are so conservative and calculated, but this time you made a grave mistake, I think. You cannot control her."

"Our Advisors are just that, people we choose to advise us, to keep us grounded and in contact with the Great Pack. They are not supposed to be carbon copies of ourselves, nor should we treat them like slaves, Celine." Jason's tone was mild, but his irritation was evident in the disdainful way he looked at her.

"Well, you explain to her why we need to keep this debate between the Councils. As it is, some of our Councilors have taken a very dark route, and this is why we are here tonight, no? Because one of you is a traitor?" She fixed Etain Feehery and Glenn Murphy with her beady, brown gaze.

Councilor Murphy had been doggedly applying himself to his meal, but now he set down his fork and gave her his full attention.

"Declan Byrne is the one on trial," he said and Celine's mouth curved into a sardonic smile.

"Yes, and hopefully during the course of this tribunal, the truth will come out and he will identify the person who planned this."

"You think one of us plotted to assassinate Councilor Allerton? But we're all Guardians." Etain Feehery's sherry-brown eyes were cold.

"Jason Allerton has begun a campaign against his own side. He has ruthlessly exposed several peripheral people, mostly among the grandmothers and grandfathers, but there has been more than one Regional Council member who has also gone down. If he were removed, someone like you, Etain, could come to the forefront and champion the Guardians and direct them at your discretion. Perhaps you approve of the murders." Ducharme played with the stem of her wineglass, her face alight with malicious pleasure.

"You overestimate my influence among the Great Council, Celine, if you think I could ever hope to take Jason's place," said Etain Feehery with a laugh. But I could tell by the hard glitter in her eyes that she was furious. Why? Because Celine Ducharme had insulted her? Or because she'd hit the nail on the head?

Celine took a leisurely sip of her wine and grimaced as if it tasted bitter. "Or you, Glenn. An open slot on the Great Council could mean elevation of your status. You've been on the Regional Council for several years and would be in line for consideration."

"I think if Jason's slot opened, someone from an American Regional Council would be selected." Glenn continued to fork lamb into his mouth as if he and Celine were having a trivial dinner conversation.

"True, but if someone more sympathetic to your version of the cause were to ascend, all the better, no? You have the motive, Glenn. So do you, Etain. Why don't you make it easy on us all and confess now. We can judge you at this same tribunal."

"Any number of Councilors could have gotten to Declan Byrne and Mick Shaughnessy," said Glenn Murphy. "England, Wales, Scotland, anyone there could have pulled their strings."

"Ah, but proximity makes it more likely it was one of you two. We shall hopefully find out during the tribunal.

"And now, Constance," Celine turned her gaze back to me. "Now do you understand why this must be kept from Mac Tire? From the Great Pack? What do you think would happen if they could no longer trust their

Councils? We are supposed to be above reproach. We are the upholders of our laws, and we administer justice. Do you really suppose our Pack would be better off to know the truth? That there are traitors in our ranks who betray everyone in the mad attempt to hold back the future?

"I think not. And, now, if you'll excuse me, I have a headache, and would like to go to bed." She rose to her feet and left the dining room.

Save for the sound of cutlery on china, silence reigned at the table.

Chapter 17

After dinner, Jason picked up his glass of Irish Mist and gestured for me to do the same. I followed him out onto a large, sloping terrace just outside the dining room. We sat on a stone bench overlooking the gray lake and sipped our liquor without speaking.

Sunset was nearly over, and dusk enveloped the trees and castle in shadow.

"Do you believe whether or not the Pack reveals itself should be decided solely by the Councils?" I asked. The Irish Mist was sweet on my tongue, but my thoughts were dark and heavy.

"I do," he answered. "Stanzie, a decision as monumental as this was precisely the reason the Councils were established. We are the guardians of the Great Pack and administrators of justice. This debate has been ongoing for nearly a decade now."

Surprise must have shown in my expression because he smiled wistfully.

"These decisions aren't made lightly or hastily. It's taken this much time for it to pick up serious momentum. At first the idea of announcing ourselves to Others was barely tolerated, but it's gained support in the past several years. Enough to alarm me."

"Ryan said you're the leader of the Guardians. The founder."

He nodded. "I am. But if I'd told you that nine months ago, you would never have become my Advisor."

"Why is it so important that I am?"

"Because you'll be Alpha of Mac Tire someday, and after that you'll be on the Regional Council. And someday I have every expectation that you will join the Great Council. Possibly to replace me."

"Me?" I scoffed. "Not Murphy?"

"I think he'll go far too, but you're the one I'm watching."

A cold shiver drifted down my spine. His confidence was daunting. What did he see in me that I couldn't see?

"So I'm supposed to fight the ones who want to reveal us? Be a good little foot soldier until I'm promoted to general?"

"The members of Pack First aren't our enemies. Can't you see that? Our enemies are the ones who take matters into their own hands and murder Pack members. Grandfather Tobias, Callie Olstrom, Grandfather Mick, Declan Byrne. They're the ones to fight." He took a sip of Irish Mist. "Some of my closest friends and confidants are Pack First."

That was too much. Jason read my incredulous expression and smiled sympathetically.

"Someone you're close to is a staunch proponent of telling the Others who we are." He took another sip of his liquor and gazed through the gathering dusk at the tranquil lake.

"Who?" I sat up straight on the bench in shocked dismay. "Besides Celine Ducharme, I don't know anyone who wants that. I didn't even know that was the real issue until a few days ago."

"Think about it. It will come to you." Jason finished his Irish Mist and rose to his feet. Tall and handsome, he seemed like some sort of demigod, although I knew well how flawed and human he really was. "Good night, Stanzie."

He disappeared inside, but I sat on the stone bench until full dark descended, unable to comprehend the complexity of everything he'd shared with me.

* * * *

Back in my room, I dug my cellphone out of my purse. No messages from Murphy. I called him again, and the phone rang three times.

I was bracing myself for voice mail when he said, "I just got Fee to sleep for the first time, and if you woke her up I'm gonna be friggin' pissed. Forgot to shut this damn phone off. Everyone wants something from me, and I'm telling you, I've got nothing left for anybody but Fee. So whatever it is you're wanting, I'm pretty sure I can't give it to you, but try me anyway. I doubt it, but it could be your lucky day."

My brain stuttered for a moment. I went hot, then cold.

"I'm sorry," I whispered. "I didn't know. I don't want anything, Murphy. I just wanted to hear your voice." Lie. I wanted him to tell me who I should trust and what the hell to do, but how could I ask him that now? "You should go back to sleep. I—it's just you never called me back, and I—oh, hell, I'm sorry. Goodbye."

"Stanzie!" His tone was sharp, and I froze. What had I done now? "I didn't know it was you. Your number's not programmed into my phone. I'm so fucking tired I can't think." I heard a door open and then shut. He'd moved rooms. Hopefully that meant Fee had not woken.

"Then I won't make you stay on the phone. Please," I floundered. I tried to remember his mouth, hot on mine, his arms tight around me, but he was a stranger again. One I barely knew.

"How's everything going with the fucking tribunal?"

I wanted to tell him about Celine Ducharme and what we'd discussed at dinner, and Jason being the founder of the Guardians, but I couldn't. It wasn't fair to burden him with more than he already carried.

"I'm a witness. And the accuser. I don't have much of a role. I hope they won't keep me here for it. I want to help you."

"You can't." His voice was heavy with fatigue. "She doesn't want anyone but me near her. Not even Siobhan." He didn't say his father's name. How had his interview gone today if Fee didn't want anyone around her but him? I waited for him to say something about his father's possible involvement, but he didn't, and I sure as hell wouldn't.

"I love you," I said, the only thing I could think of to help him.

"I gotta go." His voice was apologetic but firm. He hung up without even a goodbye.

Why hadn't he said he loved me back? My damn insecurities went into screaming overdrive, and for a moment I couldn't breathe because of the tears that clogged my throat.

I needed some sort of connection, something, so I scrolled through my contacts and called my cousin, Faith.

She answered on the second ring, her voice cheerful and upbeat, and for a moment I couldn't speak. Somewhere someone was happy. Would I ever be happy again?

"Did you know he was dying in the dream?" I heard myself ask her, but until I spoke I'd had no idea what I would say.

A dreadful pause rang between us.

"Oh, Stanzie, your Alpha's dead?" Her voice was a small, horrified whisper.

"Yesterday," I confirmed. "Stabbed in the stomach. Did you know? You thought it was Murphy, and that's why you said I should go to him, right? So I could say goodbye?"

"He had blood on his teeth." Her voice shook. "I didn't know he was dying, just badly hurt. But I kept hoping…"

"I wish you'd told me. Goddamn, I wish you'd told me."

"Could you have changed it?"

"Has anyone ever changed any of your damn dreams, Faith? No, I couldn't have changed it. I could have been prepared maybe. All I know is he's dead and I couldn't do anything."

"Who stabbed him? How did it happen?"

"It doesn't matter, does it?"

She began to cry, and then Scott's voice was in my ear.

"Who is this? What the hell is going on?" Protective fury radiated from his tone.

"Scott, it's me. Stanzie,"

"Why is she crying?" he demanded.

"My Alpha's dead," I answered baldly, and I heard him suck in his breath.

"Oh, shit. Stanzie, I'm sorry. That fucking dream? It came true?" His voice was filled with a superstitious dread.

"One of the grandfathers tried to kill Councilor Allerton, and Paddy stepped between them." How long would it take before I could explain what happened without flashing back to that moment? Without seeing all the blood and feeling so utterly helpless?

Scott's voice snapped me back to reality. I had no idea what he'd just said, but it didn't matter. Meaningless platitudes, expressions of horror, nothing would bring Paddy back, would it?

"I'm sorry I made Faith cry. I shouldn't have called." If Murphy had just said *I love you* back I wouldn't have. Spreading misery was something I was good at.

"Do you need anything? Do you need us? We could be there tomorrow." Scott really meant it. He'd get on a plane for me. He'd clear out his bank account to buy tickets to Dublin just to make me feel better.

My spirits lifted a fraction, not enough to wipe away all the grief, but somehow it was bearable.

"No, you don't have to do that, Scott. But thank you so much for offering." My voice broke a little, and Scott said, "We're family, Stanzie. Anytime you need us, you just ask, and we'll be there. You'd do the same for us."

He was right. I would.

A small glow ignited in my heart and spread warmth through my cold body. I did have family again. I had people who cared about me. It had been so damn long. Hot tears spilled down my cheeks, and I wiped them away with my fingers.

When I could speak again, I said goodbye to Scott and got into my pajamas.

Just as I was about to pull back the covers on the massive bed, someone knocked on my door.

When I opened the heavy oak door, Ryan stood in the stone corridor. He looked so strange and grief-stricken, I didn't hesitate to bring him inside.

"Stanzie, this is gonna sound dumb, I think, but I gotta ask you." His Irish brogue was thick and I could hardly understand him. He could barely look at me with his mournful brown eyes. "I keep thinking about Paddy, and I feel so awful and alone. Everybody in the pack has somebody to be with right now, but we're stuck here in this horrible castle away from everyone else and I just thought—this isn't a seduction or anything, not that I wouldn't..." A crimson blush stained his cheeks, and he floundered to find his place. "Jaysus, I just wanted to know if I could sleep with you tonight? I mean just sleep. In the same bed. Maybe you could put your hand on my arm or something. Anything so I know someone from my pack's there and I'm not alone?"

He looked very young at that moment. I wondered how old he was.

"Come on." I took his hand and led him to the bed. He helped me pull back the covers. He wore a pair of sweat pants, a t-shirt and a pair of socks. He climbed onto the bed and curled into a miserable ball.

I shut off the light, pulled the covers over us both and settled into the groove of his spine. When I put my hand on his arm and hooked my ankle over one of his, he gave a great sigh, and some of the tenseness left his body.

In times of trouble, Pack always turned to Pack.

Chapter 18

I woke with a craving for butterscotch squares. Ryan was gone, the space where he'd slept still warm. All through my shower and as I dressed in a conservative black skirt and gray blouse, I fantasized about butterscotch squares.

Allerton was the only one left at the breakfast table in a sunny room near the kitchen. He sipped coffee as he stared out the window at an herb garden.

"Kathy Manning," I said as I slipped into the chair beside him with a plate piled high with scrambled eggs and sausage I'd put together from the buffet table near the door. He reached out for a carafe of coffee and filled a cup for me. "She's a member of Pack First."

I recalled snatches of conversation she and I had exchanged. How she wanted her son to graduate from an Ivy League school with a business degree so he, with her guidance, could run a company. How she didn't need the Great Council to achieve her goals.

I suspected she'd use all her influence on the Regional Council to persuade the other members to see the so-called benefits of revealing ourselves.

"Yes," he agreed pleasantly as he passed me cream and sugar. I fixed my coffee and took a sip. Elixir of the gods.

"That's the real reason you blocked her from the Great Council, wasn't it?"

"Part of it," he allowed. "I truly did love her and wanted to bond with her."

"So you could keep an eye on her and squash her influence as best you could." I forked up some scrambled eggs, although, woefully, no ketchup was in evidence. I stole a look at him through my lashes. The man was a cold-blooded monster. Or was he desperately trying to protect our Pack? Heroes made sacrifices. Was Jason Allerton a hero?

"Is that why you chose her in the first place? To be your mistress?" I guessed. Eggs without ketchup were disgusting. I reached for the toast rack. "You figured out she was Pack First, and you went after her with all the weapons in your arsenal."

A small smile quirked the corners of his mouth.

"You ascribe the most underhanded motivations to me," he murmured. "But what if I told you that you had a point? I didn't expect to love her. That threw a wrench in everything, and I knew better than to play that game. I regret it now. Do you believe me?"

"Regret loving her? Sure, I believe you." I spread marmalade on my toast and took a crunchy bite.

He snorted. "I regret playing with her emotions the way I did. I thought I would keep it strictly pleasurable business. I thought I could persuade her to my side of things or failing that, yes, block her ascension to the Great Council. She was first in line, although I wish you wouldn't repeat that."

"If she'd switched sides, you'd have supported her appointment?" I ate a bite of sausage.

"Possibly. If I'd believed she was genuinely in support of it. She might have turned the tables on me and merely pretended. We used to spend more time in bed debating Pack politics than..." He trailed off, but not before I saw the amusement in his smile. My expression must have verged on horrified. I so did not want to hear intimate details about Kathy Manning and Jason Allerton in bed. "She's under no illusion why I did what I did. I'm surprised she let you believe I blocked her so she would bond with me."

"She knew I had no clue about the real nature of what's going on, remember?" I piled some eggs on a piece of toast and some sausage, then another piece of toast to make a sandwich. Perhaps the eggs would be palatable with toast, butter and sausage to mask their taste? "Nobody bothered to tell me about the existence of Pack First or the Guardians. This whole thing is like peeling an onion. Layer after layer, and the deeper you get, the more it stinks." The egg-and-sausage sandwich was pretty decent. I took another bite and chewed reflectively.

Allerton sipped his coffee and returned to his contemplation of the herb garden.

"Do you think Murphy's been agonizing about his father's involvement in all this ever since he came back here?" My question drew Jason's attention back to me. "Because I think he has. From what I can gather, nobody liked Sorcha except him, of course. Killing her maybe wasn't so hard to do."

"But pushing his own son out of the Alpha position wasn't?" Jason didn't seem convinced.

"Some fathers don't stand behind their children. Some fathers do all they can to undermine them." My voice was bitter, and I put down what was left of my egg sandwich.

"I don't think Glenn Murphy's one of them." There was compassion in Jason's expression, but I didn't want any from him. I picked up my coffee cup and moved toward the doors that led out into the garden. He followed me as I knew he would, damn him.

"Then Etain Feehery, your ex-whatever she is, wanted to put Paddy into the Alpha slot. That makes more sense since she's the one who recruited his father who then got Paddy into it."

Jason looked as if he struggled against inappropriate laughter, but he couldn't keep the gleam of amusement from his blue eyes. "You'll never miss an opportunity to throw my ex-mistresses in my face, will you?"

"I doubt it." I found a stone bench, warmed from the morning sun, and sat. Jason joined me. I could discern the gleam of the gray lake behind a screen of trees beyond the garden wall. Ireland was fucking beautiful. With a pang, I wondered if Paddy had ever sat on this bench and thought the same thing. My eyes filled with tears, and I took a hasty sip of coffee to shield my face from Jason's prying gaze.

"Murphy was Alpha. Why didn't Glenn try to recruit him?" The sun glinted off the surface of the lake, and my eyes were dazzled for a moment.

"Who's to say he didn't?" Jason's words were soft, but they hit me like a bomb.

"No. No way. Murphy told me once that the only connection he had with the conspiracy was fighting to end it. He had no idea about the Guardians or Pack First until Paddy told him about it."

"No idea that people within the Guardians had taken a dark turn in their methods," Jason said. "But I suggest he knew about both Pack First and the Guardians through his father although he refused to join, preferring to stay neutral. What then, Stanzie?"

"Then we're back to his father plotting to remove him as Alpha, and we're back to him keeping secrets from me. Like you did. Like my father

did. Like everyone has." Tears spilled down my cheeks, and I didn't
bother to brush them away. "You're wrong, Jason Allerton."

But was he?

* * * *

I had to compose myself, so I headed for the sanctuary of the gardens
where I wouldn't have to walk through the breakfast room and confront
any of the others.

Halfway along the grassy path to the lake, I spotted Glenn Murphy. His
pipe trailed a plume of cherry-scented smoke as he headed toward me.
He'd likely gone for an after-breakfast stroll, maybe to prepare himself
for the beginning of the tribunal.

I dashed the last of the tears from my cheeks in a no doubt futile
attempt to hide the fact I'd been crying, and mustered a smile of greeting.

It would have helped enormously if I knew I could trust this man. He
was Murphy's father and I understood I was a bit jaded with fathers after
what I'd experienced at the hands of mine. Jason's infuriating ambiguity
also didn't help.

"Good morning," he said as he drew closer. The smile on his face faded
as he obviously realized I'd been crying. "Are you all right, Stanzie?" His
voice, so like Murphy's, made me want to cry harder. And fling myself in
his arms for comfort. Damn it.

"I'm fine," I said. I tried to move around him so I could pretend I'd just
been on a walk, but he moved to block me.

"It's a terrible thing to lose an Alpha," he said, and that did it, the
floodgates opened again. Paddy's face rose up to haunt me and once again
I felt horrible for every bad thing I'd ever said to him.

Glenn reached out for me and drew me into his embrace. Up close he
smelled of cherries and Pack. I sobbed into his shoulder. He wore a tweed
jacket and the fibers scratched my nose.

"We'll get through this," he promised as he patted my back. "We're
strong. We're Mac Tire and we won't let this break us."

I thought I might already be broken, but he sounded so confident, even
as the grief stripped his voice of most of its power.

He gave me a brisk shake and fished in his pocket for a tissue, which
he handed to me. I wiped my eyes and blew my nose while he smoked
his pipe.

"Ready?" He held out his arm and I tucked my hand in the crook of his
elbow. We didn't talk on the walk back to the castle, and I wished I knew
the truth about anything.

* * * *

The tribunal began at ten. I just had time to retreat to my room to wash my face and redo my makeup. As I opened the door, I noticed a small gold plaque bolted to the wood at eye level.

Liam Murphy and Sorcha McClanahan. Her name coupled with his left a nasty taste in my mouth. What the hell was this? For the first time, I saw all the doors in this wing of the castle had gold plaques. Were they names of pack members?

The plaque on the next door down read Padraic O'Reilly and Fiona Carmichael. Paddy's face flashed before my eyes and I leaned my forehead against the plaque. As close as I could get to him now.

Homesickness surged through me. I wanted to go home. Tears threatened, but somehow I held them back.

The plaques must be the names of current and former Alphas. This must be the Alphas' wing of the castle. Older plaques must give way for newer ones as time passed. Would my name replace Sorcha's someday? A sobering question and one I didn't have time to contemplate.

I passed into my room and heard my cellphone chirp. It was Murphy. I stared at the phone for several seconds, paralyzed. Could I talk rationally to him right now, or would I sling accusations and sob again like a fucking baby? Sorcha's name on the damn plaque coupled with his hurt.

I let the phone go into voice mail and went into the bathroom to wash my face.

* * * *

"You will tell us who instructed you to provide Michael Shaughnessy with a knife, *Monsieur* Byrne." Celine Ducharme worked her usual charm as she ruthlessly questioned Declan Byrne.

The tribunal took place in a large, echoing chamber that added a disconcerting counterpoint to the bitch queen's interrogation. A table, several horribly uncomfortable wooden chairs and a few rugs and tapestries did nothing to muffle the sound. The windows were mullioned and set with opaque glass so nobody could distract themselves with anything pleasant, like nature.

Three hours of torture and I wasn't even the one on the hot seat.

Ryan and I had notebooks where we ostensibly would take meticulous notes of the proceedings. How many times, though, could I write the same damn thing? Ducharme had already asked a variation of her question, but was a single-minded bulldog who refused to be sidetracked.

Declan's standard answer—silence. Attempts by the other Councilors to ask different questions had been venomously rebuffed by Celine Ducharme. This was her show.

Etain Feehery tapped her fingers on the edge of the table and sneaked glances at her watch. Glenn Murphy sat stony-faced and listened. Jason steepled his fingers and appeared lost in thought, but I knew he missed nothing. He never did.

Beside me, Ryan's stomach gurgled loudly, and he crimsoned.

"Councilor Ducharme, it's past one o'clock, and I believe we would like to take a lunch break." Etain Feehery's tone was impatient, but her expression remained bland.

Celine Ducharme threw her hands up in the air and sighed so gustily it was a wonder the tapestries in the room didn't flutter.

"If we must." She pushed back her chair, with effort—the goddamn things weighed a ton—and stalked from the room, her Louboutin heels clacking on the slate flooring. Today she wore the same peep-toe pumps I remembered from the chateau. They must be her favorite interrogation shoes. Her navy blue pencil skirt was tailored, as was the matching jacket. Her straw-blond hair was rolled into a no-nonsense chignon at the base of her skull and with her hair drawn back, her face became even more arrogant than usual.

I couldn't find any sympathy for Declan Byrne under the circumstances, but I still hated the woman and her relentless methods.

As I struggled with my damn chair, Declan Byrne's gaze swept over me, his expression full of contempt.

"Enjoying yourself, you self-righteous slag?" he asked.

"I'll enjoy it more when I watch you die," I said with a nonchalant shrug. I made a mental note to look up the meaning of slag. Whatever it meant, it couldn't be good.

His face darkened, but before he could spring out of his chair, Ryan Kelly and Glenn Murphy were at his side.

"Sit down. What are you thinking?" Glenn Murphy growled, and Declan Byrne sank back into his chair.

"I'm hungry," he said. "Surely, prisoners get their bread and water."

"Oh, shut your feckin' mouth, Byrne," snarled Ryan.

"You think you're better than me, but you're not. You just haven't gotten caught," muttered Byrne.

Ryan flushed scarlet and his hands bunched into fists. "I'm not a fucking murdering traitor. Get outta that chair, you frigging coward, and back up your words with your fists. Otherwise, shut the fuck up."

"Ryan." Etain Feehery didn't raise her voice, but Ryan dropped his fists to his side, and a frustrated sigh burst between his lips. "Declan Byrne is facing a tribunal. Your fists won't settle this, the Councils will.

He'll get what's coming to him, never you worry, but you need to put your anger aside. Now's not the time or place for it."

"I had nothing to do with this, Etain. I can't have him insinuating I did."

"Maybe I'll tell that fucking skinny bitch French Councilor you helped me," said Declan Byrne with a grin. "She's convinced somebody did. Why not you, Kelly?"

Etain Feehery paled, and her mouth tightened into a thin line.

"You'll tell the truth and nothing less, Declan." Her tone was harsh and uneven.

For the first time I felt a small measure of sympathy for her. If she truly had nothing to do with Paddy's murder, and her son did, how awful it must be for her to sit and wait for Declan Byrne to crack under Councilor Ducharme's pressure.

She already had to condemn her cousin and if Declan implicated Ryan, she'd have no choice but to move against her own son. Had I done the right thing to bring Declan up before a tribunal? I remembered Jason telling me he'd support me in whatever decision I made. The minute I saw the photographs, I hadn't thought of any alternative but to bring Declan Byrne before a tribunal for justice. But what if there had been other ways to handle it? A dark alley and a knife? No one the wiser for why he died except a precious few who would never breathe a word of the truth?

What had I brought down on Mac Tire? No. Murder was murder, no matter who did it or why. I'd done the right thing. So why did I feel so goddamn guilty?

* * * *

After bolting a few mouthfuls of lunch, I escaped outside and walked to the shore of the gray lake, where I scavenged flat rocks and skimmed them across the lake's smooth surface.

The sun was warm on my skin and the cool breeze carried scents of water, grass and flowers. Once a small fish broke the surface, perhaps drawn by the noise and motion of my skipping stone.

I wanted to be wolf. She tugged at me even though she had no way to come out. Ryan and I should have had sex the night before. We could have had the release of our wolves if we had.

But, I wanted Murphy. Not the stranger, the one who told me he loved me one day and turned away the next, but the kind man I knew from our time in America. Maybe I hadn't known he'd loved me back, but he'd been patient and calm and he'd always been there.

It wasn't fair to build somebody's hopes up the way he had mine. I'd been alone and then he'd made me see how lonely I'd been and showed me what I might have. He made it seem as if it were mine for the taking, so when I reached out and grasped nothing, it hurt like hell.

My best was five skips, but I thought it was mostly a fluke, not skill. I didn't want to return to the tribunal, but my watch and my internal sense of justice prompted me to return to the castle.

The summer breeze caressed my face as I walked along the pathway. Ireland smelled so different than Massachusetts. The plant life was not the same, the water had a strange, though not unpleasant sensory texture, and even the air was unique.

These woods would become my hunting ground for the most part from now on. The condo in Boston would be a vacation destination, not home. Wistfulness clouded my eyes with tears. What would Dublin be like without Paddy? What would Murphy be like?

"Goddamn you, Declan Byrne, and everyone who helped you," I snarled beneath my breath as I mounted the stone steps to the castle entrance.

I hadn't even reached the main staircase before Celine Ducharme pounced on me.

"Where have you been, Constance?" Her tone was accusatory, and resentment turned me sullen. What the fuck business was it of hers? I wasn't late. I still had ten minutes before the tribunal was due to reconvene.

"None of your business," I hissed, and her predatory face darkened.

"That is where you are wrong. It is my business. What did you do to Declan Byrne's food? Or was it in his coffee? You know we'll analyze everything. You, of all of us, here, have the herbal knowledge. Did you act alone or were you acting on someone's orders? You cannot convince me you had nothing to do with it. Not this time, *madame*."

What the hell? I stared at her, completely baffled. A thread of fear squirmed down my spinal column. Analyze his food? Herbal knowledge?

"Are you trying to say something happened to Declan?" I managed, past the mounting anxiety threatening to close my throat.

She snorted and gave a contemptuous toss of her head. The fine lines that bracketed her thin lips were more pronounced than the last time I'd seen her, nine months ago, at the chateau. Although she could easily pass for mid- to late forties, she was aging. She couldn't age fast enough for me. Grandmothers didn't serve on the Great Council. Was retirement next year for her? Or did she still have a decade left? It was never really clear with Pack. We held our own against the aging process for sometimes over a hundred years before we looked old.

"You could say that. He's dead. There was poison in something he ate or drank for lunch. You didn't stay to lunch with us. You barely managed to warm your seat before you were gone. Where did you go? Up to his room, perhaps? To the kitchen to put something in the food on his tray?"

"Are you insane?" I took a step back from her as if she might reach out and grab me with one of her skeletal claw hands. I reeled at the knowledge Declan Byrne was dead. "Why would I bother to murder him when I was the one who brought charges against him and wanted him to stand before a tribunal? It doesn't make any sense, Councilor."

"That was before he threatened to expose Ryan Kelly as an accomplice. I saw him come out of your room this morning. You are sleeping with him, and you want to protect him." Celine's smile was chilling.

"That's bullshit," I said. Movement on the stairs distracted me. Etain Feehery and Ryan Kelly stood frozen between one step and the next. Obviously they'd heard us.

"He didn't sleep with you last night? What was he doing creeping out of your room at six in the morning then?" Celine Ducharme asked.

Etain Feehery's expression was one of bewildered fear. Ryan Kelly flushed.

"We just slept in the same bed," he said.

"It's none of her business what we did or didn't do, Ryan." I was pissed and scared, not a good combination. "I didn't poison Declan Byrne. I was at the lake, skipping stones."

"A likely story," said Ducharme. Her gaze moved to the stairs. "But if Constance didn't poison him, perhaps your son did, Etain. He had the motive. Declan Byrne was about to reveal him to the tribunal." Her beady eyes shone with malevolence. She was enjoying this, the bitch. God, I hated her so much. Why couldn't someone poison *her*?

"How do you even know Ryan had a so-called motive?" I demanded as Etain Feehery's face paled to the color of skim milk. She clutched at the railing either to keep from falling or from throwing herself at Councilor Ducharme. "You weren't even in the room for that conversation."

Ryan looked guilty. Why did he have to look like that? Had he poisoned Declan Byrne?

"Because Declan Byrne told me when I brought him his tray," replied Councilor Ducharme.

"You brought him the tray? So you had the best opportunity of all," I declared.

"Declan didn't tell you definitely Ryan was involved, did he?" Etain Feehery ground out. I thought for sure she was going to faint. Ryan thought so, too, because he moved closer to her and put a steadying hand on her shoulder.

Celine Ducharme smirked. "Oh, he insinuated he might be willing to implicate someone after all. He suggested I ask your son what he was keeping back. He said Ryan Kelly had more knowledge than he was admitting to. I want to know what it is, Etain."

"Of course you do," snarled Etain Feehery. She turned to her son helplessly. "Ryan, do you have anything to say?"

Ryan gulped. My heart sank. He did know something. I didn't want him to be involved in this. Had I slept with my arms around a traitor last night? Had I let one of Paddy's murderers into bed with me? I felt sick.

"No." Ryan abruptly turned and floundered up the staircase.

"What a liar, Etain," observed Celine Ducharme with a complacent smile. She inspected her flawlessly manicured fingernails for a moment. When she looked up, her eyes were like flint. "I want to see everyone in the conference room in fifteen minutes. We will get to the bottom of this—do you understand? And if we don't, I'm calling in more Councilors, and Mac Tire will be in a worse, more awkward situation than it already is. I'm sure you don't want that, Etain. Your family's fingerprints are all over this crime. How do I know you aren't the mastermind behind it all?"

Councilor Feehery's mouth tightened, but she said nothing at all.

Chapter 19

No one had an alibi. That became clear after ten minutes in the conference room with Celine Ducharme leading the charge.

Jason's expression gave away nothing. Apart from offering a brief explanation of his whereabouts after lunch—it turned out no one had stayed long in the dining room, although I had been the first to leave—he fell silent, fingers steepled on the tabletop.

Ryan was miserably defiant. He kept his head down and refused to speak.

"Your silence is damning," remarked Ducharme after thirty minutes of badgering. "I believe I will have to call in other members of the Great Council. And press formal charges against you, *Monsieur* Kelly."

"Really?" challenged Etain Feehery. "Exactly what charges have you in mind, Councilor Ducharme?"

"*Alors,* the usual. Conspiracy against the Great Pack. Attempted murder of a Councilor. Declan Byrne's words are enough to get things started."

"It's interesting that only you heard these supposed words," said Jason in a quiet, musing tone.

"Ah, Constance herself admitted there was another conversation about Ryan Kelly. One I believe you were privy to yourself, Councilor Allerton. So there are two conversations. Enough to go on," crowed Ducharme.

Jason looked startled, but only for a second. Short enough time to make me doubt what I'd seen. However, the reproachful glance he sent me was long enough to make me feel like complete and utter shit. Me and my fucking big mouth.

Glenn Murphy's expression reminded me of one I'd seen on his son's face when he tried to mask his anger.

"I can't believe my Advisor has anything pertinent to do with this fiasco, Councilor Ducharme. Bring on your damn Councilors. They'll all be in your pocket, of course, and my man won't stand a chance, but if he says he's not involved, he's not, and it'll be on your conscience what happens to him."

"The problem is, Councilor Murphy, your man hasn't said anything either way. He has yet to deny or confirm any of my suspicions. He's tying my hands." Celine Ducharme looked positively elated at this fact.

"Then tell the Councilor you're not involved, son," demanded Murphy's father. The timbre of his voice jolted me with its familiarity to Murphy's.

Ryan gave his Councilor an agonized look and then bowed his head.

"Mother of God." Glenn Murphy shoved his chair back. "I can't help you if you won't deny the charges."

"Yes, Ryan. Say something," begged his mother.

Instead, Ryan fled the table even though he had not been excused. That was probably a smart, although doomed, move. He hadn't yet been formally charged but his own actions made it just a matter of time.

I escaped the conference room before Celine Ducharme could corner me for yet another imagined transgression.

* * * *

In the hallway outside of my room, a suit of armor stood guard complete with a jaunty plume atop the metal visor. This castle was almost a frigging cliche. I examined the armor and thought it seemed incredibly small. I doubted even I could don it. Medieval men had been impossibly short, I decided, and turned to go to my room.

Ryan was sprawled across my bed on his stomach, face turned toward the window. He scrambled into a sitting position when he heard me enter.

"I needed a place to escape everyone." He got to his feet.

"It's a castle. You pick my room as the only hiding place?" I wasn't sure I wanted to deal with him. I had to think about everything and sort my feelings. His presence complicated everything because when he looked at me with his soulful brown eyes, all my thoughts that he might be complicit in Paddy's death seemed stupid and unfair. Goddamn, I sometimes hated gorgeous men.

Always attracted to the shiny surface, never the substance beneath, I heard my father's lecture in my head for perhaps the thousandth time in my life.

Ryan's cheeks flushed, and he looked so young and terrified, my traitorous heart melted.

"How old are you?" I demanded as he headed for the door. He stopped and looked at me for a moment before he answered.

"Twenty-three."

A fucking baby. Goddamn it.

"You want some whiskey?" A decanter and glasses decorated one of the small tabletops. I shuddered at the thought of sipping the stuff, but Ryan's eyes lit up with hope, and he nodded.

We took our glasses to the cushioned window seat that overlooked the front of the castle. From this bird's-eye view I could see the fountain and the precise spot where Paddy had fallen as he'd clutched at the stab wound in his stomach. My gut clenched.

We drank in silence because I didn't want to interrogate the poor bastard, and I'd bet he sure as hell didn't want to talk to me about any of it. We sat with our knees touching, and I saw tears glimmer in his eyes, although he didn't let them fall.

"What's going to happen to me?" he asked as he neared the bottom of his glass and his fears got the better of his tongue.

"What do you think? The Councilors who Ducharme will ask here will condemn you, and you'll be put to death," I said. I knew I was brutal, but he had to hear it. Maybe it would make him think.

He paled, and one of the tears in his eyes slipped down his cheek. Goddamn it.

"Tribunals suck, Ryan. I should know. I've been through two of them. You don't want to go there if you don't have to."

"I'm the one who took the photographs you brought to An Puca," he confessed before he leaped to his feet and escaped. He dropped his whiskey glass on the slate floor as he ran, and it shattered. Just like his life.

The pressure of my fingers around the crystal whiskey glass turned to pain. The pungent scent of the alcohol burned the insides of my nostrils.

Ryan took the photographs. He wouldn't have done that if he were a part of the plot. He must fucking know who set everything in motion, and he was protecting one of them—his mother or his mentor, the man for whom he worked as Advisor. He'd had just enough doubts to take the photographs, but even now, with his life on the line, he maintained his silence rather than betray the person responsible for Paddy's death.

Why was he protecting that person? Because he'd been ordered to, or because he was a scared and confused young man whose ideals and naivety combined to render him helpless to figure out what to do?

He'd turned to me as if I could untangle the fucking web and make it all right again. What a fucking laugh. What a colossal joke.

I heard him in my head telling me he wanted to become a Councilor, just like his mother.

What kind of selfish mother would let her own son take the fall for something she'd done?

"It doesn't make sense," I whispered. Avoiding the shattered pieces of glass and the spilled whiskey, I ran after Ryan. Maybe it wasn't too late to catch him and beat some goddamn sense into him. I couldn't help the idiot if he wouldn't tell me which Councilor he was protecting, could I?

* * * *

I nearly knocked Glenn Murphy down the stairs. He was coming up as I tried to plunge down.

"Whoa, watch yourself, woman," he cautioned and grabbed me so I wouldn't fall. He sounded so much like Murphy, but he didn't look like him.

Anger gripped me so hard I choked. Ryan Kelly couldn't possibly be one of the Guardians who used murder to fight the debate. He was too young, too idealistic. He wouldn't willingly help kill his Alpha or a Councilor. But I thought he might cover up for an idol that did. Or try his damnedest until his fear overcame him.

When he broke, he'd betray everything and everyone who meant anything to him. I couldn't let him do that to himself. It was the kind of thing nobody could ever really recover from. It would haunt him all the rest of his life.

He would cover for his mother, no question. But would she let him?

He would also lie to protect his mentor, the man he served as Advisor. And that was a person who might let him—might even expect him to.

"Ryan Kelly has nothing to do with this shit, and you know it," I snarled, and Glenn Murphy let go of my shoulders, his expression cautious.

"Then why won't he say that?" he countered.

"Because he's protecting you. He's covering for you. You're one of his idols. He thinks that's what you'd want him to do."

"You don't know what you're talking about." Glenn Murphy's eyes darkened. "Does my son know you're fucking my Advisor?"

What an interesting defense. Cloud the issue and go after my vulnerability—my feelings about Murphy and his about me.

Was he really the outraged father, or was he the calculating member of the underground movement?

I said, "What difference does that make? We're Pack. We can fuck whoever we want."

His lip curled. "You're just like her, aren't you? Sorcha, the bitch cow from hell. She fucked practically the entire bloody pack, and Liam just stood there watching."

"The entire pack? Including you?" I wondered, and he hit me so hard I tasted blood.

"I never touched the bitch!" Glenn Murphy's face mottled red with rage.

My next words spilled from my mouth without a pause, as if my brain were on autopilot. To think—to reason—would be to lose the momentum. I'd never been an analytical thinker. I always operated best in the moment when choices narrowed and there wasn't time to consider things from all angles.

"No, you got Grandfather Mick to do your dirty work for you. You may not have fucked her, but you murdered her. How the hell do you sleep at night?"

"I sleep fine. You're mad, you know that? My son bonded with a lunatic. I tried to give you the benefit of the doubt. For Fee's sake and Liam's, but anytime Jason Allerton sticks his nose into Mac Tire business, we all get fucked over, and this is no exception."

"It's snowballing out of control, Councilor. You got away with Sorcha's murder, but you won't get away with Paddy's or Declan Byrne's, and you won't get away with Ryan's. He took those photographs of Declan and Grandfather Mick. He made sure those got into my hands, but he kept the ones he took of you. But not for long because I'll make sure Councilor Ducharme gets them." I had no idea if there were compromising photographs of Glenn Murphy, but it stood to reason, didn't it?

"What did he tell you? He has nothing he can tell you. Get the hell out of my way. I'm sick of the sight of you."

I knew I was right when I saw the fear leap into eyes. Just a flicker quickly contained, but a dead giveaway nonetheless.

Rage boiled through me. I hated him just like I hated my father. Weak, power-hungry, grasping bastards.

"What kind of a father makes sure his own son loses the Alpha position? But then I guess you didn't care because you had your daughter waiting in the wings to take over. You're disgusting. Why would you do something like that?"

"At least I would know that any child Fee bore would be true family, not like the bastard Sorcha carried. Do you think I'd stand by and watch my son's bond mate have Colin Hunter's baby and ruin any chance Liam had of having his own child?" Glenn Murphy's lips peeled back from his teeth in a feral snarl. "Better that he lost the Alpha slot and had the chance to get it back again someday with a good, loyal woman, than become broken-hearted spare to the pair to that treacherous bitch. Only look what he's done to himself with Jason Allerton's frigging help? He's tied himself to the same sort again. As if once wasn't enough.

"Well, you're not gonna ruin Liam's life any more than I let Sorcha ruin it!"

By the time I realized I was in danger, it was too late. He had his hands wrapped around my throat, thumbs digging into my larynx, and I couldn't fucking breathe. The pressure hurt so much I wanted to scream, but I couldn't drag air enough to inflate my lungs.

I kicked and struggled, but Glenn Murphy was a strong man, and I couldn't find leverage.

My vision narrowed until all I could see was Glenn Murphy's mouth. Everything else went black. My coordination deserted me. I could no longer remember how to move my arms and legs. We fell to the carpet, or maybe it was just me. His mouth disappeared, and all I saw was one of the buttons on his shirt. It was small and white. The thread was one shade darker and I could see the machine perfection of it.

I wanted Murphy so badly. I wished I'd answered the phone when he'd called. I wished I'd had that one last chance to tell him I loved him.

The button turned pinkish red, which puzzled me, until I realized it must be a burst blood vessel in my eye. I shuddered, and it seemed all at once that I could see myself on the blue-and-green diamond-patterned carpet and the back of Glenn Murphy's head as he bent over me.

Out of body. I was free of my physical shell. Where would I go? Was there really an otherworld? Would Paddy be there? Grey? Elena? Or would I be eternally alone?

A terrific jolt shoved me back into my body. I felt my amorphous self force its way back into the top of my skull and work its way down until I felt my arms again, my stomach, my knees and then my toes.

The air tasted like fire. It had never hurt so much to breathe. Something was wrong with my throat. I felt like a fish out of water and flopped bonelessly on the carpet.

What the fuck had happened? Was I dead? I could see everything again, although it wavered in and out of focus, but one thing I couldn't see was Glenn Murphy.

I tried to stop shuddering. Pain flared like a noose around my neck.

Someone groaned. I wasn't the only one in pain.

"Liam?" I tried to say his name, but the noose of pain around my throat prevented me. I couldn't make a sound.

I reached out for the wall so I could brace myself and maybe sit up.

Another groan. The sound was below me, but not too far. Down the first flight of stairs perhaps? On the landing as it twisted around to the second flight?

I dragged myself to the edge of the stairs, appalled at how weak I was.

Two figures sprawled across the small landing. I recognized Glenn Murphy's shirt. He wasn't moving. At first I couldn't make out who the figure beside him was, but then I focused on the mahogany-brown hair. Ryan. It was Ryan.

I tried to say his name, but again could make no sound. I couldn't stand up. I was too weak. So I crawled down the stairs, intent on getting to him, although I didn't know why. All I knew was I had to go to him. My fingernails sank into the rough nap of the carpet and I braced my shoulder against the cold wood of the railing to keep from pitching headlong down the stairs.

Glenn Murphy's eyes were wide open but empty. His head rested at a strange angle on the slate floor of the landing, and it took me a moment to place where I'd seen that awkward angle before.

Elena's head had flopped on the stalk of her broken neck the exact same way. The fall down the stairs had killed him just as the back of the Mustang's seat had killed her.

Ryan's eyes were closed, but his lashes fluttered as he struggled to open them. Blood pooled beneath his head. He'd fallen, too. Why?

I reached out a shaking hand to touch the blood. It was warm.

"Oh, *mon Dieu*," said a woman. She was on the stairs below us, one hand on the railing, the other clutched to her throat. Her hair was straw yellow and her lipstick was coral. She had on Louboutin peep-toe pumps. *"Tu es tombés? Tu es blessés?* Constance?"

Of course I couldn't answer her. I wanted to tell her, no, I didn't fall. No, I am not hurt. But I couldn't speak.

She hissed when she saw the blood and Glenn Murphy's vacant stare. When she touched my throat, I winced and tried to scream but couldn't.

"*Mon Dieu*," she said again and was gone, heels clattering on the stone stairs.

Chapter 20

My throat was swollen and bruised so badly I could barely swallow the honey-infused tea Celine Ducharme brewed for me. Jason had applied compresses and given me a shot of something that made me feel floaty and disconnected. Thoughts burst like fragile soap bubbles inside my brain and made it impossible to string together any coherence.

I wouldn't stay in the bed, so Jason sat with me on the window seat and we watched the sunset as Celine Ducharme fretted in French and forced hot tea on me.

They spoke sometimes, and I gradually pieced together the knowledge that Etain Feehery was with Ryan, still unconscious from his fall down the stairs. Ducharme had not yet pulled in any other Councilors, and Jason was patiently attempting to dissuade her, but most of his attention was focused on me.

I knew by the intensity in his blue eyes he believed once I regained a decent grasp of the situation and myself, I would shrink away from him. Blame him.

"No more damn tea." My voice was shredded. Every other word didn't even make a sound, and the ones that did were distorted and came out in a frightening whisper.

"Don't talk," Jason ordered. "You need to rest. Your larynx was nearly crushed and if you want to recover with undamaged vocal cords, you need to be silent for at least a week."

Ducharme made an impatient clucking noise. "Ah, but how will we know what happened? You expect me to wait until Ryan Kelly regains consciousness? Perhaps he never will. I know—we can have her write it down." She began to search for pen and paper.

Alarm surged through me, and I tried to bolt, but Jason caught me around the waist and dragged me down. Celine Ducharme must have thought I was trying to get to her, because she danced backward out of reach, her Louboutin heels loud on the slate floor.

"Ryan," I croaked. I took Jason's face in my hands and made him look at me. His skin was warm, and his cheeks were stubbled with five o'clock shadow. His usual perfection was slightly off, and it unnerved me the way it always did.

Jason had been too preoccupied with me to shave. Surely, he'd been smooth-shaven in the conference room today. Was it still the same day? Confusion sparked fear.

"Is she trying to tell you Ryan strangled her and Glenn Murphy tried to rescue her, or was it the other way around as Etain insists?" babbled Ducharme.

"Celine, I am not a mind reader." The pent-up frustration in Jason's tone scared me, but his blue eyes were kind as he gazed at me. He gave my shoulders a gentle squeeze. "Don't speak, Stanzie. Nod. Who attacked you? Ryan?"

I shook my head violently in negation. No! Something flickered across his expression. Relief? Triumph? I couldn't tell, it was too fast.

"Glenn Murphy tried to kill you?"

I nodded confirmation and there was no triumph this time, just profound sadness. Tears stung my eyes, and he pressed his cheek to mine.

"I'm sorry, Stanzie," he whispered.

"Liam," I choked.

"I'll have him here tomorrow. We're going to break the news to him and to Fee and Siobhan. They and Paddy's family are coming here tomorrow to plan Paddy's funeral. We'll tell them about Glenn when they arrive."

"Before," I insisted, and he sighed.

"Liam before," he compromised. "But not until tomorrow morning because if I tell him now, he'll come here, and Fee needs him."

I needed him, too, but I only nodded.

"Good girl." He beamed approval at me. I still held his face between my hands, and his cheeks were warm against my palms.

"Ryan." My ruined voice made him frown.

"Please don't talk," he requested, and Celine Ducharme snorted.

"You'll sooner make stones sing than persuade this one to do something she doesn't want to do. Constance, she listens only to herself. Selfish."

I turned my head to glare at her, and she flashed me a predatory smile. Was that approval on her face? I had to still be high from whatever drugs Jason had shot into my system.

"How on earth did you get Glenn Murphy, a seasoned Councilor, to confess, or so severely compromise himself, that he lost all reason and tried to kill you? You were relentless, weren't you? Went for the jugular and accused him, didn't you? Interrogated him?"

Horror engulfed me. I *had* interrogated him in just the same fashion as Ducharme herself used. Had used on me.

"*Alors*, you will, perhaps, some day make a decent Councilor after all," she said.

"Celine," remonstrated Jason when he realized how tense I'd become.

"That's how you do it, *cherie*," said Celine. "You take your own experiences, and you learn from them. Turn them to your advantage. And always, always let your anger serve you. But you must work on your sense of self-preservation. Never confront a potential enemy without allies. You should have come to me. I would have helped you."

"Celine," said Jason again, but she only laughed.

"I begin to like her, Jason. If you're not careful, I shall take her away from you and persuade her to be my Advisor. I think her politics may lean in my direction rather than yours. My side does not resort to murder within our own ranks." Her smile was toothy. "Or without them. You fight a losing battle, you know. Your own side is so divided against itself you lose momentum and credibility by the day.

"I wouldn't be surprised if Glenn Murphy hasn't delivered your side a death blow from which you cannot recover. He single-handedly may have advanced the decision by months, if not years. And your prized Advisor will help it along no matter which side she chooses."

The sound of her triumphant laughter continued until she closed the door behind her and was gone.

I wanted to tell Jason that no matter what I believed, I would never, ever become that bitch's Advisor, but he put a finger to my lips to remind me I wasn't supposed to talk.

"You need to rest. Go to bed," he ordered and when the panic flared in my eyes, he added. "I won't leave you. I'll be right here all night. I'll sleep in a chair by your bed."

He settled me beneath the covers and then dragged one of the lighter chairs to my bedside. He switched off all but one small lamp, which shed muted light onto a side table across the room, and settled into the chair. After a moment I felt his fingers comb through my hair.

"Is the pain too much? Do you want another shot?" he offered, and I shook my head. I did not want my thoughts muddled. It would make me more vulnerable than I already was.

Chapter 21

I couldn't swallow much of the chicken broth Jason gave me for breakfast, but I took another mug of honey-infused tea to the window seat and looked down into the courtyard and the fountain.

I could see the phantom image of Paddy's bloody body on the gravel if I tried hard enough.

At ten o'clock a group of grieving people made their way down the path. Murphy led them around the opposite side of the fountain so they wouldn't tread where Paddy had been attacked.

Fee, fragile and pregnant, clutched his arm. Siobhan, their mother, followed closely behind, flanked by the curly-haired brunette—Paddy's mother, Maureen O'Shea—and another man I didn't know but suspected must be her bond mate. Behind them came Colm O'Reilly, Alannah Doyle and the woman from the pub who had sat with Colm, the petite beauty with coal-black hair that hung in a shimmering mass to the small of her back. Deirdre. In heels she might come to Colm's chin. Maybe.

Jason and Etain Feehery met them just beyond the fountain. Etain went straight to Siobhan Carmichael, and a moment later I saw Siobhan's face crumple and through the cranked-open mullioned window of my room I could not escape her cry of grief.

Tears poured down her face, and Maureen O'Shea moved to her side. Fee's face went very white, but she didn't cry. Murphy's expression was blank, and that, more than anything, broke me.

I raced out of my room, down the staircase and out the French doors of the small room where we breakfasted. It wasn't until I splashed into the gray lake and the icy water penetrated through my jeans straight into my bones that I stopped. For a moment I stood there, knee-deep in water, before I retreated to the shore. I sat on the rough sand of the beach, drew my knees to my chest and stared into the gray water.

* * * *

I heard footsteps a few moments later but didn't turn around. The person was cautious on the rocky sand as if uncertain about footing. The beach was strewn with small stones, but not enough to give someone Pack that much pause.

However, as the footsteps drew closer and the wind shifted to bring me the person's scent, I understood.

Fee lowered herself next to me, using my shoulder for support. Up close her grief-ravaged face was pale and drawn, her eyes so red-rimmed they were swollen.

My own eyes burned in sympathy, and if she hadn't needed my shoulder, I would have bolted. I could be such a coward.

Once seated, she leaned against me, this time offering me her support. I took it gratefully and bowed my head so it touched hers. Our fingers laced together, and my breath caught in my throat. The comforting power of an Alpha, even a grief-stricken one, wasn't something I could explain in words, but it meant everything to experience it.

"I wanted to ask you if you'd play the harp tomorrow. After Paddy's funeral." Fee's voice didn't falter, but I knew how much the words cost her.

I nodded. My damaged throat had squeezed so tight it was impossible to speak even though I desperately wanted to.

"And during the bonding ceremony. Please?"

Bonding ceremony? I tried to speak, but only a distressed sound escaped me.

"It's true that my baby will be born well within the three months I have to find another bond mate, but I need to make sure he or she has a place in the pack. I don't have time or the inclination to search for somebody I— for somebody. So I'm going to bond with Colm and Deirdre. Something positive can come from all this. She won't have to abort her baby.

"Everyone's letting me do what I want. I'm milking their sympathy all I can so I can protect Colm and Deirdre. Besides, I like the idea of another baby related to Paddy running around the pack, and their indiscretion would have knocked them out of contention for the next Alpha election.

"Which brings me to this." With her free hand, Fee thrust something into mine. I looked down at a silver pendant in the shape of a Celtic circle. A peridot gleamed from the center of the circle, and my stomach clenched. "Paddy made it," Fee said, and I wanted to scream and howl my grief, but I only sat there like a frozen idiot and stared. "That's what he did, you know, in the pack? He and his family are all artisans. He designed and made jewelry, silver mostly. He sold and fashioned bond pendants at the Regional and Great Gatherings. You, Stanzie, you're an artisan. The musicians fall into that category, too.

"Liam and I, our families, we're the investors. We buy and sell real estate, play the stock market, help the Alphas run the pub. The investors are generally well-off, especially in this pack because it's so old. Liam's a whiz at the stock market, and I'm really good at managing properties. I used to let Paddy believe he was keeping the books for An Puca, but it was really me." Her smile was wistful, and I squeezed her hand.

"Anyway, you need to put this on the same chain as your bond pendant. I'll help you do it now. I want everyone to see it before and right after the funeral so nobody will say a frigging word. Alphas get to choose the duos or triads in contention for the Alpha slot. The pack gets to vote, but the Alphas choose the candidates. And I want you and Liam to be the next Alphas of Mac Tire. I'm not sure who will be your competition, Colm and Deirdre will choose, but I want you and Liam. Paddy wanted it, too. That's why he made this. He was gonna give it to you when you took the pack bond, but now I'm the one to give it to you."

Fee moved aside the black scarf I'd used to cover my bruised throat and gasped.

"Jaysus," she said, and burst into miserable tears.

We held each other as tears soaked our cheeks.

"Allerton took me and Liam aside to tell us the truth. Da really did try to murder you." Fee stopped crying before I did, and her fingers gently explored my bruises. I held still and tried not to wince.

"Da tried to recruit us both into the frigging Guardians. We said no. We thought it was just one of those issues the Councils keep themselves busy with. It seemed so damned far-fetched, the idea of coming out to the Others. We never thought it was serious, that it would ever get enough traction within the Councils to become possible. Da told Liam and me both about it when we became Alphas, and we both told him we didn't want to be involved, to let the Councils work it out."

Jason had been right. Murphy had known about the conspiracy the entire time I'd known him. And never told me.

I flashed back to a night at the Hartford safe house. Murphy's lip bleeding from the fight he'd had with Colin Hunter. He'd told Jason he wouldn't be his puppet. Always, there'd been subtext beneath their interactions. Murphy had always suspected Jason had an agenda, only he'd had a much better idea of what it was than I ever had.

Murphy had sworn to me he hadn't anything to do with the conspiracy except fight against it. Yes, that had been the truth, but only part of it. He fought the conspiracy within the movement, he was against those who harmed Pack, but all along he must have known Jason was part of the original movement, and he'd never breathed a word.

He'd known his father was involved with the movement before Paddy ever had.

All his cards had never been on the table. His or Jason's. Meanwhile, I was an open book, floundering along, not trusted to know the full truth. Left behind when things got dangerously ugly.

"I'm sorry, Stanzie. I don't know what Da was thinking. This issue has gotten so much bigger, so out of control. Maybe if Liam and I had worked with him as he'd wanted, we could have kept him from doing the appalling things he's done."

I wanted to tell her it was Sorcha's liaison with Colin Hunter that pushed her father over the edge, but I couldn't talk. Besides, that may have been the match that lit the fuse, but he'd always been capable of going there. If not Sorcha, something else would surely have provided him with the excuse.

"Fiona Carmichael, what are you thinking of to be sitting on the cold, hard ground in your condition!"

Fee stiffened at her mother's voice and hastily rearranged the scarf around my throat.

"She thinks it was a heart attack," Fee whispered into my ear. "She has no idea of the truth."

And now I was being enlisted as a conspirator who would work to keep her in the dark.

Rebellion tasted like dirt in my mouth, but I couldn't talk so what would I do? Rip off my scarf and let Siobhan stare at my bruises in utter incomprehension? Fuck.

"And you, Constance Newcastle, you ought to be ashamed of yourself," lectured Siobhan. "Can you not see your Alpha's pregnant and shouldn't be sitting on the ground? You're as selfish as Sorcha ever was, aren't you? Instead of meeting your grieving Alpha at the door like any civilized, intelligent person would have done, you force her to find you sulking at the lakeshore. And not even a welcome hello to your own bond mate, let alone your Alpha. He's lost his best friend and his father in the space of three days, and you're wallowing in your own grief, shallow as it has to be. You didn't know either of them, yet here you are crying. For shame!"

Fee and I scrambled to our feet and faced her. I could feel the tears, wet on my face, and resisted the humiliated urge to wipe them away as if that could fix things.

Siobhan's own grief was stamped hard on her face, but her eyes were dry. She moved to Fee's side, shoving me away in the process, and I nearly fell but caught myself against the back of a black boulder.

"Ma," remonstrated Fiona. "Didn't Stanzie work hard to bring Declan Byrne to justice for Paddy? Hasn't she been supporting Mac Tire all along with her efforts? And I know she didn't know Paddy long, but they formed a bond, and her grief is as real as yours and mine."

"A bond?" Siobhan's expression was contemptuous. "Paddy never could keep his dick in his pants, could he? Show him a pretty face and he was off. How you put up with it, I'll never understand. He was blatant about it, rubbed your face in it."

"Siobhan!" Fee's voice was icy. "You'll not be lying to me and telling me Glenn never dipped his wick in another woman's willing hole, will you now?"

"No, but he was discreet. He didn't come back and brag about it to me."

"Paddy didn't brag. We compared notes," Fee said, and Siobhan shuddered. "I was just as blatant as he was. You know the first thing you said when I told you I was pregnant was 'Do you know who the father is?' Don't be a hypocrite, please."

"Well, what the hell are you looking at?" Siobhan yelled at me. "You go find your bond mate and tell him what a selfish, wicked bitch you are. He'll forgive you. He always forgives the ones he loves. He lets them trample all over him. And he doesn't fuck around. He's faithful, that one, and if you've got to be shagging other men, Constance Newcastle, you might have at least tried to resist his best friend. Even Sorcha didn't go there."

"Paddy wouldn't touch her. She tried to seduce him, but he fucking hated her like poison." Fee's face was livid. "You stop harassing Stanzie. So what if she fucked Paddy. I hope she made it good for him and he enjoyed it. I'm so big I wasn't much fun lately, and I hope he and Stanzie went at it for hours, I do!" Fee burst into tears again, and I wanted to crawl under the black boulder and never come out. This was fucking hell.

"See what you've done, you pathetic bitch?" shouted Siobhan, and that was it, I couldn't face either of them anymore. I ran.

* * * *

Murphy had his face buried in his hands as he sat on the edge of the bed in my room when I burst through the door.

Startled, he jerked his head up and I froze. We stared at each other. His bond pendant gleamed from around his throat. It hung on the outside of his shirt, and I saw the small Celtic knot with a pearl at the center beside the peridot and pearl.

My peridot knot was still somehow clenched in my fist.

He had my bond pendant in his hands. He must have found it on the dresser where Jason had put it. One of the bruises on my throat was the perfect imprint of the silver chain and at the base of my neck, the clasp.

I could tell by his expression he didn't understand it was Jason who had removed it. He thought I had deliberately stopped wearing it.

I'd never returned his phone call, and he hadn't said he loved me back at the end of the one phone call we'd had. His father had tried to kill me with his bare hands. Jason must have told him about how I knew everything now, all the lies, even if most of them had been by omission.

"Nine months ago I asked you to wait until your birthday. I told you if you still wanted to leave me, I'd let you go. You weren't there with Allerton and Etain when we got here. I saw this first thing when I walked in. I guess this is your answer. I don't blame you. You never wanted to bond with me in the first place, I know. And I'm sure you never wanted to love me. Maybe that's gone, too, after all that's happened the past few days." At first he'd looked up at me, but now he dropped his gaze to my bond pendant clutched in his hand.

"I trust you to make the right decision. You always do. You must think I'm such a frigging hypocrite. And I am. I know I am. Three days ago I told you to your face I wasn't a vigilante, and what's the first thing I did when I saw Grandfather Mick with a knife? I took it from him and stuck it in his heart and twisted the blade for good measure. Watched him die on the ground like a dog." He looked up at me and his eyes were haunted house dark.

"Allerton gave you the photographs of Declan Byrne, and I know what he told you. He said you could do anything you liked with them and he'd back you up, the same as he backed me after I murdered Mick Shaughnessy. If I'd had those photographs, no question, I would have taken Declan out in the back alley and beaten him to death. Maybe by myself, maybe I would have made it worse and brought someone like Colm with me. You could have shown me the photographs, let me kill Declan, but you accused him in front of the whole pack and used your Advisor authority to take him in to face a tribunal. The right thing.

"I let Sorcha's death twist me. You didn't let yourself get warped after Grey and Elena. You crept away to lick your wounds, and you came back looking for happiness without them. And you always seemed to see the best in me, not the worst. I tried to hide the worst, but you found it. How could you not? Sorcha saw it right away, it's why she couldn't love me.

"I'm not worth your time, Stanzie Newcastle. That's why I left you in Boston." He dropped his gaze again and tightened his fist around my bond pendant.

"I always meant to kill Mick Shaughnessy. Paddy's been holding me back for months. Trying to keep me away from him, trying to pay him off. Trying to protect us all. And I wouldn't let him go to Allerton or Etain or my father. I wanted to do things my way. Like I always do. And now Paddy's dead, and I've lost you as well.

"I thought revenge would feel good. Only, it feels like shit. When you came into An Puca waving those photographs and doing it the right way, I knew I'd lost you. I knew it, and yet I still hoped." He took a deep breath and lifted his chin.

"I love you so much, but I threw it away, didn't I? Revenge has cost me everything. My best friend, you, and it didn't make anything better. The stupid thing is, I didn't even think of Sorcha when I was killing him. I was thinking of Paddy and my sister—and you.

"My best friend gets stabbed, and you and I, we both start running. I went after that fucking old bastard, and you went to him, to Paddy. You did the right thing, the way you always do. I traded my opportunity to say goodbye for an empty, meaningless…" He couldn't finish because tears wouldn't let him.

He cried as if he had nothing left. Nothing at all.

The paralysis that had me rooted to the floor broke, and I ran to him. He went unresisting into my arms, but didn't hug me back at first. It wasn't until he felt my lips in his hair that his arms stole around my waist.

His mouth burned against mine. I dug my fingers into his hair and pulled him closer, so that our teeth clicked and our tongues barely had room to wrestle. I climbed onto his lap, and he slid his hands beneath my shirt. I let go of him only long enough to allow him to strip it off me.

He hissed when he saw the bruises on my throat, and such horror filled his dark eyes that he lost all momentum until I knocked him on his back and straddled him, one knee on either side of his hips. I kissed him again and his touch was tender at first, but soon enough he had me my on back, his fingers deftly unzipping my jeans so he could slide them down.

I thrust my hips up, desperate to connect with him, but he was still fully dressed. Frustrated at the barrier between us, I tore at the button on his fly. He took off his shirt as I found his zipper, and a moment later we both cried out as he slid inside me.

"Oh, God, I love you. I love you so much," he told me between kisses. He burned a trail of them down the side of my face, to my neck, my shoulder, down my arm, to my wrist, and then he gently pried apart my clenched fingers so he could kiss my palm.

He found the Celtic knot, and I felt his chest hitch as fresh tears soaked in my skin.

"Liam." I tried to say his name, but my voice would not respond. He traced the bruises on my throat with his tongue.

I wrapped my legs around his waist and dug my heels into the small of his back. We moved together, slow at first, and then faster and faster until I couldn't breathe.

He screamed my name as he came. I buried my face in his shoulder and bit him as my own orgasm rocketed through my body. I found the indented scar on his arm left behind by my wolf and pressed my palm to it.

* * * *

We lay entwined on the bed. Legs, arms, fingers, anything we could wrap around each other.

Layer by layer, secret by secret, I was discovering Liam Murphy. His motivations, his past, his ideals, his demons. Love made it hard to breathe, hard to concentrate. All I wanted was to lie there in his arms forever.

"It's very disconcerting, this strange, silent you," he remarked as he stroked the skin of my hand with his thumb. I ran my foot up his calf and then back down again to his ankle. "But I think I'll take what just happened as you telling me you're not going to leave me."

"Never," I managed to croak, and his face lit up with indescribable happiness, even as he pressed his mouth to mine to shut me up.

"Don't talk. It sounds like you have a throat full of broken glass. I don't want you to hurt, Stanzie. Not more than you have to. Talk with your body, not your voice, okay?"

I smiled against his mouth and drew my finger along the curve of his ear. I reached my other hand between his legs, and he caught his breath for a moment and then chuckled. At least for a moment, until I straddled him and used my hand to guide him back inside me. He was rock hard the second after I began to move, and this time we took our time.

Chapter 22

It rained during the funeral. The faces of the people of Mac Tire ran with raindrops indistinguishable from their tears.

Although it was a complete travesty, Glenn Murphy and Paddy O'Reilly's ashes were scattered at the same time. Declan Byrne's had been spread across the earth earlier by his bond mate and his parents. Fee had not attended. Murphy and I had gone, but we'd refused to touch his ashes. We were there as witnesses only. So were Jason, Celine Ducharme, Etain Feehery and Ryan Kelly.

Ryan had regained consciousness, and although his memory was spotty, especially as concerned events just before he'd tackled Glenn Murphy and they'd both fallen down the stairs, he did recall walking around the corner to see Glenn with his hands wrapped around my throat. He'd thought I was dead, too late to save, and when I'd walked into his room hand in hand with Murphy, he'd burst into relieved tears.

We'd hugged each other for what seemed like hours. He didn't remember telling me about the photographs, but he told the Councilors Glenn Murphy had been acting strangely and he'd been concerned. On impulse, he'd followed him one afternoon and saw him speaking with Declan Byrne. Saw him hand him the knife that Declan then gave to Grandfather Mick.

He'd taken photographs of the exchange, although he hadn't been sure why, and then when he'd heard Paddy had been stabbed, he'd been too damn scared and horrified to talk to Glenn about what he'd seen.

Miserable and conflicted, he'd printed the photographs and left them for Jason to deal with. He'd been sure Glenn's motives had been good and that things had gone wrong even as the evidence pointed in the exact opposite direction. Much of the idealism had been knocked out of him, leaving him breathless. I knew that feeling so well and I hated that Glenn Murphy's selfish acts had done such damage to those around him.

The Councilors declined to bring charges against him for withholding evidence. Even Celine Ducharme had not wanted to go for his throat. I was shocked and suspicious. The woman was up to something, and being lenient must serve her agenda. I refused to believe she had a compassionate bone in her scrawny body.

Alannah Doyle had not cried as she'd let the ashes of her bond mate drift to the ground. Her emerald-green eyes had been dry. She saw the Celtic knot next to my bond pendant, and the hatred that convulsed her face made her ugly.

The rain began as we'd walked with Paddy's and Glenn's urns through the woods surrounding the castle.

We formed a huge circle, more than one hundred and fifty strong, and those who went to the center to scatter ashes had to shout so their voices would carry.

Of course, I couldn't speak, but I did step into the circle. Not too many of us did. Fee limited it to immediate family, their bond mates and the Councilors.

I couldn't avoid Glenn Murphy's ashes, but I did not want his ashes to come into contact with Paddy's, so I picked up Paddy's urn first. It was swirled in a blue-and-brown pattern reminiscent of his different-colored eyes.

I remembered how his eyes, glazed with pain, had stared at me as he lay broken and bleeding on the gravel. I heard him ask me if I believed in him again. He'd been dying, and he knew it.

"I'm scared," he'd told me. "Don't leave me."

Tears scalded my face. The mourners in the circle became a blur.

I wanted to scream, but I couldn't. Instead, I took a handful of gray ashes and carefully let them sift through my fingers. Rain battered them into the mud.

Glenn Murphy's urn was white. I made myself stop crying before I picked it up. I knew everyone had to wait while I composed myself, but fuck them. I would not cry over this man. Not even for the innocent family he'd left behind.

We wouldn't be here right now if not for him and his pride.

Why did men like Glenn Murphy and Paul Benedict get to live to bring up their children while good men like Paddy died before they ever had the chance to look at their baby's newborn face?

Plastic gloves prevented me from touching the ashes with my bare skin, but I couldn't get Glenn Murphy's off my fingers fast enough. As soon as they were gone, I rushed from the circle, stripping the gloves off as I moved.

Murphy took me into his arms, and I shuddered against him. Although it was August, the rain made it cold, and goose bumps rose on my skin.

I didn't listen to what the Councilors said as they scattered the last of the ashes, but the second Etain Feehery set down Glenn Murphy's urn and began to strip, I let go of Murphy so I could undress, too.

He helped me with the zipper to my dress and we both made sure to tuck our bond pendants into our shoes to protect them.

All around us, people dropped to all fours. Murphy and I held hands as we knelt in the mud and the rain beat down on our exposed backs.

The shift swept through me first, but I clung to his fingers as long as I could, until my hands were more paws than anything else, and then I blinked into the other dimension. Once again it flashed silver, and then it was gone, and I was my wolf.

* * * *

Sad. I am still me, but today I am one with my pack. We howl our sadness together. Our Alpha is dead. We sing for him. We remember him. Friend leans against me. His voice is strong. Mine will not come. I have no song for my Alpha, but I try. I try so hard. Now we run, we run slow because Alpha Fee cannot run fast. She is big with young. We protect her. We keep her safe. We roll to her, give her our throats and bellies. We did not keep our dead Alpha safe. We have failed them both. We are full of sadness.

Alpha Fee takes my throat in her mouth. I wait for her to bite. I wait for punishment, but she does not make me bleed. She licks my muzzle and cries. I lick her back, get to my feet, let her lean against me. We breathe together. She cries in my ear. I try to sing, but I cannot. Friend leans against me, too. He cries so loud it hurts. He hurts. All come together, press together. We are Pack. We are strong together, sad together. Our song rises high to the clouds, but our dead Alpha does not hear. Never again.

* * * *

In dry clothes, with a mug of honey-laced tea, I gazed at the harp. It was very old. Would it be in tune? I hadn't had time to rehearse, but it didn't matter. I could take a few moments if I needed them.

The pack was subdued, and the whiskey flow had turned many of them maudlin, especially the ones who hadn't thought to bring dry clothes.

I was worried Fee was going to collapse. Maureen O'Shea's bond mate, a tall man with a pleasantly homely face, argued with her in a corner. As I watched, he gestured to Jason, who moved adroitly through the sluggish crowd.

A consultation, I decided, as Jason took Fee's hand and instead of giving it a squeeze of commiseration, instead placed his fingers against the underside of her wrist and took her pulse. It clicked suddenly. The tall man must be Andrew Brody, the pack doctor.

Murphy was close by with Paddy's mother, Maureen, who sobbed helplessly while Murphy held her.

It wasn't just Fee who turned to Murphy in a grief-fueled crisis. So many pack members seemed to want to touch him, speak to him or simply be close to him. He was Paddy's proxy. Maybe they remembered when he'd been their Alpha. I understood then what a good Alpha he'd been to them and that he knew and touched the very heart of Mac Tire.

I moved a comfortable chair closer to the harp and began to make my way toward Fee. She'd wanted to listen to harp music. Maybe I could persuade her to sit down and listen, and Andrew Brody would be satisfied.

"...upstairs and lie down just for an hour, Fiona, please," I heard him say as I approached.

Someone cut me off and blocked my path. Siobhan Carmichael. Her ravaged face bore an uncanny resemblance to her son's.

Impulsively, I tried to hug her and offer her some comfort. She stiffened and pushed me away.

"Don't ever touch me unless I reach out first." Her tone was furious, as if I'd done something heinous.

"Sorry," I whispered through my bruised, aching throat, and tried to step around her, but she moved with me.

"Stay away from my daughter," she ordered. "Today is for family. Go play the harp and make yourself useful."

Hurt, colored with humiliation, washed through me. I reminded myself I'd indirectly caused her bond mate's death. Only she wasn't supposed to know that part. Did she? If I'd had my voice, I would have asked her.

Instead, I took as deep a breath as I could, which still hurt my throat, and retreated to the harp.

People were grieving. They said and did things in that state they were sorry for after. I should let it go and do what I could to make things better.

Tears pricked at my eyes. I *was* family. Wasn't I?

I let my fingers choose the song and closed my eyes at first so the music could flow within me and out. *Carolan's Farewell.*

Some of the people here had heard it the first time I'd played at An Puca, but most of them had not.

The low murmur of voices ceased as attention focused on me, only I was beyond it, ensnared in the musical shimmer of the notes as they burst like bubbles from the strings.

I thought of Paddy and pictured his face as I played. I heard him tell me I was the pack's new bard.

A teenage girl of perhaps thirteen crept close as she dared. Her green eyes sparked with grief mixed with incredulous delight. I saw her fingers twitch as she listened, her head tilted so her fiery red hair fell away from her face. She played, I could tell.

Did the pack's bard teach the children how to play music? I hoped so. I'd never taught anyone how to play the harp, but I remembered Lauren teaching me. She'd told me one day I would teach my own daughter or son how to play, and I'd believed her then, before my wolf had complicated the issue.

I chanced a look in Murphy's direction. He was with his mother and Fee, one arm around each of them. His wistfully sad smile tore at my heart. He looked as if he was listening to something beautiful he couldn't share.

Don't worry, I wanted to tell him. *Paddy heard me play this before.*

* * * *

Three songs later, the red-haired girl brought me a frothy glass of Guinness and a plate of cheese and fruit. Shy but eager, she offered them to me, and I accepted both.

"I'm Gwenith," she introduced herself as she watched me sip carefully at the beer.

"Stanzie." My voice was a shredded whisper. A black scarf tied strategically around my throat covered the bruises, but there was nothing I could do to disguise my ruined voice.

"Are you sick?" Her nose wrinkled doubtfully. I didn't smell sick. If her senses were sharp enough to know the difference between healthy and ill, she was probably older than thirteen. I revised my estimation of her age up by two or three years. The onset of puberty produced more than physical changes in Pack. Our senses sharpened as our bodies developed.

Instead of answering, I gave her a weak smile and sipped more beer. I couldn't eat the cheese or fruit. I was still on a liquid diet.

I gestured to the harp, offering to let her play, and she flushed.

"Oh, I'm not good enough to play in front of all these people. Declan says...said I was hopeless."

Amy Lee Burgess

Anger burned through me. Gwenith stared at me, her green eyes huge. "Play." I pointed to the harp.

"Ah, it's so old," she began doubtfully, but she sidled closer, drawn against her will.

Her fingers hesitated above the strings as she bit her lip. A shudder went through her entire body as her desire struggled against her fear.

Desire won.

Her playing was tentative, but sound. She had the basics down and all she needed was encouragement to find her own interpretation of the music. Afraid to make mistakes, she muzzled her own creativity. I could see Declan's teaching in every hesitation, each tense muscle and held breath. Her eyes filled with tears when she made her first mistake, but when I smiled, she continued.

"I know that was awful, but..." she began at the end of the song, head down as she waited for me ream her out.

What the fuck kind of a teacher had Declan been? I couldn't wait to show this girl her true potential.

Siobhan stalked over, her black skirt stiff as her outraged expression. "I asked you to play. Gwenith's not advanced enough to play in front of the pack."

Gwenith's face turned bright red, then stark white, and with an inarticulate cry of apology, she dashed away.

I glared at Siobhan.

"And frankly, I've never heard *Carolan's Farewell* played the way you did it. I'm not sure I liked it, and maybe you ought to practice more so it sounds the way other people play it. If you're not sure of the music, don't attempt the song. No more classical music. We're Irish, and we like Irish music. Do you need me to find you some sheet music? There's got to be some. Declan never needed it, but it's apparent you do."

She gave me a searching, puzzled look of contempt. "Honestly, the way Paddy and Fee raved about your playing, I was expecting a lot more."

For a moment I could only stare. I fantasized about throwing my Guinness in her face, but reminded myself people grieve in all different ways. Siobhan Carmichael was full of fury she didn't know how to get rid of. I was the most convenient target.

Damn, it was hard to convince myself not to react.

I set down my drink and cheese plate and went back to the harp. Irish music. I didn't know much Irish music, and what I did was on the lighter, cheerier side, hardly appropriate for a funeral, even if it was an Irish one.

I replayed *Carolan's Farewell*. I played it the way I thought Siobhan Carmichael would want it. It felt like a cheat and a lie, but I did it.

* * * *

My fingers were bleeding. I wiped them on my black skirt and decided I was done playing the harp for the day. Siobhan Carmichael had unearthed a music stand and several sheets of appropriately anguished Irish music.

I was starving, thirsty, and felt about as low as I'd ever felt in my life.

Fee bonded with Colm O'Reilly and Deirdre Collins. None of them smiled as they exchanged bond pendants and boxes. Celine Ducharme, as the ranking Councilor, performed the ceremony. Almost everyone cried.

I'd tried to join the line that formed in front of them so I could hug Fee, but Siobhan shooed me back to the harp with a flap of her hands.

What was I? The fucking paid help?

Bleeding was the last straw. I escaped into the courtyard. The rain had eased, but a light drizzle sifted down from the sky. I didn't give a shit. I crunched my way across the gravel to the fountain and sat where I could see the spot where Paddy had fallen.

I felt alone. Bereft. Murphy spent the entire day with his family, surrounded by his pack. I'd played the fucking harp in the background. Sure, Murphy listened to me play. I'd felt the power of his love from a room away, but it wasn't the same as a touch.

I knew Siobhan Carmichael was angry. I suspected she knew the truth of her bond mate's death and blamed me. I understood Alannah Doyle hated me and maybe it was better if I'd kept away from the center of things because she was there with Fee almost every minute and no one wanted a confrontation today of all days.

I couldn't think of a way to circumvent Siobhan and my fingers hurt almost as much as my heart. If I could just sit here in the rain for five minutes, maybe I could think straight again.

Shoes crunched on the wet gravel. I looked up to see Jason Allerton. He had a black umbrella, which he graciously extended to cover me as well, but I was already soaked and past caring about it.

"I've got to leave," he said. "I've got reservations on a flight to London. The Great Council is convening tomorrow to discuss what's happened within Mac Tire."

I bit my lip.

"I wanted to say goodbye. Liam informed me today that he no longer wishes to be my Advisor. I wondered if you felt the same way."

"Guilty," I croaked, damning my stupid throat. Jason leaned forward, his brow crinkled in confusion. "Murphy," I tried to clarify. "He feels guilty. For killing Mick."

"Ah," said Jason, his face clearing. "Are you saying he feels he doesn't deserve to be an Advisor?"

I nodded vigorously.

"So I shouldn't take his resignation seriously?"

I kept nodding.

"Does this mean you'll talk him around for me?"

More nodding. Jason gave me a blinding smile that made him look ten years younger. Younger than me.

"So you can't possibly resign either under these circumstances. Not without being a hypocrite. It's settled then. I have two Advisors still."

"I want to keep the Pack safe." Every word felt like acid in my throat, but I forced them out. "Like you do."

Relief and affection lit up his face, and before I knew it I was in his arms, the umbrella dropped to the muddy gravel, so he could spin me around in a giddy, undignified circle.

Jason Allerton, man of surprises. For once I was not dismayed by the break in his facade of control and perfection. He was a man as well as a Councilor. It had only taken me a frigging year to figure it out.

Epilogue

"I'm dying!" Fee, sweaty hair plastered to her face, clutched at my hand and gritted her teeth as another painful contraction swept through her.

"You're not dying," said Siobhan. "You keep mentioning death, Fiona Carmichael, and I'll kill you myself. You think this is bad, try having twins."

Fee gave her mother the finger with her free hand, and Siobhan swatted her bare calf but didn't take her attention from between Fee's legs.

I, on the other hand, steadfastly avoided looking in that general direction. This whole experience had been bad enough before the baby's head crowned, but ever since then, I'd been in a constant struggle not to puke.

Maureen and Siobhan, the baby's grandmothers, seemed unflappable. Fascinated, even. Alannah Doyle, the baby's aunt, looked a little green around the gills. That didn't stop her from shooting me death glares when she thought no one was looking.

In the weeks since her bond mate's death, her hatred had intensified. I was shocked she would even deign to stay in the same room with me, but apparently she was not going to let me witness the birth of our niece or nephew without being in attendance as well.

Siobhan Carmichael had not warmed up to me in the intervening weeks either. Glenn was a taboo subject. She didn't talk about him to me. Murphy didn't. Fee didn't. It was as if he'd never existed. The same with Declan Byrne. They'd betrayed the pack.

Everyone talked about Paddy, though. Every day his name came up at some point. Sometimes I could even talk about him without crying. Baby steps.

Maureen O'Shea, Paddy's mother, bent closer to the baby's crowning head. I tried not to gag. Birth was supposed to be beautiful, but it so wasn't. Not even close. It was disgusting, actually.

"Just a few more pushes, Fee," Maureen said, and Fee groaned as another contraction rippled across her huge belly. Revolted, I couldn't tear my gaze away.

"You're next, you pussy," snarled Fee and dug her goddamn nails into my wrist.

"Fuck you," I retorted. "You think I'm going to go through this bullshit?"

"I do." Fee's grin was malicious. "And I hope you have triplets, you horrible, horrible bitch. I'm gonna be there laughing."

"Less talking, more pushing," suggested Siobhan. The look she directed at me was cold. If she could have sent me from the room for instigating childbirth rebellion, she would have, but when she'd originally tried to say the room was too crowded, Fiona suggested she ought to be the one to leave. And since then I'd been tolerated, but I had a feeling a lot of Irish cursing of my name was going on beneath the breath.

"Fee, do you want to stand up, darling?" Maureen was the calmest influence in the room. I liked her, but I wasn't sure how she felt about me. Her black, curly hair was piled on top of her head in a careless knot, and her dark eyes were compassionate. I wanted to talk to her about Paddy, but I didn't know how to begin. I thought maybe after she and Andrew had bonded with Siobhan she would approach me, but so far she hadn't.

Deirdre Collins, Fee's new bond mate, rushed back into the room with bottles of water. She saw the baby's head and blanched.

Her pregnancy hadn't started to show yet, and every time I tried to imagine her four-foot-ten body attempting to expel the child—or children—of six-foot-six-inch Colm O'Reilly, I shuddered.

The men—Murphy, Colm and Andrew Brody, waited in the living room of the apartment the Alphas shared. I suspected there was a lot of Jameson's being handed around. Andrew was standing by to help if necessary, but so far the birth had been nearly textbook and we women were handling it. I wished I could have had a shot of Jameson's but instead I took a bottle of water from Deirdre and made do with that.

Fee's glazed gaze sharpened as another contraction hit her. I looked over my shoulder for the fifth or sixth time that hour, but nobody was there, even though the space between my shoulder blades itched as if somebody was staring at me.

"You see him too, huh?" Fee's face contorted as she tried to breathe. She looked straight into the corner, past me. "You ought to be in the other room with the men, you feckin' idiot!" Her tone was exasperated, yet affectionate.

Shivers went down my spine.

Maureen and Siobhan exchanged looks and said nothing.

Alannah's face pinched in on itself.

"Never tell me he's here. Only the miserable ones walk. He's miserable, Paddy is, and he's gonna haunt us forever, isn't he?" She let out a wail and covered her face.

"Alannah," remonstrated Deirdre. "You're not helping."

Alannah bit back a sharp retort. Deirdre was her Alpha.

"She's not lying. Restless spirits walk. They don't go to the otherworld. I keep waiting for Paddy to go, but he won't. Wretched bastard." Tears streaked Fee's blotchy face, and Maureen winced.

Deirdre rushed to Fee's side and smoothed back some of the sweaty hair from her face.

"Don't you fret about this. He's here to watch his child born. Then he'll go, you'll see. Won't he, Stanzie?" Deirdre appealed to me as if I would know.

"Maybe I'm dying. Or the baby will die, and he's here to bring us to the otherworld," speculated Fee in a sepulchral tone.

"For fuck's sake, Fiona," I yelled. "You're not gonna die. Nobody with a mouth as big as yours is dying."

"Piss off." Fiona pinched me, and I pinched her back. Deirdre bit back a smile.

"You tell him to go then, you sanctimonious bitch. Tell Paddy he's breaking my heart. I want him to be safe in the otherworld, not fucking floating around in this one. He can't talk, he can't touch me—he just fucking hovers there staring. You tell him to move on, Stanzie. You think you know everything."

"I don't see spirits," I said.

"You don't believe he's there?" A sly look spread across Fee's face. "Why are you casting looks over your shoulder every fifteen minutes then? Looking right at him in the corner if you don't see spirits. You're a fucking liar, Newcastle, you know that?"

"He'll go when he's ready." Maureen O'Shea looked wistfully into the corner where Paddy supposedly hovered. I didn't see a fucking thing. I don't think she did either.

Fee burst into tears.

"I don't want him to be alone. I wish I would die so I could be with him."

"Fiona!" Siobhan's cheeks paled. "Please don't say things like that. Your baby needs you. You had your time with Paddy and now you're with Colm and Deirdre and you're Alpha of the pack. We need you strong."

"Then tell him to leave. Tell him to rest," Fee begged and thrashed in the bed as another massive contraction took over her body. She screamed, and I felt the bones in my fingers cracking beneath the pressure of her grip.

The stench of blood filled my nostrils. Blood and other fluid. Maureen and Siobhan put their hands out, and Alannah covered her face again. Deirdre watched for a moment and then turned her face to mine.

"I think I'm going to pass out," she remarked conversationally and slumped across the bed.

Alannah grabbed for her and dragged her to a chair.

"Oh. Jesus God, what am I doing here?" I groaned beneath my breath.

"Fuck. You. New. Castle," Fee managed to say between screams.

Thin, reedy wails filled the air. More blood and fluid.

"It's a boy," cried Siobhan, jubilant. Tears poured down Maureen's cheeks as she cradled the newborn for a moment before she handed him to Siobhan.

I saw a small scrap of a baby with a huge mop of black hair. He had more hair than anything else, and when Siobhan laid him on top of Fiona, I saw his eyes. One was blue, the other a cloudy indeterminate color between blue and brown that I was sure would resolve into pure brown. Just as I was certain the hair on his head would curl.

Fee let go of my hand so she could touch her son. I stumbled away from the bed. My hand hurt like frigging hell, and I flexed it to get the circulation moving again.

Nobody stood in the corner that I could see, but I stopped just short of where I thought maybe his toes would be.

"Okay," I said through the tears that clogged my throat. "He's born, he's safe and he's going to look just like you, the poor little thing. Now you can go. It's like Alannah said, only miserable spirits walk, and you'd better not be miserable, Paddy O'Reilly. We love you too much for that. Nobody as loved as you can be miserable. It's the law, you bastard.

"I swear I'll look after Fee and when your son's old enough, I'll initiate his wolf like I promised. Paddy, I don't even know if you can hear me." I grimaced and felt like an idiot, but then something weird stole through me. A feeling as if I weren't alone. I swore I smelled Paddy's cologne, but that was impossible. I swallowed the tears in my throat. "Jesus, Paddy, no matter how many Alphas I ever have, there will always be a piece of me that belongs to you. Always. Now go on, get the fuck out of here. Move on. Please."

I still didn't see a damn thing, but I swore I felt the tip of someone's tongue in my ear, and a shiver danced up my spine.

I turned around and saw Fee surrounded by her pack mates, her son in her arms, but her gaze was fixed on me not him.

Her lips parted and formed two words. *Thank you.*

I curled my fingers around my bond pendant and the Celtic knot Paddy had fashioned for me and let the tears fall. They hurt, but they were good tears, cleansing tears.

After a moment, I went back to the bed.

"Here." Fee held out the baby. He was so fucking small, my heart hurt. I'd never held a baby that little. I took him as gently as I could and he trembled in my arms as he struggled to find comfort. "We're gonna call him William. Will for short. Paddy wanted that name. When we were growing up, he always said our son's name would be William and Liam's would be Patrick and they'd be best friends the way we all were." Her glowing face dimmed, and unbearable grief made her eyes dark. "I just always thought he'd be here to help me raise him."

"You've got the whole pack to help you raise him," I whispered. One of Will's tiny fists waved in the air, and I reached out a finger. His fist closed around it with surprising strength, and my heart missed a beat. "It'll be all right, Fee. You just wait, okay?"

"But it'll never be the same," she said, her gaze far away.

"No," I agreed. I thought of Grey and Elena and my former life. "But you're wrong if you think the best is in the past. You'll find new happiness, Fee, I know you will. I did, and so will you."

I tried to hand the baby back, but Fee shook her head.

"Go clean him up and show him to Colm and Liam. Tell them his name. Watch Liam's face when you do. Tell me what he says."

* * * *

"Hi, Will." Murphy very carefully took his nephew in his arms while Colm watched. "God, he's gorgeous, isn't he?" Murphy's face softened, and his smile was indescribable.

I nodded.

"Stanzie, if we ever have a son…" Murphy began. I loved him so much I couldn't breathe. He tore his gaze away from his nephew, and when he looked at me, I felt how much he loved me in return. His love was a blaze of warmth I felt from the inside out.

"We'll call him Patrick, and he'll be best friends with Will, and they'll do all the things you two did," I told him. He grinned at me and looked back to the baby.

"And they'll be old grandfathers together someday," Murphy leaned against me when I brushed my lips across the side of his face. "Because we're going to make sure they have that chance. Right, Stanzie?"

"Right," I agreed. I was damned if I wouldn't make it so, in any way I had to. Whatever it took.

Meet the Author

I blame Stanzie for making me break one of my cardinal rules in writing: No conspiracies! They get so tangled up and hard to manage, but nothing is worse than one that is too simplistic and black and white. I have to admit, though, I am enjoying the ride. Maybe I should break my rules more often?

Other rules I have are--in no particular order--never mix supernaturals. No werewolves with vampire friends. No elves elbowing out warlocks. Always put out the yellow towels on Friday. Avoid highways and take surface streets as often as possible. Never name characters after exes. Lock the bedroom door when watching The Walking Dead. No singing aloud in public.

I started out life in New England and moved to New Orleans on a whim with my fiancé when I was thirty. We endured fires, floods, four cats and the peculiar stench that drifted from the river every spring.

Katrina scared me into relocating to Houston where I currently live with two dogs and a very elderly computer.

Stanzie journey is one that shows me, time and again, what it takes to start over and become better. Now if I could only shift into a wolf like she can!

I love to hear from readers, so please email me at amyleeburgess99@gmail.com. I'm also on Twitter @amyleeburgess

Turn the page for a special excerpt of Amy Lee Burgess's

Across the Line

Solving problems is her job...even when it may cost her life.

When Councilor Allerton sends Stanzie to investigate a territory dispute between tiny pack Stony Fell and the British branch of much larger Mac Tire, it seems routine until someone sets a bear trap. A young Stony Fell man pays with the loss of his leg and now it's up to Stanzie and Murphy to figure out who set the trap--and why--before more members of the packs are maimed.

Add a pair of star-crossed lovers, one love triangle, a grief-stricken bond mate with jealousy issues, and bad blood all around and the resultant twisted hell brew reveals the darker side of inter-pack politics that could prove too difficult--and dangerous--for even Stanzie to untangle.

On sale now!

Chapter 1

The red dress on the back of the bathroom door called to me. Short, but not indecent, filmy but not see-through. Sexy but not trashy. I stared at it from my vantage point in the tub and couldn't help but smile.

I loved to wallow in my favorite mint-scented bathwater until my fingers and toes pruned, but I couldn't ignore the siren song of that dress.

Tonight marked an entire year since Liam Murphy and I had exchanged vows at the Great Gathering bonding ceremony.

Once on the bath mat, I toweled off, never taking my gaze from the new dress. The peridot and pearl bond pendant Murphy gave me that night shifted around my throat as I drew the towel across my arms.

Murphy didn't know it, but I'd made reservations at an expensive French restaurant in the heart of Dublin. If we didn't hurry, we'd be late.

A pang went through me as I briskly rubbed the towel through my wet hair. All day I'd waited for him to remember the date, but so far he hadn't said a word. Thankfully, it wasn't one of his bad days—when he brooded about Paddy and his father, but it wasn't a great day either.

He'd spent most of it behind his laptop connected to the stock market. He made money for our pack, Mac Tire, that way. For us, as well.

For all I knew, he might have been using his work as a shield against grief—it wouldn't be the first time, but I preferred it to the days when he sat on the sofa with a cold cup of coffee and stared into space. Those were the days I hated.

I'd managed to smuggle the red dress into the bathroom so he wouldn't see it until I had it on. The cherry red stilettos I planned to wear with it were from Paris. I'd worn them the night we'd met.

I smiled, remembering that moment. Polite, yet reserved when we'd been introduced by Councilor Jason Allerton, Murphy had obviously resented my presence at the table. He'd barely glanced in my direction until one of the other people there asked me if I was the Constance Newcastle who'd killed my bond mates in a stupid, careless car accident. Then Murphy looked at me and his polite facade crumbled, replaced by disgust. He'd left the table and stranded me in a sea of British pack members who, after they'd had their fun making me squirm, cold-shouldered me out of subsequent conversation.

To hear Murphy tell the tale, he'd been smitten the moment Jason Allerton led me to the table. One of the stories he told people about us featured my red dress and how he'd known from the moment he saw me in it, we were destined to bond.

I didn't all the way believe him, but maybe the truth was somewhere in between. All I knew was that he'd protected me at the Great Gathering and saved my ass by bonding with me.

Now a year later, we both had admitted our love for each other, but instead of wine and roses, we had grief and an invisible wall.

We talked—about inconsequential things. *What should we have for dinner? How about this movie tonight? Jesus, the weather's awful, isn't it?* But if I brought up Paddy, Murphy would shut down as if he were one of those animatronic robots at Disneyworld and it was closing time at the park.

Fee couldn't make him talk about Paddy either, but he listened to her talk about him. Listened and held her when she sobbed against his chest while I dealt with Fee's new baby, Will.

Four nights out of seven Fee and Will slept at our apartment—Will in his portable crib, Fee, Murphy and I tangled together on the bed.

What must it be like to have a twin? Murphy was endlessly patient with his sister and she relied on him with a faith that must weigh so heavily, but he never said a word of reproach.

This morning, after Fee packed up Will's crib and his diaper bag and left to go home, I'd held my breath waiting for her to return. Usually when she left, she stayed gone for at least twenty-four hours, but with Fee it was hard to predict. All I knew was she'd be back, I just didn't know precisely when.

So when I heard her voice in the living room, just as I reached for the sexy bra that went with the dress, my heart sank. Should I get dressed? Could I? How could I walk out there and remind her I had something to celebrate and she didn't?

Paddy had been dead for three months. Fee was swamped with pain and guilt she hadn't known he was in trouble, that he hadn't shared his fears with her. I kept waiting for her to turn on Murphy in anger because he'd known everything, but so far she hadn't. Murphy and I knew the stages of grief from bitter experience. We'd both lost our first bond mates to the conspiracy.

The bitter conflict between the Guardians, who wanted our world to remain as it was and Pack First, who wanted the Pack to reveal itself to Others killed them as it killed Paddy. Fee, Murphy and I were members of an exclusive, horrible club. Devastated survivors because our bond mates paid the ultimate price. I was determined the ranks of this club would not swell with more reluctant members.

That was why I was Jason Allerton's Advisor and worked to reveal members of the Guardians, who took matters in their own hands and murdered Pack First members or sympathizers.

In the living room, Fee's voice rose to a shrill pitch. I winced. Murphy's murmured response was meant to soothe her, but she overrode him and now I discerned the thread of anger. She was bitching about her bond mates, Colm and Deirdre, especially him and since that was nothing new and I'd heard it all *ad nauseum*, I didn't pay much attention to actual words. I was too busy mourning the fact my night out with Murphy had been torpedoed. So much for my red dress and fancy dinner reservations. Most likely it had been a bad idea anyway.

In the bedroom, I hastily hung the dress at the back of my side of the deep double closet. As always when I saw my shoe collection piled in a sorry-ass heap beneath my dresses and skirts, I heaved a sigh and mourned the loss of my walk-in closet in Boston. Dublin had taken a lot of getting used to and sometimes the lack of a walk-in closet seemed the deepest cut.

I threw on a pair of jeans and the red hand-knitted sweater Paddy's mother, Maureen, made me. She ran a small mail-order clothing line. Sweaters, vests, jackets, baby clothes—all knitted by hand. Some of the other members of the pack contributed their talents and recently one built her a website. The website made me nervous. Too high tech for some of the Guardians. I hoped we'd rooted the bad ones out with the deaths of Grandfather Mick, Declan Byrne and Glenn Murphy, but didn't know for sure. So I kept an eye on Maureen and the girl who'd designed the website, just in case.

When I walked into the main room of the apartment, Fee still stood in the doorway, her face flushed red with fury. Will dangled in his car seat from one of her clenched fists and made fussy noises indicative of hunger.

Did we have any breast milk in the refrigerator? With Fee so caught up in her anger, the last thing she probably wanted to do was take a time out to nurse.

I didn't bother to say hello. She'd left not even seven hours earlier. Instead, I tacked right, into the galley kitchen.

Score. Three bottles of breast milk and all of them within the expiration date. I popped the oldest into a cup of hot water to warm and walked over to where Fee stood yelling at Murphy.

She'd crossed the line from shrill to shout in the space of time it had taken me to get the bottle. Murphy listened to her patiently. He had one hand on her shoulder. Touch was important to Pack. Did he derive as much comfort from the touch as she did? Did she even know his hand was there?

Perversely, I was glad to see her mad. For the first time in ages she was angry. A good sign she was beginning to move on in her grief. But I predicted it was going to be loud around our place for a few weeks.

Will's little rosebud mouth puckered into a bow as he let out a protesting wail when I lifted him from the warmth of his blanketed car seat. Fee had bundled him up in one of Maureen's knitted jackets and a blue cap with an adorable white yarn puff on top.

"You greedy, hungry baby, you just wait a few more minutes," I told him as I struggled to hold his small arm still so I could take off the jacket. The heat was too high in the apartment again but Fee was always cold so we kept it up. Neither of us had remembered to turn it down. Murphy had been wrapped up in the stock market and I'd cleaned. Guests with babies left an awful lot of disarray in their wake. I suspected Will had more blankets, binkies and clothes here than he did at the house Fee shared with Colm and Deirdre.

I found one of his cloth rattles—the one in the shape of a lamb—and shook it in his face to distract him from the fact he was hungry and there was no food. He was having none of it. His face scrunched up into a miniature red-cheeked version of Fee's and he let out another indignant blat.

Born three weeks after Paddy's death, he was just over two months old. He mostly slept and ate, but when I spoke to him, he swiveled his head in my direction, and I swore, listened to me. Did he recognize my voice? He'd spent much of his young life cradled in my arms as Fee wept in Murphy's.

His eyes had settled into their permanent color. Left eye blue, right eye brown. Just like his father. His hair was growing in black and curly, also like his dad's. Otherwise, he was a carbon copy of his mother. He would have her quicksilver good looks. She and Murphy closely resembled each other, so maybe when Will grew up he'd look like his uncle Liam. That thought made me smile, and I pressed a kiss to his wrinkled little old man forehead, which made him squirm. He cooed, his earlier temper tantrum forgotten. If only adults' bad moods could be as swift and mercurial as babies'.

Occupied as I was with Will, I'd tuned out most of Fee's impassioned diatribe, but once he was settled in the crook of my arm, greedily sucking on his bottle, I spared some of my attention for her.

"He's just doing it to be difficult, because he knows damn well I don't want to fuck him. I don't want to fuck anyone at this point, Liam."

"I think he's doing it for the pack's sake, Fee," Murphy told her. "Think about this for a minute. None of us seem to be getting over the shock and pain very well. This could help us."

"I don't want to get over the grief. Do you hear me, Liam Murphy?" The tendons in Fiona's neck stuck out from the force of her shout. Will gave a convulsive jerk in my arms and the nipple slipped from his mouth. He added his scared wails to her angry shout and I hastily plugged the nipple back in and hoped the poor thing wouldn't choke.

Jesus, could she not take three minutes to calm down and let her poor son drink his milk?

"Getting over the grief doesn't mean forgetting him, Fiona," I said.

Both Fee and Murphy turned in my direction as if surprised to find me there. That was nothing new. Half the time I thought I must invisible to them. Just a ghost who took care of the baby. A housekeeping ghost who put food on the table they rarely bothered to eat then cleaned it all up again.

I told myself to be nice because I knew what it was like to lose loved ones.

"I won't be forced into this. You know that sonofabitch has called the hunt for tomorrow morning? Without my consent, he's called the hunt and all the pack has known about it for days now. He finally bothered to inform me an hour ago. Bastard."

"I didn't know about it," Murphy said. He took a deep breath.

"It was posted on the pub wall, and he's been making phone calls. But he didn't call you, Liam, because the gobshite knew I was here with you."

"Why did he leave us out? Why is calling a hunt so awful, Fee?" I was confused. A hunt sounded like fun to me. Since Paddy's funeral, Murphy spent most of his time with Fee and on the computer. Also, many, many members of Mac Tire managed to drop by to see him or ask him to go somewhere so they could talk.

Everyone knew Murphy and Paddy had been best friends. Mac Tire was reeling from the blow of losing their Alpha male and also their Regional Councilor, Glenn Murphy. It was a one, two punch nobody seemed able to deal with.

Murphy knew how to listen. He knew how to say what was needed. He guided, advised and sometimes just lent a shoulder to weep on. I'd watched him do it a dozen times and more these past three months.

Consequently, we didn't have much time together. We'd made love exactly twice since Paddy's funeral and neither time shifted because Fee showed up before we could get to the forest.

I'd hoped tonight after a leisurely dinner, I might seduce him and we would shift. That wouldn't happen now because it would take hours to calm Fee down. But a hunt tomorrow could make up for losing out on the dinner seduction scenario tonight.

I wanted to let my wolf free. She was gloriously normal now and last time she'd run with the pack, it had been at Paddy's funeral and it had been a sad, solemn, gut-wrenching hunt. I wanted something upbeat and blood-stirring. I missed Paddy like hell, but we had to go on. Things like hunts would be small steps in the right direction.

"Because the high-handed bastard intends to administer the pack bond before we do, that's why, Stanzie. And he needs my blood for it. Are you that stupid, I have to explain it to you?" Fee's voice dripped sarcasm, and I gulped.

Pack bond. A terrible chill swept through my body. My fingers slackened enough around Will's bottle that it slipped out of his mouth again. He wailed as the bottle slid with a wet thump to the hardwood floor at my feet.

"Now you've done it." Fee swept across the room to snatch her son out of my limp arms. She rocked him and crooned something in Irish as she fumbled with one hand to unbutton her jacket and blouse. "And how old is that fucking milk you've been poisoning him with?" She gave the bottle a contemptuous kick with her boot so it skittered across the floor somewhere beneath the dining table.

"I...it's not old. I checked the date first." My lips were numb. Was I going to pass out? Everything seemed so oddly bright and yet frighteningly dim.

"It's all right, Stanzie," said Murphy. He sounded so kind. So understanding. Could he possibly understand the tumult of emotions gripping me right now?

My wolf was normal. Free of the yoke of the unactivated pack bond my father forced upon me when I was a baby. I'd shifted three times since it had been lifted. Once when my wolf was out of control because it was the first time she'd ever been free of the pack bond. That had been a giddy, scary, roller coaster of an experience. Once after Paddy's murder when she and I had been wracked with grief and then again at his funeral. She'd never run free and unfettered just for the hell of it. I'd waited and waited, patient because if anyone understood the grief of losing a loved one, it was me.

But now a new pack bond would be thrust upon us, While intellectually I understood it wouldn't hurt her, cold terror settled in my heart.

"A pack bond right now would be the best thing for Mac Tire." Murphy stepped around Will's car seat so he could sit beside me on the sofa.

"You don't understand a feckin' thing," shouted Fiona and Will, who had been calming down, gave another frightened wail. Fee shushed him by sitting in an arm chair and giving him her breast.

Paralyzed, I couldn't turn my head to look at Murphy. I wanted to see his face, but couldn't move.

"Stanzie, if you can't stop stinking up this room with your fear, can you please go somewhere else?" Fee glared at me. I couldn't see her face, but the burning wrath of her gaze was hot on my cheek. "What the hell are you scared for anyway?"

"The pack bond, Fee," Murphy reminded her. He stressed her name as if to jog her memory. Maybe it was a reproach too because she sucked in her breath as if struck.

"For fuck's sake," she snarled. "We don't have time for your petty little fears right now. Get over it. A pack bond won't hurt your precious wolf and you know it. Why can't you sympathize with me and what I've got to go through instead of wallowing in your own self-pity?"

"I've been wallowing in yours for three months. Do you suppose I could have two minutes for myself?" The words rushed from my mouth before I could take them back.

Again I told myself she was grieving. She'd lost Paddy. Sick to my stomach, I remembered what it was like to lose Grey and Elena.

Shocked silence for a beat, then Fee burst into ugly tears. Will howled and Murphy cursed beneath his breath.

Tears pricked my eyes. Poor Murphy. I'd made his night even harder because now it would take much longer to talk Fee around. I was such an idiot. Fee was right. I had no time for self-pity or fear. I needed to suck it up and deal. The pack bond would supposedly help everyone. I had no idea how because I thought they were devices from hell, but I was a member of Mac Tire and if they took a pack bond, so would I.

My lips trembled and I leaped to my feet, brushing away the hand Murphy stretched out to me. He didn't have time to deal with me too. He needed to concentrate on Fee.

"I'm sorry, Fee." My voice was choked. "I'm sorry."

She refused to look at me and buried her face in Will's sweet-smelling hair. I retreated to the bedroom and curled up on the bed.

* * * *

"Want to talk about it?"

I jerked in the bed and rolled over to see Murphy assembling Will's portable crib. He'd switched on the desk lamp and the yellow light spilled across his tired face as he worked.

I must have dozed. A glance at the clock on the nightstand revealed it was the middle of the night. Nearly one o'clock.

"Fee?" I whispered.

"Sleeping in the chair finally," he answered. "I'll carry her in after I settle the baby."

"I'll get him." I slid to the edge of the bed and rubbed my sleep-encrusted eyes.

"Will you be all right? Colm's determined to do this thing tomorrow. I called him and couldn't get a word in edgewise. Five minutes of impassioned screaming. In stereo. One ear was him, the other Fee."

"I must have slept through it." I yawned guiltily.

He cast me an amused look, but he looked so damn worn out. "Good for you."

He finished setting up the crib and turned toward me. "Will's in his car seat and they can both sleep where they are for now if you want to talk."

"What about?" I tried to find a brave smile, but was fresh out of such luxuries.

Murphy scrubbed along the edge of his jaw. His fingers rasped against his beard stubble. When was the last time the poor man shaved? He'd verged past sexy stubble two days ago and was now closing in on unattractively prickly.

"Really, it's the best thing for the pack," he said. "All this fucking grief, we're mired in it. We're not moving forward. A pack bond will help." His tone was wistful, as if he only half believed in his own bullshit.

I swallowed hard and slid off the bed. I wanted to talk to him in the worst way, but it wasn't fair. It was one o'clock in the morning and he was flat-out exhausted.

"I believe you," I said, and his smile turned affectionate. He took a step toward me, as if he meant to hug me, but Will chose that moment to cry out. The poor thing disliked his car seat intensely.

"I'll get him." I darted out the door and across the living room floor to rescue him before he roused Fiona.

She was sprawled in the arm chair, still with her jacket on, blouse buttoned wrong. Tears had left shiny streaks across her cheeks and her sandy blond hair was lifeless and bedraggled around her shoulders. She looked so pathetically alone, tears rose in my eyes.

What the hell, Paddy? Why did he fucking have to die? Irrational anger bloomed within me. *He* was supposed to have given me the pack bond. I trusted him. I loved him. I didn't know Colm O'Reilly and the thought of drinking his herb-infused blood sickened me. Terrified me.

I scooped Will from the car seat and bounced him against my shoulder, cradling his little head in my hand.

As soon as his face pressed against my skin, he quieted. Pack children needed touch. Hell, so did Pack adults.

Murphy lifted Fee's limp body and moved ahead of me into the bedroom. He set her down gently on the bed while I placed an already sleeping Will in his crib. As I looked at him, he gave a hitching, little sigh that tore at my heartstrings. This little boy would never know his father. He'd hear stories and see pictures, but he'd never, ever know his father's touch.

Anger bloomed inside me again and I beat it down. Pointless. Useless. What was done was done and now it was time to pick up the pieces and move on.

By the time I turned away from Will and the crib, Murphy was stretched across the bed next to Fee, sound asleep. He hadn't even undressed or crawled beneath the covers.

I shook out a blanket and drew it over him. When I smoothed the back of my hand across his stubbly cheek, he murmured something in his sleep. My name. This time when tears choked me, I let them fall because no one else could see them but me.